# THE DNR TRILOGY VOLUME 2

## NO GOOD DEED

## Don W. Hill, M.D.

ISBN 978-1-969268-13-7 (paperback)
ISBN 978-1-969268-14-4 (hardcover)
ISBN 978-1-969268-12-0 (digital)



This is a work of fiction. All of the characters, names, incidents, organizations, and dialogue in this novel are either the product of the author's imagination or are used fictitiously.

Scriptures marked KJV are taken from the KING JAMES VERSION (KJV): KING JAMES VERSION, public domain.

Printed in the United States of America

# TO THE FLAGS

Colonel Benjamin Terry: Tell the Texas Rangers that I'm the proud curator of their sacred standard, the Lone Star and Bars. Although the colors are long faded, and it's been tattered by a volley of musket fire, the fly end is still heavily encrusted in human blood. From a forensic analysis, it's quite obvious that the bearer was blown out of the saddle and clutched this flag as his life ebbed away. I can scarcely look upon it without weeping. I promise to pass this on to a future generation of Texans who may still remember that there was once a time when a man would charge forward, fight, and if necessary, die for what he believed in, be it right or wrong. Harry McCarthy sends his regards. He bears no ill will to the Rangers for the riot they caused down in the French Quarter back in September '61. After all, Texans will be Texans.

William Barrett Travis: I know where the flag is. I'm not joking! It's currently held under lock and key in the Chapultepec Castle at the compound of the *Museo Nacional De Historica* at *Ciudad de Mexico*. Despite the fact that the flag rarely, if ever, goes on display, it doesn't appear that the Mexicans are inclined to give it back. They still appear to be a bit steamed about that whole unpleasant Estado Tejas-Coahuila ordeal from a few years ago. In any event, if I ever get my mitts on that flag, I promise that I'll personally swim with it across the Bravo myself, and I'll return it to the Cradle of Liberty in Bexar where it rightly belongs. Give my warm regards to David, Jim, and the 180, and some-odd other Texans who are up there with you at the big Celestial Chili Cook-Off.

## TO THE RUSSIANS

Ilya Anisimov and Andrey Galyutin: This author has often wondered what it would have been like if Peter the Great decided to abandon the use of Cyrillic letters, which evolved out of ancient Greek script, and had decided to employ Roman letters instead during the remote time when he updated the Russian alphabet many centuries ago. After all, to most Americans, the Russian language is extraordinarily complex. Nonetheless, the Russians appear to be extremely skilled at cursing and hurling insults. Nice! My fictional character, "Russian Bear", thanks you both for your expertise in providing the appropriate nasty Russian expressions that I decided to utilize in this novel. Oh, by the way, thanks loads for your help in getting President Trump elected! Nice work. The American people owe you one.

# CONTENTS

# 1

## BASEMENT MEMBRANES

Irene Segulla was previously the charge nurse on the day shift of the med-surg unit at the medical school, but the wheel of fortune in life had ironically and irrevocably taken a spin for the worse. As she was now a critically ill patient with devastating injuries to her face and generalized head and neck region, which occurred when she was victimized in a botched carjacking attempt, she was no longer able to function in the capacity of a caretaker. Sadly, the nurse had just suffered from a life-threatening cardiopulmonary arrest as a consequence of aspirating her gastric contents deep into the recesses of her own lungs. Her jaws were previously wired shut by the team of medical specialists from the trauma service in conjunction with the maxillofacial surgeon who had valiantly attended to her care after she was violently assaulted in the employee parking lot at the Gulf Coast College of Medicine.

Irene had looked upon J. D. Brewster as a "surrogate son," and she tried to protect the troubled young man from the pitfalls that could blindside a medical student during the emotionally stressful and arduous clinical clerkship rotations. Wracked with cumulative guilt, Brewster blamed himself for the physical assault that had befallen Irene. After all, he was standing in the very same parking lot where Ms. Segulla had sustained her severe injuries only a few moments before she was attacked by two vicious thugs.

Brewster was painfully aware that Irene's caustic stomach acid would start to immediately digest the very lining of her pulmonary tree. As the medical student and the floor nurse, Missy Brownwood, performed CPR on the patient, Brewster could only wonder what was taking the Code Blue Response Team such a long time to get to Irene's bed side to assume management of the emergency situation.

"Where in hell is the code team?" Brewster demanded as he continued rapid chest compressions on Irene Segulla. "Did they stop and pick up a pepperoni pizza on their way here, or what?"

"I don't know, but I'm getting a lot of resistance on this Ambu-bag!" Missy explained. "I … I'm running out of steam, Brew! Let's swap out on the count of three. I need you to man the vent bag for now. Do the countdown!"

"Okay, here we go," Brewster commanded. "One, two, three— swap out!"

"Smooth work," Missy said as she took over the administrative duties of chest compressions while Brewster assumed the responsibility of attempting to aerate the patient. "Tell me … do you feel a lot of back pressure on the Ambu-bag?"

"This is bad, Missy," Brewster said in a panic. "Her lungs must be filled with shit!"

"Keep bagging her, Brew," Missy said. "It sounds like the code team is just now rolling up. They must be just right down the hallway."

"Well, it's about time!" Brewster exclaimed. "They need to take over right now. After all, I have a new mission in my life, Missy."

"What are you talking about?"

"If the police detectives working on Irene's case can't get the job done," Brewster explained, "then I'm going to hunt down the two bastards who attacked her. I'll do it all by myself if I have to. I'll make absolutely certain that justice is served. I swear on it—if it's the last damned thing that I ever do!"

"Okay by me," Missy said while panting from fatigue. "Let me know if you need help."

Half a year prior to J. D. Brewster's enrollment in medical school, the hostile competition between the Cardiology Service under the leadership of Dr. Adonis Portland and the Emergency Medicine Division lead by Dr. Frank Barber was about to turn into open warfare. Although there was no overt bloodshed per se, the conflict nonetheless resulted in an administrative nightmare for the Gulf Coast College of Medicine. Both department heads had aggressively pursued the contract from the parent institution to develop the Code Blue Cardiopulmonary Resuscitation Protocol.

Whichever medical specialty division that would eventually be awarded the contract would also have the responsibility for the implementation of a CPR Code Blue Response Team. The plan was for the development of three separate teams to cover each eight-hour hospital shift on a rotating basis. There was a considerable amount of money at stake via departmental funding allocations in addition to bragging rights for the specialty service that would be fortunate enough to successfully woo administrative favor.

Prior to January 1977, if a patient suffered a cardiopulmonary arrest at the university hospital, the resuscitative efforts that were brought to bear were sadly haphazard and non-standardized. The obvious trend amongst many hospitals in the late 1970s was the development of a specific and highly trained on-call medical team that would be responsible for intervention in such medical emergencies in a timely and proficient manner.

Dr. Adonis Portland's particular claim to fame was that he was a pioneer in the field of post-cardiac transplant medical management. Portland and his team of clinical research scientists achieved considerable notoriety for successfully developing moderately effective treatment regimens to help thwart the complication of immune-modulated host-versus-heart tissue graft organ rejection. This success was achieved through the work he was involved with in South Africa in the late 1960s. A notoriously pompous, misogynistic, and egomaniacal womanizer, Dr. Portland's reputation in clinical medicine (and also in the boudoir) had widely preceded him.

As all is fair in love and war, the head of the Emergency Medicine Division, Dr. Frank Barber, had no qualms about exploiting these foibles that had characterized his chief competitor to the benefit of his own Emergency Medicine Department. Much to the embarrassment of the medical college, inquiring minds throughout East Texas were suddenly and thoroughly captivated by a series of rather unflattering and scandalous published reports concerning Dr. Portland's sexual exploits, which unfortunately landed the cardiologist in front of a very angry board of medical ethics.

"Tell me something, Frank," Dr. Portland asked as he privately confronted his political adversary in the doctor's lounge. "Are you the one responsible for this rash of shit that's being printed up about me in the tabloids? I'll have you know that every relationship I've ever been in has been consensual and mutually satisfying. When in hell are you going to climb down from your high-horse, holier-than-thou, load of crap?"

"Am I talking to the same Adonis Portland who has a restraining order filed against him by some skirt named Hilty Skankenberg? She was the cardiology fellow from Corpus who did an externship with you last year, was she not?"

"Stop right there, Frank. If you keep it up, you're gonna' get a fat lip."

"You need to refresh my memory about something, Adonis," Barber asked. "Was it just a bad case of venereal warts, or was it an exotic, juicy, chancroid ulcer that rotted your pecker off at the hilt?"

"How do you know about that?" Portland asked.

"A little pussycat told me that you're a dirty bird," Frank Barber answered. "In fact, if the truth be told, I heard that you're a downright filthy rooster that got kicked out of the chicken coop."

"Is that so?" Adonis Portland asked. "The same little femme feline told me that you need to watch your back, buddy boy!"

A basketful of dirty laundry about Adonis Portland saw the light of day in several human-interest articles that somehow found their way into *Gulf Coast Monthly* magazine. Mysteriously, the articles appeared just prior to the time that the hospital and medical school administration had to make a decision as to what specialty department would be awarded the contract to implement the new Code Blue Cardiopulmonary Resuscitation Protocol.

When Dr. Portland was publicly shamed by the magazine articles, his campaign to secure the CPR contract for the Cardiology Service was effectively sunk by a torpedo. Sadly, as the flagship circled the drain, the cardiologist didn't have a life preserver to afford him even the slimmest of chances to survive a perilous dip in the shark-infested drink.

As it would turn out, Dr. Barber's endeavors were a pyrrhic victory at best. Within six weeks of his department being awarded the honor (and also the financial windfall) of developing the Code Blue Cardiopulmonary Resuscitation Protocol, Dr. Barber and his wife, Nancy, simply disappeared from the very face of the earth while they were on vacation in San Antonio. At that time, Dr. Barber was slated to give a voluntary presentation to a local community charitable organization on the correlation between health and hygiene. As expected, no good deed goes unpunished.

The local authorities found Frank's car in a parking lot at El Mercado, and oddly enough, the keys were still in the vehicle's ignition. The dried blood that was caked upon the steering wheel and dashboard strongly suggested that Frank and his wife were victims of foul play, but it remained only speculation to the Federal Bureau of Investigation for the longest time as to what really happened to the couple. Although never substantiated, rumors were prevalent that Dr. Portland was somehow responsible for initiating what was essentially an act of political sabotage against his bitter rival.

Upon the arrival of the CPR Code Blue Response Team to room 3:16, J. D. Brewster was able to give a brief overview to the Code Blue team captain, Dr. Bailey, about the clinical circumstances contributing to the patient's acute aspiration that directly resulted in Irene's cardiac arrest. Of course, the attending knew very well who Irene Segulla was. In fact, prior to Irene's critical injuries, she was the usual day shift charge nurse of the med-surg unit, so *everybody* knew her.

Brewster erroneously believed that the better part of valor would be for him to slip out of the patient's room and allow the Code Blue Response Team to carry out their duties. However, the medical student was certainly surprised when he was drafted by Dr. Bailey to help out with the code.

"I just don't feel a pulse. I want Horace on chest compressions," Bailey ordered in a calm yet firm and direct manner.

Brewster's anxiety about Irene's circumstances receded with Bailey's authoritative command of the code team. J. D. stood behind the attending to wait for further orders.

"Mary's on the stopwatch, so we'll be able to keep track of how deep we go into this code. Since the patient's jaw is wired shut and we can't ram down an ET tube, I want Buck to man the Ambu-bag for ventilation. Explain something to me," Dr. Bailey asked as he turned his head toward Brewster. "What happened when you tried to bag her before the code team arrived?"

"Resistance," Brewster answered, "and a ton of it."

"Damn. I was afraid of that." The attending applied a thin, adhesive-wired electrode to the right upper anterior chest wall and another on the left lateral rib cage and then subsequently turned on the cardiac monitor to note a prolonged, slow, but nonetheless potentially lethal, ventricular fibrillation.

"Slow V-fib! Juice the paddles," Bailey said. "Let's move it, people; we've got a life to save!"

"The bag isn't working!" the man named Buck proclaimed as he attempted to manage the Ambu-bag. He turned to the medical student and asked, "What's your name, junior?"

"Brewster!" Although terrified, J. D. was ready to comply with any task that the team needed assistance with.

"Get your ears on this lady's chest," Buck ordered, "and then tell me if you hear any air movement!"

Brewster placed his stethoscope upon Irene's anterior chest wall and listened intently. "Sounds like somebody threw a monkey wrench down the kitchen sink disposal!"

"Charged up!" Dr. Bailey placed the electric paddles from the defibrillator upon the patient's chest. "Clear!"

At that moment, all the members of the code team stepped back from the patient and raised their hands to indicate they were not touching the patient or the metallic bed railing. In unison, the team members replied, "Clear!"

Irene's body briefly convulsed forward as the electrical current from the defibrillator was successful in jump-starting her heart. "Good news, boys and girls; we've got a sinus!" The Code Blue team captain reported. "Hold the compressions, Horace, and grab a BP. Keep pumping the Ambu-bag, buckaroo, before her rhythm deteriorates back into V-fib."

"This isn't working worth a tinker's damn!" Buck said. "Her mouth is full of vomit, and it seems like the only thing I'm doing is driving a truckload of shit down into her lungs. Either we need to do an emergency bedside tracheostomy right now to get a patent emergency airway or we better get some damned snips in here to free up her jaw and snake in an ET tube. I guess it would be too much to ask to see if we had any wire cutters on the crash cart."

"I don't see any," Missy Brownwood reported, "but Harper from the maintenance department is down the hall. He's changing out a burned-up GFI plug in the utility room."

"Go get that wire clipper, Missy," the attending ordered. "No! Better yet, just grab Harper and drag him down here with his entire tool kit. Be quick about it. Brewster, I want you to flip on the wall blower and grab the tonsillar suction. I want you to extract all of that vomit and shit out of Irene's mouth."

"No dice," Brewster explained. "Missy and I tried it just before your team arrived, and the wall suction's apparently broken!"

"What the hell is wrong with you, dumbass!" Bailey said. "The adjacent patient room is empty. You and Missy should have moved Irene over there when you found that the wall suction was malfunctioning. Why didn't you do it before we got here?"

"I'm sorry! With all of the excitement that happened when Irene quit breathing, I guess my mind just went blank for a moment."

"Somebody told me at one time that you were one of the brainiacs," the attending said. "Well, you can't prove it by me. Wake up, Brewster! What are you waiting for? Get that empty bed next door rolled out into the hallway so that we can move Irene over to a new room. Did anyone ever tell you to your face that you're an idiot?"

Were these allegations of clinical malfeasance rendered upon Brewster by the captain of the code team indeed true? If so, Brewster realized that he would be culpable for any future untoward clinical outcome that might befall Irene Segulla after her cardiopulmonary arrest. If Irene failed to recover from this calamity, Brewster knew that he would never be able to forgive himself.

The Dalton twins were big fans of disco dance and disco music, and they were both grieved and prematurely nostalgic when this happy era was coming to a close around 1980. The twin sisters were drop-dead gorgeous with bright green eyes, and it was rather inexplicable to everybody why their skin tone was quite a bit fairer than either their mother or their father.

D' Shea and D' Nae Dalton were taking summer classes before entering their junior year at the University of Houston, and they were renting a small basement apartment near the university campus. Scholarships provided an eighty percent tuition ride for them both, and it was fortunate that their parents were able to pay the balance including books, supplies, and miscellaneous university fees. The only stipulation was that if the young ladies had ever made the big jump to live off campus, the financial responsibility for that decision would be on their dime. Needless to say, their parents were somewhat nervous about their precious offspring spreading their wings in what was essentially a very dangerous and crime-infested city.

Except for being carjacked and physically beaten by two thugs at the point of a lead pipe during their freshman years back in 1978, life was good. Being assaulted can be a life-changing experience, but as the twins were "black, free, and twenty-one", the event had only hardened them. The young women were now licensed gun owners, and they were trained in the use of matching chrome, faux ivory grip, .25-caliber automatics that they had tucked neatly into their handbags.

The future looked bright, and the twins had no worries—except for the fact that D' Shea was starting to experience troublesome headaches. "Okay, enough of this, baby girl," D' Nae said. "I'm now seeing you vomit every day from those headaches."

"I'll be just fine," her twin sister replied. "It just comes on once in a while."

"Just once in a while?" D' Shea scoffed. "Well, it was 'once in a while' a month ago. Now it's every damn morning when you get out of bed. There's something the matter with you, and I'm going to drag your carcass down to the student health center. I'm telling you right now, you need to see a neurologist. I've seen some folks who've had migraine headaches before, but migraine headaches don't strike day and night and without end in sight."

"You need to back off right about now," D' Shea replied as she pressed the palm of her right hand against the frontal and lateral aspect of her skull. The young woman intuitively realized that something was wrong, but perhaps this problem would just go away in the same fashion that it had just suddenly appeared. "I have summer classes to attend. We'll be graduating in two years, and I just don't have time to be sick."

"Is that so?" D 'Nae asked. "Perhaps you can explain to me why you're having trouble holding onto things with your left hand from time to time. You better not keel over on me with a stroke—or I'll open up a can of whoop-ass on you, baby girl!"

"Be cool, Sis," D' Shea said. "I just need some fresh air. Let's take a drive to the grocery store and pick up a few things. Trust me. I'll be okay."

The twins dressed and looked alike. In the spring of 1980, they had even decided to sport close-cropped hair as opposed to the large, gravity-defying, perfectly round Afro-style coifs that they had chosen as their signature image for the previous six years. The new hairstyles they had chosen were elective yet reluctant acts that acknowledged a changing of the guard. When the Manhattan-based dance discotheque, Studio 54, had closed its doors in February 1980, the writing was already on the wall. Sadly for the twins, if the disco era was not already declared dead, that style of music and dance was on advanced life support with a documented and notarized DNR code status. Popular music was clearly moving in the direction of what was called "new wave" and "punk," and it sounded very much like angry (warning: a literary double entendre is approaching) white noise to the young ladies. It was a sound that was diametrically opposed to the now passé, snappy, and carefree disco music that was rapidly disappearing from the radio airwaves. If the times were a-changin', then so be it. If the changing times dictated that the twins should also change their appearances, then so be it.

D' Shea and D' Nae had just completed their grocery shopping for two weeks of provisions to stuff into the small pantry in their basement apartment. As they loaded the sundry goods into their trunk, D' Shea realized that she had forgotten to pick up an important item on their shopping list. The two closets in their apartment were infested with small voracious moths that were drilling holes into their wardrobes. Since the landlord disregarded multiple requests to have the apartment fumigated, it was clearly necessary that the twins would have to purchase mothballs or moth cakes for the closets. If the pesky insects were to be eradicated, two young women would have to embark on the paramilitary interdiction of arthropod extermination on their own accord.

"Hold the fort, baby girl," D' Shea said. "I have to pop back in and pick up a bug bomb and some moth cakes."

As D' Shea stepped away from the trunk of the car, something strange caught her eye. Two men were walking briskly toward them from the front of their automobile, and one of the men was holding a lead pipe. Although they were disguised in Columbia blue Houston Oiler football jerseys and late 1960s-style silver helmets, the young woman immediately recognized them as the ones who had carjacked and beaten them two years before. D' Shea couldn't believe her eyes; she and her sister were about to be assaulted yet again by two life-long career criminals who predominately preyed upon the Black community. Utilizing debasing and intentionally derisive insults, they insisted upon calling themselves "Big Nig" and "Smeg Nog"!

D' Shea calmly said, "Check out these two fools who're about to roll up on our doorstep. I'll bet they don't even recognize who we are. Pull out your piece, baby girl, but hold your water until they get to the front of our car."

"I'm already on deck," D' Nae replied. "I've been praying for an opportunity to have a nice little chat with these animals one day."

The two thugs had no idea that they had overplayed their hand when Big Nig said, "Ma'am, 'scuse me. My man here and I needs to ax you a question. Where da white wimins at?"

At that moment, the twins stepped from behind their car with the chrome-plated automatic pistols and leveled the barrels down on the approaching carjackers.

D' Nae said, "I'll show you! I have five of them in this clip. Come take a peak down the barrel, and I will introduce them to you."

"There must be some type of misunderstanding, lil' sister," Smeg Nog said. "Let me just get a bit closer, and I'll man 'splain things to you."

D' Shea said, "Take one more step—and I'll drop you."

"You gonna' shoot me?" Big asked.

"You stupid bastards don't even recognize who we are!" D' Nae exclaimed.

"Don't make me laugh. Is that a cap gun?" Nog asked. "It ain't ladylike to be messin' with a boy toy. I don't think the big man and I have ever met you girls before."

"Well, we know who you are. That's for damn sure. Now my pistol doesn't have sights, but I can knock a can of Billy beer from the top of a fence post at thirty feet. Go ahead. Test me. It's your call." D' Shea was serious. Dead serious.

The two would-be carjackers sprinted away, shedding their pitiful disguises as they ran.

"At that distance, why didn't you smoke a round through his left eye?" D' Nae asked. "All you had to do was to pull the trigger. If you had done so, I would've greased the big boy next. Easy-peasy."

"There was a time in my life when I tried to be a good Christian, just like you," D' Shea answered wistfully. "I was taught in Sunday school to turn the other cheek, just like you. I'm ashamed to say that I'm just not like that any longer. However, maybe someday I'll find my way back home."

"As long as you can see the light."

"Can I get an 'amen,' baby girl?" D' Shea asked.

"Amen, baby girl," D' Nae answered. "Let's go back into the grocery store. You pick up the moth cakes, and I'll go over to the pay phone and call the cops. After that, I have one more phone call to make."

"Are you going to call Mom and Dad and tell them what happened?" D' Shea asked.

"I'll get to that, but first I need to call that fat-ass, dipshit owner of the Houston Oilers, Bud Adams. I'm going to tell him it'll be necessary to give his football team a big juicy raise so they don't have to moonlight as gangsters!"

The twins gave each other a high five and had a good laugh.

Big Nig and Smeg Nog collapsed with exhaustion in the empty warehouse they used as their chop shop near the Fourth Ward.

"The cupboard is empty, Papa Bear," Smeg Nog noted. "I think we need a new strategy. I do believe it's time that we start carrying hardware."

"No, you're wrong," Big replied. "We just have to learn how to separate business from pleasure. Shit, son! It made me laugh when we made the white nurse up and bleed in that parking lot at the medical center when we crushed her face like it was an empty cardboard box."

"A hoot to boot!"

"Putting a pipe upside the head of Snow White was pure, unadulterated recreation," Big admitted, "but if we're out and about on the job to pull inventory, we have to stay focused."

"So, you sayin' we have a problem?" Nog asked.

"Well, to tell the truth, it ain't *we* who has the problem. *You* are the one who has to stay focused."

"Wait a minute … are you disrespectin' me?" Nog asked. "Sounds like the pot calling the kettle black. It be *you* who has trouble staying focused on the job. The only reason you don't want to carry hardware is because of what happened at that cigar shop on South Main that we hit back in '68. After you greased the old white lady and the colored man working behind the counter, you found the colored man's daughter hiding in the stockroom."

"My memory must be a bit foggy about that matter."

"Is that so?" the smaller man asked sarcastically. "When you got all stoked up for a little serious extracurricular activity, we almost got caught. By the time we got out of there, the pigs were rolling down the street with their sirens a-blowin'. That was all on you, bro."

"I'm not your brother," Big said.

"That's right!" Nog replied. "You ain't my brother, 'cause you ain't shit to me. There ain't no statute of limitations on what we done. We gots to be smart when we be out pickin' up inventory. I sez we use hardware, and we is in faster and we is out faster. That is, of course, only if you be the one who up and figure out a way how to separate da business from da pleasure."

Big didn't see where this conversation was headed. This was all ancient history, as the raid on the cigar store on South Main was the first job the partners in crime had executed well over a dozen years earlier. "Stay cool, little man. You pitched the piece into Braes Bayou after we hit that cigar shop. If there ain't no gun, there ain't no evidence."

"I have to 'fess up about something," Nog sheepishly stated. "I never pitched the piece. I still have it. I wanted to keep it because it was a World War II Walther. That's why I think we should start carrying hardware again. I already have a piece."

"If I get pinched because of some dumb-shit thing that you do someday, I'm going to kill you. Am I clear?" Big Nig gritted his teeth and sneered at his junior partner. "I'm not going to the big house because you're careless."

"Be cool," Smeg said. "I'll do it."

"I'm serious," the big man said. "Get rid of the damned gun now—or I'll get rid of you. For now, our business transactions will continue to be executed with a lead pipe. Here be our next course of action. We need to lay low in da weeds for the next few weeks, and then we up an' hit the Texas Medical Center once again."

"So soon?" Nog asked. "We'll be goin' against the grain."

"We've struck out in the past like this, so it's no time to panic," Big claimed. "I know we'll bounce back. All you have to do right now is keep your pecker dry and get rid of that gun once and for all."

Smeg Nog paid lip service to the order from Big Nig, but the junior partner actually planned on keeping the gun secretly stashed. After all, the weapon just might come in handy someday…

In the basement of the Gulf Coast College of Medicine, the research biologist named Rip Ford and his colleague, J. D. Brewster, left the primate lockdown kennel after paying another visit to the great apes. The head of the MD/PhD dual training program, Dr. Harrison Reed, was coming down hard on the two men for their obvious procrastination on the non-A, non-B hepatitis research study. Understandably, however, Brewster and Ford had very serious qualms about the next phase of their experimental endeavors, which would involve the injection of the great apes with a potentially lethal viral entity.

Ford had returned to his section of the lab to try to figure out a way to forestall the inoculation of the great apes with a non-A, non-B hepatitis viral load harvested from the blood, serum, and ascites fluid from infected human subjects. In the meantime, Brewster was over-due to follow up on the condition of Mrs. Segulla after her harrowing cardiopulmonary arrest and near-death experience. Upon Brewster's arrival to Irene's new room in the intensive care unit, Dr. Marek Cannon and his Internal Medicine Team #4 were in attendance.

Dr. Cannon had the diaphragm of his stethoscope placed firmly against the thorax of Ms. Segulla and was listening carefully to her respiratory sounds. Irene had not fully recovered from her harrowing cardiopulmonary arrest, and she was back on mechanical ventilator support.

Dr. Cannon had a look of grave concern when he looked up and realized that J. D. Brewster had arrived. "Come here, brainiac. You need to listen to this. Where are your ears?"

"I'm not a brainiac anymore. I received a field commission rank of stud, but I don't have my ears," Brewster replied. "Maybe somebody on your team would be so kind to allow me to borrow their stethoscope." He extended his left hand to one of the students on the team. "Lend me your ears."

The student members of Internal Medicine Team #4 glared at J. D., and nobody was willing to pass over a stethoscope to Brewster, even for a moment.

"Who in hell gave you that field commission—and how did you skip the rank of scut puppy?" Dr. Cannon asked.

"The GI fellow, Dr. Colima, gave me this rank," Brewster replied. "I had two clinical rotations salted away during my year of research, and he felt that I deserved to be a stud."

"I find that unacceptable," Dr. Cannon said. "And I need to check the rules. In any event, if I ever catch you on one of the wards again without your stethoscope, I'll demote you on the spot. You understand? Take my stethoscope and listen to the right mid-lung field of this patient. If you leave any nasty wax on my set of ears, I'll sling your sorry ass back down to the laboratory basement so fast that your unit will shrivel up fall off at the short hairs. Listen carefully. The crackles you hear on expiration are called 'rales' and I want y'all to line up and listen in."

Brewster had never heard rales during the auscultation of a patient's chest, but he correctly surmised that they must have been associated with pneumonia as a consequence of the previous aspiration event just prior to Irene's cardiopulmonary arrest.

"Don't ever forget what this sounds like," Dr. Cannon explained. "Everybody in this room needs to memorize that sound. If you put your ears on a patient's chest and hear the sound of a dog turd being wrapped up in cellophane, something bad's going down."

A portable x-ray machine was rolled into the patient's room, and the stat CXR confirmed to all present that Mrs. Segulla was starting to have a "whiteout" of her right middle lung field.

Dr. Cannon said, "Irene, I know you can still hear me, so I don't want you to panic. Let me explain what's going on. You're developing aspiration pneumonia in the middle lobe of your right lung. I was hoping we could start weaning you from the ventilator today, but your oxygen-saturation levels are quite poor, and we'll have to postpone that plan. We'll get some additional antibiotics on board. Don't be scared, darlin'. We still have a good chance of getting your chestnuts pulled out of the fire."

When Brewster left the patient's room, he was rightly concerned about the current circumstances complicating the clinical course of Ms. Segulla. Although he had great faith in the advancements of modern medicine, the pneumonia was a major setback. J. D. considered the funny, frumpy, middle-aged lady a friend. He had suppressed his guilt about Irene's situation, but intrusive thoughts of recrimination and self-doubt were yet again knocking on his front door.

As he was leaving the ward, he encountered a very large woman in the hallway outside of Mrs. Segulla's room. At about five feet seven inches tall, it appeared that she was pulling down about a deuce and a quarter in dry body weight. She was wearing a threadbare, cream white halter top that looked like a doily. She was also adorned in an anachronistic short purple paisley skirt that was far from the realm of haute couture. With four or five plastic daisies embedded in her disheveled blonde hair, she appeared to be in her early thirties.

Even without a formal introduction, this woman must have been Mrs. Segulla's niece, Stella Link. Brewster was immediately smitten. Her face was so round that it must have been blueprinted by a protractor, while her bosom was an amorphous mass that lacked clearly definable boundaries. Neatly polished symmetrical toes peeked out from leather cross-strapped Roman sandals, and a fringed fanny pouch completed her presentation.

Brewster imagined that Stella Link would have looked good in a Viking hat festooned with giant bovine spikes that had been harvested from the skull of a burnt orange longhorn steer. A shorter set of horns would even be acceptable under the circumstances, as any bony protrusions emanating from a relic helmet from the dark ages that would make a Brahma bull proud would still be most alluring. She could be a Brahma momma! Brewster had imagined that her corpulent body had been adorned with a tattoo of an anchor on her bulging right forearm and a flaming skull on the other. She would have looked perfect carrying a mace or a trident. This was actually J.

D. Brewster's dream of a beautiful version of the angel of death. *The opera ain't over until the fat lady sings,* he thought.

Brewster was determined to muster up the courage to formally introduce himself to Stella Link. Little did he know that all he had to do was to pull the trigger.

Brewster thought that his own life would wind down as a consequence of his left main coronary artery being clogged up with a thick, greasy, atheromatous plaque. He had specific fantasies about his own demise: he wanted a huge blonde woman in a Viking hat with long braided hair and a battle ax to take him down for the ten count. He had hoped she would just throw him right down on the ground and plop her morbidly obese frame smack dab on the middle of his sternum. As she crushed the life right out of him, maybe she would sing a dramatic Wagnerian number in the mezzo-soprano range. If that exceeded her vocal limitations, perhaps she would at least serenade him with Led Zeppelin's "Stairway to Heaven." Hopefully, it would be the long version. *Yeah, that's the ticket!* Brewster had hoped he would take a one-way trip into the great beyond while a fat Viking lady angel of death was sitting upon his face. When it was his time to finally shoot through into the blue, that's exactly how he wanted to make his exit from this plane of existence known as life.

Brewster had always been attracted to moderately fat girls, but they had to meet certain criteria for him to become seriously interested in them. First, a fat girl must not be so big that she had her own area code. Nor could she possess the gravitational fields approaching the magnitude of the giant red star, Pachyderm, which had been recently discovered in the distant constellation commonly known as the Big Pork Rind. It would have been a bit unsavory to have dated a giant fat girl who had smaller, sweaty, fat women in perpetual orbit about the giant. These sweaty satellites would likely be voyeuristic chunky monkeys—nonsolid planetary giants comprised of methane, ammonia, and other noxious gases, much like what can be found up in Uranus.

Also, a potential fat girlfriend could not be so gargantuan that smaller creatures such as moths and spiders would be able to hide underneath the woman's abdominal pannus. This intertriginous fold of skin and adipose tissue was a potentially dangerous netherworld of pure, unadulterated, cheesy funk. This particular criterion was an absolute prerequisite. Those caveats aside, Brewster contemplated the prospects of actually going out on a date with Irene's niece.

Stella Link smiled and vigorously waved at J. D. Brewster as he left the floor. She was desperately trying to get his attention. Although Brewster's mind was filled with outrageous fantasies, he was nonetheless quite shy. He pretended not to notice her as he scampered to the elevator that would take him back down to the safety of basement laboratory.

The music on the elevator happened to be the bossa nova standard, "The Girl from Ipanema" by Astrud Gilberto and Stan Getz. Although he knew the lyrics by heart, he had never really appreciated the meaning of this song. If only Brewster had paid attention, he would have been hit in the head with a cosmic two by four. As per usual, he failed to see the big picture.

Upon Brewster's arrival back at the basement laboratory, Rip Ford had a message for him. "Dr. Rabbi came along and wanted me to invite you to join him in a new research project. He wants you to help him work on a new shingles vaccine project."

Brewster slowly shook his head and said, "No, I don't think I'll be going down that rabbit hole."

"Why not?"

"Knowing the Rabbi, I'll bet that any research project on a shingles vaccine will run a prolonged course," Brewster said.

"Of course it would!" Ford exclaimed. "You boys would be starting from scratch."

"Don't you see? That's the problem," Brewster explained. "When I was one of the few students who got accepted into the MD/PhD program, I was determined to wrap up my training in six years. I want to be on the launch pad to blast off in 1983."

"Now that the hepatitis B vaccine study that you previously worked on with the Rabbi has come to a dead end, why don't you just expand your horizons and add this project to what you're doing now?"

"No, damn it!"

"You and the Rabbi could make something of it. What are you afraid of? Don't you like it here?"

"If I take on something with the complexity of a shingles vaccine project, I suspect I'll be stuck here at the Gulf Coast until I'm half past dead. That's why."

"It's your life," Ford said. "Feel free to squander it any way you choose."

"Aren't you a fountain of joy? Thanks, asshole," Brewster said. "By the way, where's Uncle Hank?"

"He's a hermit crab," Ford said. "No hide nor hair, I tell you!"

"I thought he'd be back to work after he got his skin and lymph node biopsies done."

"Nope," Ford noted. "You don't think it's a harbinger, do you?"

"What—of bad news? Perish the thought," Brewster answered. "I'm sure he'll be fine."

"Well, I sure won't be fine once we start inoculating the big primates."

J. D. Brewster had prayed hard for some act of grace to deliver him from the burden of doing experimental studies on the great apes, but he felt that God was no longer listening. He and Ford had to have a plan for what to do as soon as the head of the non-A, non-B hepatitis virus isolation study returned from his prolonged sick leave. That man was Dr. Hank Holcombe, and the two young research scientists hoped his return to work was imminent.

An act of grace appeared in the form of an enormous black man who was knocking on the door to the basement laboratory. He was wearing a short-sleeved shirt underneath the short, white consulting jacket and navy trousers that were typically worn by male medical students at the Gulf Coast. He filled the entire doorway, and he spoke with an obviously exaggerated black southern dialect. "Lord, have mercy on you white boys down here. No wonder you have no functional melanocytes in your skin. You're all a bunch of damn vampires! No, I'll bet you're Mexican vampires. Are you boys 'high-spanics'?"

"I'm cracker white," Brewster said. "As far as my colleague, Rip Ford, his ethnicity is definitely in question. In fact, I am not even sure if the son of a bitch is a human being."

"Bite me, Brew," Ford said. "Tell me more about these 'Mesikin' vampires."

"They're called *vampiros*," the big man answered. "They happen to be the most dangerous subtype of parasites known to mankind."

"Even more dangerous than a bloodsucking member of Congress?" Brewster asked.

"Oh, by far! I met one out west in New Mexico quite a while back."

"A congressman? Frankly, that would scare the shit out of me," Brewster replied.

"No," the big man replied. "A *vampira*! Pay attention."

"Did she suck you off?" Ford asked.

"She wouldn't back off until she drained a quart."

"Sounds like she's a keeper to me," Brewster noted.

"Not so much," the giant said. "Although she was a deluxe babe, she wasn't very smart. A taco shy of a combo platter, I tell ya!"

Ford said, "At the risk of sounding like a pig, I don't give a shit anymore if a girl is smart or not. Do you still have her phone number?"

"The she-beast became my love slave for a time being. She could suck the chrome off the bumper of a '59 Caddy!"

"Wait a minute," Ford said. "I just now realized that you maliciously accused my colleague and me of human vampirism!"

The man pulled two ballpoint pens out of his jacket pocket and formed them into a cross. "Back! Get back to the depths of hell, you bloodsucking agents of Satan!"

Brewster and Ford had no idea who this guy was, but it was clear that he wanted to jaw. He wanted to BS. He wanted to grapple. He wanted to crack some *cojones*. He wanted to play. Brewster thought, *Outside of locker rooms, black and white people rarely interact this way anymore. It would be too dangerous.*

"How come there aren't any ladies around?" the big man asked. "Oh, yeah. I forgot. There's just a bunch of pasty *vampiros* locked up down here in this basement. Well, you can stop the presses. Tell them all that Willy the 'Wooly Mammoth' Mammon is here."

"I have no doubt that your surname, 'Mammon,' has a direct lineage that can be traced all the way back to the evil demigod of avarice and lust for wealth," Brewster said. "Do you possess any of those ignoble attributes of your disreputable namesake?"

"Would a rose by any other name smell as sweet?"

"Oh, hell no!" Brewster answered. "If a rose was named *feces,* it would smell like, well—like shit!"

"Nice!" the big man said. "Did your momma ever have to wash out your mouth with a bar of soap when you were a youngin'?"

"From time to time," Brewster answered. "What's your angle?"

"It should be plain to see," the stranger said. "I'm here to satisfy what everybody is hungry for."

"Ford, the pizza guy's here," Brewster said with a grin. "This mountain man says he's going to satisfy what everybody's hungry for. Flip him a Hamilton and get him the hell outta' here. Make sure the big sumbitch didn't forget the anchovies. I'll square up with you later."

At six feet and five inches, the Wooly Mammoth was huge— even if he didn't tip the scales at 325 pounds. "A little respect is in order here, my man. When I come into town, I'm riding on a pogo stick that's the size of the Hemisphere Tower."

"Excuse me while I grab a nap," Brewster replied.

"Pay heed to what I'm preachin'! I keep it all spooled up on a fishing reel. When I need to break it out, I'll only let it down by the yard. Then, I'll loop it up really good and let it fly like a lasso."

"What's this guy's game?" Ford asked as he turned to Brewster.

"Beats the shit out of me," Brewster answered. "Maybe he's a door-to-door peddler who wants to sell us an encyclopedia set."

The Mammoth made a motion as if he was swinging an invisible rope around his head, and it was then thrown at a distant, invisible target. He let out a high-pitched buzzing sound like a fishing line would make when cast out by an angler. "Just like that, my man.

"Brewster turned to Ford and said, "Well, here it is. Unsubstantiated hyperbolic braggadocio about the black man's alleged sexual proclivity."

"It's all fact, my man, and no brag," Willy continued with his proclamations of prowess. "Where are you, little momma? Your salvation is on the scene. Of course, a man of my stature needs to be careful when I let it rip or else I might get backlash in the line. Getting the knots out of it can be a beast, know what I mean?"

"Wow," Ford said. "I'd pay good money to see just that."

"I have to pay very close attention when I'm out clipping the lawn" the Mammoth added. "On a hot and humid day, the big boy will often reel down on his own accord just to air out a bit. I have to keep a close lookout or else I might end up running him over with the mower."

"Ouch," Brewster added. "Need a Band-Aid?"

"One time I drained the radiator, and when I flushed, it got snaked downstream to the water-treatment plant. The big boy ended up at the Houston Zoo, and they put him on display in the python exhibit. Do you feel me?"

Finally, Brewster had met a man who was full of as much BS as he was. "Feel you? That's never going to happen. You keep that nasty trouser snake under wraps. While it's true you black boys may pack some bodacious beef, here's something straight up: black chicks will always dig me over a guy like you for two reasons."

"Okay, I'll bite," the Mammoth said. "What are these two alleged reasons?"

"It's quite simple," Brewster replied. "First, I've never been to prison. Second, I'll have a job someday. Dollars to doughnuts, there's no black fellow I know who can make that same claim!"

The Mammoth's smile was broad and gleaming. He entered the lab and bent over slightly. With a forward motion of the fingers of each hand, he offered Brewster and Ford an open invitation to get scrappy.

Ford leaned back in his chair, crossed his legs on the top of his desk, and interlaced his fingers behind his head.

"Don't you dare!" Brewster proclaimed. "You'll suck all the breathable air out of this room, and I'll die a horrible death from hypoxia!"

The big man pancaked out his huge frame against Brewster and pinned his arms against his side.

Brewster turned to Ford and said, "Tonto, the Lone Ranger here could use a little backup!"

"No way, Kemosabe," Ford said with a laugh. "It looks like you just about have everything under control. Besides, if I help you out, I'll be the one who'll end up getting spanked! Don't forget that no good deed goes unpunished."

The Wooly Mammoth grabbed Brewster's head and secured it in the crook of his arm. With the knuckles of his free hand, he started to give the misfortunate Brewster noogies on top of his scalp. The Mammoth started to sing a lullaby as he tormented the smaller man: "I wish, I wish, I had a fish. Go tell Aunt Helen, I want a watermelon. Go tell Brother Nye, I want some pecan pie."

"I surrender, damn it!" Brewster said. "Uncle! Uncle!"

The big man patted Brewster on the head and said, "Don't you worry, my man. Your hair will likely grow back in a few months."

Brewster checked his scalp and was relieved to see his hair was still intact.

Ford pulled a Mr. Pibb out of the mini-fridge and handed it to the Mammoth. "I've always enjoyed a good medieval donnybrook, especially when the cupcake over here is on the receiving end. How may we be of service to you, Mr. Willy Mammon?"

The big man held the cold beverage on high as if making a toast and nodded in appreciation as he sat in an open chair facing the other two men. "I'm here to talk you, Mr. Brewster. You don't remember me, do you? It was twenty years ago when I last saw you. You must have been about three years old, and I was only about ten. My father and I came over for your dad's funeral."

Brewster said, "So, what happened? Did you hoodlums come over and ransack the place while my family and I were off at Forest Lawn getting my old man interred?"

"No, dumbass!" the Mammoth replied. "We also went to the funeral. My father is Rudolph Valentino Mammon. He used to work for your father up until the very time your dad passed away."

Brewster flipped through his memory Rolodex, but he couldn't recall anything about the folks with whom his father had worked with in the past, and that included people who were white, black, brown, or otherwise. "I'm indeed sorry, but I'm drawing a blank. I was only three years old when my dad kicked the bucket. Although I do remember a lot of things from that time, I just don't recall meeting you or your father."

"Rudolph Valentino Mammon went to work for your father early on in the 1950s, but apparently they knew each other long before that," Willy said. "They were both in the navy during the war and served on ship together in the Pacific Theater. As I understand it, your father was the LT, and my dad was the cook."

"After the war, in what capacity did your father work for my old man?" Brewster asked.

"At first, my father was apparently an informant, but he also worked as a liaison between the white and black community at that time," the Mammoth said.

"How so?"

"After your father left the FBI, my dad became a torpedo for your old man. I don't want to speak out of school, but they got into some kind of sinister gangster shit together. Runnin' numbers? Don't know for sure."

"Stop right there," Brewster said with a scowl. "Sounds like bullshit to me. After my dad left the FBI, he became the assistant district attorney for Houston, not a gangster."

"True, but maybe he was simmering a pot of spicy chili on the side," the Mammoth said.

"Enough!" Brewster exclaimed. "My father worked in DA's office up until the time that he was elected to the city council—just a week or so before he passed away."

"Well, I don't want to get you all riled up, but my dad's still very much alive, and he claims that he was involved with more than just a few sketchy business endeavors with your father along the way. Pops won't say much about it, but perhaps he'll let you know more if you have a chance to talk to him."

"Am I to believe that my father had a dark side?" Brewster asked.

"If I'm not mistaken," Ford said with a smirk, "I once told you that the apple didn't fall far from the tree."

"Shut up, Ford!" Brewster demanded. "This sure as hell doesn't involve you."

"All I've been told is that your dad was a player in the black community over near Hobby Airport," Willy said.

"Why are you telling me all of this?" Brewster asked. "I don't even really know who you are."

"Hey, stud! Don't forget for one minute that *you* were the one who asked *me* what kind of working relationship your father had with my dad. Buck up and deal with it. Why are you looking at me like I have two heads?" Willy asked. "I'm on the square, my man."

"I have to process what you are telling me," Brewster said. "Frankly, it's a lot to take in.

"You have an older brother named Bill," Willy Mammon said. "He was about five or six years old when I last saw him. When my father went out on a job for your dad, he would leave me at your house."

"I swear that I really don't recall any of this," Brewster said.

"Well, I certainly do. I remember you boys had a tan little terrier dog named Electron that I played tug-of-war with using a kitchen towel. You and your brother got the dog the day after your father passed away. I only met your dog one time when my father and I came over to your house in Bellaire for your father's wake. As I never had a pet, I immediately fell in love with that little dog."

"The dog's name was actually Electra," Brewster said. "Maybe you're on the square after all."

"You see? If I'm lyin', I'm dyin', Brew. There's more—your dad had an olive green '59 Cadillac when he died," Mammoth added.

"Now, I do indeed remember that old car," Brewster said. "It had fins!"

"When your father died, he owed my dad some money, so your mom sold that Cadillac to my family at a big discount. We still have that car to this very day! It's now a collectible classic. Back then, I'll have you know, it was a major status symbol for a black man to drive a Cadillac."

"How so?" Brewster asked.

"It meant that somebody had 'made it' if they had that kind of car. When you meet my father, he'll tell you all about it. He's proud of that old Caddy. He's now the assistant to the head groundskeeper at the Astrodome, and he'll straight up tell you that your dad's old Cadillac helped secure that position for him."

"Be that as it may, I'm sure there's something else on your mind to bring you down into this basement above and beyond the pleasant opportunity to reminisce during our personal twenty-year reunion," Brewster said.

"The world is small, and everything in the universe seems to be connected somehow. If your father and my dad successfully collaborated in the past, be it for good or bad, then perhaps lightning can strike twice. Perhaps you and I should collaborate together during the clinical clerkships that are approaching in July."

"Hang on there," Brewster said. "As I'm enrolled in the dual training program, I'm currently engaged in scientific research. I'm concentrating on the PhD arm of my education. I'm definitely not planning on enrolling in the clerkship rotations any time soon."

"Is that so?" the Mammoth asked. "The word is out that the Gulf Coast pulled the plug on the hepatitis B vaccine study you were working on with Dr. Rabbi."

"Sad, but true. It looks like the Merck pharmaceutical company beat us to the punch—and they're already several years head of the research we have done thus far."

"In addition, it's no secret that you boys have run into a brick wall with Dr. Holcombe's non-A, non-B viral isolation study."

"Not a brick wall per se," Ford explained. "More like a crisis of conscience."

"So I've heard," Willy said. "Frankly, I don't envy your situation if it is all going to come down to subjecting the great primates to inoculation and subsequent vivisection in the name of science. Maybe it's time for you to shift gears and set your PhD research on the back burner for a while. You can get back to it someday, but for now, I think it's time for you to roll up your sleeves and enter the formal clerkship rotations. I'm just now finishing my second year of medical school, and I'm up to bat to start on two years of direct patient contact. I think it would be a good idea if you would do the same."

"What's in it for you?" Brewster asked.

"When your mom sold that Cadillac to my family, it changed our lives," Willy Mammon said. "It helped my father get to what I would call the 'next level'. Perhaps you could do the same for me if you're one of my clerkship partners. You know the ropes. I don't. To be frank, I'm nervous about what I'm going to face on the wards. I've known medical students who ended up getting their dicks broken off at the nubbies. It's brutal out there."

"I am flattered that you hold me in such high esteem," Brewster responded, "but there's a good possibility that I'll only get both of us into some deep kimchee."

"How so?" Willy asked.

"I've been told that I don't play well with other children," Brewster explained. "Just ask Ford. So, instead of grabbing onto my coattail, it might be the other way around."

"I can live with that," Willy added. "I'll be the pulling guard, and you can just grab onto my jersey while we're making an end sweep!"

"Fair enough."

"My dad has access to Astro tickets. The Cincinnati Reds are coming into town for a three-day series starting tomorrow, and I would like to invite you all out to the game. We can talk more about all of this. I can have my pops leave tickets at the will call window. J. D., I want you to call your brother and invite him to come along. The Astros are going to the World Series this year!"

As it would turn out, the Mammoth gave a prognostication that would fall a little short. Although the Astros arguably had the best team they had ever assembled at that time, which included the finest pitching staff in the entire Major Leagues in 1980, they would not make it to the championship series.

"So, are you up for a baseball game, Rip?" Willy asked.

"Hoorah!"

Rip Ford's enthusiastic expletive set Willy back on his heels. It had been many years since the big man had heard this particular expression. It was a term that was generally utilized by only those who had served in the military. "I need to know something, Mr. Ford." Willy studied Rip's face. "Were you in the 'Nam?"

Ford looked down to the floor and slowly nodded. "After Tet, when things turned to shit in a handbasket. Air force. Cameron Bay. I was on the ground crew, and I loaded nape and snake on the fast movers. How 'bout you?"

"I was an in-country bush grunt," the Mammoth replied with a forced smile. "I was a sapper, I tell you. Come to the game tomorrow night, and we'll all have a few laughs about it."

Mammon and Ford peered at each with a deep, unspoken understanding of death, grime, and chaos. Despite what Willy had said, neither of the men would ever find warfare to be a subject they could ever have "a few laughs about." The act of killing another human being, for whatever reason, is and should always be a serious, life-changing event. Obviously, that is the case for the person who is being killed, but it remains just as true for the individual who committed the act. That's a fact whether one is looking into the eyes of an enemy combatant while a sharpened Ka-Bar is being thrust into the adversary's heart or being the one who loaded the napalm and sidewinders onto the undercarriage of an F-4 Phantom.

Angst and regret can sometimes be compartmentalized, but the Vietnam War never came to a conclusion for either Rip Ford or Willy Mammon. As a matter of fact, it never would. Sadly, intrusive nightmares and recrimination over ancient sins would ensure that they would be caught fighting in this maelstrom for the rest of their lives.

Brewster was just getting off the telephone with Bill at the Tenneco Company. J. D. was pleasantly surprised to learn that his brother did indeed remember Willy Mammon. Bill was happy to be invited to a baseball game, but he insisted that J. D. would have to drive the hot rod '68 Mustang to the Astrodome. J. D. readily agreed.

Willy Mammon was a gentle giant who unfortunately had more than a few cracks in his armor. "How did the most powerful country in the world ever lose a war? I will never be able to figure that out. It's okay because the Astros are going to the World Series this year. I'll see you gentleman soon. I'm sorry, but I have to get out of this basement. The dark hallways down here are, well—I just have to get out of here right now!"

Before Mammon left the laboratory, he studied the dim and dank hallway for a moment, as if he were a man peering through the vines and ferns of a steamy and dangerous tropical jungle.

Brewster was unable to grasp the meaning of the big man's peculiar mannerisms when Willy fled the basement, but it was all too clear to Rip Ford as to what was happening. As the Wooly Mammoth quietly slipped into the hallway and headed toward the elevator shaft, he mustered enough bravado to say, "You pasty *vampiros* need to promise me that you can find your way out of this damned basement!"

# 2

# HOME SWEET DOME

At 7:40 a.m. on the last Friday in June 1980, J. D. Brewster received an emergency phone call from the nurse, Missy Brownwood. The patient, Irene Segulla, was now septic.

It's implicit that a patient afflicted with the clinical condition known as "sepsis" is about to be steamrolled by a systemic infectious process. The consequences of the septic state will result in a high risk for morbidity and mortality and it can occur when any infectious process gets out of control. The signs and symptoms of sepsis include high fever, shaking chills, tachycardia, hypotension, cool and clammy skin, dysfunction of major organs, and also the obtundation of mental faculties. As sepsis is a life-threatening condition, Brewster sprinted to Irene's bedside. He truly believed that his omissions were at least partially responsible for her clinical decline.

Dr. Cannon's team had already placed Mrs. Segulla into the Trendelenburg position to try to maintain brain perfusion while they added antibiotics in a shotgun fashion. As Irene needed pressor support to drive up her blood pressure, she was started on a relatively new drug, dobutamine, which was a direct sympathomimetic, beta-1 agonist. It was a powerful drug, but if not used judiciously, it could end up restricting the blood supply to her hands and feet. If that happened, Mrs. Segulla could end up getting gangrene in her extremities, and she would slowly begin to rot from her fingers and toes toward the inner, proximal sanctum of her core.

Brewster tried to be of help at the ICU, but he was booted out of the room because he was only in the way. When he left the patient's room, he was gravely concerned. It was a major setback for the funny, frumpy, middle-aged lady who Brewster considered an ally.

Brewster made a point of finding one of the brainiacs, Joyce Hennigan, and her mentor, Dr. Rockstroh, in the basement laboratory. The two research scientists were involved in a project investigating the use of naloxone in the setting of septic shock. Naloxone had long been available to overcome opioid overdose, but the animal models that Joyce and Dr. Rockstroh employed strongly suggested that the catastrophic hypotension that can occur in septic shock could possibly be mitigated by blocking the opioid receptors in the brain.

Joyce greeted Brewster with a strong handshake. "I wondered how long it would take you to hunt me down and interrogate me about the septic shock research I'm involved with. Look, Brew, I know you and Mrs. Segulla are good friends, so I need to let you know that Cannon is worried that she's about to circle down the drain. We're going to try to keep that from happening. One of her only living relative is her niece, Stella Link, and she's given us the green light to go down like Custer did at the Battle of Little Bighorn. For now, this is a full-court press, although the niece did ask about when a DNR code status should be entertained."

"Do what you can, Joyce," Brewster said. "Let me know if I can help you with anything."

When Brewster rejoined Rip Ford in the basement, he tried to create a superficial distraction to suppress his anger and guilt about Irene's situation. At that moment, it was imperative for Brewster to escape the confines of the medical school campus.

"The corrections officer, Arby Fuller, and I are going over to have lunch at the Buck Wong Oriental Buffet," Brewster said. "I want to get out of here and clear my mind. I'm really in a foul mood right now, and I have to get the hell out of here until I get my head bolts tightened down. You're welcome to come. I'm buying!"

"Thanks for the invite, but I want to get some work done before the game tonight," Ford said.

Brewster left the medical school campus, went to the remote student parking lot, hopped into his yellow 1968 Mustang coupe, and drove about a mile to get to the restaurant in North University Place.

Arby Fuller was saving a place for Brewster in a line that snaked outside the establishment. A brute of a man with powerful forearms, the corrections officer had just recently become friends with Brewster. It was Fuller's responsibility to transport nefarious convicts between the Sharpstown Correction Center and the Gulf Coast University Hospital when the prisoners needed specialized medical care.

The two men shook hands and entered the restaurant to attack the buffet table.

"How are things, Arby?" Brewster asked. "Are you surviving the rat race—or are the rats winning?"

"I'm still swinging for the fences," Arby said.

"Keep on your toes," Brewster cautioned. "Maybe, on some days, you eat the rat, and on other days, the rat eats you."

"You know, I'm feeling pretty good right now," Fuller replied. "I've submitted my application for the police academy. I think I might be better suited to that line of work instead of babysitting a bunch of incarcerated low-life thieving thugs, drug dealers, and even the one random, scum-sucking, baby rapist on odd occasions."

"You have a baby rapist locked up?"

"Oh, yeah, but he is not in lock*up*," Arby explained. "He's in lock*down*—for his own protection from the other inmates. The nasty bastard even humped some family's pet pooch before he buried the kid and the dog in his own backyard while they were all still very much alive."

"Nice," Brewster replied. "I think you should resign immediately from the Department of Corrections. A change would do you good," Brewster replied. "To be honest, you've been a bit surly of late."

"Pot calling the kettle black as far as I can tell," Arby said. "I want to know who put a burr up your ass. Seems to me you're a powder keg. To make matters worse, your fuse is on a fast burn."

"I'm coming up to a crossroads in my life, and I am not sure what I should be doing in regard to the only research project I have left," Brewster confessed.

"A man should take care if he should ever find himself at the crossroads," Arby cautioned. "The Devil has been known to dwell at such precarious locations!"

"Arby, I need to ask you a question. If you were in my shoes, how would you feel about doing experimental studies on chimps?"

"Fat chance, Junior," Fuller answered. "If you ever get involved with monkey lovin', I'd just as soon not know about it. Speaking of monkeys, I escorted a convict to the psychiatry department yesterday and I happened to run into Stella Link. That broad is a beast! If you slapped a blonde wig on my own head, I could actually pass as that woman's dwarf sister! What's the matter with you? It seems to me that Stella could put the hurt on you—and in more ways than one."

"Hey!" Brewster exclaimed. "Don't be a dick."

"What do you see in her?"

"Well, I happen to like large women. *Very* large women, as a matter of fact," Brewster said. "You should know, however, that I'm rather discriminatory when it comes to these matters."

"This should be interesting," Fuller said with a laugh. "Please elaborate!"

"If hairy legs are found on a fat girl, that would be a definite no-no as far as I'm concerned," Brewster said. "I once encountered a fat woman who wore silk stockings over the luxuriant beaver stole that sprouted from her lower extremities. It occurred to me that if she had ever wanted to tame her hirsute foliage, it would have required a gas-powered Weedwacker!"

"Knock it off. I'm fixin' to have lunch," Arby protested. "Are you done yet?"

"Not yet," Brewster said. "Not by a long shot. The hair on the legs of that previously mentioned brute would bristle through her stockings. Her fur, somewhat reminiscent of a greasy platter of burned curly fries, could be seen wafting gently in the breeze like cilia. If the hair that was growing on that fat girl's legs could have ever writhed about on its own accord, as if acting under its own depilatory volition, then perhaps it could have assisted her in in the difficult management of her rather limited mobility when she walked about."

"Stop!" Arby exclaimed.

"I'm quite certain that the woman was little more than an enormous di-flagellated prokaryotic microbe," Brewster postulated.

"You're starting to scare me," Arby warned.

"Although a modest amount of flexibility and perineal tidiness in a fat girl might be an attractive asset, it would nevertheless be somewhat inappropriate for a man to ask a potential consort to bend over and grab her ankles," Brewster said.

"You seem to be an expert in this rarified genre of bovine feminine beauty. Would it be appropriate to ask a fat girl about her ability to achieve the various positions documented in the treatise known as the *Kama Sutra*?" Arby asked.

"Have you no manners?" Brewster asked. "The answer to your question is a resounding no. However, there are indeed surrogate biological markers that could help answer such pertinent questions. I'd likely take a pass on a fat woman with nasty feet. If a fat woman had prehensile toes that could peel a banana or scaly fissures and splitting of the skin around the heels of her feet, that would indeed be a bad prognostic indicator."

"Isn't that why God made paper bags? A woman like that sounds like a bona fide double-bagger," Arby noted. "One to wear over your head and another one to put over the head of the ugly love monkey that you're about to doink!"

"Why do you need two bags?" Brewster asked. "If a girl's actually that fugly, one bag should do the trick."

"You're way off base, buddy boy. If you're going to nude-up with a two-ton Tessie," Arby explained, "each party participating in the lovefest should be wearing a bag just in case one of the bags accidentally breaks."

"You're missing the picture," Brewster said. "There's a lot more to it above and beyond the fact that a fat girl might have a pretty face, an ugly face, or something in between. The condition of a fat girl's feet is paramount, and that alone trumps what her face might subjectively look like. Rapier-like toes that would enable a fat woman to scale Mount Everest without spiked boots would be a clear indication that the woman was too corpulent to bend over—or to even address the inevitable, lower-regional hygienic concerns that chronically plague most obese and likely diabetic humans."

"Okay, Brew," Arby said. "I think I have heard just about enough about funky, chunky monkeys for the time being!"

Before Arby Fuller and Brewster could approach the buffet table, the kitchen doors swung open, and the two men took a quick peek of the restricted area where the food was prepared. What they saw was shocking. On the counter, a loop of bowel was coiled up on an aluminum tray. The bowel had a very small diameter, only about as big around as a fifty-two-ring Churchill cigar. The bowel was way too small to have been harvested from a farm-raised bovine or porcine source.

"Come with me, Arby," Brewster said. "We have to check this out."

When Brewster and Fuller walked straight through the swinging doors that separated the restaurant from the kitchen area, a middle-aged man of Asian ancestry who was wearing a chef's hat began to scold them in an unintelligible foreign tongue.

"Shut up for just a minute," Fuller demanded as he pointed at the cook. "What in God's name is on that aluminum tray?"

The cook appeared befuddled and failed to answer Arby's question. Suddenly, a smartly dressed Asian woman burst through the swinging doors and started to yammer away at the two Anglo intruders.

Finally, the cook turned to the two men and said in broken English, "It bow."

"I can see that it's bowel!" Brewster noted. "I want to know what kind of animal that bowel came from."

"It cow bow! Cow bow!"

"That bowel did *not* come from a cow," Arby said. "You tell us right now what kind of animal that bowel came from—or I'm going to call the health department."

"I wong!" the cook stammered. "It peeg bow. Peeg bow."

The Asian woman, who was presumably the manager, added, "You go now. Eat free—then leave. Leave fast. No come back."

"Well, I bet this is far from kosher," Brewster said.

"I am telling you right now, we shouldn't eat here," Arby said. "I don't give a shit if they plan on giving us a comp on our meal or not. Let's bail. This is one nasty-ass place."

"True, but no self-respecting medical student on the face of this earth would ever turn down a free meal. As long as it's not a rodent— or something that's still alive and squirming around on my plate— I'll eat it come hell or high water. As I've already elaborated this indisputable fact to you *ad nauseam,* I do indeed have extraordinarily high standards. All you have to do is to grab onto my coattails, and I'll personally guide you past the buffet line minefield."

Arby said, "Okay, but if I get food poisoning here, I'm going to kick your ass! Do you still have that silicone cockroach I gave you?"

"I do indeed. It's nestled in my top pocket. I'm just waiting for the right time to play a nasty prank on somebody. What are you thinking?"

"It's time to throw that roach on the buffet table and call your cousin at Your Witness News! If we're lucky, we might score of few pesos out of the deal."

"No dice," Brewster said. "I heard about a man who was thrown in jail last year when he tried a similar stunt at the Taco Hell restaurant over on South Main. Trust me—there's enough stuff going on here that we don't have to fake it. So, tell me, Arby, do you still want to meet my cousin? I can make it happen."

"I would very much!" Fuller replied.

"Keep my place in line," Brewster said. "I'm going to go call 1-800 EAT-SHIT and get her consumer protection team over here ASAP. Maybe the Health Department will show up also."

When Brewster made the call, he was patched directly to his cousin. He told her about the nasty loop of bowel in the kitchen area.

Antonia explained that the Buck Wong establishment was already on the studio's consumer protection bureau radar and that they were just waiting for somebody to make a formal telephone complaint on the "Roachaurant Nightmares Hotline" at the television station.

Brewster asked what kind of monetary compensation he and his friend could expect for making this report, and Antonia replied that it would be negotiated upon the arrival of the TV crew.

After Brewster and Fuller worked their way through the buffet line, they sat down to partake in the all-you-can-eat luncheon special—but things were about to go from bad to worse.

Fuller started to sample the house special—moo goo boo foo—and bit into something hard. He pulled a small bone out of his mouth and showed it to Brewster.

As Brewster had been performing experimental studies on mice and rats for the better part of a year, he immediately recognized that the femur bone belonged to an animal that was consigned to the order *Rodentia*. Specifically, it appeared that the leg bone likely belonged to a creature that had been given the ignoble taxonomic nomenclature *Rattus norvegicus*. Sadly, this lower-tiered mammal appeared to have met a tragic, premature demise. The misfortunate rodent, also known as the common brown rat, had probably fallen into the pot of stew after it had tripped and stumbled from a ceiling rafter. It then was cooked alive and served up in the buffet. Nice.

Fuller waved the rat bone in Brewster's face. "What in the hell did I bite into?"

Upon examining the bone, Brewster lost vision in his left eye, which happened whenever J. D. was severely stressed. His vision recovered within a few seconds, and he was able to answer Fuller's question by vomiting all over the table. In between the episodic projectile vomiting, Brewster said, "It's a rat bone!"

As soon as Brewster evacuated the contents of his upper gastrointestinal tract, Fuller also began to vomit violently. When the two men had puked to the point of having dry heaves, the television crew from Your Witness News arrived as if on cue.

Antonia walked up to the table with a microphone, while a television cameraman followed directly behind her.

As Brewster and Fuller continued to retch, tears strained from their eyes and mucus poured from their nostrils. Their bodies vigorously attempted to purge any rat fur, rat turds, rat viscera, rat gonads, rat eyeballs, rat brains, and any other noxious, organic, rat subcomponents that the two men had inadvertently ingested. By then, all the other patrons had fled the restaurant in abject horror.

Antonia lifted her microphone and said, "It would appear that these two men dining here at the Buck Wong Oriental Buffet found something unpleasant in their meal. Would either of you gentleman be so kind as to tell us what you found in your food that seems to have you both so upset?"

Brewster and Fuller were unable to speak because they were still afflicted with unrelenting and uncontrollable nausea and retching that was all being caught on film.

Without looking up or saying a word, Fuller handed up the bone to the reporter and her cameraman. He wanted them to inspect the evidence for themselves. What happened next was truly amazing; both members of the television crew also began to vomit uncontrollably.

The Buck Wong Oriental Buffet, which was about to go permanently out of business, was about to become designated on an upcoming television segment of the Roachaurant Nightmares installment as a bona fide "Vomitorium Maximus Establishment". This kiss of death would be bestowed upon Buck Wong by none other than the famous consumer advocate, Martin Zinfandel. Martin, who looked like a Baptist preacher with a pure white pompadour, was Antonia Alabaster's boss on the local affiliate's consumer protection bureau.

Upon the arrival of the Health Department, the inspector went straight into the kitchen. From behind the kitchen doors came the unmistakable sound of uncontrollable projectile vomiting could again be heard. Brewster, Fuller, and the two members of the television crew harvested the courage to cautiously wander into the kitchen to see what was awry.

In the back freezer, cats and dogs had been skinned and hung on small meat hooks, which would explain why there were no stray animals in the vicinity of North University Place.

Along the back wall in a partitioned area were three small chicken-wire animal cages. The first cage was occupied by four non-venomous yet nonetheless agitated gopher snakes. The adjacent prison cell incarcerated no less than a half dozen Mexican free-tailed bats that were flittering about. These misfortunate beasts likely had no idea that they were on a clandestine exotic lunch menu. It was the rather peculiar, sullen, and emaciated animal dwelling in the third cage that quickly caught the attention of Arby Fuller, however.

"Good God, that critter looks like a nuclear-powered armadillo! What in hell am I looking at over here, Brewster?"

The medical student scrutinized the oddity for but a moment and then proffered a robust response. "That is possibly the only mammal with scales extant on the planet earth. It's called a pangolin, and to my knowledge, it's on the endangered species list!"

"These animals are what-grub?!" Arby stammered in astonishment.

"Presumably so," Brewster replied.

"Different cultures, different customs," Arby mused. "Who am I to pass judgment in this situation?"

"Fuck that noise!" Brewster replied. "I have no qualms about being the judge, the jury, and executioner right about now. What we're looking at here is wrong on so many levels. If you ask me, it's time for these heathen scoundrels at the Buck Wong Oriental Buffet to have a serious 'come to Jesus meeting' at this very moment!"

The cook and manager tried to book out of the backdoor of the restaurant, but Brewster and Fuller quickly tackled the two miscreants.

Brewster said, "I'm not going to wait for the police. I want to take these two people behind the woodshed and put the hurt on 'em!"

Fuller realized that Brewster was quite serious, and he pulled J.D. away from the melee. It was already too late; everybody had heard his threat, which legally could be construed as an assault. "J. D., you better calm down right now. The police have been called and are on their way."

"You better get him out of this kitchen now," Antonia said. Brewster wrestled away from the grasp of Arby Fuller and said, "After my father passed away when I was a kid, I had a terrier named Electra. It was the best dog in the world, and it helped fill a void that made my miserable life more bearable. It meant everything to me and my brother. I can't imagine that anybody could do something like this to a dog or cat. I've heard people spew the argument that all cultures are created equally. What do you think of that?"

"You need to zip it right now!" Ford said.

"I'm sorry, but that's pure horse piss," Brewster raved. "Anybody from a low-life culture where it's believed that dogs and cats are an acceptable dietary staple should be forever banned from coming into our country. Fifteen years ago, new immigration laws appeared that were specifically designed to make the United States look like the rest of the world at large. Well, anybody with half a brain could have predicted that this kind of shit would eventually happen right here in our own country sooner or later."

When the cook and restaurant manager were finally hauled off to jail by the police, the health inspector nailed a big poster on the front door of the restaurant: "Closed by Order of the Health Department."

The television crew sat down with Brewster and Fuller, and everybody cleaned the vomit off their clothing as best they could in an effort to appear more dignified.

"I think this restaurant is going to be looking for new management," Brewster said.

"I have some ideas on how to rename this place," Arby said. "How does 'Hot Dogs and Cold Cats' sound to you?"

"How about 'Puppy on a Pole'?" the cameraman asked.

"How about 'Honey, I'll Wok the Dog'?" Antonia asked.

"That was a good one, but I prefer 'Pet-pourri'!" Arby Fuller noted.

"I hope everybody at this table realizes that we are all going straight to hell," Brewster added with a scowl. "Well, Antonia, what do you think this cover story would be worth to your television station? I certainly hope that my friend and I will be able to stuff an Andrew Jackson or two in our wallets."

"This will be the very best Roachaurant Nightmares segment that will ever be aired," Antonia boasted. "I checked with my station manager, and he wants to know how a thousand dollars apiece sounds."

The deal was agreed upon, but nobody was inclined to shake hands at that time.

Antonia said, "J. D., let me know if you encounter anything weird at the medical school when you begin your clerkship rotations."

"Like what?"

"Anything out of the ordinary," Antonia explained. "My crew is always looking for a good story. Bill told me that you are running into some complicated issues with your research studies. Maybe it's time for you to back out of your PhD program for a while and start your clerkship rotations. After all, you'll have to get your clinical rotations done sooner or later."

"I don't recall asking for your advice," Brewster said.

"Well, I'm giving you my advice nonetheless. Get the clerkships under your belt now!" Antonia said. "As a consumer protection journalist, I want to cover a lot more than just filthy restaurants, so keep me posted when you run into something at the hospital that's, well, hinky or kinky."

"I'll do my best—as long as I get a finder's fee."

"By the way, you need to pay a visit to Uncle John. I know for a fact that you never go by to see him anymore."

"Fine," Brewster replied. "I'll get to it."

"What's the matter with you?" Antonia added after a thoughtful pause.

"Well, it is not like I have a lot of leisure time," Brewster said.

"That's not what I'm talking about, J. D." Antonia said. "Are you okay? You were always a bit, well-volatile, I guess. To be perfectly honest, I've never seen you get so amped up like that. I was afraid you were going to beat those two restaurant workers to death with your bare hands. What happened back there?"

"Nothing," Brewster answered. "I can assure you that not a damned thing happened back there."

"You're becoming a hermit. Make it a point to pay Uncle John a visit, okay? In the meantime, you need to chill out. If I ever see you go schizo like that again, I'm going to start calling you Captain Queeg."

In *The Caine Mutiny*, Humphrey Bogart played Captain Queeg, a deranged naval captain who rolled two large ball bearings in his palm to suppress anxiety and hostility during his court-martial for dereliction of duty.

"Someday, I am going to give you two brass ball bearings to play with," Antonia said. "Maybe, just maybe, that'll help keep you calm if you ever fall back into the pressure cooker. After all, it's bound to happen to you from time to time."

Brewster had to pick up his brother, and if they were going to make it to the Astrodome for the start of the game, he was going to have to leave soon. He had to go home, shower up, and throw on some clean duds.

As Brewster said goodbye to everybody, Fuller remarked that he would never allow the medical student to make a restaurant selection ever again. He suggested that the next advancement in human evolution would be the ability to generate energy through photosynthesis. If that were to ever actually occur, the horrible events at the Buck Wong vomitorium would be a thing of the past.

After Brewster picked up his brother, he made a quick U-turn and headed toward the Astrodome.

As the two brothers shook hands, Bill said, "You look like hammered shit. Did you have a bad day?"

"You have no idea," J. D. replied. "I'm coming to a fork in the road of life. I want to stay on track with the dual training program, but I just don't think that I can take the hepatitis study into the next phase of animal experimentations."

"If you don't believe you can inoculate the big primates, for God's sake, don't do it. It's that simple. You don't want to commit an act that you know deep down inside is wrong. You can never take a sin like that back once you've crossed that threshold. You won't get a mulligan if you do it."

"Maybe so."

"Besides, it's time for you to set aside research and get on with your clinical clerkship rotations. Try not to get too worked up about things. Take the problems you encounter in stride. Somedays, you eat the rat—and somedays the rat eats you."

Traffic was terrible, but they were able make it to the Astrodome for the beginning of the National Anthem.

Bill picked up the tab for parking, and the tickets were waiting for them at the will call window. The Wooly Mammoth, Rip Ford, and an elderly black gentleman, presumably Mammon's father, were already seated.

Rip Ford said, "J. D., I've given this a lot of thought. When Holcombe comes back, I'm going to tender my resignation. You should do the same. It's time for you to start your clerkship rotations and get out of the PhD training program for now."

The Wooly Mammoth extended his big hand. "Welcome, J. D. I assume this is your brother. You boys used to call me Chilly Willy, but now I'm known as the Wooly Mammoth."

Bill extended his hand to the big man and shook it vigorously. "I remember you. You got huge since I last saw you." Bill turned his head toward the elderly man. "Is this your father?

"Hello, boys. I'm Rudolph Valentino Mammon. Please call me Rudy. When Willy told me that J. D. Brewster was in the class ahead of him at his medical school, I couldn't believe it! What a small world. Somehow, it seems everything in the universe is connected somehow."

"It is indeed," Bill said.

"Your father and I were tight many years ago," Rudolph continued. "Out of respect to him, I wanted to see you boys again. Look at you fellows now—all grown up and everything. You kids were so young when your father passed away that I don't suspect you've ever had a full accounting as to what he was all about. He was a good man with a good heart. I want to let you know though, that he was no white knight. In fact, there was a time when he and I were both a little, well-gray around the edges, I suppose."

"What do you mean?" Bill asked. "Please fill us in."

"After he left the FBI and joined the DA's office, he got bit by the gambling bug. He was a frequent visitor to the black community off of Wayside and not too far from the Hobby Airport. Are you boys sure you want to hear about all of this?"

J. D. and his brother nodded.

"Well, we both figured the best way to shake the money tree was with a little sports book biz that was tailored to the colored folks. We followed the odds from Vegas, and we were straight up. We took bets on football, including NFL and college games. We took bets on Major League Baseball and boxing. In the last year of your father's life, we even added AFL games."

"Frankly, I'm surprised to hear any of this," Bill said.

"I remember every damn fool in the black community wanted to bet on George Blanda and the Oilers, no matter the spread. Your dad and I had both known Blanda back in the day. That's a fact. If your dad had lived long enough, we probably would have added bas-ketball at some point."

"If you're still running a sports book, I'd like in on the action!" Ford interrupted.

"That was another time and another life, young man," Rudy said. "Anyhow, things started to change once Wilt the Stilt came along. People started to become more interested in the game of hoops. Anyhow, your dad was always square with black folks. He limited bets to a hundred dollars. He would've felt bad if he thought he was taking food out of some baby's mouth. He wouldn't let some fool lose his shirt. People respected your dad and rarely tried to welch. When they did, they'd get a visit from me."

"How exactly did you know my father?" J. D. asked.

"When I first met your father, it was during the war. We served in the Pacific Theater," Rudy explained. "Although he was white and I was black, we were both from Houston, and that made us both

Texans. We felt connected that way, but I remember telling your father one time that I didn't feel at times like I was being treated like, well-like an American."

"What did my dad say to that?" Bill asked.

"Woody told me that if an injustice happens to one group of Americans, then it's an injustice that happens to all Americans. After all, we all salute Uncle Sam, or at least we should. After all, white folks and black folks share the same history. It's just different sides of the same coin."

"I'm not black," J. D. said, "so I'm not sure I can relate to what you are saying. I'm surprised, however, that you stayed in touch with my dad after your time together in the Pacific."

"After the war, Wood was with the FBI organized crime task force, and I was an informant. When we started the sports book, I was the bag boy. In fact, I was a torpedo, I tell you. Your father and I did a fifty-fifty split. He treated me like a man. A man, I tell you. Your dad and I only got into real trouble one time, but it was a scary time."

"What happened?" Bill asked. "Did you guys get rolled?"

"No, it was nothing like that," Rudy replied. "One night, we were at a nightclub called the Blue Tone, and Lilly and Iris Bacon showed up. Your dad was flirting with them, and that didn't sit well with Lilly's boyfriend. He was a longshoreman named Pete Dalton. There was no way that he was going allow his girlfriend to flirt with a white man, much less doink him. That was totally unacceptable."

"Not much different in this day and age, I guess," Willy said.

"Rightfully so," the senior Mammon said. "Anyhow, Dalton cracked a beer bottle across your father's jaw. I tried to stave off what was coming next, but I just got swatted aside as if I was a pesky moth. He dragged your father outside and beat the hell out of him. I ended up taking your father to the emergency room. I was the one who had to call your mom and tell her what happened. She never did cotton up to me very much to begin with, and after your dad took a beating, that didn't help matters in the least."

"Do you think my father was having an affair with those two young women?" Bill asked.

"I'm not rightly certain," Rudy answered. "If I knew for sure, I'd tell you. Well, that's not the right thing for me to say, I suppose. Even if I did know the answer to that question, maybe I wouldn't tell you after all. What I do know is this: when your dad died, the Bacon twins rolled into the funeral service, and they were all dressed up in tight red dresses and fishnet stockings. They were gussied up to the nines! They even had matching beehives, I tell you. To this very day, I haven't forgotten that they left a huge splay of flowers and a sympathy card that simply had the words 'Senza Fine' written on the note. I never did figure out what that meant, but your mom, being Italian, was none too pleased."

"I don't imagine so," Bill said. "In English, it means, 'Never Ending'."

"Your mother caused a big fuss and made the Bacon twins leave pronto. I thought fur was going to fly. It was sad what happened to one of the Bacon girls. Iris came down with brain cancer and died just a year or two later after your father passed away."

"What happened to her twin?" J. D. asked.

"Lilly ended up getting married to Pete Dalton, and they now have lovely twin daughters named D' Shea and D' Nae. Did you know twins can run in families? The twins were drop-dead gorgeous with bright green eyes, and it was inexplicable to everybody as to why their skin tone was quite a bit fairer than their mother or father. If it wasn't for their nappy hair, I'd swear that they could both pass for white girls with a nice summer tan. They're entering their junior year at the University of Houston. Pete no longer works down at the docks. He's a member of my ground crew now. So, what does that story sound like to you two boys?"

J. D. Brewster was visibly upset. Could it possibly be that his father had an affair with two young black women? Oh God! What if his father was not careful when he was out and about, bumping and grinding? Could it be that J. D. and Bill had mixed-race siblings running around? J. D. was a Texan and a southerner. How could he ever explain something like that to anybody else if it was true?

"I'll tell you how the story sounds to me," J. D. said. "It sounds like my old man was having a tag-team match with two wild black women at the same time! Perish the thought."

Rudy Mammon patted J. D. Brewster on the leg and said, "Relax, son. White men have always found black women to be alluring and exotic. They've felt that way since, I don't know, I guess forever. Jungle love. Forbidden fruit. Truth be told, black men probably feel the same way toward white women. Human nature, I guess. I think sometimes that people are not much different than cows. We try to stick our heads on through the bottom of the barb wire fence and taste the grass that's growing on the other side."

Willy said, "Daddy, you need to tell these boys the story about what happened when their father entered politics."

"The following is my most favorite story about your old man," Rudy said. "Your dad got elected to the city council only a week or so before he passed away, but he never had a chance to serve. During his political campaign, there were rumors that were coming out. Nasty stories, I tell you. Gossip was spread far and wide by one of his political adversaries that your father was cavorting with black girls and was involved in gambling. Something like that would usually sink a politician's political campaign, but Wood was able to overcome all that bad press with humorous radio advertisements that I think helped him get elected. One spot on the radio said, 'It's good to have Wood.' Boy, was that funny—or what?"

"Pretty scandalous," Bill said. "Times being what they were."

"Straitlaced people did not understand the double meaning of that radio commercial, but hip people sure did. Your dad was hip!" Rudy said.

J. D. Brewster was embarrassed. "I'm not certain what my father's political orientation may have been, but it sure as hell sounds as if he behaved like a typical, horny liberal who lacked any moral fiber."

"If the shoe fits," Rudy said. "How is your mother doing? Is she still alive?"

"I guess she's fair to middlin'," Bill replied. "She never really got over the death of my father, and she's been chronically depressed for the past twenty years. She doesn't like being around other people and has become quite a recluse."

"Your mother never took a shine to me," Rudy said. "She was always suspicious that I was trying to drag her man down into a dark hole. Maybe she was right, I tell you. She was so suspicious of me that she never let me pee inside the house when I went over to do some business with your dad. She made me go outside into the back-yard and pee on an oleander bush. That was kind of embarrassing to me. I guess she didn't think that colored folks exactly knew the proper mechanics on how to operate a flush toilet."

"Wow," J. D. added. "I'm frankly too embarrassed to look you in the eye right now, Mr. Mammon."

"Water over the dam," Rudy said as he shook his head. "Nonetheless, after your father died, I'll always be in debt to your mother for selling me your dad's Cadillac. I got my first job as a groundskeeper at Rice after your father had passed away because of that car. I took a stencil plate, spray-painted my name on the side of that car, and declared that I owned my own landscaping company. I'm certain that is what got me hired by Rice University in the spring of 1961. That car showed everybody that I had made it. I was some-body. I jumped over here to the Astrodome four years later when it opened up in '65. Just look at me! I just got awarded my fifteen-year work pin and a polo shirt with my name embroidered over the front pocket, I tell you!"

Willy Mammon turned to his father and added, "I am so proud you, Pop."

"I have a treat for you boys," Rudy said. "I'm personal friends with the man at the concession stand who sells the coldest foam in the dome. Why don't you come up the stairs with me, J. D.? Let's get everybody some refreshments!"

When Brewster reached the top of the mezzanine stairwell, Rudy took him aside and said, "J. D., my boy is bright. He's book smart, but he's bashful. He's not sophisticated. He's had a simple life, and he likes simple things. Except for being in the military and going off to college, he's not been exposed to very much in society even though he's already thirty years old. There's something else; when he came back from the 'Nam, he was, well, different."

"How so?"

"He became all quiet and moody," Rudy answered. "Something bad happened over there. Real bad. He never told me what he did in the war, but I know for a fact that he has night terror about something he saw or did. I'm ashamed to say it, but he's sometimes afraid of the dark."

Brewster thought, "*Someday, I'll find out exactly what happened to Willy when he was in the bush.*"

"I can't say it in so many words," Rudy added, "but I know he's awfully nervous about starting this thing called the clerkships. He's afraid he'll come across as a colored bumpkin. There are a lot of rats out there. I know I'm asking a lot, but I'm talking to you with a cap in hand. I was hoping you can set aside this research business you're tied up in and join my boy Willy on the clerkships. I'd be most beholden if you could make sure he doesn't get bit by a snake."

Brewster was frustrated. He had prayed hard to get an answer from God as to what course of action he should take at this juncture in his life. The more he prayed, however, the more pressure he was getting from people like Ford, his brother, his cousin, the Wooly Mammoth, and now even from Mr. Mammon! Everybody was pushing hard for him to postpone his research program and start his clinical rotations. That's fine and dandy, but why wasn't God saying anything to him?

Brewster always had a hard time seeing the big picture. "I'll take that under advisement and give it serious consideration," he said.

Mr. Mammon nodded and said, "That's all I ask. I know you'll do the right thing." After Rudy obtained complimentary beers and nachos for Brewster and his colleagues, he popped onto the down ramp and quietly disappeared. The medical student had a lot to think about, but he could not draw any conclusions at that time as to what course of action his life should take.

J. D. returned to his seat and dispensed the adult beverages and snacks.

"How did you like meeting my old man?" Mammoth asked.

"Very illuminating," Brewster answered. "Tell me, Willy, what happened over there in the Southeast Asian War Games?"

"You just can't roll up on a vet and ask him about the 'Nam, you dip shit," Ford said. "You could open up a can of bad vibes. Be polite."

The wooly one waved Ford off and said, "Brewster, I'll tell you all about it tomorrow, but not tonight, my little buddy. It's time for song and merriment! Now, as you're the lead vocalist for that rock band called DNR, do you know any songs by the late, great, Sam Cooke?"

"All of them," the music trivia savant confidently answered. "His entire catalogue, as a matter of fact."

"Including the tune, 'Good Times', I trust?" Willy pleaded.

"From July, 1964," Brewster answered as he rolled his eyes. "Johnnie Taylor provided the back-up vocal work. The lyrics are ironic and haunting, as this was one of the last tracks that Sam Cooke ever recorded. He was only thirty-three years old when he met a violent and premature demise just a few months after this R&B classic became a hit."

"The song, 'Good Times', was one of the standards we sang on the munitions line at Cameron Bay," Ford wistfully reminisced with a sad and distant gaze.

"Excellent! I'll take the lead and you boys feel free to chime right in," Willy said before he began to sing.

"It might be one o'clock, and it might be three. Time don't me that much to me. I haven't felt this good since I don't know when, and I might not feel this way again."

As the others joined in the chorus, nobody noticed that Willy's eyes were welling up with tears…

GUAIAC
DICK
DK

# 3

# PULL THE PLUG

The following morning, Brewster paid his customary visit to Irene Segulla in the ICU, and he found the resident, Dr. Lawdy Garth Penn, and two senior medical students in the room. Ms. Segulla remained hypotensive despite continued pressor support, antibiotics, and the experimental naloxone drip protocol. She was also now anuric. Although a Foley catheter was in place, there had been no recorded urine production during the previous shift. It appeared as if Irene was suffering from acute tubular necrosis in her kidneys.

When Brewster looked at Lawdy Garth for answers, she shook her head and sat down in a chair in the corner. She motioned for the two medical students to pull down the covers and allow Brewster to observe what was occurring.

Her skin was mottled, and her hands and feet were dark purple. Ms. Segulla was dying. A nurse entered the room and turned off the cardiac monitor.

Dr. Penn said, "I'm sorry, Brew, but she's now DNR. She has metabolic acidosis, and we can't drive the ventilator any higher. We thought if we could blow off more carbon dioxide, we could try to balance out her pH with an artificially induced respiratory alkalosis, but it's just not working. Neither are the amps of bicarb that we've rammed home."

"Have you seen her niece?" Brewster asked.

"You just missed her," Dr. Penn noted. "She was the one who agreed to abandon aggressive management. You're welcome to stay for a while, but Dr. Cannon has already signed off on the case. Stella doesn't want to be here when we turn off the vent. According to the rules and regulations of the hospital, I must officially wait for the respiratory tech to pull the plug. Everything must go according to Hoyle since this is a case that is going to go to the coroner."

"The coroner?" Brewster asked. "She's pretty far out from her original admission, is she not?"

"Doesn't matter one lick!" Penn said. "Technically, Ms. Segulla will die from the complications of her physical assault. Whenever the police collar the bastards who did this to her, they'll be charged with murder. Whether it's through the legal criminal justice system or our own vigilante clinical justice system, which incidentally mysteriously manifests itself around here from time to time, there must be retribution someday. I'm done here. I'm taking these two studs over to the break room for a cup of coffee. Coming?"

Brewster was somewhat surprised when he heard Dr. Penn speak openly about a "clinical justice system." Since the initiation of the Gulf Coast College of Medicine less than a decade earlier, rumors had swirled through the hallways that evil or violent criminals who had been hospitalized at that facility would occasionally come to an untimely demise. As a matter of fact, Brewster had heard Arby Fuller talking about the "clinical justice system", but he had quickly put such thoughts out of his mind. Brewster believed the reports were probably just rumors.

"Thanks, but I'm chock-full to the gills with caffeine right about now," Brewster said. "I think I'll stay for just a little while. Before you leave, I have a question to ask you, Dr. Penn. If Ms. Segulla was made DNR, why is the crash cart still in her room?"

"That's a good question," Lawdy replied. "Gather around, team. Here's a learning opportunity. It looks like I need to fill in the blanks on a few things. Officially, there are only three resuscitation designations. Each of these is known as a 'code status' in the official hospital vernacular. The first, of course, is referred to as a 'full code' at the Gulf Coast, and this is also known as a 'full-court press' in medical slang. If a patient has a full code designation and suffers from a cardiopulmonary arrest, then everything that can possibly be done will happen to try to resuscitate the patient."

"Such as?" the other medical students asked.

"This includes intubation, ventilator support, chest compressions, and if necessary, an electrical cardioversion may be attempted," Dr. Penn said. "Intervention with emergency medications as dictated by the situation at hand is also the standard of care."

"What's next?" another student asked.

"The second is referred to as a 'Do Not Intubate' or DNI code status," Lawdy explained. "If a patient has a DNI designation and suffers a cardiopulmonary arrest, then everything that can possibly be done will happen to try to resuscitate the patient but *not* to the point of putting in an endotracheal tube and placing the patient on a mechanical ventilator. In this situation, only a hand compression Ambu-bag will be utilized to support oxygenation, and that would only be a temporary intervention during the actual resuscitation attempt. Does anybody know the slang term for a DNI code designation?"

"Bag code," Brewster answered without hesitation.

"You nailed it," Dr. Penn said. "At the Gulf Coast, this is also known as a 'bag code' as Brewster noted. Sadly, it's rarely successful in effecting resuscitation in a true cardiopulmonary arrest situation. The last, of course, is DNR. Everybody knows that this means the code team allows Mother Nature to take its course, and no medical intervention is initiated to alter the course of a patient's pending demise."

"Well, is there other terminology that has been used concerning a patient's resuscitation status?" Brewster asked.

"The three official resuscitation designations are not the only ones that exist," Dr. Penn said. "What you've learned from me thus far are the official resuscitation designations utilized when a patient suffers from a cardiopulmonary arrest, but that's not the whole story. What I am going to tell you now must remain within the confines of this cubicle. There are two other unofficial resuscitation designations that you need to learn about that exist only to treat the *family*, not the *patient*."

"I have no idea what you're talking about," one of the senior medical students said.

"This will all soon make sense to you," Dr. Penn answered. "These unofficial codes that I've spoken of are meant to damper the anguish of family members when a patient who has been deemed to be terminal finally expires during the unpleasant social circumstances when the family still insists that everything must be done to try to keep the patient alive."

"Why would this ever be the case?" Brewster asked.

"This usually occurs when the relatives of the dying person have serious, unresolved family issues," Lawdy explained. "There are many times when a patient *should* be DNR, but family members refuse to make such a declaration in the mistaken belief that a full-court press is always the right course of action for their loved one. You see, the general population at large doesn't fully appreciate that there are a hell of a lot things far worse than death."

"Are you saying that this institution occasionally runs resuscitation codes that are planned to fail from the outset?" Brewster asked. "That doesn't seem ethical to me."

"So, did the pontiff die? I'd guess by your pomposity that that the College of Cardinals ordained you to be the next pope!" Penn asked.

"No, but—"

"Yeah, so get over it already," Lawdy replied. "These two secret designations are only, at best, a 'dog and pony show' performed on somebody who really should have a DNR status to begin with. The first is called the 'slow code,' and it has also been referred to as a 'chem code.' In this situation, a half-hearted resuscitation attempt is made when the patient undergoes a cardiopulmonary arrest. The crash cart is broken into, a few choice medications are administered, but no chest compressions, electrical cardioversion, or ventilation by either Ambu-bag or intubation is attempted."

"Wow," a student commented. "There's another sham procedure in addition to a slow code?"

"The last head fake is known as a 'Mr. Pibb code.' This is when the house staff and the official members of the code team will address a cardiopulmonary arrest by going outside the hospital, smoking a cigarette, sucking down a soft drink, and then strolling around Hermann Park for a while before the code team actually shows back up on the ward to auspiciously attempt a lame-ass, broke-dick, half-hearted stab at revitalizing the dearly departed." Penn explained. "This is done to make absolutely certain that the patient is stone-cold dead and on the threshold of rigor mortis before any of these sham efforts of resuscitation are initiated by the Code Blue team."

"Mr. Pibb is a soft drink," Brewster noted. "What does that have to do with cardiopulmonary resuscitation codes that are real, sham, or otherwise?"

"I'll give you the short version of a long story," Penn said. "Mr. Pibb is an acronym for 'Positive Intracranial Bilateral Blowout.' Up until about a year ago, a Mr. Pibb code was only referred to as an attempt at a futile resuscitation on somebody who was already brain-dead from an intracranial hemorrhagic or a catastrophic thrombo-embolic cerebrovascular accident. The term has now been expanded to include any dead body that warrants a sham resuscitation attempt to smooth the ruffled feathers of hostile family members."

"Can you give us an example of when either of these sham codes might be utilized?" Brewster asked.

"Pay attention," Dr. Penn replied. "A slow code is utilized when the family members are in the room when the patient has a witnessed cardiopulmonary death event. In this situation, the family members are quickly shuttled out into the hallway for about twenty minutes. After the family members are isolated in a remote location, the slow code takes place. In this situation, it is absolutely necessary to make the room look like a catastrophic mess before the family members come back in to visit their friend or relative who just croaked!"

"The purpose being?" one of the students asked. "None of this makes sense to me."

"Simple," Dr. Penn explained. "It's done to create an illusion for the surviving family members that the medical staff individuals who were on the code team actually gave a shit about the stiff that just kicked the bucket. The friends and family members have to actually *believe* that actual resuscitative efforts had taken place to try to revive Uncle Joe or Aunt Mary."

"What methods are employed to create this illusion? Knowing this kind of information will clearly make me a more sensitive and compassionate physician in the future!" One of the medical students eagerly inquired.

"One good technique is to drop the Ambu-bag onto the floor along with several glass ampules of medications and opened packages of gauze. Throwing some water on the floor and pouring some water upon the groin area of the dead patient can also be a bonus. Doing so gives the impression to the surviving family members that a serious effort had been undertaken to try to resuscitate the individual."

"Why pour water onto the groin of the dead patient?" Brewster asked. "That sounds absurd!"

"Think about it. Doing so would make it appear to the surviving family members that old Uncle Joe was hit with enough juice from the shock paddles to make the poor bastard piss his pantaloons! Upon the return of the family members to a post-code hospital room that looks like a rummage sale, the surviving relatives of old Stiffy Jiffy are invariably pleased at the presumed herculean resuscitative efforts that had been undertaken, but nonetheless failed!"

"How about a Mr. Pibb code?" Brewster asked.

"A Mr. Pibb code is a completely different kettle of fish, and it can only be engineered if *all* the family members and visitors are absent from the hospital at the onset of the Code Blue emergency announcement," Penn explained. "You can't pop open up a can of Mr. Pibb if the patient is not alone or if the family members are still lurking about in the hallway. The *only* way to pull off this type of a sham code is to make absolutely certain that there are *no* witnesses— or else there'll be hell to pay."

"Does this actually work, as you say, to treat the family?" Brewster asked.

"You can bank on it," Penn said. "In regard to why the crash cart was already in Ms. Segulla's room, the niece wavered back and forth between a full-court press and a DNR code status. If push came to shove, it was our original intention to break out a Mr. Pibb and guzzle it down if Irene's niece wanted us to go down swinging at the plate. Fortunately, at the very end, the niece finally came to terms with our recommendations to abandon aggressive medical intervention altogether."

At that juncture, a respiratory therapist arrived at Irene's bedside.

"Are you here to pull the plug?" Brewster asked.

"Don't be rude," the therapist replied. "A little respect is in order here, stud. I'm here to turn off the ventilator in order for nature to take its course."

"I anticipate Ms. Segulla's respirations will begin to slow, and within the next hour, she'll simply 'brady down' and then she'll check out," Penn said. "I'll keep the vent tube in place since the coroner will need to confirm its location during the postmortem examination. My team and I are out of here."

"I learned a lot from you," Brewster said. "Frankly, what you taught me today was righteous and actually quite inspirational."

"You need to consider quitting your research program and start on your clinical clerkships, Brew," Lawdy Garth said. "It would seem to me that you have great potential, as you already have enough cold-blooded cynicism and distain for other human beings to be truly successful at this line of work. With just a teensy bit more abrasive erosion of the little residual moral fiber that you may still foolishly possess, you could one day be a real superstar here at the Gulf Coast. That being said, I think that you'll miss out on quite a bit of important clinical experience if you stay entrenched in the PhD program. In any event, I'm truly sorry about what happened here. I heard from the other staff members that you were friends with Ms. Segulla. I wish things had turned out differently. I'll be back to make the declaration once she shucks this mortal coil and gets transferred to the eternal care unit."

As Brewster sat and thought about the pending demise of Irene Segulla, Sister Buena entered the room with a vase filled with twelve perfect, yellow, long-stemmed roses. "Madam, I believe we've met before, have we not?"

"Of course we've met!" Sister Buena replied. "I'm a floating nurse from the temp pool. I'll be most upset if you don't recognize me."

Brewster feigned recollection to avoid embarrassment. "Well, of course. It's good to see you again. Who sent the lovely flowers?" Brewster said in an attempt to divert the woman's attention directly away from his poor memory and equally shabby social skills. "Irene once said she hoped she would get a bouquet of roses someday, and here they are!"

"They're from her fiancé," the woman replied. "I have orders from my Boss that this patient's going home today."

"You're obviously in the wrong room," Brewster remarked. "Your boss must have made a mistake. Besides, Ms. Segulla's fiancé was lost in the Korean War."

"Yet that a man is lost, he can still be found," Sister Buena said. "Remember that. Also, my Boss doesn't make mistakes. Ever. Would you like to stay and say a prayer with me for Ms. Segulla?"

"No, God's busy today," Brewster said. "I checked His schedule, and he's got a lot on His plate right about now. I don't want to be any bother. As a case in point, I've prayed over a serious matter concerning my less-than-stellar career in medical research for the last two weeks. As of yet, I've had no reply. Besides, I've come to believe that God's backed the wrong primate. I no longer think that human beings are worthy of any attention whatsoever."

"Don't put limitations on God," Sister Buena marked. "The answers to prayers are sometimes so obvious that people need only to open their eyes to see, open their ears to hear, and open their hearts to feel. How can a man such as you, so blessed with the gift of intelligence, be so utterly dense at the same time?"

For some reason, Brewster was not particularly offended by this rather sharp rebuke as he left Irene Segulla's bedside in the ICU for the last time. Perhaps this strange floating nurse from the temp pool was on to something…

Upon Brewster's departure from Irene's bedside, there was a commotion going on in the adjacent ICU stall. A young woman struggling with cancer was about to be intubated for pulmonary support after developing a complication of pulmonary infiltrates from the chemotherapy drug known as bleomycin. Brewster stopped and observed the mechanics of hooking up somebody to a ventilator for oxygenation therapy and the procedures involved with adjusting the settings of a mechanical ventilator. After the misfortunate patient was finally stabilized, Brewster was notified that he had a telephone call at the clerk's desk in the ICU. It was the research scientist, Rip Ford.

"Holcombe is coming today," Ford said.

"I'll believe it when I see it," Brewster said. "You and I have heard these types of rumors before. As far as I can tell, Uncle Hank is still missing in action."

"Nonetheless, you best get down here pronto," Ford replied. "Besides, we have a visitor who would like to see you."

Just outside of the ICU, Brewster encountered a florist with the largest splay of flowers he had ever seen.

The florist said, "I'm supposed to deliver these flowers for the cancer patient in stall number six, but they won't let me in because they're doing some kind of procedure on her."

"Let me see if I can help you out," Brewster said. He looked at the card that had accompanied the huge floral arrangement: "If you have been injured from your cancer treatment, our team is more than ready, willing, and able to represent your interests in malpractice matters. Spankham, Tilley, and Hertz, atty. @ law."

*Scumbag ambulance chasers? Well, to hell with that horseshit.* Brewster was a scoundrel of the first degree, but he had an opportunity to kill two birds with one stone. In one fell swoop, he could throw a wrench into the gears of a malpractice legal firm that was out trawling for a new client, and he could also deliver a beautiful flower arrangement to express his sympathy to Stella Link upon the demise of her beloved aunt.

"Don't worry," Brewster said. "I'll make sure these flowers get delivered today."

As soon as the florist turned the corner and was out of sight, Brewster took the flower arrangement upstairs to where Stella Link worked in the office of Dr. Corka Sorass, the head of the Psychiatry Department. When J. D. got there, the psychiatrist was present, but there was no sign of Stella. He asked Dr. Sorass if he could leave the flowers for Stella, and the chief of psychiatry replied that Stella was only using the restroom. He anticipated that she would be right back—and Brewster would be welcome to sit and wait for her if he preferred.

J. D. lost his nerve and decided the better part of valor would be just to leave the flowers and then disappear. He was almost out the door when he remembered that he had inadvertently left the tacky greeting card from the attorneys embedded within the floral arrangement. He quickly reached into the splay of flowers, grabbed the greeting card, and then jammed it into the wastebasket under Stella's desk. He took a blank index card from Stella's desk and wrote a note of sympathy. He stuck it on the plastic trident in the arrangement and quickly fled the scene before the object of his romantic fantasies returned to her desk.

Upon Ms. Segulla's transfer to the eternal care unit later that morning, the hospital had announced that there would be a sponsored memorial service for her to be held before the upcoming Fourth of July holiday weekend.

When Brewster returned to the basement, he was pleased to see that Willy Mammon had come down to the laboratory for another visit. It appeared that Willy and Ford were having a serious existential conversation, and Brewster didn't want to interrupt. Ford was getting the lowdown on Willy's hardscrabble existence.

"I graduated from high school here in Houston back in '67," the Mammoth said. "I played football, and I was a pretty big boy at six feet four inches, but I was relatively skinny at 220 pounds. I wasn't very mobile either. I wanted to go to college, but I didn't get a football scholarship. My grades were only good enough to get partial scholastic scholarships at South Texas State and Prairie Baptist University.

"What was the holdup?" Ford asked.

"Sadly, my family didn't have the financial resources to cover the partial scholarship shortcomings. The United Negro College Fund was going to step up to the plate and help me out, but Uncle Sam called me up. I was personally asked to keep the dominoes from falling. As best I can tell from Sam's intonations, I was supposed to do it all by my lonesome! It was up to me to save the entire world from insurgent Communist hegemony. I was soon shipped off to a lovely, luxurious tropical vacation spot that was known as Vietnam."

"Hello, Willy. Don't let me interrupt you," Brewster finally said. "I'm sure Vietnam was no vacation."

"Last night at the Astrodome, you asked what happened in Vietnam. Look, Brew, I want you to work with me on the clerkship rotations that are starting in July. You have to know *who* I am—and exactly *what* I've been through. Full disclosure."

"Sounds to me like this isn't going to be a happy-ever-after bedtime story," Brewster said.

"No," Willy said. "Not hardly. There are things that happened over there that I just can't get over. In late '67, my platoon stumbled upon a VC tunnel complex, and we got into a nasty firefight. Two of our boys got greased along with four ARVN. I have to tip my hat to Victor Charles. They were fierce, fearless, and innovative. During that firefight, we must have killed about a dozen of the Cong, and another dozen or so probably escaped into the bush. I fired away with my M16, but to this day, I think I just killed a bunch of ferns and vines. We were just about to bring in the engineers to nuke the underground complex, but first we sent down a midget 'tunnel rat' to scope things out."

"You couldn't get me to go down a VC tunnel for all of the tea in China," Ford said.

"Me neither," the big man said. "We thought there was probably quite a bit of munitions down hole. I guess we got there before the dinks set up any booby traps, and I'm glad we did. We found three prisoners of war in tiger cages. They were frail, cachectic, and completely flat and vacuous of any discernable emotions. Their eyes were open, yet it seemed as if they were incapable of even blinking while they cowered back in the dimly lit enclosure."

"American soldiers?" Brewster asked.

"Check this out, man!" the Mammoth explained. "This is what creeps me out about the whole ordeal to this very day; the three men were *not* Americans. They spoke no English. Listen to me carefully; they were *French Foreign Legionnaires*! Holy shit! They'd all been captured before the fall of Dien Bien Phu in '54. After the French got their asses kicked, they booked out of Vietnam, but the dinks continued to hold onto these men as prisoners of war. What disturbs me is that it appeared that these men were going to be held as prisoners of war in perpetuity."

"I know where you are going with this, but you can't think this way," Ford said. "Let it go. The French are the French, and the Americans are the Americans. Don't draw conclusions from what you saw!"

"Hard not to though," the Wooly Mammoth said. "On my second tour, one of my buddies, Clifford Spiro, disappeared into the jungle and was presumably captured. To this date, I don't know if it was the Communist North Vietnamese or those godless Vietcong animals that may have had their way with him, but he never came home. God forgive me, but I pray that he died quickly. I know exactly what happened to our American servicemen who were interrogated by the enemy during the war. You know, a lot of those prisoners of war of never came home."

"Stay frosty, big man," Ford said. "It happens in *every* war."

"You don't think that any of our boys are still being held by those Communists after all of these years, do you? For what purpose could our boys still be held as captives? Well, what else can I say? The French fries that we had found ranged from thirty-three to forty-one years old. However, they all looked to be in their late sixties. As best I can tell, our enemy hated us even more than they hated the French. As you see, the French were simply imperialistic in regard to their own nationalistic world view. That makes sense. Predominantly, they only had economic goals and a plain, straightforward plan for the exploitation of natural resources."

"As if we didn't?" Brewster asked.

"Americans are *different*, Brew," the wooly one said. "We're ideologues. We were bringing in foreign concepts of freedom, capitalism, and nation building to a part of the world that wanted none of that. You know, my family has voted for Democratic Party candidates all of their lives, but it's clear to me that LBJ ramped up the Vietnam War. I can never forgive that jug-eared bastard for doing that. I hate to admit it, but that man was from Texas! All I know is that I'll never vote for a Democrat again for the rest of my life."

The three men sat in silence for a moment before the big man continued. "So, Brewster, you said you want to know about the war. Well, they say that confession is good for the soul. I don't know about all of that, but I want to tell you a story that my father doesn't even know about. Tell me, Brew. What do you know about the Ho Chi Minh Trail? Well, at least that's what we called it."

"I know that our military could never pull the plug on that damned thing."

"The enemy called it the Truong Son Strategic Supply Route. It brought munitions, men, and material from North Vietnam into the South where most of the fighting was taking place. Traversing through Laos, it had numerous obscure entry points into South Vietnam. Try as we might, we could never eradicate the damned trail. It was generally comprised of a bunch of narrow dirt roads, and when we bombed the shit out of it, the enemy simply filled in the holes with more dirt. The trail passed through rugged mountains and thick, steamy jungles."

"Yesterday, you described yourself as sapper," Ford noted. "Did you and your colleagues practice the various deadly and well-honed skills of your particular trade on the Ho Chi Minh?"

"That was a nice euphemism, Ford," Willy said. "The best we could ever do was ambush the enemy when they came through the jungle. If our intel or the ARVN had found where a leg of the trail had crossed the border into South Vietnam from Laos, that's where we would try to catch the dinks with their pants down."

"Is it safe to assume that you were an *ambush predator*?" Brewster asked.

"Yes, you could say that," Willy admitted. "One day, our squad was waiting at the border beside a trailhead. Suddenly, an ox-drawn supply cart and three men showed up, and it appeared as if they were taking a Sunday stroll through the forest. These guys were armed with greasy Chinese SKS rifles. Low-quality crap, I tell you. Probably Korean War surplus. They were wearing black jammies just like Victor Charles, but—check this out—these dudes were wearing pith helmets complete with little, NVA red stars on the front of their lids. Weird, I tell you. Were they Vietcong or North Vietnamese Army regulars?"

"A dink is a dink," Ford said. "In your own words, would a rose by any other name smell as sweet?"

"You're right," Willy said. "It didn't matter. We were determined to exterminate them all. Nobody gave the order to fire—we just blasted away. Have you ever seen those nature films where a pack of wolves coordinates an attack on a baby moose? They come in from all sides at the same time. What unseen force in nature can possibly drive the wolves to know how and when to do exactly what they do?"

"Mother Nature is a bitch on wheels," Brewster proclaimed.

"Precisely," Willy said. "The wolf pack splits up, and they can't see each other in the woods. What trigger gets pulled to make these canines attack like that? Some unseen force, no doubt. The very same question should be asked about the nature of human beings. What kind of trigger gets pulled to make human beings instantaneously and simultaneously strike out without saying a word?"

"Maybe there's something dark and primal in us," Ford said. "Maybe, this is why human beings have such an affinity to be around dogs and keep them as pets and vice versa. Maybe, when it comes right down to it, humans are not much more than two-legged wolves."

"Maybe, when it comes right down to it, God just backed the wrong primate," Brewster said.

"So it would seem," Willy said. "What happened up until that point was just the start of what would turn out to be a very bad day."

"It just sounds like war to me, plain and simple," Ford said.

"Nothing more and nothing less."

"No, Mr. Ford," the big man countered. "It turned out to be much more than that. When we wasted the ox, it bellowed out with a long, low moan of agony as it fell to its front knees. I went over, took my right foot, and pushed hard against its hip until it fell on its side, pulling the cart over with it. Two of the enemy died where they stood, but the third man managed to take cover behind the cart. Somehow, the third soldier appeared to be uninjured. Before we grabbed him and tied his hands behind his back, he waved a white piece of cloth. In perfect English, he shouted, 'Surrender! Surrender!' He said this over and over again, I tell you."

"Good," Brewster said. "Perhaps this enemy combatant would be a valuable intel resource."

"One would think," Willy said. "We charged forward to secure the scene. The cart was loaded to the gills with crates of magazines and a single crate of RPG rounds, I tell you. Jackpot! We tied up our prisoner of war, pitched the two dead men into the woods, and untethered the dead ox. It took the strength of the entire squad to pull that damned thing off of the trail."

"You're a big boy," Ford joked. "I bet you could have picked it up all by yourself."

"I swear to Jesus—it must have weighed two thousand pounds," Willy recalled. "Once done, we rolled the cart back up into its upright position and started to pack up the scattered munition crates. The radio man sent off a status to HQ. We needed instructions on what to do with the captured munitions. More importantly, what should be done with our new prisoner of war? Eyes on the trail said another oxcart loaded up with weapons was about two clicks upstream and was headed our way. They told us to wait for the next shipment that was coming down the trail and take it out, too. However, the other orders we received from HQ were as ambiguous as they were clear."

"I don't understand," Brewster said. "What does that mean?"

"They wanted us to blow the crates of munitions, but they didn't need the prisoner of war for interrogation. They suggested that we should just somehow make him, well, disappear. It was more important for us to continue on with our ambush mission. They would never give us an illegal order over the radio, but what they had done was exactly that: they had given us an illegal order over the radio, if you understand my meaning. We had to carry it out. Once again, we became a pack of wolves. No verbal communication was necessary. We were going to pull the plug on some poor bastard who was willing to fight and die for something he believed in, just as we were."

"Both sides of that conflict couldn't be right," Brewster said.

"I hold that conviction to this very day," Willy said. "As a matter of fact, I have to. If I didn't think that way, I wouldn't be able to live with myself. Hell's bells, boys; I can barely live with myself now! Anyhow, the sergeant simply pointed to me and Clifford Spiro. Sarge never even bothered to point at our prisoner of war or even look in his direction. Nonetheless, we knew what we were supposed to do. Clifford had unsheathed his Ka-Bar, and he and I walk over to the prisoner who was bound but not gagged. He had a slight frame and looked to be about my age when I went off to the war. The prisoner smiled, bobbed his head up and down, and said, 'Surrender.' Perhaps that was the only English word he knew."

"I see where this is going, Willy," Ford said. "I suspect the prisoner probably figured out what was about to happen to him next."

"No, sir! He most certainly did not. He never saw it coming. For certain, he had no idea what was going to happen until we laid hands upon him. I pressed against his torso to instruct him to lay back. He did this without hesitation. To this day, I remember seeing a small silver crucifix that he wore around his neck. This man was a Christian. Maybe he was even a Catholic. We were told that the enemy were all a bunch of Godless atheists and that it would be proper for us to kill as many as we possibly could. You don't think that our very own government ever lies to us, do you?"

"Every day of the week—and twice on Sunday," Brewster said.

"I'm not sure if I want to hear any more of this."

"Please!" Willy said. "Somebody has to hear what I have to say. Anyhow, I used to wear an olive-green towel around my neck when I was in the bush. It always came in handy when I needed to wipe the sweat out of my eyes. It was a giant handkerchief if I ever needed to blow a nasty leech out of one of my nostrils. It could be a great makeshift pillow if I ever needed to grab a nap when the bag monster was knocking on my eyelids. One of my buddies once got greased when his right carotid artery and jugular vein got a blowout from RPG shrapnel. He had bright red blood blasting out of his throat. I held this towel over the gaping wound in the right side of his neck to try to keep him calm until the angels came down from heaven and hauled him away."

"You should have burned that towel after your friend got wasted," Ford said. "Bad Karma, big man!"

"Maybe so," Willy said. "I can't help but think about that now and again. No doubt about it, that old towel was very handy, but it stank. No matter how many times I washed it, I just could never get the funk out of it. P-funk, baby! It was pure and unadulterated funk, I tell you. I can't even begin to describe the odor, but if I smelled it today, I would recognize it in an instant, and it would probably make me vomit. The closest thing that I could describe it to, I guess, would be the odor that emanated from the meat loaf that went bad in my fridge when the power company cut off my juice because I couldn't pay the electric bill."

"Oddly enough, I know exactly what spoiled meat loaf smells like!" Brewster said. "I also happen to know exactly what spoiled meat loaf tastes like, and I want to vomit just thinking about it."

"Well, then, you get it," Willy said. "I took this towel from around the back of my neck and I put it under the head of the prisoner of war. He smiled and bobbed his head ever so slightly up and down. He thought that what I had done was an act of kindness. I got down on my knees beside his head and threw my body across his face to muffle his screams. My buddy took his bayonet and slowly, but thoroughly, thrust the knife in an upward direction right below the prisoner's breastplate. With each thrust, he would swing the handle up and down as if he was shifting the gears on the tranny of an old Mustang. Of course, we had to do that to make certain that the heart of our victim was thoroughly lacerated to ribbons. There was no coming back from what we had done."

"He was a prisoner of war, Willy!" Brewster protested. "He surrendered to you, for God's sake!"

"As best I can recall, God wasn't in the 'Nam. Nowhere to be found, as a matter of fact. I turned my face away because I didn't want to watch a man being butchered, but I could still feel copious amounts of warm, thick blood pouring out of the hole in his heart and soaking through my shirt all the way down to the right side of my rib cage as I continued to lay across his face with all of my might. Suddenly, he worked his hands free from his bindings."

"Did he put up a fight?" Ford asked.

"One would think," Willy said. "At first, his arms were thrashing about wildly. It reminded me of *Lost in Space*. Do you remember the robot that would flap his arms around like a bird? He would shout, 'Danger, Will Robinson, danger!' That always cracked me up."

Brewster had a transient diminution of vision in his left eye. With each episode of déjà vu, it was becoming painfully clearer that everything in the universe was connected somehow.

"Before the prisoner of war died, though, he did something odd," Willy said. "He reached out and held my hand. Why would he do something like that? We were committing an act of cold-blooded murder, but at the very end, our victim tries to hold my hand. That has always bothered me. What did it mean? That's always bothered me a lot. In any event, within just a few moments, his body became very still. That was it. It was finished."

Brewster thought, *"Forgive them, Father. They know not what they do."*

Ford said, "I'm sorry for all of that shit you went through, big man, but you need to learn how to let this go somehow and in some way. You need to learn how to forgive yourself."

"I would like to, Ford, but how am I supposed to do that? It wasn't so much that I got blood all over me when we murdered that boy. Frankly, I deserved that. The problem is that I have never been able to wash off the stain that was left over on the right side of my rib cage." He stood up and pulled out the tail of his shirt. "See? It's right here. Can you see it?"

Brewster and Ford looked at each other and then back over to the big man's anterolateral thorax. There was no sign of any stain, blood, plaque, macular eruption, bruising, petechiae, papular outbreak, hematoma, solar or seborrheic keratoses, abrasions, nevus, ulcerations, excoriations, geographic rash, erythema, rubor, pallor, hypopigmentation, hyperpigmentation, or anything else to speak of. Nada. Zip. Nothing.

Brewster proceeded to tell a lie to his new friend. "Yes, Willy, we all see it. Maybe it's just something you have to live with."

Willy Mammon said, "I knew it was there! I can see it whenever I look at myself in the mirror! Well, I guess I deserve this stain too. In the end, I turned out to be no better than the dinks who were holding those French Legionnaires in the tiger cages for all those years."

"You were just following orders," Ford said.

"Yeah. That is right, Rip. We were just following orders. We waited by the trailhead for several hours, and nothing else came out of the jungle except for a small deer. We wasted Bambi, too. Cut it right in half. I guess, since nobody else came down the trail, we could have taken that young fellow into headquarters as a prisoner of war instead of, well, you know… That bothers me. That bothers me a lot. In retrospect, I think I was given a test in life long ago, and I failed."

"It's behind you now," Brewster said as he reached out and rubbed the Wooly Mammoth on the back of his neck. "Take a deep breath."

"On my second tour in the 'Nam, I was a medic," Willy said. "I guess that's what inspired me to eventually apply for medical school. I was seriously wounded after I stepped on a booby trap of punji sticks. Do you know that Victor Charles would lace the spikes with human feces?"

"Biological warfare?" Brewster asked.

"Precisely," Willy said. "I ended up getting osteomyelitis, and I eventually needed to have the second metatarsal bone of my left foot resected. I was on antibiotics for a long time, but the injury knocked me out of the war. I was eventually able to go on to college as I had always originally planned at Prairie Baptist University."

"Thank God for the GI Bill," Ford added.

"I ballooned up to 280 pounds, and I became a walk-on offensive tackle. I would like to think that I was pretty good at protecting the quarterback, but after I injured my left foot in Vietnam, I was only mediocre at best as an up-field blocker on running plays. Anyhow, I was never particularly fast to begin with. Straight up, I think a snail could beat me now in a race!"

"I could have gone through my entire life without hearing *any* of this," Brewster said. "I feel like I need to take a wicked shit and a hot shower right about now."

"Well, I guess that's it, Brewster," Willy concluded. "Now you know all about me. You'll need to decide very soon if you are going to jump into the clinical clerkships. You'll have to make a decision before the Fourth of July since all the rotations will ramp up on July 7. I hope you'll be able to let me know as soon as you decide what to do with your life. Anyhow, there's nothing else I can ever really say about that place called, well, you know— Vietnam..."

After Willy Mammon left the laboratory, Ford and Brewster found themselves in a very dark place. They had to get out of the basement and find some restorative sunshine and a breath of fresh air.

As Ford and Brewster sat on a bench across the street at Hermann Park, J. D. lit up a cigar. He would spit after each puff as if he were trying to purge something nasty and evil that he had inadvertently ingested.

Rip Ford picked up a stick and started to draw a crude figure of a fish in the dirt.

"In my humble opinion, I think your fish needs an eyeball," Brewster said. "After all, I took a course in college on art appreciation, and I'm therefore certainly qualified to offer such a sophisticated critique on your dexterity and artistic skills, or lack thereof, as the case may be."

With that comment, Ford rudely pulled the cigar butt out of Brewster's mouth and jammed it into the dirt to make an eyeball in the correct anatomical position for the drawing of the fish that he had just rendered. "Well, Brew, how does my masterpiece look now?"

Brewster replied, "I do believe that if there are any disciples of a certain itinerant rabbi from Nazareth that are lost and still lurking about in the Roman catacombs, they would be most proud of your artistic endeavors."

"We've had several false starts," Brewster observed from the safety of his laboratory cubicle, "but let's see if Dr. Holcombe actually shows up today. It's gotten to where he never even answers the telephone at his house anymore."

"I have it on good authority that he's on his way in as we speak," Ford replied. "He wants to meet with us, Zip Talbot, and the rest of the research group in the conference room as soon as he gets here. Apparently, our boss has some very important information to share that will have an immediate and long-term impact on our hepatitis research. He promised, come hell or high water, that he would make a guest appearance to talk to everybody and fill us in on what he's been up to."

"His prolonged absence from work has certainly been a big mystery," Brewster said. "When he shows up, are you really going to resign from the non-A, non-B hepatitis study as you've been threatening to do?"

"I will indeed if push comes to shove and we're forced to inoculate the great apes. I just wouldn't be able to do it," Rip Ford said. "How about you?"

"I'm still looking for deliverance."

"I hope you find it," Ford said. "Tomorrow is the Fourth of July. Are you going to do anything to celebrate?"

"Why in hell would I want to celebrate the 117th anniversary of the fall of Vicksburg to the goddamned Yankees?" Brewster said with a laugh. "Actually, my band, DNR, will be performing our very last performance at the Guaiac Dick nightclub in Bellaire. As you know, our guitarist, Blow Colima, is completing his postgrad training, and he'll be moving away from Houston."

"Does he have a job lined up?"

"Beats me," Brewster answered. "With his pending departure, we've decided to pull the plug on our band after our last performance. I'll be sad and lonely when it happens."

"You're an idiot, Brewster," Ford proclaimed. "I know that Irene Segulla just passed away, but why don't you ask her niece out for a nice date this holiday weekend? After all, you talk about her all the time. I don't know why you're attracted to fat girls, but it's not natural. Knowing you, I'll bet dollars to doughnuts that you've never even been on a real date before."

"I do indeed like fat women, but I have to be careful about who I go out with," Brewster replied.

"How so?"

"Before I ask a fat girl out on a date, I have to make absolutely certain that she's not so huge that her toes are splayed out into a 180-degree arc in order for her to ambulate in an upright fashion."

"Can a woman ever get that big?"

"Absolutely. I took a girl of such gargantuan proportions down to the beach at Galveston on a Saturday afternoon date a few years ago. As we walked upon the beach, amateur paleontologists followed the woman's tracks as if she was a resurrected wooly mammoth. I must admit that it was rather embarrassing when several of the interlopers started to take plaster of Paris castings of the woman's footprints. I'll have you know that I made a gallant, yet futile attempt to shield the misfortunate behemoth from the other beachgoers when they began to hurl spears of contempt at her. The poor rotund monster bellowed out in anguish. It was all very sad."

"Well, that's what I get for trying to have a normal conversation with you," Ford said. "Of all the people I've ever met in my entire life, you're the first person I've ever known whom I truly despise."

"As well you should," Brewster said. "After all, it should be self-evident to you by now that also I truly despise myself."

"You're a pig," Ford said as he looked upon Brewster with disgust. "Never said otherwise."

"So, you admit it?" Ford asked. "You're going to stumble on your own shoelaces someday and fall down headfirst into a deep, dark shithole. When that happens, nobody's going to miss your sorry ass when you suddenly disappear."

"Well, neither would I."

"Fine, then," Ford added. "Be a jerk. What do I care? It's your life."

"No," Brewster said, "but that's the point. It's not my life that I'm living. This life is a test. It's only a test. If this life was meant to be my *real* life, then it should have come with a better set of instructions."

"Maybe so," Ford said. "However, if that's the case, and this abbreviated personal existential journey that you're currently on is nothing more than just a dry-hump preseason test run, then you're miserably failing the audition."

"Well," Brewster added, "at least I don't have to worry about it until if and when God's in the house. If he ever finally shows up and gets around to raising the curtain on the big show, I promise you that I'll have my song and dance routine nailed down tight by the time that I pirouette upon the scene, stage left. The ovation—or is it ovulation?—from the audience will be deafening!"

"Dick wad!" Ford exclaimed. "For you, it's not stage *left* or stage *right*. It's stage *wrong*.

"You need to ease up on the starch in your shorts, Rip. You'll have nobody to blame but yourself when you singe your own short hairs and your blazing blue balls blister up on you."

"I'm not laughing. You're sittin' over there like a turd-chompin' possum. Everything's just a big joke to you. Stand up!" Ford grabbed Brewster by the lapels. "I'm fixin' to bust you up."

"Go ahead," Brewster said as he arose from his chair and stood with a malevolent sneer. "I deserve it. I'll even let you take the first poke. Once you get started however, you better finish me off. If you don't pull the plug on me right here and right now, I'll come back at you and make you bleed."

Brewster closed his eyes and abducted his arms while awaiting the first blow from Rip Ford that never came. "That's what I thought," Brewster said momentarily. "You're a pussy willow. All you had to do was pull the trigger. I assure you, the both of us would have felt better if you had …"

The research associate, Zip Talbot, was eavesdropping upon the hostilities while he stood in the hallway. After becoming a witness to the verbal barbs that Ford and Brewster freely exchanged, it was time for Talbot to interrupt the skirmish before things got any uglier. "Knock it off! Pay attention, my fellow thespians on the stage of life, or perhaps I should say, my fellow lesbians on the stage of irrelevance?"

"What gives?" Brewster asked as he pulled away from Ford's grasp.

"As for you, Brew, I guess God's finally in the house because the curtain's just about to go up," Talbot answered. "It's time for everybody who's been involved with the non-A, non-B hepatitis research project to congregate in the basement. I ran into Dr. Holcombe upstairs, and as we speak, he's headed down to the conference room. If I could make an educated guess, gentleman, I believe that the fat lady's about to sing."

Upon his arrival to the basement laboratory conference room, it was rather obvious that Dr. Holcombe appeared to be pale and frail. He was clearly suffering with the stigmata of an acute and serious illness. During the time of his prolonged absence, he had lost about twenty pounds and was suffering from alopecia totalis. All his hair had fallen out after he received his first dose of systemic chemotherapy that included the anthracycline mammalian antibiotic that was euphemistically referred to as "The Big Red". His skin had the color of a manila folder, and he was sweating profusely.

Brewster's worst fears had come to pass as some dreadful malignant illness had obviously befallen his mentor. Dr. Hank Holcombe had been diagnosed with lymphoma, a cancer arising from the immune system.

Initially, the nomenclature that categorized the diseases aggregated under the heading of "lymphoma" was an unsophisticated system based entirely on light microscopy histopathology. An early attempt to pigeonhole lymphoma under different subheadings had been conceived by Dr. Rappaport in 1966. In 1974, an updated system by Kiel would try to separate lymphomas into diseases to be categorized by "B" cell and "T" cell designations. It would not be until 1982 that a more intelligent conception of the nature of the myriad subtypes of lymphoma could be categorized into what was called the "working formulation." The limitation of the working formulation was that it applied to strictly "B" cell diseases.

Toward the end of Brewster's career many decades later, the nomenclature for lymphoma would become so complex that keeping track of the different subtypes of the lymphoid malignancies was akin to seeing a modern quarterback trying to keep track of his team's fifty or so potential offensive plays during a football game. The successful execution of the schemes found in a football playbook could never be considered a rote, brain stem function. A modern quarterback now finds it necessary to tape the list of plays onto his non-dominant arm during the course of a game to keep track of the strategy needed in any given situation. Similarly, a modern oncologist needs immediate computer access as a reference to sort out the complexities of the malignancies that may arise in the lympho-reticular system, and the appropriate up-to-date managements thereof.

"Well, I have bad news, boys," Holcombe said as he addressed his research colleagues. "I was trying to keep this medical problem that I have under wraps. I wanted to see if I could get this illness cooled off and get back to work without anybody knowing what was going on with me. After all, having some type of cancer might be interpreted as a sign of weakness, and the Gulf Coast College of Medicine doesn't tolerate any signs of weakness."

"Spill it, Hank," Denny Sassman, one of the research scientists, demanded.

"As far as keeping anything about my situation on the QT, that just won't be the case any longer. I have lymphoma, Denny," Hank Holcombe said. "Things have been rough thus far. I tolerated my first course of systemic chemotherapy quite poorly. In fact, the crab-pickers beat the dog shit out of me."

The chief veterinarian who oversaw the animal research lab asked, "What happened?" As Dr. Caleb was accustomed to only working with animal specimens, he was not readily versed in complications that could arise as a consequence of chemotherapy treatment.

"It was bad, I tell you," Dr. Holcombe said. "I had severe nausea and vomiting the likes of which I had not seen since that fateful day when I found a floater in my bowl of moo goo boo foo at the Buck Wong Oriental Buffet! My skin itches so badly right now that I now have to alternate applications of scalding hot water and ice packs just to try to find some kind of peace."

"Do topical steroids help at all?" Brewster asked.

"I might as well be pissing in the ocean," Holcombe answered. "The crab-pickers tell me I have advanced stage IV-b, T-cell mycosis fungoides with lymphadenopathy. This disease has features consistent with the Sezary syndrome, as I have bone marrow involvement. These abnormal T cells are now working their way out into my bloodstream."

"What are the crab-pickers hitting you with?" Zip Talbot asked.

"I've started CHOP chemotherapy. The free radicals are going to try to spot-weld some of the large plaques on my skin with XRT. I hope and pray the treatment might buy me some time, but I'm afraid about what I'm up against. I must admit it's a bit sobering to know that it'll be 'box city' for me sooner than later."

"You shouldn't talk like that," Ford said.

"Why not?" Uncle Hank asked. "It's the truth. Are you afraid that I'll jinx the situation? How could my predicament get any worse than it already is?"

"Frankly, Ford's correct," Brewster said. "It could get a lot worse. Your proclamation could become a self-fulfilled prophecy."

"I'm just trying to be objective about my particular situation," Holcombe said. "Damn it to hell; I'm not even forty years old—and I might have to squeeze out thirty years of living into just about a year or so."

Talbot said, "If that's the case, you better make that time count for something, Hank."

"I don't know about this premonition that I've had for a while," Dr. Holcombe said, "but for some reason, I think that I am getting closer to the finish line of my life."

"Well, I can't speak on behalf of the other people in this room," Brewster said, "but maybe Rip and I can help you get you to that finish line in life that you spoke of."

"Thanks, J. D.," Holcombe said. "Don't be surprised if I call on you boys someday and ask y'all for a big favor. My only regret is that I missed a chance to be loved. If it had happened, even for a fleeting moment, I think I would truly feel that my life was complete. I guess it just wasn't meant to happen for me. It's the awareness of our own mortality that gives our very lives any meaning at all. What do any of us have? If a person is lucky, maybe he or she will have about a number of four score or so spins around the sun. That's it. That's all we get."

*Déjà vu!* These disturbing and surrealistic cosmic messages were becoming more frequent for J. D. Brewster as he vigorously rubbed his left eye.

"I can't help but be philosophical about all of this," Holcombe added. "I believe that we're all called to find some tangible mission that is righteous and good. Once we recognize that this divine calling may be our destiny, it is then our duty to try to accomplish this calling to the best of our God-given abilities."

"You've done that," Sassman noted. "Be proud of your accomplishments, my friend."

"I hope that's true," Holcombe concluded. "After all, this commission to such a purpose gives our lives a deeper meaning. This is my conviction. Should we not also surely strive to pursue love and happiness? I suggest you do the same."

Rip Ford asked, "Uncle Hank, do you have somebody, anybody, with whom you might be able to stay with while you're undergoing cancer treatment? You might need some help along the way, especially if the chemotherapy is going to be this hard on you."

"No, I don't, but it's not just about me. None of you fellows are married, nor to my knowledge, even have a girlfriend. From my fresh perspective on this matter, that's not a good thing. Far from it.

Nobody wants to die alone. I hope that doesn't happen to you too. When I start to spin down the drain, I pray that I'll be brave enough to ask somebody to pull the plug. I just need somebody willing to do it. No person ever comes into this world with a set of blueprints. None of us are given instructions on how to be born, how to live, or how to die."

Although Brewster couldn't agree more to what Dr. Holcombe had just said, dying is a mysterious event. It's also very much an individualized and personalized transition. Dr. Holcombe had not yet realized that when it comes right down to it, *every* human being will eventually die *alone*, even if a person may be fortunate enough to be surrounded by loved ones at the terminal moment.

Dr. Caleb waved about his right arm about as if he were man trying to chase away a pesky moth. "What about the research project?"

"For the time being, I'm going to pull the plug on our hepatitis study, Dr. Caleb. I want you and Zip Talbot to continue taking care of the great apes in the lockdown kennel until we figure out what to do with them. As for you, Professor Sassman, I hope you find Bigfoot someday. I respect your noble quest. After all, I've seen you go out into the thicket and look for this mythical biped every spring. Personally, I don't believe the damned thing even exists, but I know you do. Listen up, Rip. I want you to start working on this new illness called 'GRID' that's starting to sweep through the homosexual community."

"I'm on it like bluebonnet, Hank," Rip said. "It probably won't be too hard a transition from the research that we've been doing up until now."

"This GRID business might be a virus, but there's a distinct possibility that we're dealing with a noninfectious etiology. Anyhow, Dr. Bookman and his brainiac, Parker Coxswain, have been working on this project for the last year. I want you to go help them out. I know for a fact that Parker is a smart fellow, but he's as crazy as a bedbug. It will be your job, Rip, to keep this guy tethered to the planet."

"What do you envision for me?" J. D. asked.

"As for you, Brew, I want you to surface for a breath of fresh air. It's time for you to start your clerkship rotations and get on with life."

Holcombe shuffled toward the conference room exit. "Goodbye, good luck, and God bless you all." Dr. Holcombe left the basement without making any further eye contact with his research team. Nobody had a chance to shake his hand or even say goodbye.

In the course of scientific research at the Gulf Coast College of Medicine, it was the first time that J. D. Brewster could ever recall Dr. Holcombe speaking without employing his signature, exaggerated, Trans-Pecos, West Texas dialect. In the course of life events at the Gulf Coast College of Medicine, it was the first time that Dr. Holcombe had ever told somebody that he was facing a terminal illness. After Hank Holcombe's departure, the members of his research team sat for several moments in stunned silence.

One by one, the scientists slowly left the laboratory, suddenly transfixed by the thought of their own eventual mortality.

"Dr. Holcombe is a top-shelf research scientist," Ford noted, "but more importantly, he's a good and decent human being. Hank was only trying to make the world a better place."

"So, will that be his epitaph?" Brewster asked.

"Fitting, I believe."

"Maybe so," Brewster concluded, "but sadly, no good deed goes unpunished. If Hank tried to make the world a better place, I guess it's no surprise that he got dealt such a lousy hand of cards to play in this life."

"You're a cynic," Ford said as he looked at Brewster with dismay. "No," Brewster answered. "I'm just a realist, and I understand how the world works. Our beloved bumpkin just took a direct hit. Nobody saw it coming, but he just got bombed from high altitude with atomized and aerosolized shit, and there's not a damned thing that we can do about it."

"Hang on, Brewster," Ford said. "Perhaps you haven't been paying attention to current events. After all, Dr. Holcombe is taking cancer treatment as we speak."

"That's not the point! Can't you see? Did Hank deserve any of this? Sadly, bad things happen to good people all the time. That cold, hard fact is—and likely always will be—part of the human condition. If that's indeed the case, come to think of it, maybe all of us deserve to be shit upon with a ton of bricks!"

Brewster and Ford shook hands, but neither one knew exactly how to verbally say goodbye. When Dr. Holcombe pulled the plug on the non-A, non-B hepatitis research study, it was as if an albatross had been cut from the neck of Rip Ford. After all, he absolutely had no intention of ever proceeding with hepatitis inoculation experiments on the big primates.

"You get off the hook, Ford," Brewster said.

"Well, you did too."

"I'm not talking about our recent altercation," Brewster replied. "That's not important now, although I'm glad you didn't bust my chops. No, it's more than that," Brewster replied. "I just squandered an entire year of my life. I have no choice but to postpone the PhD track of my professional education and enroll straight away into the clinical clerkship training program. I guess the die has been cast, whether I like it or not. Assuredly, I don't like it. Nonetheless, I have to try to revitalize the only thing I have left that's still going for me. If I stay tightly wired, I still might have a chance to get my MD degree by '82."

Brewster found Wooly Mammoth and asked him to investigate which clinical rotations were still available at such a late date. The first clerkship was scheduled to start on Monday, July 7, which was only four days away. Most of the good slots had already been taken, but Willy told Brewster there was still room for both of them to start out on the surgery clerkship on Dr. Street's burn service.

Nobody in their right mind wanted to tackle that particular rotation, unless they were forced to at the point of a gun. Dr. Blaze Street had a well-deserved reputation for being a sadist. The only other person who had signed up for that rotation with J. D. Brewster and Willy Mammon was another student named, Ben Fielder. He would be joining them on the burn service and also on the next two mandatory surgical rotations that would follow in August and

September. Despite these challenges, the Wooly Mammoth was quite delighted and most relieved that his new friend, J. D. Brewster, would be there to share the common misery that they were about to experience.

"We're about to see some fireworks! Are you ready to become the new love monkey at the Gulf Coast College of Medicine?" Dr. Bryan asked Brewster before the band went on stage for their final performance.

"Am I ever!" Brewster exclaimed. "Dr. Bryan, I recently learned that you're originally from Bryan/College Station."

"My father was a macro-economics professor at Texas A&M," the emergency room physician answered.

"I was just wondering if your sir name traces all the way back to the 19th century in East Texas and if you're a direct descendent of the patriarch who founded Bryan/College Station."

"I am in deed!" Dr. Bryan proudly replied. "My third great-grandfather was a city father."

"Pretty cool," Brewster said. "I'm sure you're proud that your remote ancestor was a Bryan."

"No, dumb shit," Dr. Bryan said with a smirk. "His last name was College Station."

"What?!"

"Have another brew, Brewster, "Dr. Bryan suggested. "You're just too damned sober to go on stage for our last gig!"

It was now late in the evening on the Fourth of July at the Guaiac Dick nightclub in Bellaire, Texas, and it was finally time for Brewster and his band members from DNR to perform the very last song of the very last set that they would ever do together as a group. As a promise to the GI fellow, Blomeo Colima, the last song was going to be Dylan's masterpiece, "My Back Pages," performed in the style of the Byrds, complete with Blomeo's mighty, new, *atomic* twelve-string "Ric".

"Ladies and gentlemen," Brewster spoke into the microphone, "I must sadly announce to you that this will be our very last performance, and we're about to perform our very last song for you tonight. Our lead guitarist, Dr. Blomeo Colima, has completed his post-graduate medical fellowship training and will be leaving Houston. Tonight, we'll pull the plug on our band, DNR. On behalf of the band, I can say without a doubt, that we definitely had a good run at it. It's been a blast. Goodbye, good luck, and may all of you have a happy and safe Fourth of July holiday."

The band members were a bit startled when they were suddenly greeted with a loud chorus of jeers.

As the finale had drawn to its sad conclusion, Brewster belted out the last verse of "My Back Pages" into the microphone: "My guard stood hard when abstract threats, too noble to neglect, deceived me into thinking there was something to protect. Good and bad, I defined these terms, quite clear, no doubt, somehow. But I was so much older then—I'm younger than that now." As planned, Brewster repeated the last line over and over again until he began to cry. "I was so much older then—I'm a lot younger than that now."

It finally worked. As the tears began to stream down Brewster's face, the women in the audience were mesmerized.

One of the fat, aging hippies pointed up at Brewster and proclaimed, "Oh my God! He looks so—so sensitive!"

"Take them!" another woman declared. "Take them now!"

Suddenly, the women in the audience rushed the stage, and the band members were pulled down into the crowd. Brewster watched in amazement as Blomeo Colima was swept away into the audience as if he were merely a tray of beverages hoisted on high by waitresses in a busy pub. That was the very last time that J. D. Brewster would ever see Blomeo Colima. The GI fellow, along with Brewster's other bandmates, simply disappeared into the crashing wave of an estrogenic tsunami!

As predicted by Dr. Bryan, the drummer in the band, the fireworks were about to start. For some reason, the only person left abandoned on the stage was Brewster. As the crowd plowed out of Guaiac Dick's, Brewster was left alone on stage. He was totally bewildered by his unexpected solitude. After all, Dr. Bryan professed that Brewster was about to become the new "love monkey" at the Gulf Coast College of Medicine. What went wrong?

While he stood at the open microphone and scratched his head, an obese woman with plastic daisies in her hair emerged out of the darkness and bravely approached him. She reached out and handed him a plastic flower that she had taken out of her unkempt mane. "Hello, Brewster. I believe you already know who I am. My name is Stella Link. I think that it's time that you and I get to know each other a bit better. We should find a quiet place somewhere. I believe you and I need to have a nice little chat!"

# 4

## THIRD DEGREE

On Monday, July 7, the gates of Hades opened. Three unwitting medical students were about to experience a day they would remember for the rest of their lives. It all started when they were introduced to a young man named Billy Joe Jarvis.

Billy Joe was going to be a high school senior, and he held a prized summer job at a nearby lumber yard where he was employed as a "go-fer." He was also the shop's "air quality control engineer." In other words, he was the scut monkey who swept up the sawdust that would accumulate at the rough-cut table saw that was in near-continuous operation at the establishment. His job was to keep the work area and restrooms in a tidy state. He enjoyed his work, but he was starting to have some concerns about the constant high-pitched tinnitus that would molest him at night when he tried to go to sleep.

He was not a particularly gifted athlete, and his paws were about as deft as scrap plywood. His notoriously poor hand-to-eye coordination rendered him the nickname "Hands" on his high school football team. Despite these shortcomings, he was fleet of foot. Stride for stride, he was able to pace any black wide receiver in a forty-yard dash, and this made Billy Joe an invaluable defensive back who could readily swat down passes thrown in his general direction. Sadly, he had not intercepted a single pass during his high school football career — not even in practice. This was even the case when the team's quarterback threw the ball directly at him instead of the wide receiver

87

during practice sessions to try to give the hapless defensive back a bit of encouragement. Billy Joe was determined his upcoming senior year would be different, however, and he was right; his senior year was about to be different, and tragically so.

Billy Joe lived in the town of Alief, and he was making the seven-mile commute to his summer job on a bright Monday morning in July. On his trek to work, a flock of wild turkeys gathered on the right side of the road as Billy Joe sped toward them in his old beater sedan. He stopped his car to allow the avian aggregates to cross the road. Twenty or so turkeys sprinted over to the left side of the road, leaving only one of the birds behind.

Billy Joe hit the accelerator and tried to proceed with his journey when the moronic flock decided to rejoin their witless solitary companion, which was aimlessly pecking away at pebbles on the other side of the street. The last thing Billy Joe wanted to do was massacre a flock of wild turkeys, but no good deed goes unpunished. He panicked and pulled the steering wheel hard to the right, which caused his car to flip. The vehicle landed on its roof in a culvert.

Billy Joe didn't experience any injuries, but he was trapped inside the vehicle. Since he was wearing his seatbelt, he was suspended upside down. He was frustrated that he could not move, but he was hopeful that his boss at the lumber yard would not can him for being late to work. His frustration turned to terror when the gas tank erupted into flames.

Good Samaritans quickly arrived on the scene and tried to extricate Billy Joe from his perilous predicament before he was overtaken by the inferno. When the flames enveloped the interior of his car, Billy Joe tried to valiantly bat away the fire with his free right arm. His efforts were futile, and he sustained extensive third-degree burns to his right hand, right arm, and face.

Before the fire department arrived, one of the rescuers took a large rock and bashed in the driver's side window. They pulled Billy Joe from the wreckage only seconds before the gas tank blew. Many years later, Billy Joe would wonder if it would have been better if he had just died in the accident back in the summer of 1980.

When the emergency medical technicians arrived, they quickly realized the serious extent of his burns. They called in the cavalry in the form of Dr. John "Wayne" Gray's very own brainchild: the helicopter air ambulance service that had been initiated at the Gulf Coast College of Medicine. Reportedly, the helicopter was just minutes out.

Billy Joe was strapped to a gurney and loaded onto the helicopter for the trip back to the Texas Medical Center. Billy Joe was met by the surgical burn team when the chopper landed on the roof of Gulf Coast University Hospital.

In the specialized surgical suite that was referred to as the "Tank Room," the remnants of the nylon jersey that had melted onto his body were cut away. During the transfer to the surgical suite, Billy Joe's IV site was lost.

"I need to get a new line going!" Dr. Street barked. "Where's my new team of grunts? Get them in here, damn it!"

There was no time to waste, and the dead flesh on Billy Joe's body had to go away—and it had to go away pronto.

"New line is in and running, Dr. Street," a nurse reported.

"Hit him with the ketamine," Street ordered. It was time to render Billy Joe into a semi-obtunded state to facilitate his survival in the chamber of horrors that was known as the Tank Room.

Brewster was having a hard time comprehending all the instructions demanded by Dr. Kelvin. "Heads-up. The only garments you need to wear right now are scrub pants and scrub tops with hair net, mask, and gloves. We won't have a scrub nurse to help us get dressed, so you're on your own here."

"Wait a minute," Brewster said. "In what order do we gear up?"

"Watch and learn," Kelvin answered. "Debriding a burn victim is a procedure performed in a non-sterile environment. In fact, it's usually quite a contaminated setting. During this procedure, nobody wears a full surgical gown. I don't have time to explain everything. We have to hurry. Do as I do—and do it right the first time. I am going to scrub up at the sink and then glove up. You boys better snap to it. Dr. Street is waiting out there for us, and if we don't perform, we're all looking at getting a new asshole by the end of the day."

"What are we going to find on the other side of this door?" the wooly one asked.

"There's a teenage boy on the other side of this door who got badly burned when his car rolled over," Kelvin explained. "We're about to strip off his dead flesh. This will be a nasty and brutal procedure. I can't lie to you about that. Dr. Street is a nasty and brutal man. I can't lie to you about that either. Keep your mouth shut. Don't speak to Dr. Street unless you're directly spoken to. He won't pimp you, but don't piss him off unless you want to get clobbered."

Ben Fielder found a package of latex gloves and said, "My left glove must have deteriorated in the package. It broke at the wrist. There doesn't appear to be another set here in this scrub room that's my size. What should I?"

Dr. Kelvin waved him off and said, "Suck it up, buttercup. There's no time to re-glove. You're going to get blood, slime, and dead shit down through the hole in your glove and onto the palm of your hand. Deal with it. Just follow my lead."

The resident burst through the doors of the tank room with the three medical students in tow. Billy Joe was moaning and sitting in a stainless-steel tank of murky water that covered him up to his chest.

"Fresh meat!" Dr. Street said. An angry, bipedal, fifty-five-gallon oil drum with a ruddy complexion, Dr. Street was not known to be a particularly patient or forgiving individual. "Quit diddle fucking around, and get to work. Now, damn it!" He looked at Ben Fielder who was a lanky ectomorph with deep-set blue eyes and thick, black, straw-like hair. "Listen to me, you beanpole. Take the scrub brush to this patient's right arm and clean away all of the eschar and black tissue. I want to see oozing raw flesh when you're done."

The surgeon turned to the Wooly Mammoth. "Get over here, King Kong. I want you do the same thing to his right hand, and I can tell you right now that his hand will take a lot of work to get it cleaned up." Looking at Brewster, he said, "Your turn, dumbass.

Tackle this kid's face. Dr. Kelvin, I want you to supervise with me. Let's see what kind of job these simpletons can accomplish."

General anesthesia can't be used during a debridement procedure. Patients need to be sedated, but they must *not* be fully unconscious. If they were, the respiratory drive mechanism would be completely shut down. Patients cannot be intubated since they may need to be moved about while they're in the scrub tank. Allegedly, at the time, ketamine was the best agent to achieve this conscious sedated state. Anybody who's witnessed the debridement of a burn victim under the influence of ketamine might have a reasonable doubt about that claim.

As was the case of Billy Joe Jarvis, patients would often cry out in pain and moan in agony during the debridement procedure. Dr. Street insisted that patients under the influence of ketamine during the debridement procedure may very well feel severe pain at some level during the process, but hopefully they wouldn't remember it. That assessment however was not particularly comforting to the three musketeers who were just starting their first official clinical rotation together.

"Dr. Street, I'm scrubbing away at this young man's face, and it's very charred. I'm afraid he might lose his ears!" Sadly, Brewster had just violated the primary rule that he was not allowed to speak to the attending unless spoken to first.

Street became livid and started to scream at Brewster within just a few inches of his face. "So, you're afraid that he might lose his ears? Let's take care of that problem right now!" Dr. Street walked over to the Billy Joe, grabbed his ears, and pulled them off the young man's head like he was peeling away the outer skin of a banana.

Billy Joe screamed and then started to whimper.

"Here you are, numb nuts!" Dr. Street said. "These are the kid's ears. Why don't you put them in an envelope and save them for the poor bastard? That way, he won't ever lose the damned things! Don't forget to label what's in the envelope when you're finished, because we'll soon have more charred body parts coming your way soon."

Dr. Street grabbed Brewster's left hand and put the ears in his palm.

Brewster lost the vision in his left eye, and he started to sway back and forth. He stumbled briefly when his proprioceptors failed and his very own spatial orientation to the planet's gravitational forces became untenable, but nonetheless, he stood fast and didn't collapse.

Dr. Street and the two nurses howled in laughter and pointed at Brewster.

"Here, boy," one of the nurses said as she approached the stunned medical student. "Let me help you." She swatted the ears out of Brewster's hand, and they fell to the floor.

Confused, J. D. reached down to pick up the ears, but Dr. Street took his right foot and pushed hard against Brewster's hip, causing the traumatized student to fall to the floor. His face landed directly upon the charred ears that now adhered to the tile floor.

Street and the nurses convulsed with laughter yet again.

Dr. Kelvin and the Wooly Mammoth gently reached down and helped Brewster back up to his feet.

Dr. Street was furious. "Leave him there on the floor and get back to work."

"He's my friend, and I'd never do that," Willy Mammon replied quietly. "I wouldn't even leave a man like *you* on the floor if you had fallen."

"Get out of my way, Mammon!" Dr. Street said. "I told you to debride this man's hand—and what have you done? Nothing, as best I can tell. I'm taking over this spot!" He pushed Willy aside and started to talk like Sergeant Carter from the old *Gomer Pyle* television show, which was popular in the 1960s. "Billy Joe Mud-flap, can you hear me? You're going to have to say bye-bye to the fingers on your right hand." Dr. Street took a large pair of bandage scissors and started to cut off the fingers of Billy Joe's right hand at each interphalangeal joint. He performed each crude amputation joint by joint, and finger by finger.

Every time Dr. Street clipped off a digit, Billy Joe cried out.

With each snip, Dr. Street said, "This little piggy went to the market!" When Dr. Street reached the metacarpal-phalangeal joints, he encountered fresh bright red blood that suggested the tissue proximal to that region was still viable.

"Look, Billy Joe Mudflap," Street exclaimed. "I've left you with some nice little chicklets on this useless stump so you can still wave your hand and say bye-bye! As best I can tell, your biggest problem is that you'll never be able to give somebody the finger if you ever get cut off in traffic. Say bye-bye, Billy Joe. Say, bye-bye, damn you!" He held up Billy Joe's fingerless right hand and started to rapidly flex and extend the hand at the patient's wrist, as if Billy Joe was electing to sadly take an abrupt and unexpected departure from all the warmth and gracious hospitality that was afforded to him by the empathetic and compassionate medical personnel within the confines of the tank room.

As the ketamine started to wear off, the patient began to respond to Dr. Street's relentless taunting. Billy Joe finally said, "Bye-bye!"

"I can't hear you!" Street exclaimed. A quid pro quo demand-and-answer chant began between the patient and the doctor. It got louder and louder with each cycle.

"Bye-bye!"

"I can't hear you!"

"Bye-bye!"

"I can't hear you!"

"Bye-bye!"

The wretched nurses laughed and clapped as if they were demon spawn watching a macabre marionette matinee.

Dr. Street finally dropped the fingerless hand and oozing, skinless arm back into the scrub tank.

Brewster was still petrified with fear as he watched Dr. Kelvin attempt to decompress the volatile Dr. Street. "I need a word with you in private, Dr. Street. Now, if you please. Let's take a breather for a moment, shall we?"

The medieval spectacle was finally over—at least for now.

While Dr. Kelvin attempted to pull the attending toward the empty hallway, Dr. Street bared his teeth and turned his head to sneer at the three students yet again. "Get Billy Joe Mudflap cleaned up—and then get some Silvadene cream on those open wounds," Dr. Street barked as a final order. "Tomorrow, we start grafting."

After taking a shower and dressing, the three stunned students congregated on a bench in the locker room. They sat in silence for several minutes.

"Should we say something to somebody about what we witnessed today?" Willy Mammon asked. "Perhaps we need to talk to administration. I'm serious. We just saw some evil shit going down, and I don't think I'll ever get that out of my mind. I was in the 'Nam, I tell you, and I know evil shit when I see it."

"We can't tell anybody about any of this," Ben Fielder said. "I'm certain that the administration already knows Dr. Street is an industrial strength dirtbag. This is our very first clerkship rotation. If we start complaining now, we'll look weak. The Gulf Coast has a reputation for breaking out a weed eater and cutting down any students they believe are not strong enough to take it. We have to prove we can take it."

"Well, I can't take it, Ben," Willy confessed. "After all, I can barely live with myself as it is. What are we going to do, Brew?"

"Shut the hell up!" Brewster exclaimed. "You boys need to pipe down. If we're going to retaliate, we're not going to talk about it."

"What do you have in mind?" Ben asked. "We better not get blowback from whatever crazy shit you might be planning."

"The first order in the delicate business of retribution is that you clamp your pie hole tight," Brewster said. "I know exactly what to do—let me take care of this. I make a solemn vow to you boys here and now that someday I'll have sweet revenge."

"I want in on it," Willy said.

"No dice," Brewster said. "In the not-too-distant future, an opportunity for clinical justice will avail itself. You'll know it when it happens. Just don't ask me about the details. In the meantime, gentlemen, we need to create an impenetrable firewall of plausible deniability. Am I clear?"

The three students sat in silence for several minutes.

Finally, Brewster whispered, "What the hell happened in there?"

"Nothing," Fielder replied. "I assure you—not a damned thing happened in there today."

By mid-rotation, the students had become quite proficient at burn debridement and were learning how to utilize the electric-powered dermatome to perform skin grafts. Part of the daily chore was rounding on the patients who were confined to the burn unit. This task was invariably done with the resident, Dr. Kelvin, as the attending, Dr. Street, only made "chart rounds." He would just sign off the work that had already been done by the resident and students.

One patient on the burn unit, Christopher Crider, warranted a great deal of medical attention. Dr. Street had derisively given the nickname "Crispy Critter" to this chronically malcontent individual. After all, the stubborn, cantankerous old man had accidentally set himself on fire while using oxygen therapy and smoking a cigarette at the same time.

At the end of his career, it was hard for Brewster to believe that there was a time when passengers on commercial airlines were allowed to openly smoke cigarettes and cigars in flight. It was also hard for him to believe that there was a time when patients were allowed to smoke in their hospital rooms at certain institutions. Well, 1980 was such a time—and the Gulf Coast University Hospital was such an institution.

Mr. Crider had been hospitalized with chronic obstructive pulmonary disease as a consequence of his hundred-pack-year smoking history. Pack-year history is calculated as the product of multiplying the number of packs of cigarettes smoked per day times the number of years an individual has actively smoked.

While hospitalized previously under the care of Dr. Cannon, Mr. Crider was instructed that he would not be allowed to smoke despite the hospital policy that allowed patients to consume tobacco if they had so desired. Mr. Crider was a rigid and quarrelsome individual, and he was not about to pay attention to the order that was given to him by the attending physician.

Several weeks prior to his transfer to the burn unit, Mr. Crider decided to sneak a cigarette while on oxygen therapy. He held the nasal cannula delivering oxygen to his nostrils in his right hand and a lit cigarette in his left hand. He would alternate a hit of oxygen with a subsequent puff of tobacco smoke. Well, it doesn't take a genius to figure out what happened next. In a simple act of discoordination, he accidentally put the nasal cannula and the lit cigarette onto his lap at the same time. Ouch! Houston, we have a problem.

While making rounds with his colleagues, Ben Fielder said, "Tell me, when you go off to the scrub tank and get debrided, is it a painful experience? I know they give you ketamine to sedate you for the procedure, but does it still hurt?"

Mr. Crider—who had been crusted over like a blackened redfish at an upscale New Orleans restaurant—replied, "Do bears shit in the woods? Why, most certainly! Do alligators shit in a sluice of gradeaux? Why, most certainly! How would you feel if your own balls exploded like popcorn while they were still safely nestled within the confines of your very own nut sack? Do you think that would hurt?"

"Why, most certainly!"

Years ago, when the aging bull elephants were erroneously culled from the herd at a popular game preserve in Africa, something most unusual occurred. The adolescent male elephants that were left in the herd went on a rampage and proceeded to kill a variety of other animals in the game preserve. Sadly, the murder victims included a rhino and several docile vegetarian ungulates that had been misfortunate enough to have crossed the path of the juvenile delinquent pachyderms.

It would appear that across a wide range of mammals, adult supervision is required to keep the adolescent members of the species from getting into trouble. Perhaps a lesson can be learned from this observation. In adolescent human beings, much like in adolescent elephants, high testosterone levels are present, but the prefrontal lobes of the brain, which tamper destructive and aggressive behavior, are not fully developed.

Sadly, the prefrontal lobes of sixteen-year-old Billy Bob Barton were not fully developed on the third weekend in July 1980. His parents had gone out of town to celebrate their twentieth wedding anniversary, and they foolishly entrusted their adolescent son to behave and keep an eye on the homestead during their absence. What does a young man do when his parents go out of town for the weekend, especially when there's an unlocked liquor cabinet above the wet bar? Well, it was of course time for Billy Bob to host an afternoon pool party. As music from the Cars and Journey blasted out from the stereo speakers, the liquor flowed. The teenagers at the party became quite rowdy. The suburban swimming pool became a clothing-optional skinny-dipping party.

There's a troublesome tallow tree that grows along the Gulf Coast area of Texas that has a beautiful green canopy, but it litters like a three-year-old riding in the back of the family sedan. At any moment, a candy wrapper will likely fly out of the back window. As it is deciduous, the tallow tree drops a heavy burden of leaves every fall. In the summer, it drops nasty green berries that have a malodorous and sticky white sap. The branches are weak, and it is commonplace to have stems and branches break off with only the slightest provocation.

Other than providing shade, the tree is useless. Even when the wood is dried out, it will not sustain a burn in a fireplace or render even a halfway decent flavor in a backyard smoker. Anybody in Houston who has a swimming pool and nearby tallow trees will need an array of aluminum extension poles and baskets to keep the swimming pool free of debris.

Billy Bob Barton's home was no exception. What was an exception, however, was the high-tension line that ran across his property line in the utility service right-of-way behind his house. This easement separated his posh neighborhood from an adjacent, less-affluent, middle-class subdivision.

As several of his male guests became inebriated, they challenged their host to see what it would be like to have some fun with the aluminum extension pole and basket that was used to clean the swimming pool. His malicious "friends" dared him to extend the aluminum pole as far as it would go and then touch the high-tension line that could be reached across the backyard fence.

Billy Bob was up for the challenge after taking four shots of tequila. Unfortunately, for the adolescent, this turned out to be a very bad idea.

The three medical students followed Dr. Kelvin into the tank room where Billy Bob was waiting to get his first debridement. What happened to the sixteen-year-old was unspeakable. How he survived thousands of volts passing through his body was inexplicable. His arms and legs had exploded off his body, and his remnant extremities appeared to be hot dogs that had been cooked in a microwave on high power for five minutes.

Unlike the thermal burns they had grown accustomed to seeing over the past three weeks, Billy Bob's body lacked the classic stigmata of the black crusty eschars that one would expect from a third-degree thermal injury. As with all the other patients who were debrided under what was called "conscious sedation" with ketamine, the adolescent would wail woefully when the debridement started.

Dr. Street barked out instructions as to what appendage he wanted each member of his team to tackle. He had new implements that the team members had not seen before. They were large, stainless-steel shears that would have been at home in a garden shed. Street would personally debride away the dangling sinew that had exploded on Billy Bob's right arm, and he wanted Dr. Kelvin to tackle what was left of the patient's left arm. Ben Fielder and the Mammoth would clean away the dead tissue from the right and left leg stumps respectively.

"It appears that this idiot also fried his penis," Street said. "Brewster, I want you to take a pair of bandage scissors and start trimming back his penis, starting from the corona end and working your way down to the curlicues. I want you to trim off a half centimeter of his penis at a time until you find fresh red blood. After you get done trimming back this boy's tally-whacker, it looks like he's going to need a permanent suprapubic catheter for the rest of his miserable life. I want you other fellows to do the same thing to his extremities with the heavy shears. However, whittling off what's left of his extremities at two-centimeter increments will probably be acceptable."

"Should we fill up the tank and get this patient ready for a scrub down?" Dr. Kelvin asked.

"Not yet," Dr. Street replied. "Let's surgically debride a lot of his dead tissue first and then we'll scrub him up."

With envy, Dr. Street scrutinized the boy's rather handsome facial features. "Do you know what we're about to do to you, pretty boy? We're going to turn you into home plate! That's right! Since you won't have any arms or legs, the Houston Astros will be able to use you out on the diamond at the Dome during their drive to win the National League pennant this yar."

Billy Bob could only respond by generating a soft, unintelligible gurgling sound.

"Mr. Brewster here is also going to cut off your penis with a pair of scissors," Street continued. "You won't even be able to get laid! Your rich mommy and daddy won't even be able to hire a prostitute for you to give you a hum job. You turned out to be one sorry sack of shit!"

"Ease up, boss," Dr. Kelvin pleaded.

The members of Dr. Street's burn service initially thought it was perhaps a bit odd when the attending physician started to smell what was left of Billy Bob's right arm and hum the theme song to the old television show, *Bonanza*. "Boy, this incinerated flesh smells really good! I want everybody to come over here and take a sniff of this kid's lumpy stumpy. I want you boys to tell me what you think."

Each of Dr. Street's team members unwillingly obliged the attending by obeying his rather bizarre direct order. First, Dr. Kelvin took a sniff and said, "Shit fire, boss—it smells like burned tissue to me. Nothing more and nothing less."

When Fielder and the Mammoth put their noses close to his exploded right upper arm, they concurred with Dr. Kelvin's original assessment of the situation.

"What the hell is the matter with you people?" Dr. Street asked. "Are all of you idiots genetic mutants born without a first cranial nerve? You boys are so worthless that you probably couldn't even tell if the back-forty outhouse was going up in flames and Aunt Bessie was trapped inside! Brewster, get over here and tell me what you smell."

Brewster followed the instructions of his deranged attending, and the student cheerfully rendered an honest epicurean observation. "Well, it smells like a mesquite-wood, sixteen-hour slow-smoked brisket that's been marinated overnight in a big vat of Lone Star and then garnished with a dash of cayenne, followed by a generous black pepper-corn rubdown."

"Your nailin' it, sweet child!" Street proclaimed. "My juices are a flowin'!"

"There's more!" Brewster added as he gently fanned the critically injured patient's extremity to aerosolize a few more molecules of seared sinew. "This combo platter of smoked human flesh was finally topped off with one or more tender sprigs of fresh Mexican cilantro!"

"Yes, you're absolutely right," Street concurred, "and it smells delicious! I swear, Brewster, my opinion of you has suddenly risen rather dramatically."

Brewster proudly took a bow.

When the director of the burn and trauma surgical service pulled down his own face mask, his nostrils flared as wide as silver dollars. His tongue rapidly darted to and fro as if he was a deadly pit viper harvesting the unmistakable odor of incinerated flesh from a misfortunately injured prey item was about to become the serpent's very next meal. For a moment, it appeared as though the ogre was about to voraciously lick away at Billy Bob's open wounds. Dr. Street's own team members were quite certain they were about to witness an act of human cannibalism!

Brewster noticed that the clock on the wall indicated it was 3:58 p.m. He had no time to lose, and he had to act quickly. It was time for the student to initiate the promised act of sweet revenge that he had long plotted against the attending surgeon. Brewster had to unlock the door to the scrub tank room by 4:00 sharp. He slipped away from the stainless-steel scrub tank and cracked open the door that led to an outside hallway. Fortunately, nobody saw him as he pretended that he had gone off to relieve himself in the restroom. Upon his return to the debridement suite, he resumed the unpleasant task of performing a methodical penectomy on a living, breathing, and intermittently screaming fellow human being.

Within moments, Antonia Alabaster and her cameraman from Your Witness News crashed through the door of the tank room— and the camera was rolling!

"Dr. Street, will you tell our viewers what exactly is going on in here?" Antonia asked pointedly just before she stuck the microphone into Dr. Street's face. Unfortunately for Brewster's cousin, ambush journalism doesn't always go as planned.

Without a word, Dr. Street grabbed her by the arm and threw her out into the hallway. The cameraman attempted to beat a hasty retreat, but he met the same fate after Dr. Street stripped the television camera from the videographer's right shoulder. Dr. Street swung the recording device and slammed it against the wall. He returned to the surgical debridement suite and said, "We can never let anybody know what goes on in here, can we? Repeat after me, damn it. We can never let anybody know what goes on in the scrub tank room!"

Brewster was devastated that his planned act of retribution had failed so miserably. He was sadly resigned to the fact that he had no obvious recourse but to fall in line. As if taking an oath, Dr. Kelvin and the three medical students dutifully replied in unison, "We can never let anybody know what goes on in the scrub tank room!"

On the last day of their rotation on the burn service the following week, J. D. Brewster got an emergency phone call from his brother, Bill. Tenneco's offshore drilling platform, the *Blue Gulf Breeze*, had a blowout! Dozens of oilers were critically injured and burned. UTMB in Galveston took as many of the injured offshore drillers as they could, but many more would be diverted to the Texas Medical Center. Others would need to be flown to LSU in Baton Rouge and Tulane. Each of the major university hospitals and the other facilities at the Texas Medical Center could expect multiple patients arriving by air ambulance.

The Gulf Coast General Hospital was slated to receive a total of six patients, all of whom had reportedly suffered 100 percent third-degree burns. Unfortunately, three of the patients died while being ferried across the Gulf of Mexico. While it came as no surprise to Dr. Street and Dr. Kelvin, the three surviving oilers were purposefully left in the emergency room and not taken to the scrub tank room. The students were not able to grasp the significance of this strategy, but Dr. Kelvin explained that 100 percent whole-body third-degree burns are tantamount to 100 percent mortality. "Come with me," Kelvin instructed his students. "This isn't going to be pretty. Not by a long shot."

The first stop was to take a look at the charts at the ER desk to find out exactly which patients they would be dealing with. Of interest, they all had the exact same first names. One was Billy Ray, another was Billy Mack, and the other was Billy James. The patient identification face sheets indicated that one of the oilers was identified as being black, and the other two were Caucasian. Even late in his career, Brewster would never forget that it's impossible to ascertain the racial or ethnic pigeonholes that may encapsulate a human being if said individual actually had no skin whatsoever. That was indeed the case for the three patients he was about to meet on the last day of his rotation on the burn service.

Upon finding the three charred, mortally burned oilers in an expanded emergency room stall, Dr. Kelvin said, "Gentlemen, my name is Dr. Kelvin, and this is my team from the burn service. We're here to help you get to the finish line. I know you men have all had a very *bad* day, but sadly, I need to let you know that this will also be your very *last* day. I'm sorry, boys, but the three of you are going to die within the next few hours. You've burned off all your skin, and there is no way we can save your lives. You have no living tissue to try to graft onto your open wounds. I promise all of you this; I'll make sure that you don't suffer. If you're all agreeable with what I am saying, I'll now have you sign a DNR code status form."

"What does that mean?" one of the victims asked. "I'm afraid of dying. I've never done it before."

"This means that we will not try to resuscitate you when your heart and lungs quit working within an hour or less," Kelvin explained. "If you like, I can speed up the process and start a morphine drip. It will keep you in a twilight state, but it may drop your blood pressure— and you may die sooner than later. As a prospective overview, that might be a good thing. As none of you have any skin left, you will simply decompose very rapidly. What little bodily fluids you have left will simply flow out through your open wounds and onto the floor. After that, you'll go to sleep— and then you'll never wake up. As you don't have any skin, you'll feel cold. Very cold. When that happens, we will make sure you have warm blankets to keep you comfortable for what time you have left on the planet. If you're so inclined, now is the time to make peace with each other and also with your Maker."

They all signed the DNR form, but one of the burn victims had to give a verbal consent because he was not strong enough to hold a pen. None of the men were married, and there were no family members who needed to be contacted. They asked to see the hospital chaplain to make peace with God and each other as Dr. Kelvin had suggested. Perhaps they could even have a cold beer. After all, they wanted to make a toast to each other before they completely disintegrated into a nonviable amorphous mass of quivering goo.

Dr. Kelvin replied, "I'll make that happen—come hell or high water."

Brewster explained that he knew the cafeteria cook, Mehdi, who could help procure the cold beer.

"What you're going to do, do it quickly," Kelvin said. "I know how all of this will play out. Now, you're going to need a prescription from me. You just can't go down there and pick up a six-pack of beer. You have to take the script to the pharmacy first, and Ralph will have to sign off on it. When he does, you'll get a pharmacy requisition that you'll need to take over to the cafeteria. Once you get that requisition, you'll have to walk it over to the cafeteria by hand or else it'll never happen. After that, the cafeteria will technically 'fill the prescription' right there. The clock is ticking. Go, Brew. Go, go, go!"

"What about you?"

"I just don't have the stomach anymore to just stay here and watch what's going to happen next," Dr. Kelvin said. "I want you boys to babysit these oilers until they check out. This will be your last assignment for the last day of this rotation. Dim the lights in here. Call me when it's finished, and I'll come back and teach you boys how to do a death summary and fill out the terminal certificates. I suspect there will be millions of dollars of lawsuits against the oil company for what happened today. In light of that, once these three poor bastards expire, their bodies will need to get posted by the county coroner."

As Brewster left the emergency room, he ran into Sister Buena. She was on her way down to see the three oilers. "You're the floating nurse from the temp pool! You know, at some point, I'm going to remember your name and where I first met you." Brewster just couldn't understand why the woman never had a name badge.

"I'd like to chat," the woman said, "but I'm on a very tight schedule. I'm sure I'll see you around."

While Brewster was gone, the three critically burned men started to get shaking chills as Dr. Kelvin had predicted. A liberal use of blankets was not enough to relieve their obvious discomfort. Fielder and the Mammoth went to central supply and pulled up heating blankets. Fortunately, the simple devices made the patients feel considerably better.

When the two students returned, an elderly black woman with white hair was praying over the three patients.

"Are you the chaplain?" Ben Fielder asked.

"No, I am a floating nurse from the temp pool," Sister Buena replied. "The chaplain is busy upstairs in the ICU with a young woman who is dying from pulmonary failure. I was told she had a complication from a cancer treatment drug called bleomycin. As the chaplain can't be here right now, my Boss asked me to come down here and offer some spiritual support for these fellows. I'll be around later if they need me, but for now, my work here is done. Sorry, boys, but I have to go. I'm on a tight schedule."

The patients were starting to feel thirsty. To hydrate them with IV fluids would only postpone their inevitable demise. As they had all signed a DNR code status, nothing would be done except comfort measures. Vital signs and even laboratory work would not be performed from there on out. Dr. Kelvin had told the students that when the patient began to feel thirsty to simply moisten a washcloth and let them suck on it. Mammon and Fielder held serious reservations that something as simple as a wet washcloth could help relieve the painful thirst the three men had started to experience, but once again, Dr. Kelvin was correct in the instructions he had disseminated to the students before his departure.

Getting the beer that the three terminally injured patients had requested turned out to be a fiasco. It took forty-five minutes for the pharmacy to fill out the requisition. Upon taking the form to the cafeteria, Mehdi reported to Brewster that there was no beer to be found. That discovery was a bit of a surprise since the cafeteria usually kept at least one six-pack of beer on hand for just those types of catastrophic circumstances. Mehdi presumed that one of the other line cooks had been nipping at a few of the pilsners from time to time.

Brewster was on a mission, but the clock was ticking. He told Mehdi that he would be in touch, but there was no time for a visit at that particular moment.

Brewster left the Texas Medical Center in his Mustang and headed to a grocery store in North University Place. He bought the most expensive beer he could find and hoofed it back into the emergency room as fast as he could. By the time he got back, he was already too late. The three patients had already expired. Around their lifeless bodies was a sticky pool of mucoid, serosanguinous slime that was stuck to the gurneys and caked upon the tile floor. The faces of his two colleagues were completely flat and vacuous. Their eyes were open, yet they seemed incapable of even blinking as they cowered in the dimly lit enclosure.

In silence, Brewster passed beers to his colleagues, but the German beer didn't have twist-off bottle caps. Fortunately, the countertop had a sharp metal edge, and they were able to pop open the bottles by bracing the edge of the cap against the counter and slamming down upon it with their palms.

The students raised a toast to the patients who had just passed away. Ben Fielder actually made an effort to honor each of the dead men by pouring a small amount of cold beer into their mouths with a 50-cc irrigation syringe. Although this tribute seemed to be somewhat macabre, Brewster thought it was nonetheless a gesture of supreme respect for the three men who had just succumbed to a most horrific death.

"Maybe I made a mistake in ever thinking that someday I could become a doctor, Brew," Willy confessed. "I wonder if it isn't too late for me to follow in my father's footsteps and get a job riding a lawnmower or trimming bushes somewhere."

# 5

# THE BONE CAN CLONE

After battling alcohol abuse for several years, the research scientist, Dr. Bruce Beathard, was finally able to maintain sobriety through his long-term participation in Alcoholics Anonymous. Years ago, when Dr. Beathard was struggling through his internal medicine residency program, he would find solace in a cocktail after a busy shift. Soon, one cocktail at night was not enough, and he started having two drinks of hard liquor on a daily basis. An insidious process had begun, and his alcohol consumption began to snowball out of control.

Within a year, Beathard was soon up to two alcoholic beverages at midday and four at night. He was clearly aware that he was in trouble. If an eventual intervention had not taken place, his career— and his very life—would have been in jeopardy. Fortunately, after the twelve-step AA program, it had been at least a decade since Dr. Beathard had tasted any alcohol. Nonetheless, his history of alcohol abuse remained a secret from his colleagues. He was afraid that his job at the Gulf Coast College of Medicine would have been in peril. Being an alcoholic would have been a sign of weakness. The Gulf Coast College of Medicine did not tolerate any signs of weakness.

Despite his long-term sobriety, Dr. Beathard felt compelled to continue his attendance at weekly AA meetings. At the AA meetings, he would say, "Hello, I'm Bruce Beathard. I'm an alcoholic."

The other members of the group would smile, wave, and reply, "Hello, Bruce!"

Perhaps, using appropriate medical jargon, he could have said, "Hello, I'm Bruce Beathard. Previously, I had both a physiological and psychological addiction to ethanol. I required consumption of this substance on a daily basis to maintain the façade of normalcy. However, I'm proud to report that my disease process is in a long-term remission, and I'm likely cured of this dreaded malady at this point in time."

Alcoholics don't talk like that. Intuitively and by personal experience, alcoholics have long known that "falling off the wagon", for even one moment, could immediately result in behavior that spirals into a full-blown relapse. Scientist and physicians in the field of substance addiction now recognize that permanent neurocognitive changes take place in the brain in individuals who are addicted to alcohol or other substances, legal or otherwise.

Dr. Beathard was maintaining his sobriety, but his long-term abuse of alcohol had fundamentally changed him—and definitely not for the better. Now a spiteful and duplicitous individual, Bruce Beathard had an undeniable mean streak. After all, he was the man who was personally responsible for sinking the hepatitis B vaccine study that Brewster and Dr. Rabbi had toiled over for an entire year. What could account for Dr. Beathard's newfound malignant behavior?

The changes in the neural networks in the limbic system of the brain are likely irreversible for most people with substance addiction. These changes in the brain may develop slowly or quickly, depending on the potentially addictive substance in question. For example, there are many individuals who claim that they became hooked on methamphetamines the first time they ever tried this illicit stimulant! That's rather sobering to think about.

Can the same thing be said of individuals who are subjected to—or who are witnesses to—acts of brutality? Are there neurocognitive changes that might take place in the brain in such circumstances? Perhaps the neural networks in the temporal lobes can be permanently altered, which may account for the ability of some individuals to be able to perpetuate violent criminal behavior. Certainly, a child who is abused will have a dramatically increased risk of growing up to become an adult who is abusive. Is that simply a behavior that is learned—or is it an aberrant behavior that manifests because it is rooted in neurocognitive and neural network changes that may have occurred in the brain?

In the act of dogfighting, man's best friend is coerced into participating in a blood sport that is ultimately a fight to the death. The canines that are subjected to this lethal abuse are trained to behave in that fashion. Is this a learned behavior in dogs—or are their actions rooted in neurocognitive changes in the brain as a result of the physical and psychological abuse from their owners? Are human beings any different? After all, *Homo sapiens* may not be much more than bipedal versions of *Canis lupus*.

"I must say that you boys are certainly living the life of Riley in here," Willy said as he vigorously rummaged through the refrigerator in the designated student R&R zone. This isolated oasis, known simply as the Vinyl Lounge, was generally reserved for the medical students who held the rank of stud. "First time I've ever seen these digs. I can tell you right now—I could get used to this place pretty quick."

"Nice job, Brew," Fielder added. "Thanks for getting us in here."

"Well, having all the frozen burritos that one can eat anytime, day or night, is indeed a nice perk," Brewster admitted. "All that you and the wooly one have to do is to get promoted, and all of this luxury can also be yours someday. We even have a television in here!"

"Be that as it may, we stepped into a big, evil, steaming pile of shit on the burn unit last month," Mammon said as he pulled a cold Mr. Pibb soda out of the fridge. "Are we going to be able to scrape it off the bottom of our boots and get back in the saddle for our next rotation?"

"I hope so, but I just can't shake off what happened to us," Brewster admitted. "It's as if we were surrounded by a malevolent cloud of evil that was about to swallow us whole. It feels as if my very soul got, I don't know, *warped* somehow."

"I know," Willy said. "I felt it. It was all around us. In fact, it was actually palpable. Listen to me, Brew. You need to gather it all up, jam it into a big jar, and screw the lid down tight for now. It's time to move on."

"I plan to do just that," Brewster said. "I'm a simple man who tries my level best to travel in a straight line. Maybe if I keep my head down and get my nose back to the grindstone, I won't be influenced by external evil forces."

"Gentlemen, you need to broaden your worldview," Fielder said as he pulled his face away from the television screen that was blaring out the prophetic rants of the famed televangelist from Hope, Arkansas, named Rectal Roberts. "As I'm watching this holy-roller preacher on the boob tube jumping up and down and waving poisonous snakes over his head, I've come to the inescapable conclusion that the archaic Judeo-Christian perspective is no longer applicable in this modern, post-theistic epoch where we now find ourselves. It would appear to me that you boys have oversimplified views about love versus hate, good versus evil, and right versus wrong. Must it always boil down to a debate about nurture versus nature? Well, ladies, I believe in nature. Nothing more and nothing less. I don't think that evil is an entity *per se*. It is *not* an extrinsic force that can unduly influence us."

"What then?" Brewster asked.

"I'd like to believe these issues of right and wrong are essentially already integrated into the human condition," Fielder answered. "If that's the case, it makes *Homo sapiens* a much more complex species than what you'd readily admit."

"So, by that argument," Willy asked, "what happened to Irene Segulla was *natural?*"

"Sadly, the answer is a resounding *yes*," Fielder explained. "My belief is that the violent act of brutality that ultimately took the life of Irene Segulla was not caused by some extrinsic evil entity that stands outside the realm of human existence. Violent behavior, although it needs to be internally suppressed, is just a natural characteristic that can be easily found within the spectrum of recognized human behavior."

"What in hell are you saying?" Brewster asked.

"Simply speaking," Ben Fielder replied, "good and evil are *not* abstract concepts restricted to the realm of spirituality. They're yin and yang, buddy boy. It's what *we* are. Both good and evil behaviors are the basic noble attributes *and* the basic wretched flaws that are deeply and inexorably embedded within the fabric of the human condition. These are the essential and fundamental components of what it means to be a human being."

"Oh, for the love of penis!" Brewster protested.

"Straight up, Brew," Fielder asked, "within the context of your explicative response to my postulate, are you talking about my penis or yours?"

"Mine, of course! I can imagine years from now some idiot will come along and argue that evil is a concept fabricated out of whole cloth that's intended to only marginalize the complexities found within our fellow humans who may simply hold values, beliefs, and perspectives that are far different than our very own," Brewster suggested while he shook his head in disgust.

"Is it not?" Fielder smiled. "That argument, despite its contemptuous inflection of your own personal conservative sarcasm, has more than an element of truth to it, I tell you."

"Is that so?" Brewster scoffed. "If that's the case, I predict such a simplistic moron, crippled with denial about how the world *really* operates, will tenaciously cling to these perverse ideations beyond the juncture in time where he or she is slowly stabbed to death with long knives toted by *evil* Homo sapiens who worship a different god, or who otherwise embrace a misdirected allegiance toward different social or political constructs."

"Does that not constitute the root of all warfare? Bravo! Be that as it may," Fielder argued, "such a scenario fails to confirm what you gentlemen profess to believe. Somehow, I must convince you boys that that evil, in and of its self, is *not* a limited liability corporation, per se."

"You're right," Brewster said. "It's *way* beyond that. Evil is an extant, independent, and operational external entity."

"You're wrong, Brew," Fielder said. "There's nothing out there."

"Well, my pasty friend," Willy challenged with a raised brow as he glared at Ben Fielder, "you just got hoodwinked!"

"How so?" Fielder asked.

"Allow me to paraphrase the 19th century French poet and philosopher named Charles Baudelaire by planting a cautionary red flag at the crossroads for all to see," Willy said.

"Would this intersection of byways be the same place where the famous blues singer, Robert Johnson, allegedly sold his immortal soul to the very Devil to acquire an extraordinary, yet short-lived musical talent, circa 1936?" Fielder asked in a rather futile attempt to best J.D. Brewster in the ability to spout irrelevant trivia.

"Geographically speaking," Willy replied, "the answer would be no. However, within the realm of spirituality, the answer would be a resounding yes. After all, you can *always* find the Devil at the crossroads."

"I've often confronted the crossroads in life with a great deal of trepidation," Ben Fielder sheepishly admitted.

"Even more so than your irrational fears of pesky moths or Willy's apprehension of what might be lurking in the darkness?" Brewster asked.

"Naturally, I'm speaking in metaphorical terms about the crossroads that all of us may unexpectedly encounter on our journey through this mysterious plane of existence," Ben answered as he quickly recovered from Brewster's rebuke. "Nonetheless, that particular Faustian tale of woe regarding the Devil suddenly appearing from the depths of hell in order to purchase a man's immortal soul for a temporally restricted earthly commodity is little more than an urban myth, ladies."

"*Au contraire, mon ami,*" Willy said. "Ain't no myth, string bean."

"Now that you've got my undivided attention," Fielder replied, "spell it out for me. I don't know jack diddly about the French poet named Baudelaire, or anything that he had written in the remote past about the Devil in a blue dress and what he may have or may not have said to Miss Molly, good golly!"

"Pay attention. Here's the pitch," Willy said. "You've got blinders on if you think for one minute that the Devil ain't out there."

"Is that it?" Fielder asked as he stifled a yawn. "Are you trying to lay down some ebonic urban voodoo on me, big man?"

"The exact quotation is found in the famous treatise known as, 'The Generous Gambler.' As I recall, Baudelaire said, 'My dear brethren, never forget, when you hear the progress of wisdom vaunted, that the cleverest ruse of the Devil is to persuade you he does *not* exist!' It was published in Paris around the year 1864," Brewster added.

"Thanks, Brew!" Willy said. "You're full of such a high titer of esoteric bullshit that I should have realized you would've remembered the exact quotation. On more than one occasion, you've proven to me to be one smart sumbitch."

"Well, at least I'm a sumbitch," Brewster concurred. "The jury is still out as to whether I'm smart or not."

"Now you boys got me shakin' in my skivvies!" Fielder gasped as he feigned despair.

"Cut the crap!" Willy exclaimed. "I'm serious, Ben. I assure you; demons are close enough to reach out and touch any one of us as we speak."

"You need to reel in that crazy shit right about now and put a lid on it!" Fielder cautioned. "Otherwise, Dr. Corka Sorass from the Psychiatry Department is going to come by here with a big net and haul you off to the looney bin."

"Open your eyes, Ben!" Willy demanded as he wagged his index finger in front of his colleague. "I've had a face to face with the Devil already. I'd be the first to admit that his motives may be somewhat duplicitous. Nonetheless, he's a rather handsome looking fellow, if I may say so myself."

"If that's the case," Brewster asked, "what does he look like?"

"He looks like, well–like me," Willy replied. "I also found him to be a rather persuasive son of a gun if the truth be told. He was in the jungles of the 'Nam. He was on the parking lot where Irene Segulla was beaten to death. He was in the scrub tank room on the burn unit, whispering ever so sweetly into the receptive auditory canals of the evil Dr. Blaze Street."

"Believe what you want, but I personally reject these anthropomorphic personifications of what you claim evil may or may not be. I just happen to be intellectually enlightened—that's all," Fielder said. "Welcome to the twentieth century, gentlemen."

"I'm not certain, Ben, but perhaps you're right. Nonetheless, I just don't think you've got a handle on the full scope of the matter," Brewster said. "Maybe, just maybe, evil behavior is a consequence from an admixture of forces derived from our own internal *intrinsic* nature in conjunction with the adverse effects from *extrinsic* exogenous forces. All I know is that I'm not happy. Something's wrong I tell you, but I just can't put my finger on it. I feel as if I'm one step away from being ambushed. Is that weird, or what? I find myself looking over my shoulder from time to time."

"No," Willy answered. "It's not weird. I've got the same premonitions. It's as if I'm about to get a lead pipe poned upside the head."

Perhaps the sense of foreboding evil Brewster and Mammon felt was a consequence to recent *permanent* psychological and neurocognitive changes. Nonetheless, Brewster couldn't help but wonder if his original supposition was right all along; maybe God just backed the wrong primate.

An insidious transformation had already occurred in Brewster and his two colleagues. The three men had been adversely transformed by their experiences on their first clerkship rotation on the burn unit. They were now completely receptive to evil thoughts and completely capable of violent deeds. They just didn't realize it yet…

Out of inventory at the chop shop, Smeg Nog was determined to try to eventually strike out on his own. After all, why did he need somebody like Big Nig to constantly berate him? Why did he need to strike a pipe upside somebody's head just to steal a car? Big Nig had given specific instructions that his partner in crime should lay low for a while, and they would eventually make another raid upon the Texas Medical Center. Why should Smeg wait? After all, he had a pistol, and that fact alone would make it easier to strong-arm a victim if necessary.

Perhaps, if he was clever, he could steal a car right from under somebody's nose without employing any violence at all. Although he certainly enjoyed giving a white person the gift of a vicious beat down, pleasure should be pleasure and business should be business. He had his eye on the Fuel Stop in North University Place. The sleepy establishment was adjacent to the Texas Medical Center and was a perfect mark. Foolish patrons would often leave their car keys in the ignition when they stepped away from their vehicles to pay the attendant after gassing up.

Cars that were left off at the service station for repair work would invariably have the keys left on the dashboard. If he timed it right, it could be easy pickings. As an added bonus, the Fuel Stop had not been updated with the fancy security cameras that were starting to become more commonplace at commercial establishments throughout the greater Houston area.

The first Saturday in August was the only day off for Brewster and his two colleagues since early July. On the following Monday, they would be starting their second month on the surgery service. They would be assigned to a rotation on the urology unit, which of course was a surgical subspecialty. For now, there were places to go, people to do, and things to see. Brewster was hoping to sleep in, but unfortunately, he had been suffering from insomnia for several weeks.

When the telephone rang in his shabby apartment, he was surprised to hear Wooly Mammoth on the line.

"Hey, Brew, my dad's '59 Caddy must be having a midlife crisis. Dad says when he hits the brakes, the pedal goes almost all the way down to the floorboard, and it's becoming quite hard for the car to come to a full stop. I'm at my dad's house right now. Missy

Brownwood says you know a lot about cars, so I thought I'd give you a call for some advice."

"Missy Brownwood talks too much," Brewster replied. "I know just enough about cars to screw things up for you. If I help you work on it, you'll have to spend twice as much on the old thing to get it done right by a real mechanic by the time I'm finished with it. Obviously, you'll need a brake job. The vacuum-assist unit on the brakes might be going out, but it's hard to say over the phone what the exact problem might be."

"What else you know about brakes?"

"Most sedans up to the sixties had drum brakes all around," Brewster explained. "I suspect a full brake job, which would include turning the drums and throwing a new pair of shoes on all four corners, would not cost your dad too much. Are you going to need a lift to the service station?"

"No," Willy said. "That's okay. Ben Fielder is with me. He lives in a dungeon that's been overrun by bloodthirsty moths. Can you believe that? He's afraid of moths. I guess that's okay since I'm afraid of the dark."

"Stay frosty, big man," Brewster said. "After all, I happen to be afraid of, well—*you!*"

"As well you should be," Willy said. "Anyhow, he wants to try to find a new place to live today. I'm going to take the Caddy over to a mechanic whom I've heard good things about. His name is Arby Fuller Sr."

"Stop right there!" Brewster exclaimed. "I'm now in the twilight zone. I happen to be friends with that dude's son."

"Well, the old man is the proprietor of the Fuel Stop in North University Place," Willy said. "It's a small world indeed. Sometimes, it seems that everything in the universe is connected somehow. Be cool, buddy boy. I'll see you Monday for our next rotation."

Brewster didn't have time to ponder any mysterious cosmic confluence of the stars. He had promised Antonia that he would pay a visit to Uncle John. Brewster had been purposefully avoiding this cantankerous and erratic elderly relative for quite some time. J. D. asked for backup, and Bill agreed to go along for what would be a rather unpleasant obligatory family visit.

Uncle John lived in a run-down mid-1930s bungalow near Buffalo Speedway, south of the Texas Medical Center. Of all the homes on the block, Uncle John had the only house with an unkempt lawn, tall grass, and overgrown, unruly shrubs. A menagerie of wind chimes hanging above the front porch remained motionless in the hot and humid subtropical climate. A passerby would have likely thought that the domicile had been overrun by lazy, stoner hippies on welfare.

The doorbell was rendered inert long ago as the ringer button was heavily encrusted with a thick coat of impenetrable latex house paint. Bill knocked upon the front door to see if he could arouse Uncle John from his usual benzodiazepine-induced stupor.

It was a conscious act not to call Uncle John before the brothers showed up for their surprise visit. The boys intended to keep their conversations with the old man short and sweet. Well— at least short. After all, there was no sense in wasting valuable chitchat over the phone when such superficial verbiage could be exchanged in a face-to-face manner. Doing so would ensure that their obligation to visit Uncle John would be fulfilled for at least another six months. A telephone call placed to Uncle John prior to their arrival would have only ensured that the brothers would have most likely run out of things to say to the cranky old codger within just a few seconds after Uncle John opened the front door.

When the front door finally slipped open, J. D. was surprised to see a pretty young black woman with a perfect broad smile. She was the unofficial cousin of the Brewster boys. The moniker that had been lovingly bestowed upon her twelve years earlier was "Feral Cheryl," and it was a nickname that she would proudly carry for the rest of her life.

"Well, look what the cat dragged in! It's the Brewster brothers. I thought you boys had fallen off the face of the earth. I'm so mad at you fellows that I could just spit nails. Now, look here; Uncle John is, well, *your* uncle, despite the fact that you boys *never* come by to see him. Ever. What's the matter with you? If I didn't know any better, I'd think that y'all were trying to avoid him altogether for one reason or another!"

"Ease up, Feral," Bill said. "That's not the case. J. D. and I have been, well—busy."

"Can't prove it by me," Cheryl said. "Although John's the closest thing that I have to a living relative, he ain't my blood kin. He's your kin. You need to start treating him as such." She gave Bill a brief hug and a quick peck on the cheek. "Welcome, Cuz!" She threw her arms around J. D.'s neck and kissed him passionately. She bit his lower lip hard enough to draw a drop of blood.

She had openly pined for him since her senior year in high school. Cheryl exhaled a deep sigh as J. D. gently pulled away from her firm embrace. As Bill looked away with mild embarrassment, J. D. said, "It's good to see you too, Cheryl. Let's go find Uncle John."

"How are things on the island?" Bill asked.

Cheryl firmly clutched J. D.'s hand and led the two men inside. "Past tense now. At first, I loved Galveston, but I don't know what happened. I started to feel claustrophobic. Maybe it's because I never learned how to swim, and I know at some deep subconscious level that I'm surrounded by water. I resigned my post."

"Whoa," J. D. said. "You did what?!"

"I have a new gig lined up," Cheryl explained. "You'll be happy to know that I'll be starting on the med-surg unit at the Gulf Coast University Hospital once I complete my orientation training. What do you think about that, J. D.? From now on, I'll be working near you. I'm so excited I could just pinch myself. I'm slated to start at the beginning of September, so I'll have a few weeks off. I need you both to fill me in on what's been going on in your lives."

J. D. was suspicious about Cheryl's motives to seek employment at the same place he was going to medical school, and he had to make certain the affection they shared for each other didn't turn into a full-blown romance. Above and beyond the ethnic differences, which J. D. would be ashamed to truthfully admit was indeed a major stumbling block, he felt Cheryl was, well, *family*.

Uncle John was sitting at the kitchen table, and it appeared that he had dressed up for the occasion. Wearing a pair of flip-flops, the soles of which were no thicker than a dime, John's only other apparel was an orca-print, threadbare pair of boxer shorts. Uncle John looked up to Bill and said, "Hello, William." He scratched his beard momentarily and then turned toward the younger brother and repeated the same greeting. "Hello, William." J. D. knew there was no point in trying to correct Uncle John. After all, John had referred to J. D. as "William" his entire life.

Sitting in front of Uncle John was a bowl of breakfast cereal. Within arm's length was a plate of sliced peaches that Cheryl had prepared for her foster parent. John looked at the peaches and extended his index finger. "Fruit! Fruit!"

J. D. picked up the plate and derisively threw them on top of Uncle John's corn flakes, one slice at a time. Every time he added a peach slice to the breakfast cereal, the milk would splash over the rim of the bowl and upon the table.

Uncle John mindlessly inhaled his breakfast and intermittently issued editorial comments about his gustatory experience with the enthusiastic proclamation of an occasional eardrum-shattering belch.

While the two brothers and Cheryl filled each other in on what had been going on in their lives for the past two years, Uncle John suddenly became verbally aggressive. "I don't know what in hell y'all are talking about, but if this little colored girl over here is planning on coming back to Houston, I don't want her moving into the upstairs garage apartment. Understand?"

"What have I done to upset you, John?" Cheryl pleaded, obviously hurt by the imperial edict that the old codger had just ordered.

"I'm not going to get dressed up like this every time you decide to come down for a visit, that's all," John explained.

"No, siree! There's no sense in you getting all gussied up like this ever again, Uncle John," Bill said. "We all can see that it's such a chore for you to wear *any* type of clothing whatsoever!"

Uncle John answered Bill's critique with a window rattling fart.

"This is exactly why Bill and I are going to start stretching out the intervals of these unpleasant obligatory family visitations that cultural norms dictate we must bestow upon you, irrespective of how meaningless and spiritually devoid that any of these pathetic and mind-numbing encounters truly are for all of us!" J. D. exclaimed.

"If that's the case," Uncle John asked, "why are you still here?"

"Good question," Bill said. "My, my, my, how the time flies! We've been here all of five minutes, and it's already time for us to go. Cop a whiz if you need to before we split, J. D., and then let's get the hell out of here."

"That's a good idea, William," John said as he turned to address J. D. "Listen, William, I want to rent out the furnished upstairs garage apartment to one of your rich medical student friends. I know that I'm asking a lot for it, but my home here is close to the medical center, and that should be worth something. I want three hundred a month. I know you'll be able to help me out with this humble request, William. The little colored girl over here tells me that you're a good boy, although to be honest, I've never really liked you very much."

The one-bedroom, one-bath apartment Uncle John spoke of was directly above the freestanding two-car garage, and it was immediately adjacent to the utility alley. It was fully furnished, and it had a complete kitchen. Since the unit was built in the 1930s, it had no insulation to speak of, but a single window-mounted air conditioner helped keep the small unit cool and comfortable.

Uncle John had always rented the place to medical students since he felt they were responsible and more likely to mind their own business. For unclear reasons, Uncle John had a very hard time keeping the unit occupied with happy tenants. He rarely had any renters for more than a few months. Most would simply pack up and disappear in the middle of the night, usually without leaving any legitimate forwarding address.

"It's strange how everything in the universe is connected somehow," J. D. said. "I have a friend who's looking for an apartment as we speak, and he wants to find a place that's near the medical center. I'll get in touch with him and see if he might be interested in your apartment. In the meantime, Cheryl, why don't you come along with Bill and me? Let's see if we can find you a nice apartment to rent."

Cheryl laughed. "I have a better idea, J. D. Why don't I just move in with you at your one-bedroom apartment in Bellaire? That way, we can just commute together. We could take care of each other. It will be cozy, but I am sure we can figure out a way to make it all work."

Bill said, "Oh my! That sounds like a capital idea."

J. D. could only purse his lips and issue a hostile glare toward Brother Bill.

When Willy Mammon dropped off his father's Cadillac, Arby Fuller Sr. told him to leave the keys on the top of the dashboard. An assistant would then move the vehicle to the locked area behind the service station. If no major organ transplant procedures were required on the vehicle, the old car would be ready by Monday or Tuesday.

As Willy walked to the corner to wait for Ben Fielder, something caught his eye. A complete stranger jumped into the Cadillac and fired up the engine! Arby and his assistant ran out of the garage to try to stop the thief, but by then, they were way too late.

Before the car thief powered away from the service station, Willy grabbed the door handle and tried to enter the car before the man who called himself Nog had escaped. Wooly Mammoth was dragged for several yards before he was thrown to the pavement. He extended his left arm to try to protect his body from the impact, but upon rolling to a stop, the medical student immediately recognized that he had fractured his wrist. He was in a lot of pain when he pulled himself up from the pavement.

Ben Fielder had just arrived, and he had witnessed the whole ordeal. He got out of his car to see if his friend was okay, but Mammon yelled out a specific order: "Follow that bastard, Ben! I'll call the cops."

Within seconds, Ben Fielder's pickup was in hot pursuit of the stolen Cadillac as it zipped through North University Place.

When Willy Mammon entered the service station, he was feeling lightheaded and nauseous. Nonetheless, he had to notify the authorities about the crime. As Willy collapsed in the corner of the office, he learned that the mechanic's assistant had already called the police.

After four blocks, Nog approached a busy intersection. Since the Cadillac had no functional brakes to speak of by that juncture, hitting the brake pedal had absolutely no effect on slowing down the gargantuan land yacht. Nog was not wearing a seatbelt when the Cadillac crashed into a utility pole, causing the car thief's forehead to slam into the upper rim of the steering wheel.

Ben Fielder pulled up to the scene of the one-car accident, and he immediately suspended any previous allegiance that he might have made to the philosophical principles espoused by Hippocrates. After Fielder reached inside the Cadillac and turned off the ignition, he discovered that the front doors of the vehicle were jammed from the impact. At that point, the only way to extract the driver was to pull him out through the open window. Fielder made absolutely no effort to try to spare the injured man from a hard impact upon the ground when the student extracted the would-be thief from the wreckage. Once the thief's center of gravity passed over window-sill, Fielder allowed the Newtonian laws of physics do the rest of the work, and the injured and disoriented criminal immediately crumpled upon the pavement.

Cars continued to plow through the intersection, and people seemed to pay little attention as Ben Fielder sat squarely upon the dazed man's chest and waited for the ambulance and the police.

Nog said, "Hey, man, get off me. I can't breathe."

Fielder had already fully adopted the sadistic Sergeant Carter routine that he learned from Dr. Street on the burn unit during the previous clinical rotation. "I can't hear you!"

"I can't breathe."

"I can't hear you!"

When the police arrived, one of the officers took one look at Smeg Nog and said, "Well, well, well, we haven't caught one of *these* in a while. Let's take you back to the police station and have some fun. I don't think this old boy is going to need an ambulance. There's no question that we're going to be able to take care of this bad boy all by ourselves." He turned to his colleague and said, "Rayford, break out the Miranda card and read this joker his rights."

If there is a cosmic retribution called Karma, Smeg Nog was about to dine on a hot, steaming bowl of contrition for the long list of sins he had committed over the past twelve years. Assuredly, the forthcoming penance would be a very bitter pill for him to swallow.

At the emergency room, Willy Mammon patiently waited for the orthopedic surgery resident to come down and put the broken forearm in a cast. Ben Fielder soon discovered that J. D. Brewster had returned to his apartment in Bellaire. Once informed over the phone as to what had transpired, J. D. promised to go directly to the emergency room to pay the big man a visit.

Upon Brewster's arrival, it was already late in the afternoon. Mammon had been waiting for nearly four hours by the time the orthopod had shown up to set and cast the fractured extremity. Fortunately, an ice bag helped keep the swelling manageable. The effete non-narcotic pain medication, zomepirac, was only marginally efficacious in controlling Willy's discomfort.

The orthopedic resident, Dr. Bay, was from California. "Wow, that's some nasty break you have there, Willy. Don't you worry none. I am going to patch you up. Orthopedic surgery is such a cool sub-specialty. It's way cool, man. Dig this, gnarly dude. The bone can clone! I just have to line up everything, and like, whoa— the rest of it will be taken care of by Mother Nature. How rad is that?"

Without single word, Ben Fielder grabbed an empty urine specimen cup from the supply cart and tapped J. D. Brewster on the shoulder with it.

Brewster nodded, took the cup, and said, "Dr. Bay, do you mind peeing into this cup? I think we should check your urine for cannabinoid metabolites."

As Dr. Bay finished setting the cast, he replied, "Don't be a dumbass. I could be chilling out real mellow like on the island if it wasn't for you guys."

The emergency room nurse came by to get Willy to sign off on his discharge papers.

Willy said, "I'm just exhausted. I need to rest here for just a little bit before I go home. The bag monster has come by to pay me a visit, and I need to study the back of my eyelids for just a little while."

The nurse acquiesced to his request, but if the ER got busy and the staff needed that particular patient stall for a new, incoming emergency room visitor, she would have to give Willy and his friends the boot. After all, Saturday was always a bad day for anybody to be working in the emergency room. Also, Saturday was always a bad day for anybody in need of medical care to be treated in the emergency room. Once the sun went down, the card-carrying members of the "Saturday Night Knife and Gun Club," amongst other urban refuse, would start showing up with their rude, unreasonable, and incessant demands to have the bright red blood that was gushing from their bullet holes to get promptly plugged and also to have their gaping and festering knife wounds to get immediately cleaned and sutured. After all, if the frightful members of the Saturday Night Knife and Gun Club were nothing else, they were certainly rather impatient patients for unclear reasons.

While the big man took a nap, Brewster said, "Ben, I found an upstairs, furnished, one-bedroom and one-bath garage apartment for you to rent. It's only two or three miles south of the Texas Medical Center. My uncle owns the place, but as a matter of honest and full disclosure to you, he's asking to get paid what I think is far more than a pretty penny."

"Well," Fielder asked, "how much is he looking for?"

"Three hundred per month. That's a lot of money for what you'd get, but at least the place is furnished. It has a complete kitchen and a stacked washer and drier. There aren't any moths— to the best of my knowledge—and it is only a stone's throw from the medical center. I need to warn you, however, that my uncle is a bit, well—eccentric."

"I'll take it," Fielder said. "Your uncle simply can't be any weirder than you are."

——∘∘∘}◈{∘∘∘——

The two policemen who had arrested the car thief came by the emergency room to pay a visit to Willy Mammon. Relieved to find out that the big man had only sustained a fractured arm, they wanted to have a little informal chat with him about the options that were available concerning the dispensation of justice to the man they held in police custody.

One of the officers said, "This man who tried to steal your car has never been previously arrested, much less convicted of any prior crime. We were hoping to connect him to a series of violent carjacks that have occurred inside the loop for many years. However, what he did to you does not seem to fit the pattern of what we'd seen before. As best we can tell, this is the first time this fellow has ever tried to commit a crime like this. Now, this is how it will all play out. If you decide to have us proceed with criminal charges, the judge who'll likely hear this criminal's case is a well-known liberal. Rayford once heard the judge proclaim that he was ashamed of his own white race."

"What the hell is wrong with being a white man?" Brewster injected. "I'm just as proud about being white as Willy is about being black. It's all good!"

"The judge believes in something he calls 'institutional racism' and 'white privilege'. He espouses that if criminals are from an ethnic minority, *they* are the actual victims and therefore can't be held accountable for any of the evil crimes that they perpetrate. It's utter bullshit. I think he pulled these idiotic Marxist ideas right out of his own ass," one of the officers replied. "I can tell you right now that this low-life car thief will walk away with nothing more than a slap on the wrist."

"Is that so?" Willy asked.

"Absolutely," the officer replied. "Since this perpetrator has never been arrested or convicted of anything in the past, I can guarantee you that the judge will make certain that this guy will fly right out of jail in the blink of an eye without bail. He'll be as free as a bird! Regarding financial compensation for the injuries you've received and for the damage that your father's Caddy has sustained, you'll have to sue this bastard in civil court. Unfortunately, the Cadillac is totaled—and you'll never get a dime out of that asshole."

"You said you wanted to talk to me about options," Willy recalled. "Other than criminal charges, what other options are on the table? The only thing I care about right now is making sure this guy gets punished for what he did to my dad's car."

The two officers looked at each other for a minute.

One of the policemen finally smiled and said, "Well, we would like to propose something that could be mutually beneficial to you as a victim and to us as peace officers. We could give you an opportunity to make sure that justice will be served, and it will save us a ton of paperwork in the process. We'd like to know if you'd enjoy an opportunity to have a private *encounter* with this suspect that we have down at the jail."

"Similar to what would happen when a man might *encounter* a sewer roach crawling along a kitchen tabletop?" Willy asked. "Is that the kind of opportunity you might be referring to?"

"You're a medical student," one of the police officers said. "You're a smart man. You can figure it out. To be frank, you'd be allowed to have a fifteen-minute personal meeting with him, as long as you make a promise right here and right now that you won't kill this guy outright. We'll have him in handcuffs while you conduct your *interview*. If this sounds like a good idea to you, let me know if you need any special supplies or equipment from us to help facilitate a satisfying personal interlude. We want to make certain that your experience will be as enjoyable for you to conduct as it will be for us to watch. After all, we're your friendly neighborhood police department, and we're simply here to serve and protect."

The three musketeers gave out a loud cheer that would have made a Texas Aggie proud. Brewster and Fielder started to shout out their own recommended implements of torture, including a lead pipe, vice grips, brass knuckles, and box cutters.

"Silence, knaves! I've got this!" Willy Mammon pulled a sheet of paper from the copy machine and wrote down several items before handing the list to the officers.

The policemen laughed and nodded as they looked at the sundry list of goods and equipment that Mammon had requested to be on hand at the police station before the interview occurred.

"I think I can see where this is going," one of the police officers said. "You, sir, are a bona fide genius! Come on down to the station, and we'll have everything set up for you."

As the three students drove down to the police station, Willy Mammon was not about to reveal what he had written down on the list. He wanted to keep his act of planned retribution an unpleasant surprise.

When Willy was ushered into the interrogation area, Smeg Nog was handcuffed to the leg of a large table that had been bolted to the concrete floor. He had a piece of duct tape over his mouth. Inside the interrogation room were the items Willy had requested: a six-foot wooden stepladder, two fifty-pound weights, and two pieces of sturdy hemp rope. Brewster, Fielder, and a handful of police officers watched what was about to unfold from the other side of a two-way mirror.

Before Mammon was allowed to conduct his interview, a police detective walked into the interrogation room. He casually tossed a black backpack on the table, unzipped it, and pulled out a peanut butter and jelly sandwich wrapped in cellophane and a World War II Walther P38, semi-automatic, nine-millimeter pistol in a plastic evidence bag. "Mr. Mammon, do these items belong to you? We found them on the front seat of your father's Cadillac."

"I've never seen that stuff before. Neither my father or I have ever owned a handgun, and peanut butter makes me flatulent!"

"Yes, I think we all know who owns this stuff," the detective said with a big grin. "Fortunately, the gun has this perp's fingerprints on it, and we'll have no trouble pinning ownership of this weapon on Mr. Darrell Hewrett. Hello, Darrell. Is this your gun?"

Smeg Nog cast his eyes toward the stepladder and the other implements that were soon to be utilized in a medieval torture session, but he didn't respond to the detective's questions. After all, he had a heavy piece of duct tape applied firmly over his mouth.

"Speak up!" the detective said. "This gun has never been registered. We don't have a ballistics laboratory here, but I think we should send this piece off to see if it has been used in any unsolved crimes over the past two decades." The detective banged on the glass window. "Hey, Rayford, get this piece shipped over to the HPD detectives, Culp and Watt. Ask them to run ballistics and see if it turns up anything that might be gathering dust in the cold case files."

The detective turned back toward Smeg Nog, got within an inch of his ear, and whispered an overt threat. "Tell me, Hewrett, does it make you sweat just a little bit to know that we are going to send this gun off for a ballistic analysis? If this weapon was used in a crime to shoot somebody, we will find out about it. It will take some time, but rest assured, we'll know someday. Perhaps in the future, I'll have to hunt your ass down. I'll enjoy putting a cap in you when that happens, so don't even think about throwing up a white flag. Ain't gonna save you. Clear? The wheels of justice may grind slowly, but the wheels grind very fine indeed."

As the pistol had been previously used to kill two people in a botched cigar shop heist on South Main St. back in '68, the life of Nog had just been stamped with a pending expiration date.

The detective banged on the window and shouted, "Let the interview begin!

Twenty-dollar bills started to pile up in the observation post. Bets were going down as to what type of injury the Wooly Mammoth would inflict upon the shackled prisoner.

Without a word, the wooly one stretched out the right leg of Smeg Nog and planted the heel of the car thief's right foot on a chair. Willy took the fifty-pound weights, and using the short length of hemp rope, he tied each of the heavy weights in a proximal and distal location on either side of the criminal's knee.

When Smeg Nog's leg was held out straight and secure at a ninety-degree angle from his torso, it had been rendered completely immobile.

"Is it safe for me to assume that you've already signed a DNR code status authorization form just in case something goes awry during this technically difficult invasive medical procedure that I'm just about to perform on your nasty black ass?" Mammon asked.

The bound and gagged criminal gave Willy the middle finger, and that was all the big man needed to see before he pressed on with his astounding acrobatic performance.

Willy Mammon opened the stepladder, climbed up to the very top of the platform, and then executed a perfect cannon ball dive directly upon the top of Smeg Nog's right knee.

Although Smeg Nog's heel remained squarely propped upon the chair seat, the posterior fossa of his knee buckled, and it was soon firmly planted upon the floor. When the ligaments and cartilage of Smeg Nog's knee were completely sheared away, the ensuing disintegrating flesh produced a sharp and audible explosion. It was as if a batter had just connected with a fat changeup that the pitcher left hanging over the middle of the plate, and the ensuing swing jacked the baseball over the center field wall at the Astrodome!

Inside the observation post, the spectators profusely vocalized a discordant admixture of empathetic moans of anguish amidst bloodthirsty war cries. Money exchanged hands as the squad members looked upon the grisly scene in awe. The "peace officers" had all witnessed "private interviews" conducted between victims and their alleged assailants in the past, but none of the policemen who were present on that fateful day had ever seen such a display of raw and shocking brutality!

Nog blacked out, and he was completely unresponsive to verbal or tactile stimuli for several minutes. It took an ampule of ammonia broken underneath his nostrils to arouse him to a semiconscious state. It would be months before he would be able to bear weight on his right leg. The career criminal would never be able to flex his leg at the knee again, and he would need to wear a leg brace for the rest of what would turn out to be a very short and wretched life.

If the Mammoth had any premonition about pending interactions with this violent and evil individual, the big man would have murdered Smeg Nog on the spot. In fact, Willy should have done it regardless of any rational plea for restraint from the police officers who witnessed the act of merciless vengeance that Willy had just committed. Alas, it was an oversight that the big man would soon pay dearly for in the not-too-distant future.

After Mammon shattered Smeg Nog's leg, the big man lightly patted the semiconscious man on his cheek and whispered, "It's way cool, man. Dig this, gnarly dude. The bone can clone!"

# 6

## PICK A PACK OF PICKLED PECKERS

J. D. Brewster and Stella Link went out for a date to an Italian restaurant before the next clerkship was scheduled to start. Stella had been concerned that J. D. seemed distant and preoccupied. She was already starting to fall in love with the young medical student, even though he was ten years her junior. She was a woman who, up until that time, had always been bold and assertive. There was something fresh and different about this relationship. J. D. and Stella were starting to forge a bond that was more than a simple physical attraction. *That's how true love is supposed to work, right?* She was determined to make this relationship a permanent one—come hell or high water—but she was fearful that she had done or said something that upset her new boyfriend.

"Are you okay, J. D.?" Stella asked. "You're very quiet tonight."

"I don't know, sweetie. I'm in a blue funk, and I can't quite put my finger on what's going on in my life. I can't believe that it's already been six weeks since your aunt died. I've been thinking about that a lot lately. I hope the bastards who did that to her get caught. I have this dream that I'd be granted a fifteen-minute private interview with each of them. I know that it wouldn't bring Irene back, but at least it would certainly make me feel better."

"I think I understand," Stella replied. "I was just afraid that you were mad at me for some reason."

"No," Brewster said. "I'm jammed tight into the clinical clerkship rotations, and frankly, I'm terrified. I don't know up from down or right from left anymore. Through no fault of my own, both of my hepatitis research projects have been pulled out from under me. I'm angry, and I don't even know who to blame."

In restaurants, mistakes occasionally happen when food is *prepared*, and some patrons receive dishes they did not order. Mistakes also occasionally happen when food is *served*, and patrons at the same table might be presented with an entrée that was intended for an adjacent guest. Usually when these minor mishaps occur, it never turns out to be a big screaming deal. For the most part, the people at the table cheerfully pass their plates about until all the guests have the correct meal that had been originally ordered. The above scenario is simply part and parcel of what may occur during the adventures of restaurant dining.

The young waitress made a mistake when she served the medical student and his girlfriend their entrées. Brewster had ordered pasta alfredo, and Stella had requested pasta marinara, but the couple were presented with each other's intended meal. Instead of taking it in stride and simply exchanging the dinner plates across the table, J. D. Brewster unexpectedly blew a gasket.

Before the waitress had left the table side, Brewster grabbed the young woman by her wrist and pulled her toward him. "I would surmise that this is merely a summer job for you, and it's clearly a temporary occupation that you don't give a shit about. I suspect that you're a college student trying to make a few extra bucks before the fall semester starts in the next three weeks or so. I don't know what you're studying in school, but I can tell by this brief interlude that we've shared together this evening that your life will likely be squandered in a tribulation of meaningless, poorly compensated, and spiritually vacuous endeavors. In a best-case future scenario, your marginal intellect will eventually condemn you for the heinous mistake that you've just made tonight. As a punitive measure, I hope and pray that you'll be banished to some backwater hellhole where you'll live out your life as nothing more than an annoying, space-occupying lesion."

"I'm terribly sorry," the waitress said. "Let me make this right!"

"So, you plan to make this right, do you?" Brewster asked. "You're clearly destined to toil in a dead-end career as a useless mid-level functionary. Now, I've been served the wrong entrée, madam. Just how do you intend to make this right?"

The stunned young woman began to shake as she quickly flipped the entrées in order for Brewster to get his precious pasta alfredo, and then she fled back to the kitchen in tears.

Stella Link stared at J. D. Brewster with mouth agape. "What the hell is the matter with you? You're a pig."

"I am indeed. I won't deny it."

"Go back there right now and apologize to that young woman. Did you think that was funny? She didn't deserve to hear what just spewed out of your filthy mouth. How dare you speak to another fellow human being in such a fashion? Do it now, damn it!"

Brewster refused to budge or even look at Stella at that point.

Stella said, "Give me your wallet. If you don't do it this instant, I'll never speak to you again. Am I clear?"

Brewster pulled out his wallet and slammed it down on the table. He had forty-three dollars in his wallet, and Stella took it all and stormed off into the kitchen to find the traumatized waitress. After giving the young woman a big tip and a hug, Stella stomped out of the restaurant and hailed a cab. Stella had done nothing to make Brewster behave in such a dark and brutal manner. Something else must have happened that was fundamentally changing him as a person, but she was not quite ready to give up on him at that point.

The manager walked up to Brewster's table and said, "We try very hard to run a fine establishment here, and all our employees do their best to keep our patrons happy. Therefore, I will not tolerate the kind of abuse that reportedly just came out of your mouth. Leave now and never come back."

Brewster slithered out the front door like the venomous snake he was transforming into. Something was definitely wrong with him, and it had to be sorted out. The first order of business for the troubled medical student would be to try to make amends with Stella Link.

Without any urological procedures scheduled for Monday morning, Brewster and his two colleagues were given instructions to appear at the outpatient urology clinic at nine o'clock. They were met by the senior urology resident, Dr. I. P. Stream. Although only in his late twenties, Dr. Stream could easily pass for somebody in his forties. The heavy baggage of chronic sleep deprivation had taken a toll upon his general appearance, and Dr. Stream looked to be an older and dispirited version of the late Brian Jones who was the original founder of the Rolling Stones.

"Gentlemen," Dr. Stream said, "it's time for us to address the issue of medical student hierarchy at the Gulf Coast. I know that you've just come from the burn unit, and Dr. Street likely didn't talk to you about the rules and regulations concerning the deeply entrenched caste system found here at this institution. Well, here's the setup; you're all still mushrooms. According to the matters of rank, you can't be a candidate for a promotion to scut puppy status until you've completed at least three clerkship rotations. Once you've been assigned the rank of scut puppy, you'll need to get an additional three clerkship rotations under your belt to be considered for a promotion to stud status. There are quite a few students who've graduated from this medical school who *never* made it to the rank of stud by the time that they graduated. Frankly, that's pathetic. In my humble opinion, if you're not able to be promoted to the rank of stud by your fourth year of medical school, you're probably worthless."

"Just a moment," J. D. Brewster interrupted. "I'm already a designated stud!"

"How's that possible?" Stream asked.

"I was never a mushroom," Brewster explained. "I started out as a brainiac. During my one year of scientific research, which I just completed, I was able to get credit for two clinical clerkship rotations. Technically, I already have credit for three rotations since I just finished my month on the burn unit. I was given a field promotion before then by the former gastroenterology fellow, Dr. Blomeo Colima."

"I thought you looked familiar," Dr. Stream said. "You were the front man for DNR! I saw you guys perform your very last gig on the Fourth of July. What a very cool time. I got laid that night. I'll bet everybody in your band scored some major-league rookie nookie on that holiday, am I correct? Tell me; did you get tag-teamed by a couple of fat, sweaty, old chicks in a deadly double-header?"

Brewster shrugged and said, "A gentleman doesn't kiss and tell."

"Damnation, Brewster! What's it like to be the new love monkey at the Gulf Coast College of Medicine?"

"I couldn't possibly find the words in the English language to begin to describe to you what that's like," Brewster honestly replied with a smile.

"No wonder Colima gave you the designation of stud," Dr. Stream said. "Maybe I can hang out with you sometime if you promise to toss a few table scraps my way!"

At the Gulf Coast College of Medicine, image was everything.

"I have a steady girlfriend now," Brewster replied. "Otherwise, it would have been an honor to have made sure that you would've gotten steamrolled if you had hung out with me. I can assure you that if the opportunity had ever availed itself, you would've been treated like a true thoroughbred and not just some plow mule. I guarantee that you would've been ridden hard and put away wet, my friend."

J. D. Brewster's offer was just a line of bullshit. He was far removed from being anything like an alleged love monkey.

"Do you have the index card signed from Dr. Colima that confirms you received a field commission?"

J. D. Brewster reached into the top pocket of his white consultation jacket and pulled out the official promotion.

Stream scrutinized the card and said, "I've never seen somebody skip a rank before, but I know the official rules, and there's nothing that precludes this from happening. I guess this might very well be the first promotion of this magnitude at this institution. I offer you hearty congratulations."

"To me, this seems like a bunch of hocus-pocus bullshit," Willy Mammon said. "I presume that all the students get the same education here at the Gulf Coast College of Medicine. What difference would it make if a student has been designated mushroom, stud, scut puppy, Pontius Pilate, Peter, Paul, preacher, priest, pope, poo bear, or Grand Poohbah?"

"Not so fast, you prehistoric mastodon," Stream said. "Your presumption is most assuredly *not* correct. I'm aware that you boys probably participated in debridement and skin graft procedures while you were on the burn unit. What you experienced was an anomaly as a consequence of a shortage of manpower. After all, nobody in their right mind would want to actually work with Dr. Street. I've heard that his students have come out seriously warped. Generally speaking, mushrooms should not be allowed to do *any* procedures. As for scut puppies, they are basically glorified go-fers. If I need somebody to bird-dog a lab, I'll send a scut puppy. If I need somebody to dig up clinical information out of the library, I'll send a scut puppy. If I need somebody to drop a 'DiSPOSe' at the bus stop, I'll send a scut puppy."

"What's a DiSPOSe?" Ben Fielder asked.

"That stands for a 'drug-seeking piece of shit.' It's an acronym," Dr. Stream replied. "I can assure you that this acronym represents the lowest form of human life walking around on this planet. A DiSPOSe will usually show up in the emergency room at two o'clock in the morning looking for a fix. This creature is even taxonomically lower than a mushroom, if that's indeed a possibility."

Ben Fielder asked, "I get that, but what makes it so much better to be a stud than a scut puppy?"

"Stud!" Dr. Stream barked as he looked Brewster over. "Step forward, front and center. What procedures have you learned how to do thus far?"

Brewster turned to face his colleagues. "Well, let's see. I'm now proficient at paracenteses procedures, anoscopic evaluations, and rigid proctoscopies. I've performed an arthrocentesis a time or two on a septic knee and elbow. I've helped with several flexible colonoscopies and sigmoidoscopies, but I'll be the first to admit that I haven't flown solo yet on those more complex invasive GI procedures."

"Do you see what I mean?" Dr. Stream asked. "It's better to be a stud than a scut puppy. There's also a huge added bonus. A stud has access to the Vinyl Lounge. This is a miniature version of the doctor's lounge, and it's down by the ER. Oversized chairs and sofas are abundant, and there's a fridge stocked with Mr. Pibb and frozen bean burritos."

"Fielder and I were invited into the Vinyl Lounge by J. D. just recently," Willy said. "I must admit, it's indeed a nice place to hang out."

"So now you know," Stream said. "I suggest that you boys stay on the good side of Brewster and piggyback a ride with him to visit this small slice of heaven in the middle of hell whenever you have the opportunity. I tell you right now, if you're a stud, you're a stud."

"I'm a stud!" Brewster boasted.

"Today, we are going to be working in the outpatient urology clinic," Stream explained. "We have several consults that you can see with me, including a new prostate cancer and a new renal cancer. We also have several postsurgical follow-up visits. Later this week, you'll accompany me and the attending, Dr. Freewater, into the operating suite, and we'll expose you boys to a few surgical procedures. Let's get started."

Brewster asked, "Dr. Stream, before we roll, could you tell me what the initials I. P. stand for in your name?"

"The 'I' in my name stands for the letter 'I.' The 'P' in my name stands for the letter 'P.' As I was told, my mother named me during a time when she was taking a leak," the resident explained. "Heaven knows what my handle would have turned out to be if Mom was dropping a deuce into the porcelain pot when she was thinking of baby names. Yes, you can call me I. P. because that's indeed my name. It's actually on my birth certificate. May I call you 'J. D.'?"

"Why, certainly!"

The morning urology clinic ran behind schedule, and it was 3:16 PM before it finally concluded. There was no way Brewster would have time to leave campus to get a bouquet of flowers for Stella Link. However, Brewster did have enough time to pull off one of his patented sleazy maneuvers. The medical student meandered back into the intensive care unit during his lunch break and found a sedated VIP. The acronym stood for "ventilated, intubated patient." Almost invariably, patients who are intubated and require ventilator support also require heavy sedation. Having a tube jammed into the trachea and then being hooked up to a ventilator machine is not a particularly enjoyable experience if one is fully conscious.

Brewster found a stall occupied by a VIP, and the room was filled with flowers. Surely, this unfortunate soul would not miss one medium-sized bouquet. Brewster grabbed a splay of flowers, made sure there was no greeting card that could possibly incriminate him, and hustled over to the Psychiatry Department to see his girlfriend. He was quite fearful that Stella Link would clobber him because of his boorish behavior the night before. Fortunately for J. D., nothing could have been further from the truth.

"Oh my!" Stella exclaimed. "That's a beautiful flower arrangement. I was hoping you would come by to see me. We need to patch things up. Did you know that Ben Fielder is dating Missy Brownwood?"

"That's news to me."

"I told Missy about your behavior at the restaurant," Stella said. "She told me that you, Ben, and the Wooly Mammoth just completed a clerkship with Dr. Street. He apparently has a reputation as the nastiest attending in the entire Texas Medical Center. I've heard that students who've completed rotations with him have come out as damaged goods."

"I was able to handle it," Brewster said. "I guess it wasn't that bad, all things considered."

"Missy told me about all of the terrible things you three experienced in July."

"Don't blow this up to be something more than what it was," Brewster said. "In my opinion, no harm, no foul."

"Why didn't you tell me about any of this?" Stella asked. "You can't keep all of that bottled up inside you. I'm here for you. It's no longer a mystery to me as to why you have been sullen and walking around with a short fuse."

"Where I am right now at this time in my life, I can't afford to show any sign of weakness. Otherwise, I might be culled out from the herd. Besides, Missy Brownwood talks too much."

Stella jumped out of her chair, ran around her desk, threw her arms around his neck, and kissed him passionately.

The storm clouds that had previously enveloped J. D. Brewster were starting to recede just a bit. "I know for a fact that I was a major league bastard last night. To prove to you that I'm indeed a true gentleman and not some disreputable scoundrel, I know where I can readily pick up another splay of flowers exactly like this one. Tonight, I'll bring the arrangement over to the waitress at the Italian restaurant to make amends."

"Oh, you're so sweet," Stella said. "I know that these flowers must have cost you a fortune!"

"Don't worry, baby," Brewster said, "It was nothing."

When the afternoon urology clinic had concluded, Dr. Stream gathered the three students and said, "I want you to know that being a stud is not all fun and games. Do you see these heavy bags underneath my eyes? It probably makes me look ten years older than my chronological age. I'm perpetually sleep deprived because of the nonsense that goes on at night in the urology unit."

"Is there anything we can do to help?" J. D. asked.

"Brew, you're about to step up to the plate and help me out on this matter," Stream said. "The bane of my existence is a nurse who works on the late shift. Her name is Melba Toad. I don't know if Melba is just a fucking idiot or just fucking evil. Perhaps she's a combination of both. Invariably, I get six or eight calls a night from Mrs. Toad to let me know about the most meaningless information that you could possibly imagine. Brewster, you're going to field these calls for the rest of the month. I don't expect you to give any orders per se. As a medical student, that would be illegal—despite the fact that you're a stud."

"I can handle it."

"You should be able to discern a real problem from pure bullshit," Stream said. "If you get a call from Melba about pure bullshit, just write up a memo about it and try to go back to sleep. Tell me about it in the morning. If it's something I need to know about right away, I want you to call me immediately. I'll give you my beeper number. Do you think you can handle this task?"

Brewster gave the resident a military salute. "I've been having some insomnia lately, so a few phone calls here and there likely won't make any difference to me."

Brewster should not have been so cavalier or enthusiastic about carrying the primary call beeper for the urology service. After all, no good deed goes unpunished. Dr. Stream had been quite honest about how Mrs. Melba Toad would make Brewster's life miserable. The following is an example of the phone calls that Brewster would receive on a typical night:

Call #1. Time: 10:10 PM. Message: "Mr. Brewster, I just wanted to let you know that the patient, Mr. John Doe, is sleeping comfortably."

Call #2. Time: 12:25 AM. Message: "Mr. Brewster, I just wanted to let you know that Mrs. Jane Doe, who was admitted with the diagnosis of having kidney stones, has been asleep all night and has not had any complaints of any pain at all. Can you believe that?"

Call #3. Time 1:18 AM. Message: Mr. Brewster, I just wanted to let you know that Mr. Joe Blow is not having any fever right now and his vital signs are completely normal."

Call #4. Time: 2:51 AM. Message: "Mr. Brewster, I just wanted to let you know … oh, I forgot why I called. Never mind. I'll call you back as soon as I remember what I wanted to chat about. Please try to get some rest."

Call #5. Time 3:16 AM. Message: "Mr. Brewster, I remember now what I wanted to tell you before. The blood warmer that we use for transfusions is not working. It's okay though because nobody needs a transfusion right now. Biomedical engineering says they'll bring up a new one around six this morning. I just wanted you to know."

Call #6. Time: 3:48 AM. Message: "Mr. Brewster, I just wanted to let you know Mrs. Joe Blow said she had a very successful bowel movement. She said her stool was well formed, and she could readily recognize the small bits of corn in the fecal matter from the lunch that she consumed a week ago. She did not have to strain very hard to evacuate her bowels. This is really exciting, and I just wanted you to hear the good news."

Call #7. Time: 4:26 AM. Message: "Mr. Brewster, I just wanted to let you know that the blood warmer from biomedical engineering has arrived. Can you believe it came this early? After all, they said it would be here on the floor at about six and it is not even four thirty in the morning yet. Those fellows really work hard. I bet they don't get any rest. This is really fabulous. Anyhow, we still don't have anybody who needs a transfusion at this time, so we probably won't need this device for quite a while. I just wanted to let you know the good news."

Call #8. Time: 4:58 AM. Message: "Mr. Brewster, I have a question. Dr. Chelsea from the anesthesiology service sent over pizza to the med-surg floor last night, and I was invited to come over and have a piece. It was that Mexican-flavored pizza from that fast-food joint called Taco Hell over on South Main. I can't remember the name of the pizza. Missy Brownwood said it was called 'burrito' pizza, but that doesn't sound right to me. I'm quite certain that the Mexican-flavored pizza is called 'Mexican-flavored' pizza. Anyhow, when I eat pizza like that, loaded with up with onions and jalapenos, I can suck down an entire liter bottle of Mountain Dew in one sitting. I swear I can drink it down so fast that I don't even taste it! It actually gives me a little bit of a buzz from the caffeine. Anyhow, I just wanted you to know. If you ever have insomnia and can't go to sleep at night, you're welcome to come over for visit and have some pizza with us. In the meantime, try to get some rest."

Call #9. Time: 5:24 AM. Message: "Mr. Brewster, I just wanted to let you know my shift is about over. I am going to go home and get some sleep. You know, I'll probably sleep just like a baby as soon as I get home. I snore really loud. Do you snore? You better get up now and get showered and get ready to go to work. I heard you were going to have a busy day in the urology clinic. I know that you're overbooked, and you'll probably have to work straight through lunch today. I'm certain you won't have time to get any rest at all. Well, I look forward to talking to you on the phone again tomorrow night. You seem to be such a nice young man."

One of the things that had made the urology clinical rotation so enjoyable was the anesthesiologist. Dr. Ron Chelsea would regale his colleagues with outlandish tales of personal, hyperbolic heroism displayed during extraordinary, superhuman adventures. Of course, it was all BS, but since Ron was a Texan, it was all okay.

Once a week, Ron would provide pizza for everybody in the surgery lounge. His favorite dish was "Bandito" pizza from Taco Hell. The Bandito came with jalapeno peppers, cilantro, onions, spicy taco meat, and refried beans. Consuming even one slice could cause severe reflux and heartburn. When Dr. Chelsea would bring in the pizza to the lounge, he would sing the lyrics from some obscure, silly little song: "Who Shot That Hole in My Sombrero?"

Never missing an opportunity to insult as many ethnic groups as he possibly could at the same time, Dr. Chelsea described the Bandito as a "gustatory conglomeration where two inferior cultures come together in one death-defying taste."

The homicidal ideations that had plagued J. D. Brewster from time to time had fortunately not resurfaced during the student's rotation on the urology service. Nevertheless, it was paramount that any feelings of burgeoning hostility remain safely sequestered within the confines of his personal bottle of moral decay. During this period of his own personal "Pax Romana", Brewster had to figure out some way to punish Mrs. Melba Toad for her overtly abusive behavior before his rotation on the urology service was over…

The last week on the urology service rotation was nigh, and the pending proclivity of peculiar clinical presentations would soon convince J. D. Brewster and his colleagues that urology was a surgical subspecialty that was not their particular cup of tea. Many decades later, the trio would remember the final week on the urology service as the "Pathological Pecker Parade."

Billy Don Dilbert was a twenty-two-year-old man from East Texas who had gone camping in the woods near Lake Livingston. He had two of his best friends with him when he saw a copperhead snake near their campsite. To impress his friends, he captured the snake and tried to milk the poison out of its fangs over an empty beer bottle. The snake, however, was not inclined to cooperate and tried to shy away from its captors.

With his thumb and index finger, Billy Don tried to pry the snake's mouth open to expose its fangs in a planned attempt to milk the venom from the terrified pit viper. For reasons that remain rather obscure to this very day, Billy Don Dilbert and his friends, Billy Slim and Billy Frog, were completely naked out in the forest except for their camping boots. Billy Don was sitting in a lounge chair while he was demonstrating his alleged herpetological expertise to his two inebriated colleagues. The abused creature was finally able to wriggle out of Billy Don's hands. As it made its escape, the agitated, legless, and venomous reptile landed right in the lap of the naked redneck. It doesn't take a rocket scientist to guess what happened next to Billy Don Dilbert.

Upon arrival to the ER at the Gulf Coast General Hospital, Billy Don had an ice pack strapped across his loins, and he appeared to be quite uncomfortable. The ER physician, Dr. Frank Barber, administered the antivenin and called the urology service down to assist with the management of Billy Don's traumatized penis.

The urology team was comprised of Dr. Freewater, Dr. Stream, and three medical students. "Hello, Frank. I'm glad you're back in the saddle," Dr. Freewater said. "I haven't had an opportunity to visit with you since your dramatic rescue from the hands of the Calle Vampiro Mexican drug cartel. I'm sorry to hear that your lovely wife is still missing in action. I can't imagine the emotional turmoil you are going through."

"If it wasn't for my work," Frank Barber replied, "I'd be homicidal."

A medical student named Jorge De Santo brought Dr. Barber a lab report for review.

"All right, Jorge," Dr. Barber snapped, "you gave me the damned lab report already. Now get the fuck out of my face!"

The traumatized medical student fled, never realizing that the only crime that he had committed was being Hispanic.

"What the hell is the matter with you?" Freewater asked. "You're a pig. Go back there right now and apologize to that young man. Did you think that was funny?"

"I'm sorry," Dr. Barber said. "Something happened to me when I was a prisoner in Mexico. If I encounter somebody who's Hispanic—or if I even simply hear the Spanish language being spoken—I, well, I want to take an IV pole and shove it up somebody's ass!"

"Be careful or the hatred will burn you up," the urologist said. "It'll get to the point that every other emotion you've ever had will become eroded. You need to try to get over that feeling."

"God forgive me, but I don't know if I'll ever get over these feelings. To be honest, I don't *want* to get over these feelings. The boys in admin state that I should probably go talk to somebody in the Psychiatry Department to help me cool off, but I don't want to cool off. I want to stay angry. The rescue team that extracted me from Mexico never found my wife. Deep down inside, I know that she, in all likelihood, is no longer amongst the land of the living, so I don't ever want to get over this hatred. You're very right, pal. It would seem that hatred is the *only* thing that I know or feel anymore. To be honest, Freewater, I'm dead. I'm just waiting for somebody to come along and bury me. I'm just going through the motions of being alive."

"You need to pull it together, Frank," Freewater said, "What's on our plate today?"

"A dumbass named Billy Don Dip Shit is over in stall number four. He was trying to have a personal relationship with a copperhead when he got bit on his pecker. Dig this; Billy Don was naked at the time. What do you make of that?"

"Do you think he was trying to trouser snake a dangerous snake?" Freewater asked.

"This is Texas," Dr. Barber conceded. "Anything's possible. When you're finished, one of Billy Don's friends, Billy Slim Slacker, will also be requiring your services. He's in stall five. He managed to get his penis spooled up into the beater bar of an upright Power Pulse vacuum cleaner. It happened to be the 'Deluxe Tornado Suction' multi-vortex edition. It's a top-shelf model, as best I can tell. The thing is still strapped to his Johnson if you're at all curious about the exact model and serial number of the tool in question. It looks to be a fairly big unit, and it might still be under factory warranty. I hope you realize that I'm talking about the vacuum cleaner and not the guy's pecker."

Dr. Freewater was combing through the paperwork. "Billy Don and Billy Slim Slacker weren't alone in the forest. It says here another friend was with them both, and his name was Billy Frog Ferris. I have to ask—"

"Don't worry" Dr. Barber interrupted. "I'm a step ahead of you. Billy Frog Ferris doesn't have a problem with his penis. In fact, he doesn't *have* a penis. A few years back, he ran his pecker through a blender when he was making frozen margaritas on a hot summer's day."

Dr. Steam and the three medical students who had accompanied Dr. Freewater down to the emergency room recoiled with a collective groan.

"Don't ask, okay?" Dr. Barber concluded.

"Split up the work," Dr. Freewater ordered Dr. Stream. "Keep me posted."

Dr. Stream sent in his team to take a history from the unfortunate Billy Don Dilbert and examine the damage that the serpent had rendered upon his tally whacker.

After Billy Don explained the circumstances, Brewster said, "What I don't understand is why you were completely naked at the time."

Billy Don laughed out loud and said, "I thought you doctors were supposed to be smart people. That's a stupid question. My friends and I were naked because we were out in the forest, you dumbass! I don't want somebody as stupid as you trying to patch up my plumbing."

"How silly of me," Brewster replied. "Of course! You were in the forest! Why wouldn't you and your friends be naked? It all makes sense now. Well, there you are, boys: another verified, unprovoked, vicious viper attack on a completely innocent man from the Lone Star State. Have fun, and I'll see you later." Brewster left the patient's cubicle in disgust.

Wooly Mammoth said, "Tell me, Billy Don, what'd you do to the copperhead after it bit your pecker?"

"I threw it down on the ground—and then I took my twelve-gauge shotgun and blasted it!"

"Nice job there, Billy Don," Ben Fielder said. "You taught that damned snake a lesson that it'll never forget, didn't you?"

"You're darn tootin', I did!"

After being kicked out of ER stall four, Brewster went over to interview Billy Slim Slacker, who was patiently waiting to have his pecker pried free from the vacuum cleaner beater bar. "Well, Billy Slim, what happened here?"

"You know what happens when you run naked in the forest, right? Dog-pecker gnats, chiggers, and shit like that will set up shop in your pubies. That's exactly what happened to me, and I started to itch like crazy. My other buddy, Billy Frog, said I would be able to suck all of those nasty creepy-crawlers off of my pecker with a vacuum cleaner. Well—here I am!"

Ultimately, after several weeks of futile medical management, Billy Don finally lost his penis. It became necrotic, fell off, and got lodged in the legging of one of his cowboy boots. All was not lost for Billy Don since he was able to make a good-luck charm out of his petrified pecker. He now rubs it to perpetuate his lifelong blessings of extraordinarily good fortune, and he claims that it works better than a rabbit's foot.

Billy Slim's pecker was repaired, but he was left with trauma-induced epispadias. Although usually congenital, this is an abnormal condition where urine will shoot out from a hole from the top side (the dorsal aspect) of the penis, as opposed to its usual exit route from the urethral meatus, found on the tip of the corona. In locker room jargon, this is referred to as "pee-in-your-own-face" syndrome. To add salt to an open wound, Billy Slim Slacker would never have another erection. The good news for society at large was that Billy Don, Billy Slim, and Billy Frog had successfully, through one traumatic means or another, eliminated themselves from ever again peeing into the gene pool.

The Pathological Pecker Parade, however, was far from over. The following day, three new patients appeared who were afflicted with macerated reproductive members.

Dr. Stream assigned each student to one of the patients. He told Willy Mammon that he wanted him to see the patient in exam room number one. Dr. Stream explained, "The guy in the first exam room is black, and he's a verified DiSPOSe. Maybe you can relate to him, but I certainly can't. He's a heroin addict, and he somehow developed what sounds like an abscess in his penis. Get in there and sort out what's going on. Fielder, you take the patient in room number two. Brewster, that leaves whatever consolation prize that's hidden behind door number three for you. Good luck, gentlemen. I will be waiting out here to discuss your findings. I'll see the old established patients who are here for simple follow-up visits. You have exactly one hour, and that's probably more time than what you'll need. We'll reconvene at ten o'clock sharp in my office. Okay, boys, get to work."

The patient in room number one was twenty-seven-year-old Jamaal Pukes, and he had been addicted to heroin for nearly a decade. He ran out of IV sites to inject himself, and he was reduced to getting heroin injections underneath his tongue or into his penis. He rarely had the courage to inject his own pecker with heroin, so he'd let his grandmother take on that specific task. Granny would lube it up and work over her grandson until he had a firm erection, and then she would ram the needle into his pecker in order for him to get his fix. She would always try to jab the needle into his penis before he had an orgasm. Otherwise, that would just be wrong. Granny had standards after all, and she thought it would be sinful if she gave her own grandson an orgasm. Her timing was not always perfect, however, and Jamaal sometimes unloaded his wad to the secret delight of both parties.

Unfortunately one fateful day, Granny got pinched while trying to score a hit, and Jamaal was reduced to shooting heroin into his own reproductive member without the trans-generational, familial assistance that he had so desperately needed. This was not only for the technical assistance required to successfully execute the arduous task of jamming a dull and frequently shared nineteen-gauge dirty needle directly into the shaft of his own pecker, but also for providing a most important existential barometer to somehow justify his own miserable life that long ago had been cast into the marginalized toxic dregs of society.

Perhaps somewhere in the universe there's a tiny planet named "Opium" that's forever trapped by the gravitational pull of the giant red star known as "Addiction" which may be found within the distant "Narcosis" galaxy. Only there would a man like Jamaal Pukes be welcomed with open arms…

Sadly, unlike his grandmother, Jamaal's illicit administrative methodology was less than hygienic, and he ended up getting a bacterial cellulitis and abscess within his penile shaft. When Willy Mammon examined the patient's penis, it appeared to be afflicted with the early stages of gas gangrene.

As Pukes was black, Mammon attempted to be courteous, respectful, empathetic, and gracious to a member of his own ethnic group. "You're truly a lowlife scumbag, and you're the kind of person that gives black people a bad name! I'm going to call in the resident, and we're going to filet open your filthy pecker and scrape out all that gas, pus, and nasty shit that's accumulating in your home-boy skank shaft. Frankly, you disgust me."

Jamaal Pukes asked a basic yet essential question. "Is this going to hurt?"

"For fuck sake, I would certainly hope so!" Mammon replied. "This needs to be a punitive procedure. When we're done with your sorry ass, I don't think you will ever be shooting up heroin into your Johnson ever again."

The infection involving the penis of Mr. Jamaal Pukes was serious, and Mammon realized that urological management could not wait a full hour before Dr. Stream had a chance to evaluate this clinical emergency.

I. P. Stream had to evaluate the perilous situation immediately. Dr. Stream agreed that something had to be done before the patient became septic. It took an astounding one hundred milligrams of intravenous morphine to keep Jamaal Pukes from flying off the examination table when Dr. Stream took a number-eleven scalpel blade and split open the man's penis from one end to the other in an effort to drain out the putrid and malodorous infected pus.

In retrospect, the procedure should have been done in the operating room under general anesthesia. When Stream and Mammon were finished with the young man, his penis looked like a butterflied lobster tail at a fancy seafood restaurant. The Wooly Mammoth was right about one thing, however. After hospitalization for prolonged antibiotic therapy and opioid detoxification, Jamaal Pukes would never use heroin again.

Ben Fielder did not fare much better with his new patient in room number two. As this individual was completely deaf, he had to communicate the shocking details about his medical history by using American Sign Language. Fortunately, there was a person present in the patient's room who was there to help translate this symbolic form of communication, conveyed by complex hand gestures, into the audible and the more conventional form of the English language. Ben Fielder was about to learn that just because somebody's deaf doesn't mean that they can't still be a sexual freakazoid. Upon careful examination, Fielder soon found that the patient's penis had sustained multiple deep and painful lacerations. When questioned, the deaf man started to rapidly move his hands about to explain his peculiar circumstances.

The translator who was present explained what had occurred by carefully studying the patient's hand motions. "I was sitting naked in a hot tub spa, and I don't know what happened, but my penis accidentally got sucked into the water drain vacuum line tube. It must have been stuck in there for about an hour. I don't know why I didn't just turn off the spa right away since the off switch was right beside my left hand. I would try to thrust my hips back and forth over and over again, but my penis just kept getting sucked right back into the water drain line. The vacuum was so strong that it felt like a fat lady wearing a Viking hat was trying to yank my pecker off at the root. It was horrible!"

"Are you for real?" Fielder asked.

"Well," the patient conveyed, "things like this just seem to happen to me from time to time. The other people in the hot tub thought I was fooling around, and they wanted to stick their peckers into the water vacuum line where my dick was stuck. Try as they might, there was just no additional room in the water drain vacuum line because my penis is *so* huge as you can readily see. They were all strangers, and I didn't know any of these people, but one old bastard with a really shriveled and wrinkled unit tried to mount me from behind. He was really old… I guess he had a hard time keeping it all poned up and whatnot. That was too bad, but he gave me his phone number. Would you like his phone number? Are you circumcised? I hope so. Do you have a boyfriend?"

It was a good thing at that moment that the patient was as deaf as a post.

Ben Fielder cleared his throat and said, "Excuse me for just one second." He stood up and turned around to face the door, keeping his back to the patient and the translator. "I'm going to tie this man's pecker to the bumper hitch on my truck—and then I am going to drag him around Hermann Park until he's dead!"

Unbeknownst to Ben Fielder, the translator, by using sign language, told the patient exactly, word for word, what the student had said. The translator's commissioned duties continued all the while the medical student proceeded to belt out a host of foul expletives. In fear, the patient began to scream at the top of his lungs, but fortunately his timing could not have been more perfect. In the other room, Jamaal Pukes was also screaming in pain as his pustular and toxic gas-impregnated penile member was surgically split open in a north-to-south direction with a surgical scalpel blade.

While Dr. Stream was splitting open Jamaal's penis across the hallway, Ben Fielder left the exam room to which he was assigned to explain his peculiar situation to Dr. Freewater.

Fielder was instructed to take a thick wad of triple antibiotic ointment, encase the patient's penis in it, and then wrap it up with surgical gauze. A follow-up appointment time was given to the deaf patient, and Fielder made sure that he and his two other medical students colleagues would be long gone and off to a different clerkship rotation by the time the scheduled visit was to occur.

The third patient assigned to J. D. Brewster was a clumsy man named Billy Dog Davis. It was a hot day in late August, and Billy Dog had to repair a rip in his jeans. He put the trousers underneath his mother's Singer sewing machine and started to sew on a new denim patch. Unfortunately, Billy Dog was naked. For unclear reasons, that seemed to be a peculiar recurrent thematic element for the patients who presented to the urology clinic that fateful day with penile injuries during the Pathological Pecker Parade.

Billy Dog's penis accidentally got flopped upon the tabletop, and he accidentally activated the sewing machine with his foot—and then he accidentally ran a button stitch across his pecker. Although quite bloody, the stitch line across his penis was readily recognized.

"You're really quite skilled with a sewing machine," Brewster noted. "As best I can tell, your button stitch looks flawless."

"Why thank you, kind sir," the patient replied. "I pride myself in all endeavors that I undertake."

Dr. Freewater gave Brewster the green light to take a suture-removal kit and carefully remove the self-induced stitches from the man's pecker. Afterward, the patient was given a tetanus shot and a referral to Dr. Corka Sorass for a psychiatric evaluation was submitted.

While Brewster labored to remove Billy Dog's self-inflicted button stitch, the student said, "You're truly a lowlife scumbag, and you're the kind of person who gives white people a bad name."

When finished, Billy Dog thanked J. D. Brewster and gave him a piece of paper with his phone number on it. "I liked it when you talked dirty to me." Billy Dog put his index finger up to J. D. Brewster's lips before he had sashayed out the door.

Mercifully, it was the last day of the rotation, and the three musketeers were given permission to shower and go home early. It would be, without a doubt, the longest shower any of them had ever taken. Nonetheless, there was one unfinished task. Before Brewster departed from the urology service, he needed to engineer a malicious act of vengeance. The student was duty bound to figure out a way to somehow punish Mrs. Melba Toad. J. D. Brewster's transformation into a nasty ogre was indubitably well underway.

Whether or not Mrs. Toad was evil, stupid, or some combination thereof, she had nonetheless inflicted an entire month of sleep deprivation upon Brewster. Finally, he knew exactly what to do. Brewster went to Taco Hell and purchased a twelve-inch Bandito pizza and a one-liter bottle of Mountain Dew. He also picked up two ten-ounce bottles of magnesium citrate, a powerful, carbonated cathartic agent. At the medical school, magnesium citrate was called the "Green Bomb." It was strong enough to cause patients to poop their brains out if they consumed a bottle of the vile beverage in one sitting.

Brewster opened the Mountain Dew and happily drank twenty ounces of the soda pop for himself. The consumption of this caffeinated beverage would also help him stay awake for the entire night.

He refilled the bottle with the two bottles of magnesium citrate, and then he put the bottle cap back on tightly. At ten o'clock that night, Brewster went to the urology floor and left the pizza and the bottle of tampered soda in the nurse's lounge. He put a sign on the pizza box that thanked Melba Toad for all the work she had done over the past month. His devious plan had now been set in motion.

Brewster set up his observation post in an empty patient room that was two doors down from the nurse's station. He watched Mrs. Melba Toad consume the pizza and the bottle of the adulterated beverage. It would be just a matter of time before the magnesium citrate went to work on the nurse's lower digestive tract.

The first wave of abdominal cramps and diarrhea struck just before midnight.

Whenever Mrs. Toad ran to the bathroom, Brewster paged her. Every time Mrs. Toad was struck with a wave of diarrhea, Brewster would place a telephone call to her immediately and incessantly. The following is an approximation of the phone calls that Brewster placed that night:

Call #1. Time: 11:58 PM. Message: "Mrs. Toad, I just want you to go and check on Mr. John Doe and make sure that he's sleeping comfortably. Do it right now. I need to know this minute. I'll wait on the line."

Call #2. Time: 12:21 PM. Message: "Mrs. Toad, I just want you go and check on Mrs. Jane Doe who was admitted with the diagnosis of having kidney stones and make sure she is not having any complaints of pain at this time. Do it right now. I need to know this minute. I'll wait on the line."

Call #3. Time 1:14 AM. Message: "Mrs. Toad, I just want to check on Mr. Joe Blow and make sure he doesn't have a fever. Do it right now. I need to know this minute. I will wait on the line."

Call #4. Time: 2:42 AM. Message: "Mrs. Toad, I just wanted to ask … oh, I forgot why I called. Never mind. I'll call you back if and when I remember what I wanted to chat with you about. By the way, every time I've called you, I hear the sound of a lot of grunting and moaning. Are you okay?"

Call #5. Time 3:16 AM. Message: "Mrs. Toad, I remember now what I wanted to ask you before. Is the blood warmer that we use for transfusions working properly? I want you to immediately stop what you're doing and check on it to make sure it's functioning without any problems. It wasn't working at the beginning of the month, and I need to know if the biomedical engineers repaired it correctly. Do it right now. I need to know this minute. I'll wait on the line."

Call #6. Time: 3:50 AM. Message: "Mrs. Toad, I just want to ask you if you know if our patients are having any abnormal bowel movements. The infection control nurse sent out a memo that there is a dangerous outbreak of amoebic dysentery that's sweeping through the hospital. It's highly contagious and potentially lethal. I want you to let me know if any patient on the urology unit is having any problems with uncontrollable diarrhea. If they are, I would be very worried about it. I want you to go through the entire patient registration list and let me know if anybody is having a bad case of diarrhea tonight. Do it right now. I need to know this minute. I'll wait on the line."

Call #7. Time: 4:10 AM. Message: "Mrs. Toad, I just wanted to let you know that I gave you wrong information earlier. The diarrhea that is sweeping through the hospital is not amoebic dysentery. It is a new tropical disease called 'lack-a-nookie'. There's no known treatment for it. Stop what you are doing and go over to the fax machine. I'll send over a flier about this deadly peril. Do it right now. I need to have you wait by the fax machine until you get the memo. I'll wait on the line."

Call #8. Time: 4:41 AM. Message: "Mrs. Toad, I have a question. I sent over a pizza to you the last night. It was that Mexican-flavored pizza from the fast-food joint over on South Main. Missy Brownwood said the pizza is named 'burrito' pizza,' but that's not right. I'm certain that the Mexican-flavored pizza is called 'Bandito' pizza.' Anyhow, when I eat pizza like that, loaded up with onions and jalapenos, I can suck down an entire liter of Mountain Dew in one sitting. I swear I can drink it down so fast that I don't even taste it! It actually gives me a little bit of a buzz from the caffeine. Anyhow, I just wanted you to know. If you ever have insomnia and can't go to sleep at night, you're welcome to give me a call. I'd be happy to send over a special bottle of Mountain Dew just for you. I certainly hope you enjoyed the pizza and soda tonight."

Call #9. Time: 5:24 AM. Message: "Mrs. Toad, I just wanted to let you know my rotation on the urology service is now officially over. I'm going to go home and get some sleep. You know, I'll probably sleep just like a baby as soon as I get home. I snore really loud. Do you snore? You better go take a shower. I also recommend finding a tube of hemorrhoid cream from the pharmacy. After the night you just had, I bet you'll need it."

# 7

## SPARE PARTS

It was time for J. D. Brewster to introduce the Wooly Mammoth to Mehdi. Mehdi was a good-natured man who could make Brewster laugh, and he was always quick with a complimentary hot cup of coffee and a snack. Mehdi asked, "Who is this large, black, African, soul brother man who's with you?"

"Mehdi, I think if you had used only one adjective in your query, it would have been just peachy in this particular social circumstance. Mehdi, I would like to introduce to you an extraordinary fellow named Mr. Willy Mammon. His friends call him the Wooly Mammoth. Willy, this is my friend Mehdi."

Mehdi grabbed the hand of the Wooly Mammoth and began to shake it vigorously. "You are my new friend, my friend! Whenever you want a cup of coffee or a bite to eat, you come see me, my friend. If you are my friend, I will take care of you—and you are now my friend."

The big man appeared amused and not at all offended by the strange mannerisms of the man from Persia.

It was the first day of September—the beginning of a new day, a new month—and a new clerkship rotation.

"How are you today, Mr. Brewster?" Mehdi asked. "I want to talk to you about something strange."

"I'm finer than frogs' hair," Brewster replied.

"Is that a good thing or a bad thing?" Mehdi asked.

"It is a very good thing," Brewster answered. "What's going on?"

"I speak Farsi, as you know, because I'm a Persian," Mehdi said. "The three men at the table over there are talking to each other in Farsi. I can tell you right now, though, that they are not Persian. They're Iranians!"

"What do you mean?" Wooly Mammoth asked. "Iranians are Persians, and vice versa, no? To my way of thinking, the labels are interchangeable."

"To me, they're different," Mehdi said. "Persians are decent, proud, and honorable. These Iranians sitting in front of us have none of those qualities. From the way they're speaking, I'm certain they hate America almost as much as the evil, liberal Democrats who've sadly been elected to the U.S. Congress and Senate. Anyhow, these terrorist are loyal to the ayatollah. They seem to be hateful religious fanatics."

"What in hell are they doing in our hospital cafeteria?" Brewster asked.

"As best I can tell, they have an uncle hospitalized upstairs, and they've come to visit him. However, I've heard these three men say that their uncle must approve of their plans before they put them into action. I am not sure what they're planning, but I must tell you that I think they're up to no good."

"Well, that's not a lot to go on," Brewster said. "The only recommendation I can make at this time is that you need to keep your eyes peeled…"

Many years later, Brewster would fondly remember a song that played on the radio at that time. The song was a parody, and the inflammatory lyrics were sung to the tune of "Barbara Ann," as recorded by the Beach Boys. The title of the parody was "Bomb Iran." In fact, all of Brewster's classmates would sing the song with glee. For many years, Brewster was disappointed that the United States of America had never given Iran the spanking it had so rightly deserved.

For that reason alone, Brewster finally became politically aware, and he held President Jimmy Carter in utter contempt.

If there was any tiny consolation, Brewster would someday realize that he was honored to have been alive at a time to personally witness such historic events unfold. In retrospect, the flaccid, cowardly, politically inept, masturbatory gyrations engaged by the second worst president the United States had ever elected was truly quite a spectacle for America to behold at that time.

Brewster was under a great deal of pressure from Feral Cheryl to become involved in a romantic relationship. He considered Cheryl a family member, and now that he had a new girlfriend, he had to think of some way to divert Cheryl's amorous desires.

When Brewster and Willy Mammon left the cafeteria, Brewster said, "Willy, come with me. We have a few minutes to spare. There's another person I want you to meet. She's my 'cousin,' and she is starting as a nurse on the med-surg floor today. I promised I would come by and say hello while she's starting her career here." In short order, Brewster found Feral Cheryl and introduced her to the big man.

The Wooly Mammoth furrowed his eyebrows and looked back and forth between Brewster and Cheryl. "Now, what's wrong with this picture? So, tell me, Brewster, did somebody jump the fence here? If you indeed have any black blood coursing through your veins my pasty friend, my esteem for you has just risen dramatically!"

Cheryl looked the big man over from the top of his head all the way down to his feet and asked, "My goodness, you're indeed a big fellow! What size shoes do you wear?"

Willy said, "Well, as you can see, I'm huge. I wear a size-fifteen shoe."

Cheryl began to flutter her eyes and said, "I'm certain I know why they call you the Mammoth, but someday, I would like to see that for myself."

"Mr. Mammon here is indeed a good man," Brewster said. "However, I believe it's my duty to provide a full disclosure before you get all 'twitter-pated' on me. I just want you to know that he's well beyond his prime years. He's probably seven or eight years older than you, and over a decade ago, he even fought in the—"

"Silence! Don't make me laugh," Cheryl said. "I've been asking Missy Brownwood about you. I hear that you have been dating Stella Link. You had your shot. If you're too stupid to make a move on somebody standing right in front of you—and who would be your perfect partner for life—it is time for me to move on."

"Missy Brownwood talks too much," Brewster said.

"Little sister here needs to be looking for a mature man—and not somebody who's still wet behind the ears, white boy!" Mammon exclaimed.

Cheryl wrote down her phone number—along with a smiley face and a tiny heart—on a prescription pad and put it in the top pocket of the Wooly Mammoth's white consultation jacket.

As Mammoth and J. D. Brewster headed toward the med-surg conference room, the big man said, "You're going to have to explain to me in detail how you and Miss Cheryl know each other—and precisely why you referred to her as your cousin."

Brewster said, "It is a long story, and in many ways, it's not a very happy one. When Cheryl's father was murdered by two bandits in my uncle's cigar shop back in '68, she became an orphan. My family took her in, and she was raised by my crazy Uncle John. I'll tell you all about it someday."

"How did she get that nickname—Feral Cheryl?"

"For shit's sake!" Brewster exclaimed. "If you can't figure that out on your own accord, big boy, I can't help you."

At nine o'clock the next morning, it was time for Brewster, Fielder, and the Woolly Mammoth to start their last mandatory rotation on the surgery service. They were scheduled to meet the attending, Dr. John "Wayne" Gray, along with a resident and intern named Dr. Perkins, and Dr. Price respectively. The conference room for their meeting was beside the nurse's lounge on the med-surg service, which Dr. Gray had temporarily commandeered from the nursing staff.

After the three students arrived, Dr. Gray walked into the room and said, "Good morning, boys and girls. I can tell you right now that you're all about to be busier than a three-legged cat trying to cover up bat scat in a cat box filled with quicksand. Whowee!"

J. D. Brewster thought, "*Dr. Gray probably spent way too much time hanging around Uncle Hank Holcombe.*"

Dr. Gray walked over to a projector and turned it on. An image of a man appeared on the whiteboard. The picture looked like a newspaper clipping. The middle-aged man was wearing a prison jumpsuit, and he was shackled in handcuffs. Dr. Gray hit the button on the projector, and a new image appeared on the whiteboard. It was a newspaper headline from 1975: "Dead Child Found Buried in Neighbor's Yard!"

"I recognize that man's face," Dr. Perkins said, "but I don't remember his name."

"Is anybody else able to recognize this foul creature?" Dr. Gray asked. "In light of what's going to happen to him today, I want to make sure nobody is related to this slime wad. It's probably good that none of you recognize this convict since he's the kind of pond scum that would give you nightmares. I know about this man because I was an alternate jury member for his trial back in '76. I've ruminated over these events ever since I learned about the horrific deeds he perpetrated. This man is Lorenzo Lynch. In 1976, he was convicted of being a baby rapist and a baby killer."

"At this time, I would surmise you're telling us about this fellow because he's in need of some sort of elective surgical procedure," Dr. Price said. "By the contract I signed as an intern, I have the right to refuse to do any medical procedure that I consider immoral. I'd like to know exactly what this guy did before I decide whether or not I am going to render any type of medical care on his behalf. I don't have to form a doctor-patient relationship with this type of individual if I so choose."

"I understand how you feel, and I respect that," Dr. Gray said. "After you hear what I'm about to say, however, I think you'll want to participate in this patient's medical care. Straight up, Lorenzo Lynch is a homicidal, homosexual pedophile, although he has chosen to adopt a more benign monicker. He considers himself to be a 'minor attracted person', as if such a label would make his evil behavior more acceptable to our gender-confused society. He was convicted of raping a young boy in Vermont in 1972, but he only got three years in prison. Don't ask me how somebody who rapes a baby spends only three years in prison, but he was released from custody in 1975. Maybe you need to ask those assholes in Vermont about those circumstances. In any event, he relocated to Houston and moved in next door to a young Hispanic couple named Mr. and Mrs. Maldonado who had a three-year-old boy named Sebastian. Within a few weeks, the child and the family dog disappeared into thin air."

"I have friend, Arby Fuller, who's a corrections officer. Over lunch at a Chinese restaurant, he told me about this guy in lockdown who raped and murdered a baby and a family pet. Can't wait to meet the guy," Brewster said. "Something tells me that this story is not going to have a very happy ending."

"That remains to be seen," Dr. Gray said. "If things go according to plan, this story will have a *very* happy ending later on today! At the time that the boy and his dog went missing, there was a big search party organized, but it was initially unsuccessful. A bit of research on the part of the police soon revealed that the Maldonado family had been living directly next door to a man who was previously convicted of raping a baby. I'll bet that everybody in this room can guess what happened next."

"Lynch took the child?" Fielder asked.

"The child and the dog were found buried in the man's backyard," Dr. Gray replied. "Dig this—the autopsy revealed that the baby had not only been brutally raped, but it was also confirmed that the baby and the dog were buried while still alive! Their lungs were filled with dirt! Nice. Anyhow, I'm happy to report that Lorenzo Lynch had been convicted of first-degree baby rape and baby murder and was sentenced to death. After all, this is Texas."

"Why is he still breathing?" Mammon asked.

"He's been remanded to the maximum-security Sharpstown Correction Facility until he finally gets the big needle. As it now stands, this human turd will someday get an opportunity to take the big dirt nap, and he'll be taking it sooner than later if I have any say-so in this matter. Well, boys and girls, that day has arrived. Suddenly, this man's execution is now on the fast track."

"What are you talkin' about?" Dr. Price asked.

"There's a bug-eyed starlet out in Hollywood named, Luzanne Saranrap, who has expressed great interest in this case. This actress is a community activist who always picks the wrong battles to fight, and she recently announced that she and her lunatic Hollywood associates were going to try to petition that Lorenzo Lynch receives clemency."

"Why on earth would Tinseltown care about this guy?" Fielder asked.

"Simple," Dr. Gray said. "Above and beyond the Left Coast's aversion to the death penalty in general, the defense attorney who's representing Lynch is making the claim that his client is mentally feeble; therefore, Lynch was not responsible for the crimes he committed."

"What does this guy have to do with our surgery service?" Brewster asked.

"For the last several years, the execution of Lorenzo Lynch has been delayed by extensive legal maneuvers funded by the TEMCAL organization, but that's all about to come to an end today at exactly 3:16 PM."

"What's TEMCAL?" Willy asked. "I've never heard of it."

"I'm embarrassed to tell you that here in Texas, an organization of this nature actually exists," Dr. Gray answered. "TEMCAL is an acronym for the Texas Egalitarian Man-Child Association for Love. This is an organization that actively promotes pedophilia, and Lorenzo Lynch is the new poster boy for this despicable group. Mr. Lorenzo Lynch has just run out of any further delays in his execution. Up until now, he's been held in solitary confinement. The general population of prisoners is apparently not particularly fond of people who rape and murder babies."

"Well, what is going to happen at 3:16?" Dr. Perkins asked.

"I am happy to report that Mr. Lorenzo Lynch will be released from solitary confinement at three o'clock," Gray answered. "Reliable sources indicate that Lynch is going to have an encounter with a prisoner named 'Big Tom' and his two sons, 'Nick the Shiv' and 'Joey the Bull.' These three men are professional Sicilian 'bent noses,' and when they encounter Lynch, the evil prick is going to suffer a closed-head injury at precisely 3:16 in the afternoon."

"Is this a manifestation of the 'clinical justice system,' which is secretly embedded within the matrix of this medical school?" Brewster asked.

Dr. Gray stared at the three medical students for what felt like an eternity. "That's a subject matter that should *never* be openly discussed. I'm dead serious. I know that you're a stud, Mr. Brewster, but don't forget that I have the power to demote you at the drop of a hat. I won't tolerate any of you boys mentioning those unsubstantiated and rather salacious rumors ever again. Am I clear?"

Dr. Gray's question was met with blank stares.

"That was not a rhetorical question, people!" Dr. Gray said. "I'll ask this one more time—am I clear?"

Everybody in the conference room uttered an unequivocal yes. "Hopefully, the internal organs of Lorenzo Lynch, which include both kidneys and his heart, will not be injured at the time of the physical assault. These three prisoners are going to crush his skull with a barbell that was appropriated earlier today from the prison gymnasium. This piece of exercise equipment is currently hiding in a laundry basket in the death row cell block. Hopefully, this dispensation of justice will not result in Lorenzo Lynch suffering a full-out, cardiopulmonary arrest."

"Are you on board with any of this?" Ben Fielder whispered.

"Am I ever!" Brewster replied enthusiastically.

"As we're working with incarcerated professional consultants with whom we've done extensive mutually beneficial business within the past year, I fully anticipate Mr. Lynch will still be breathing when the air ambulance helicopter brings him to our facility," Dr. Gray explained. "We'll only have a very small window to harvest the internal organs," Dr. Price noted. "Are we going to be able to pull this off?"

"Good question," Dr. Gray answered. "The helicopter will be at the prison site by 3:45, and the EMTs will be ready to pull the trigger in case Lynch needs to be intubated and hit with the Ambu-bag before he gets loaded on the chopper. We're going to harvest his kidneys and his heart for organ transplants. There's nothing that gives me more satisfaction as a surgeon than being able to harvest spare parts for patients who are in desperate situations."

"Well, it looks like the donor is lined up," Willy Mammon observed, "but what about the patients who're going to be the organ recipients?"

"These patients have been notified, and they're already in the hospital," Dr. Gray explained. "They've been kept NPO since last night, and as we speak they've about to be surgically prepped to receive their new organs. Lorenzo Lynch has no idea that he's going to offer up his very life while performing such an altruistic act today. Since I knew this day was coming, I was able to visit Lynch a few weeks ago. For a carton of smokes, I convinced him to sign a DNR code status and an organ donor card. I feel really good about all of this. Is everybody clear on how this is all going down?"

Except for Ben Fielder, who apparently still had minor reservations about the entire ordeal, the surgical team otherwise replied with glee. Brewster was enthralled by Dr. Gray's gnostic command over the catastrophic calamity that would befall this rapist and baby murderer.

The physician who had previously overseen the terminal management of Irene Segulla was none other than Dr. Lawdy Garth Penn. She was correct when she made a cryptic reference to the "clinical justice system" that existed at the hospital, but apparently nobody was supposed to talk about it. Although the possible existence of an underground "clinical justice system" was a disturbing subject to be reckoned with, such an unofficial violent subculture should have been predictable at a place like the Gulf Coast College of Medicine.

Dr. Gray invited his team to come up to the helipad. Upon his arrival at the Texas Medical Center, Lorenzo Lynch had not been intubated, and fortunately, he was still breathing on his own accord. Dr. Gray said, "I'll do the neurological examination now to confirm that this patient is brain-dead before we take him down and harvest his organs."

"Shouldn't we have the neurology service officially make a declaration that the patient is brain-dead before we yank out his kidneys and heart?" Dr. Perkins asked.

"No, I can do this myself." Dr. Gray rubbed the patient's sternum ever so gently with a two-inch strip of a thin, lightly waxed dental floss to make certain that Lorenzo Lynch didn't respond to any "noxious" tactile stimuli.

Gray then briefly flashed a penlight into the patient's left eye and said, "Yep, this patient's brain-dead, alright! We won't need an EEG study or anything else from the neurology service to confirm that this prisoner already has acute squash rot. Let's take him downstairs and gut the son of a bitch!"

Dr. Price said, "If you ask me, that was not a particularly thorough neurological examination!"

Dr. Gray sneered and said, "For our purposes, it's the only type of neurological examination an individual like this ever deserves!"

Within two hours, Lorenzo Lynch had "donated" his vital internal organs to three individuals who were in need of spare parts. Dr. Gray and his team extracted the heart and kidneys and passed the organs off to the cardiothoracic surgery fellow and the kidney-transplant team. Dr. Gray did not actually perform organ transplants himself since his job was to procure the organs for transplant. Other surgical attending physicians would manage the actual transplant procedures.

As it turned out, Dr. John "Wayne" Gray was amazingly proficient at his job. Somehow, if there was ever a patient who was in dire need of an organ transplant, Dr. Gray was the go-to guy at the Texas Medical Center. If a spare part was needed, it would usually be found—no questions asked.

After the procedure, the team split up. The students were able to scrub in on the two kidney transplant procedures while the intern and resident were able to contribute their modest skills in assisting with the heart transplant.

For years, J. D. Brewster and his colleagues would wonder if Lorenzo Lynch was truly brain-dead when his organs were harvested and given to other patients. Personally, Brewster had his own doubts about the whole matter. He secretly thought Lorenzo Lynch was only unconscious from a concussion when his heart and kidneys were surgically removed. If that was the case, it didn't bother Brewster one iota. In fact, he had hoped that Lorenzo Lynch, at some level, had actually felt the excruciating pain of being butchered alive while his internal organs were harvested! As expected, no anesthesia was utilized by Dr. Gray's team during the vivisection.

In retrospect, baby rapists and baby murderers should consider staying far removed from the borders of Texas. The same suggestion should be given to anybody who would ever consider torturing and raping a dog, either. The act of retribution against Lorenzo Lynch sadly did not satiate Brewster's newfound thirst for revenge in the least. If the truth be told, Brewster's appetite for violence had only been whetted…

The following morning, Brewster went by the cafeteria for a cup of coffee and to visit briefly with Mehdi.

Mehdi said, "Those men are back, and they're passing photos among themselves that apparently were taken at the Tenneco fueling dock at the ship channel. They were speaking openly about their plans while I was nearby. I guess they think that I'm a Mexican and don't know what they're saying. I'm absolutely certain that I overheard them saying that they were going to 'strike a blow against the Great Satan.' I'm afraid, J. D. What should we do?"

"I'm sorry I ever doubted you," Brewster said. "It sounds like we have to act quickly. I have an idea. I need to provoke them. Take me back to the kitchen where the line cooks are preparing breakfast.

In the meantime, call security and tell them there is a riot going on down here in the cafeteria and to get here ASAP."

When Brewster returned from the kitchen, he held a Styrofoam box and walked directly up to the three Iranian men. "You boys look like you're hungry, and I want to share some of my breakfast with you." He opened up the box, peeled out strips of raw bacon, and set them on their plates.

In utter disbelief, the three men looked up from the glossy black-and-white photographs of the Houston Ship Channel that they had been studying.

While the Code Gray alert was announced over the hospital loudspeakers, the three men jumped up and commenced to give J. D. Brewster a severe beating. One of the men asked repeatedly, "Is dees pork?! Is dees pork?!"

"Yes, 'dees' is tasty hickory-smoked pork from a foul, evil, porcine quadruped," Brewster replied. "If any of you even touched that bacon, I'm going to have to tell your ayatollah. He's probably going to have to come over here and cut off your peckers with a scimitar."

Within seconds, a punch to the face knocked Brewster to the floor.

Two of the men began to strike Brewster around the head and neck, and the third man tried to kick Brewster in the groin.

Brewster covered his face with his arms and yelled, "Hey, buster, I only have one testicle. Be careful down there!"

The security team arrived and restrained the Iranian men until the Houston Police Department could arrive. The photographs of the Houston Ship Channel appeared to be quite suspicious to the police, and an emergency search warrant allowed police detectives to raid the hotel room where the three foreign nationals had resided.

Arrests were made, including the uncle who had been hospitalized at the Gulf Coast General Hospital with an acute, but mild, thrombo-embolic stroke from poorly controlled hypertension. The police could not give a tinker's damn about the medical malady that had afflicted 'Uncle Mohammed the Terrorist'. He and his three nephews were quickly hauled off to jail.

When bomb-making material was found in the hotel room, the terrorist cell was permanently put out of business. The FBI was called into the case, and the members of the terrorist cell were charged with terrorism and espionage.

In a perfect world, J. D. Brewster would have been allowed to have a fifteen-minute "private interview" with them in an interrogation room. The only thing Brewster would have needed for a successful "interview" would have been a package of raw bacon and a large plunger.

Antonia Alabaster and the Your Witness News television crew arrived, but Brewster slipped away as he was not inclined to give an interview to his cousin after he had suffered multiple head and neck contusions, a bloody mouth, and a fat lip. Brewster's injuries had warranted an ice pack application placed upon his face to make himself presentable for work. He was uncertain about how the medical school administration would respond to what he had done, but he wanted to go about his business as if nothing had happened.

On September 15, the San Diego Padres rolled into town for a two-game series with the Houston Astros. North University Place had a program where a school bus would pick up senior citizens who were no longer able to drive and take them to the Astrodome for a game. Anybody over the age of sixty-five was eligible to take advantage of this unique courtesy. The municipality would not discriminate against any senior citizen who wanted to see a baseball game, especially since the Astros were going to win the National League West in 1980. It was a noble endeavor, but they should have discriminated against Uncle John and kept him from ever getting on the bus that night.

The Houston pitching staff had given up six runs to the Padres. In the bottom of the ninth, it was clear that the Astros were going to lose. Uncle John was already agitated at the umpire and had strongly disagreed throughout the game about the seemingly generous strike zone that was afforded to the Padre pitchers, but the subjectively narrow strike zone the Houston pitching staff had to contend with.

When the Astros were down to the bottom of the last inning, a pitch seemed to be high and wide of the strike zone. When the umpire signaled that the pitch was a strike, Uncle John became unglued. He charged down the aisle and plowed over the top of the fence to get on top of the Padres dugout. He brandished a revolver and pointed it at the umpire. "I'm about to teach you what's a ball and what's a strike!"

Security forces quickly charged Uncle John to try to subdue him, but the elderly man was surprisingly fleet of foot. He jumped back over the fence and across several empty seats. When he safely made it to an adjacent aisle, he was able to book out of the Astrodome before anybody could lay a finger upon him.

"William!" Uncle John screamed into a pay phone at J.D. near the exit. "I need your help. I'm at the Astrodome, and I ran into a spot of trouble. Come pick me up. Hurry!"

J. D. found Uncle John hiding underneath an underpass south of the stadium. Six police cars raced down Kirby Drive and plowed into the Astrodome parking lot while uniformed policemen set up a roadblock outside of the ballpark.

"For shit's sake, John," J. D. asked, "what in hell's going on?"

"I tried to shoot the umpire," Uncle John replied. "Get me out of here, William!"

Brewster popped the trunk and shoved his deranged elderly relative in the storage compartment. His Mustang was facing north, and there was no way his car would be able to make a left turn onto the loop feeder. Brewster's only recourse was to motor down Kirby Drive—right past the Astrodome and the roadblock!

As an officer waved Brewster through a barricade, Uncle John started to kick at the trunk lid. Fortunately, the police didn't hear the racket.

At John's bungalow, J. D. was finally able to free his uncle from the tight confines of the trunk.

"Thanks, William," Uncle John said. "That was a close one!"

"I'm not William," J. D. said. "My name is … oh, hell, never mind."

Uncle John should have been charged with assault with a deadly weapon, but the cranky old coot would live to cause further mayhem yet again on some other day.

The interns, residents, and fellows at Gulf Coast College General Hospital were allowed to have breakfast and lunch in the doctor's lounge. The area was off-limits to the students. Dinner was only provided in the doctor's lounge during evening staff meetings.

Dr. Price was determined to get through his internship and residency without having to buy a single meal or purchase any groceries. He would enjoy a hot breakfast and lunch in the doctor's lounge, and in the evenings, he would brazenly raid the Vinyl Lounge, which was supposed to be reserved *only* for high-ranking medical students who had been promoted to the rank of stud, and their immediate guests. The refrigerator in the Vinyl Lounge was always stocked with sodas, and the freezer was invariably stuffed with bean burritos.

Brewster, Fielder, and Willy Mammon were watching the boob tube in the Vinyl Lounge when a booming voice on the television said, "Stay tuned! Lesbian, transsexual, celibate Catholic nuns who used to be male, heterosexual, pedophilic priests are coming up on the following segment. It's the television show that everybody is talking about: Live on Alonzo!"

"Boy, oh boy!" Fielder proclaimed enthusiastically. "I can't wait to see this. I love *The Alonzo Santa Cruz Show*!"

Without any warning, Dr. Price walked into the Vinyl Lounge and promptly changed the channel to a *Star Trek* rerun.

When Fielder protested, Price responded, "I have seniority here. I get to call the shots as to what we watch on television."

"Now, wait just a minute here," the wooly one said. "The Vinyl Lounge belongs to the medical students. You interns get to use the regular doctor's lounge, and we don't. Why don't you just stay restricted in your own assigned lounge and leave us the hell alone?"

"I would, but they don't have food in there at night," Dr. Price said. "I have to come over here just to eat something."

"I think you're well above your ideal body weight already, Dr. Price," Brewster said. "I think fat women are beautiful, but I think fat guys like you look like political Warsaw Pact refugees from Outer Slobovia. Maybe it is time for you to step away from the burritos for a while."

"It's taken me years to get into this condition," Price said. "I have a low coefficient of drag. I just slip right through the atmosphere with little if any friction, but I have to work at it constantly. It takes around-the-clock training to stay this obese. I have to eat, eat, and eat some more. The minute I quit eating; the weight just falls right off of me. So if you boys will excuse me," the intern said, "I'm scheduled for another round of coronary congesting mammalian fat and complex carbohydrate loading. After all, I'm trying to watch my girlish figure."

"What kind of girlish figure are you talking about?" Fielder asked. "Do you mean the nine-month pregnant look—or what?"

"We have brutal autumns here in Texas," Price said. "I've seen it get as low as the seventies from time to time right here in the Lone Star state during the month of September. I am putting on an extra layer of blubber as insulation to protect myself from the elements."

Dr. Price heated up a burrito in the microwave oven. The medical school had provided this new gadget for the small kitchenette in the Vinyl Lounge. Unfortunately, Dr. Price was not paying attention to where he was walking. The maintenance crew had recently set down sticky rat trap paper to exterminate several mice that had rudely taken up residence in the Vinyl Lounge. Dr. Price inadvertently stepped on the sticky pest paper strip that had already doomed a small rodent.

"Eek! I stepped on a dead mouse!" Dr. Price put his burrito on the counter, danced over to a chair, and pulled off his shoe. "There is nothing I hate more than mice and cockroaches!" He departed the lounge and carried his shoe with the adherent dead rodent to the men's room where he used a ballpoint pen to scrape the dead mouse off the sole of his penny loafer.

"Price is a bastard," Ben Fielder said. "Pulling rank over who gets to watch television is just bullshit. I hate that fat fuck. Let's booby-trap his precious burrito."

"Don't do it!" Mammoth said. "We could get our asses in a sling if this goes south on us."

"Don't be a wussy, Mammon," Brewster said. "I know just what to do." After all, J. D. still had the novelty silicone cockroach that had been previously given to him by Arby Fuller as a gag gift. Once Brewster stuffed the prosthetic insect into the burrito, the only thing left do was to wait and watch for the ensuing firework display. "It's time to teach this overbearing prick a lesson he'll never forget!" Brewster crowed.

Dr. Price returned from the men's room, picked up his burrito, and took a bite. When he felt a foreign object in his mouth, the intern expectorated the contents of his meal into napkin to examine what was awry. Once he saw what he thought was a large, living, six-legged coprophagic arthropod wiggling about in the napkin, Dr. Price gagged and promptly vomited.

Unfortunately for Brewster, his impractical joke backfired.

On the second occasion when Dr. Price spewed vomit, there was the sudden appearance of a copious amount of blood that painted the floor of the vinyl lounge a bright crimson red. The medical term for vomiting blood is called hematemesis, and in the intern's specific situation, it was caused by an acute internal catastrophe called a Mallory-Weiss gastric tear. A Mallory-Weiss injury is a linear rent that occurs at the gastroesophageal junction, and it can happen when a patient experiences violent vomiting. Dr. Price was experiencing violent vomiting. Dr. Price was vomiting blood. Dr. Price was in serious trouble.

Brewster and his colleagues carried Dr. Price by hoisting him from underneath his armpits straightaway into the emergency room which was directly adjacent to the Vinyl Lounge.

Cornelius T. Polyp, the new senior GI fellow who was skilled at diagnostic fiber optic procedures, was called down to address the medical emergency. A nasogastric tube was inserted, and Dr. Price received a lavage of ice water in an attempt to stem the bleeding.

When this was unsuccessful, a balloon tamponade was performed. In this somewhat archaic medical procedure, a tube is placed in the stomach and a balloon, affixed to the end of the tube, is inflated internally. Physical pressure is applied to the tube as it exits the patient's mouth in an attempt to jam the balloon against the bleeding gastric mucosal lining. As this procedure is now known to cause the tear at the gastroesophageal junction site to actually worsen on some occasions, many emergency rooms in more modern times no longer initiate this type of gastroenterological intervention.

Once the bleeding had somewhat subsided, the balloon tamponade tube was removed from Dr. Price, and the GI fellow ran a fiber optic EGD tube to see what was going on inside the intern's upper digestive tract. When the tear at the gastroesophageal junction was found, the GI fellow was able to successfully cauterize the site and prevent further bleeding from occurring.

Dr. Price was exhausted, but he hadn't lost enough blood to warrant a packed red blood cell transfusion. The emergency room physician, Dr. Bryan, recommended that the intern strongly consider an overnight hospitalization for further observation, but Dr. Price declined the offer.

Dr. Price was discharged from the emergency room and was ordered to go home and rest for a day or two. Unfortunately, Brewster and his colleagues forgot to dispose of the evidence. Dr. Price returned to the Vinyl Lounge and found out that he was the victim of a cruel joke. It could not be ascertained as to who may have tampered with his burrito, but the evidence was nonetheless turned over to the hospital administrators.

Once Dr. Price was discharged from the emergency room, the Wooly Mammoth grabbed Fielder and Brewster by their collars and banged their foreheads together.

"What in hell is the matter with you, Willy?" Brewster asked as he howled in pain. "You could have given me a subdural!"

"I told you boys not to do this—and look what happened," Willy said. "If you idiots pull another juvenile stunt like this, I am going to beat your asses and then walk away from all of your childish bullshit."

Before Brewster's very eyes, the United States was devolving into a highly mobile and heterogeneous society. It had gotten to where many Americans no longer even knew their very own neighbors. This fact is particularly problematic because many elderly people are destined to become estranged from their family members. It speaks poorly of any society where an elderly person does not have helpful neighbors or loving and caring relatives. This was true for Brewster's very own Uncle John. This was also true for a woman named Dora Garza, an elderly widow who lived in Meyerland.

Modern medicine has conquered so many diseases that human beings are now living well beyond their originally intended expiration dates. The hardest thing to deal with for many people with elderly relatives is the comorbid behavioral and cognitive dysfunction that may accompany an ancient person's latter years. It's often quite difficult to manage an elderly relative who suffers from dementia or otherwise exhibits erratic behavior, widely known colloquially by the second decade of the 21$^{st}$ century simply as the "Slow Joe Biden Syndrome". How embarrassingly sad… Oftentimes, the best way to deal with such a situation is to try to simply avoid these impaired relatives—as if they simply no longer exist. Perhaps human beings are just living too long. Perhaps our reprehensible behavior toward the elderly is just a despicable and indefensible sin, nothing more and nothing less. Perhaps God just backed the wrong primate.

Dora Garza walked out of her home to pick up the newspaper in her driveway. It was a daily ritual. However, this time, Dora never returned home. She continued to walk through her neighborhood, blissfully unaware that she was only wearing a bright yellow T-shirt and house slippers without any pants or underwear. After shuffling about for the better part of a mile, Dora became fatigued and collapsed upon the sidewalk for more than forty minutes. Automobile drivers averted their eyes and sped on past the frail and elderly individual as if they didn't recognize Dora's unfortunate predicament.

A young thug terrorized the elderly woman when he stole her slippers and newspaper. The evil miscreant actually laughed derisively when Dora became incontinent of her own urine when her precious newspaper was forcefully pried away from her bony fingers.

She was frail, confused, and disoriented, and the people passing by didn't want to get involved in such matters. As suggested by the itinerant rabbi's parable as recorded in chapter 10 of the book of Luke, perhaps human behavior had not changed all that much over the past two millennia.

A kindly individual named Sam Aria witnessed what was going on. When he came upon the elderly woman, he pulled his car to the side of the road. From the back seat of his vehicle, Sam recovered an old blanket that was employed to keep cat hair off of the car's tuck-and-roll interior upholstery. When he approached Dora, Sam gently wrapped the blanket around her shoulders. Fortunately, Dora appreciated the act of mercy, and she didn't even seem to particularly mind being suddenly covered by a generous shed coat of feline fur. "Madam, are you injured?" Sam asked. "What happened to your trousers?"

As he assisted Dora into the back of his car, Dora replied, "Oh my. I must have lost my pants. Did I leave them at your house? Did we have a good time?" Not knowing how long it would take the police or the ambulance to arrive, Sam took Dora straight to the emergency room at Gulf Coast University Hospital at the Texas Medical Center. Dora was severely cachectic. She was a relatively tall five foot six, but she weighed only eighty-eight pounds. The emergency room physician, Dr. Barber, found a palpable mass in the epigastric region of her abdomen, which was quite suspicious for a malignant process. A CT scan of the abdomen with oral contrast revealed a large tumor confluent with the inner lining of the stomach. If it was a malignancy, there were at least no obvious signs of extra-gastric metastases or peri-gastric lymphadenopathy. It seemed as if the patient had localized gastric cancer. If it was a localized cancer, perhaps it was potentially curable by surgical resection. When Dora was admitted to Dr. Gray's surgery service, Dr. Cornelius T. Polyp was called down to see if he could render an EGD fiber optic study to obtain biopsies of the suspicious gastric mass.

There appeared to be a fairly tight stricture at the gastroesophageal junction, and Dr. Polyp was unable to snake the EGD scope into the patient's stomach. Balloon-dilatation procedures were not available at the Gulf Coast General Hospital in 1980, so Dr. Polyp attempted to open a passageway between the esophagus and stomach by utilizing a progressive series of fusiform-tipped, rubber bougies to stretch out the sphincter, but this procedure proved to be unsuccessful.

After Dora was admitted to the hospital, the patient's case was presented at the scheduled tumor board where the experts rendered the opinion that the only possible course of action was an exploratory procedure, which meant using a surgical scalpel to open the stomach and then see what was inside.

During the operation, Dr. Gray and his team discovered a large trichobezoar in Dora's stomach that was encapsulated by a thick wall of mucoid slime. In layman's terms, the patient was found to have a giant, foreign wad of hair in her stomach that was the size of a baseball! The patient was literally starving to death because hair is not readily digested or easily passed through the gastrointestinal system of a human being.

After the bezoar was extracted, an intra-operative dilation of the GE junction was undertaken. Once Dr. Gray successfully finished the operation, the foreign material was sent off to the Pathology Department, which confirmed that the patient had indeed been afflicted by a large gastric hairball. The hair did not appear to be human hair however! Obviously, this was a rather disturbing revelation for the medical personnel involved with Dora's case.

A day later, the hair ball was shipped off to the AFIP national laboratory for further evaluation. All recognized mammals—and according to Dr. Sassman, even some mammals that have not yet been formally recognized—have scientific hair analyses recorded in a central data bank. This information has all been catalogued for reference purposes. The consulting pathology laboratory informed the

Gulf Coast facility that the hair ball belonged to a rather common specific species known as, *Felis catus domestica*. It appeared, for no other better explanation, that Dora had been ingesting cat fur!

With that shocking tidbit of information, it was now time for a division of labor. Dr. Gray assigned J. D. Brewster the task of finding out if Dora was licking her house cats. Ben Fielder and Willy Mammon had to contact the Social Service Department and Adult Protective Services to assay the patient's living conditions. Fielder and the Wooly Mammoth would need to personally scope out Mrs. Garza's living situation by visually inspecting her domicile.

Fielder and Wooly Mammoth discovered that Mrs. Dora Garza was destitute and that her living conditions were, at best, rather deplorable. Unread newspapers were stacked from floor to ceiling, and there were cats. Lots of cats. Some of them had died from starvation and been cannibalized by their surviving relatives. Fielder, Mammoth, and the social workers counted twenty-seven felines in Mrs. Garza's home. It took animal control and the SPCA a full day to round up all the semi-feral felines.

Antonia Alabaster and her television crew from Your Witness News aired an entire segment on the matter. The Dora Garza story was also printed in the newspaper. Since Mrs. Garza avidly collected but no longer read any newspapers, she would never know that she had become relatively famous.

Upon visiting his girlfriend, Stella, that evening, Brewster asked, "Hi, sweetie. How was your day?"

"I had a terrible day!" Stella responded. "This afternoon, I tried to give Mr. Checkers a bath—and look what he did to me." Stella's arms were covered with scratches inflicted by her pet cat.

"You know, Stella, I have a way with animals," Brewster said. "They love me. I'll be happy to make sure that Mr. Checkers gets a proper bath. All I need you to do is give me the little plastic box with the handle on it that you tote Checkers around with. If you put your cat in a box, I'll take care of the rest."

"You are such a dear to me!" Stella replied. "Wait, before you go, I want to show you the new sunflower that I am going to start wearing." Stella went off to her bedroom and returned with a giant plastic sunflower that was the size of a dinner platter, now embedded in her hair. Strategically placed behind her left ear, Stella was eager to garnish Brewster's opinion regarding her new accessory. "Tell me the truth—does this flower make my face look too big?"

"No, it looks perfect on you!"

The following day, Brewster's colleagues were waiting for him in the Vinyl Lounge.

"Pull the pillowcase off the box that you're carrying," Fielder said. "I need to know exactly what shenanigans that you're up to."

"Fat chance," Brewster replied. "Patience is a virtue."

"Whatever you're planning," Mammon said, "you better not bring a load of shit down upon our heads."

"Oh, ye of little faith," Brewster said. "Okay, ladies. Come with me."

Brewster led his two colleagues up to the med-surg unit where he pulled off the pillowcase that was covering the tote box. The student removed the frightened cat from its carrying case and then gently passed Mr. Checkers to Mrs. Garza. "Here, Dora. I have a present for you."

Without a word, Dora took the cat and started to lick it with long, deliberate, and delicate sweeps of her tongue.

"Dora," Brewster said, "it looks like you missed a couple of spots inside the cat's ears."

"No, don't worry," Dora replied. "I always save the best for last, and I won't forget to do it before I'm finished."

Brewster snorted loudly, and Ben Fielder started to howl with laughter.

The wooly one however, was not amused in the least. "You're a couple of sick bastards, I tell you. This poor lady is going to get another hair ball in her stomach, Brewster. When she does, I'll hunt you down and shove a dead cat up your ass end."

"Chill! Dig this, big man," Brewster said. "I brought along a jar of powdered meat tenderizer. After Dora is through cleaning the cat, I'll jam a couple tablespoons of meat tenderizer into her *boca* and have her chase it down with a glass of water. This will dissolve the cat hair, and she'll poop it right out. I have demonstrated to you gentleman that without a doubt, Dora Garza does indeed enjoy licking cats. When she eventually gets discharged, she should never be allowed to live alone again. I am providing a magnanimous public service with this revelation that you've both now witnessed."

"What happened to you, Brewster?" Willy asked. "You used to be somebody I respected."

"Look, this is a win-win situation for all concerned parties," Brewster said. "Mr. Checkers is enjoying a nice tongue bath. My girlfriend will be happy that her cat got groomed. Mrs. Dora Garza is clearly enjoying the lingual dispensation of customized feline hygiene. Trust me. This has turned out to be a very successful day."

Willy Mammon left the room in disgust. He informed his colleagues that he would not be working on the next scheduled clinical rotation with them. He went off to find the social worker who had been assigned to Dora's case. It was quite clear that the deranged individual should not be allowed to live alone by herself in the future. Ben Fielder had gone off to tell Adult Protective Services the exact same thing.

When Mammon was finished, he went to administration to request a change in his next clinical clerkship rotation. If Brewster was on a malignant path of self-destruction, Willy Mammon was not about to have any part of it.

Brewster retreated to the nurse's desk with Mr. Checkers safely penned up in the tote box. The medical student had to complete a clinical note, but he was surprised to find that Dora had followed him out to the workstation.

"Mr. Brewster, may I have my hair ball back?"

"What are you talking about, Dora?" Brewster asked. "Why in the world would you want it back?"

"It's valuable."

"How so?" Brewster asked.

"Well," Dora explained, "I might need it for a spare part someday."

Brewster didn't even bother to look up from the task at hand when he replied, "No, it's locked up in the hair ball vault down at the

First National Trichobezoar Bank of Bellaire. You can't have it back because now it belongs to us."

"So, it's in your possession?"

"At least for the time being," Brewster chuckled. "If you'll be so kind to excuse me, I'm a bit busy right now."

"That's fine with me—as long as you boys are able to keep it in a safe place."

"Dora, you're butt naked," Brewster said as he finally took a moment to scrutinize the elderly and confused woman standing directly in front of him. "Let's get you back into your room and get a hospital gown on you."

"Oh my," Dora said. "I must have lost my pants. Did I leave them at your house?"

"When I go back to my apartment this evening," Brewster said, "I'll make a point of checking the clothes dryer."

"Did we have a good time?"

"Oh, yes, Dora," Brewster said. "We most assuredly had a good time!"

# 8

# INFERNAL MEDICINE ROTATION

When J. D. Brewster arrived in the Vinyl Lounge, Ben Fielder poured him a cup of coffee. "Do you take it hot and black like your women?"

"Don't be a smartass," Brewster replied. "Hand me a couple of packs of creamer, and I'll be good. How are things with you now that you've moved into Uncle John's garage apartment?"

"It's perfect," Ben answered. "I'm close enough to ride my bike to the Gulf Coast when the weather is decent, and I can leave my gas-hog pickup truck parked. Your uncle's a creepy dude though."

"How so?"

"Check this out," Ben said. "On more than one occasion, I've awakened to find him peering at me through the window. I shit you not! He climbs up on an extension ladder to watch me, and he's usually only wearing nasty, worn-out, orca-print boxer shorts and a flimsy pair of flip-flops that appear to be on the threshold of a blow-out at any moment."

"What?!"

"Last night I caught him in the act. He was a Peeping Tom, I tell you!" Fielder continued, "I pulled out my pecker and I shook it at him. He seemed pleased enough by my response, but I assure you that my honest intention was to merely demonstrate my male dominance."

"I hope that you didn't upset John," Brewster said. "He can be a bit volatile."

"He eventually climbed back down the ladder and went inside his house, presumably to flog the dolphin," Fielder said. "Is that weird or what?"

"Well, I don't really know," Brewster replied. "It all seems like perfectly normal behavior to me."

"Why am I not surprised?" Ben said. "I can't believe we're starting this next rotation on the Internal Medicine Service without Willy Mammon. I always thought we were the three musketeers."

"Perhaps I went a bit overboard on the joke that we played on Mrs. Dora Garza."

"You think?" Ben Fielder asked.

"She was a sweet old lady, and she sure as hell did nothing to deserve what I did to her."

"I suppose not," Fielder concurred.

"I have no doubt in my mind that I've become an industrial-strength bastard. For the love of Jesus, I enticed a demented patient to lick a cat," Brewster said. "Sometimes, I just don't know what's wrong with me."

"Yeah, but I was in on it, too," Fielder replied. "Maybe we're both Nazi trolls. It looks like the Wooly Mammoth got butt hurt over all of that, but hopefully he'll get over it. I found out he's doing his mandatory clerkship in pediatrics this month."

"I think it would be a big hoot to watch that jolly giant trying to gently cradle a tiny baby. Do you think that he could palm a little kid like a basketball?" Brewster asked.

"No doubt."

"You could be his coach and say, 'Take it strong to the hole, Mammoth!' He'd take off from the free throw line and dunk the child through the net like Moses Malone."

"That's a sick thought," Fielder said, "but I hope it's not the last that we'll see of him. You know, that first rotation on the burn unit changed us all for the better."

"Say what?"

"Well, as far as I am concerned, it made me tough as nails. By the same token, I thought it would have made the big man a bit tougher too. As it has turned out, I found out he's still afraid of the dark," Fielder reported.

It was sad when Brewster realized that for some reason Ben Fielder believed the rotation on the burn unit had made them "better" somehow.

"Just hold on there for a minute, Slim Jim," Brewster countered. "Aren't you the same fellow who's still afraid of moths?"

"Touché, mi amigo," Fielder conceded. "Tell me, Brewster, what are you afraid of?"

Brewster thought for a moment and said, "Back in June, I was subjected to a public crucifixion when the Rabbi and I had the hepatitis B vaccine research study pulled out from under our feet. Back then, the director of the PhD program, Dr. Harrison Reed, asked me why I was trying to get through life as fast as I could on a dead sprint with the throttle wide open."

"Well, aren't you trying to do just that?" Fielder asked. "That certainly seems to be the case."

"Reed hurled an insightful accusation at me that I must have been afraid of life itself," Brewster answered. "At this juncture, I actually can't refute those brutal allegations. There must be an element of truth to what he had said."

"I just poured you a cup of coffee," Fielder said. "Take the time to enjoy the aroma before you gulp it down."

"Now that the big man has gone on to smaller and lesser things, who's going to be riding in the saddle with us for the next three months?"

"Two students from my class will be joining us," Fielder answered.

"One is Russian Bear, and the other is Felix 'Dung' Dunhill."

"So, there's a guy coming on board with us and his nickname is *Dung?*" Brewster asked while shaking his head. "You must be shitting me. What's his story?"

"Well, he tries hard … but perhaps he tries *too* hard. He's not a particularly tidy person, but he means well. I know he's the kind of guy who'll have your back. He'll definitely help you out anyway that he can."

"So, he's an industrious fellow, but he's a pigpen—or so it would seem," Brewster said. "Nice."

"You'll have to judge him by his own personal merits and eccentricities," Ben added.

"Okay, give me the lowdown on Russian Bear."

"His real name is Ilya Putinov," Ben explained. "After the Wooly Mammoth, Russian Bear will be the oldest person who'll be slated to graduate in 1982. He already has a medical degree from the Soviet Union, but their educational system is different than ours. In the USSR, medical students take an entrance exam right out of high school, and their medical school curriculum is a six-year program."

"Well, how in hell did he end up here in the land of the free and the home of the Atlanta Braves?"

"He was an exchange professor at the medical school in Havana, Cuba," Ben Fielder explained. "He and his wife, Larisa, went on an excursion to the Yucatán last year, and they both jumped ship. They got asylum in America, and Russian Bear was accepted here at the Gulf Coast College of Medicine, starting this past July. Like me, this will only be his fourth clinical rotation."

"It's not like the Soviet Union to allow married couples to go abroad together. They try to prevent defections like that from ever occurring," Brewster stated. "How did it happen?"

"I thought the same thing," Fielder said. "I asked the Rooskie the details, and he told me that he and Larisa we not married at the time. They were dating, but they were doing so in secrecy. Their defection was technically an elopement. She had a teaching position in Havana also at the school of nursing, and that's how they met. In order for Russian Bear to eventually practice medicine in the United States, it will be necessary for him to retake the last two years of medical school training on the clerkship rotations."

"Well, with his prior clinical experience, it should be a shot in the arm for the home team."

"One would think," Ben said. "A slot opened up for the clerkships after a student in my class had a nervous breakdown. The

Bear received a financial grant for tuition from some outfit called the Russian-American Friendship Society. The Texas State Board of Medical Examiners only gave him credit for his four years of classroom work in Russia, but they didn't give him any credit for his clinical rotations or his more recent postgraduate training. In any event, they certainly did *not* recognize that he already had a medical degree. It sucks for him, but that's just how it is."

"What's the story on his spouse?" Brewster asked. "Will she be able to work as a nurse here in the United States?"

"Larisa has an RN degree, and since a completely different governing body oversees nurses, I guess she's been given the green light to work here. She just passed her nursing boards and will be starting on the med-surg unit before the end of this year. I've only met Russian Bear briefly. He seems like a regular guy. For what it's worth, his English is excellent. I don't know anything about his wife, though, since I've not met her as of yet," Ben answered.

"I bet she has one big, furry Slavic hedgerow that crosses her entire brow ridge. She's probably a simian, Siberian, beast of a woman! Just the thought of a woman that beautiful is making my forehead start to sweat. I'm already conjuring up the romantic fantasy that she's a huge hairy monster! I wonder if she and Russian Bear would ever consider a three-way tag-team match with an 'Amerikanski'."

"You're a pig!" Ben Fielder said. "I don't know why I ever bother trying to talk to you."

"Relax, Slim. I'm just jerking your chain." If the truth be told, Brewster was suspicious of new people and new situations. "So, should I surmise that this Russian guy is a hard-core, godless atheist who lacks moral principles?"

"Something tells me that rudimentary Christianity and Judaism might have somehow survived in Russia over the last sixty-three years, despite the official policies of the Communist Party," Fielder replied. "Russian Bear is likely no better or worse than any other human being on this planet. He's probably just some poor, dumbass stumbling blindly through life like the rest of us, but I guess that remains to be seen. There's one other thing I need to tell you that will no doubt brighten your day."

"What might that be?"

"We'll be working with the intern, Dr. Price, again," Fielder explained.

"Wait!" Brewster exclaimed. "How could that be? We're entering the internal medicine clerkships, and he was an intern on the surgery service. I don't understand why a surgery intern would need to do a rotation on an internal medicine team."

"Well, come to find out," Ben answered, "Price was *not* a surgery service intern after all."

"What is he then?" Brewster asked. "A jack-shit intern in some jack-shit specialty?"

"The son of a bitch is doing a *general* internship, and he's not going to pursue a specialty at this time in his life."

"Swell," Brewster added. "I heard that some idiot stuffed a silicone cockroach novelty toy into his burrito a while back. Rumor has it that Price ended up puking his guts out. That's not something he's likely to forget about anytime soon."

"Time will tell," Fielder added. "I know damn well that if he ever figures out that you and I were somehow involved with that little comic caper, there'll be hell to pay, amigo."

In October, the sweltering Houston humidity finally started to abate. By 8:50 a.m., Dung and Russian Bear had finally arrived at the Vinyl Lounge.

Felix Dunhill was a chain-smoker. Surprisingly, in 1980, the Gulf Coast College of Medicine and University Hospital had no rules or regulations against smoking on campus. Dunhill would smoke during classroom lectures and clinical rounds. In retrospect, it was quite astonishing that such behavior was permissible, but that was indeed the case.

When Dung entered the Vinyl Lounge, a lit unfiltered Morley cigarette was dangling from his mouth. It was well recognized by his colleagues that once one of these unfiltered smokes was tightly clenched between his lips, Dung would never pull one of the lit cigarettes away from his nicotine-stained teeth—not even to feign the effort to flick off the ashes. As such, his shirt, necktie, and white consultation jacket were always peppered with charred pinholes from the hot cigarette cinders that would invariably fall from the tips of the perpetually burning coffin sticks. Oddly enough, for some reason, Dunhill would rarely even bother to brush the smoldering ashes off of his tattered clothing either!

If any of his colleagues were ever annoyed enough to comment about his unkempt appearance, only then would Dung make a point of sweeping the malodorous ashes from his clothing, and he'd dust the debris directly upon the offended party. His shirttail was never tucked in, and the patchy five o'clock shadow on his face was a perfect complement to his coif, which could only be best described as "Sunday-brunch bed hair."

A rumor circulated through the medical school that Dung was accepted into the 1978 entrance class at the Gulf Coast College of Medicine because his father was an attending physician on the Gulf Coast University Hospital's rehabilitation unit.

"Wow, Dung, I like your necktie," Ben Fielder said. "Do you have to pay extra for ones that have the tiny pinholes burned right into your garments already? Maybe it's like buying a pair of faded, prewashed blue jeans."

Russian Bear remained at attention as Brewster approached him. J. D. ran his hands over the Bear's scalp. "I don't have any horns coming out of my skull," Russian Bear said. "However, if you want me to drop my trousers so you can see if I have a pointed prehensile tail attached to my coccygeal bones, then you're going to have to kiss my ass. I can also assure you that I have five toes at the end of each foot, so you won't find evidence of a cloven hoof hiding in my shoe."

Brewster smiled and said, "If that's indeed the case, I think we're going to get along just fine. There's just not enough room for two demons on this rotation."

The four new colleagues headed up to the med-surg unit to meet their team leaders and start their new clerkship rotation. The new attending was Dr. Marek Cannon, and the resident was Lawdy

Garth Penn. The intern on the team was none other than the overbearing, corpulent Dr. Price.

After recovering from a gastrointestinal bleeding event that was a consequence of an impractical joke gone awry, Price rotated over to work on Dr. Cannon's internal medicine service.

"Well, well, well," Dr. Price said as he eyed Brewster and Fielder with considerable suspicion. "It's indeed a very small world."

"And indeed a very bad one to boot," Fielder countered.

"I'm quite surprised that you don't seem to be particularly happy to be working with us again," Brewster said. "On behalf of Ben Fielder, it's certainly an honor to have a chance to collaborate with you on this new rotation."

"Stow it." With a malevolent smile, Dr. Price leaned forward and whispered, "Listen to me, you monkey-fucking son of a bitch; I happen to know exactly what kind of man you are. Rest assured, I'm going to be looking for any opportunity to rip your head off and shit down your neck hole. I just can't prove it yet that it was you or maybe Fielder who put that rubber cockroach in my burrito."

"Dr. Price," Brewster said, "I just don't know what you're talking about. If you don't recall, it was Fielder, Mammon, and I who saved you when we got you down to the emergency room pronto. We even stood by to assist while Dr. Polyp shoved a fiber optic scope up your ass."

"It was down my throat," Price said, "not up my ass."

"Whatever," Brewster said. "Six of one and half a dozen of another as far as I can tell."

"Enough, dickwad!" It was clear that Dr. Price was fully capable of making the internal medicine rotation a miserable experience for the four students on Dr. Cannon's team.

"It looks like I owe you an apology Brewster," Dr. Cannon said. "It appears that you were telling me the truth when you said that you were already promoted to the rank of stud. How about you other three gentleman? Now that all of you have completed three other rotations before you came to my service, I surmise that all of you are at least scut puppies by now. Is that the case?"

Russian Bear and Ben Fielder confirmed that they had been promoted to the rank of scut puppy, but Felix was still stuck at the rank of mushroom.

"Well, if you do a good job here, you might have a chance to advance in rank," Dr. Cannon replied. "It's time to get started. I'll have the resident and intern divide up the patients between the four of you, and I want you to round on them this morning. We'll reconvene this afternoon to discuss the cases."

After Dr. Cannon departed, Dr. Penn gave the patient census list to Dr. Price and instructed him to divide up the seventeen patients on the service. Since Brewster held the rank of stud, he was assigned five patients, and his three colleagues received four patients each.

Lawdy Garth Penn wanted to have a private word with Brewster before she left for the library. "Give me the dope on the Irene Segulla situation. Any arrests made?"

"It looks like the case has gone cold," Brewster answered. "It's been four months now, and the authorities are apparently no closer to finding who was involved in her assault."

Dr. Penn handed the reins of the service over to Dr. Price upon her departure. The intern looked over the four students and said, "If I ever catch any of you two assholes getting involved in any monkey business, you're going to think that your rotation on the burn unit was a walk in the park. For you, this will not be an 'internal medicine' rotation. If you screw up, I assure you that it will turn out to be an 'infernal medicine' rotation."

Dr. Price turned to Dung and said, "Good grief! You're one sorry sack of shit. What in hell is the matter with you? You smell like an ashtray and look like a hobo. If you don't shape up, you'll never make it to the rank of scut puppy. I'll make sure of that. It's time for a game of pimp and pone."

Dr. Price pointed to Felix Dunhill and said, "Batter up, dirtbag. Here's the first pitch. Sixty years ago, gastric adenocarcinoma was one of the top causes of cancer related death in the United States. What common household appliance—in conjunction with the development of an electrical power grid in this country—was introduced in the 1920s and coincided with the sudden and dramatic decline of gastric cancer in our nation?"

"May I use a pinch hitter to help me with this pitch?" Dung asked. "Yes, you may, but this will be the only pinch hitter you'll be allowed to call upon during this round of pimp and pone."

Felix looked to his three colleagues for help, but no assistance was forthcoming.

"The answer is *refrigeration*," Dr. Price interjected. "After human beings figured out how to keep food from spoiling so quickly, gastric cancer became a relatively rare disease. You're pathetic, Dunhill. With the hints that I threw out from the bullpen, you should've been able to figure out that answer. Here is the second pitch. What volume of air is necessary to be rapidly and forcefully injected into a person's vascular system to induce an acute, fatal pulmonary embolism?"

"Are you mad?" Russian Bear asked. "How could such information ever be relevant unless a student was planning on killing a hospitalized individual or staff member?"

Price squinted at Russian Bear and said, "Shut up, Rooskie! In the game of pimp and pone, the fans in the bleachers are not allowed to participate unless they're called upon as pinch hitters. If you must know an answer as to why I asked such an esoteric question, it's simply because there are two specific medical students on this rotation that I truly despise. Is that not that correct, Mr. Brewster?"

"I have no idea what you are talking about," Brewster said. "Do you not?" Price said. "You see, as I already explained, I know what kind of man *you* are, Brewster. Now, with that second pitch that I just threw out to Mr. Pigpen over here, I just wanted you and Mr. Fielder to know what kind of man *I* am."

"Is that a threat?" Fielder asked.

"Take it any way you see fit, beanpole." Dr. Price turned back to Dunhill. "I'm waiting. I've thrown out another pitch, dipshit. Mr. Pigpen, I command you to now answer the question."

Again, Dung couldn't come up with a reply.

"Fifty to one hundred milliliters of air rapidly pushed into a person's vein should do the trick," Price said. "The bolus injection of that much air would likely lodge just past the right ventricle at the bifurcation of the right and left pulmonary artery. Theoretically, it should cause a sudden-death event that would be nearly *impossible* for a forensic pathologist to ever discover! If you ask me, that would be the perfect way to murder somebody in this hospital and then get away with it! Strike two, Dung."

"I must say, that seems to be pretty valuable information," Dung said as he glared at Dr. Price with unbridled hatred.

"Here comes the third pitch. Name the top three types of viruses that are thought to be responsible for causing the common cold."

Fortunately, Felix Dunhill was able to avoid complete humiliation. "Subtypes of the rhinovirus are thought to cause about eighty percent of the cases of common coryza, while fifteen percent of cases are thought to be caused by the coronavirus, and another five percent are thought to be caused by adenoviruses."

Price was clearly disappointed that he wasn't able to pitch a shutout. "You'll be stuck as a mushroom for the rest of your miserable medical school career if you don't do better than that. Here's the list of patients you all need to see. Get to work, morons."

Wooly Mammoth had his cast removed from his arm and wanted to celebrate by taking his new girlfriend out for dinner at an Italian restaurant. While enjoying a cup of coffee and splitting a plate of tiramisu for dessert, Cheryl asked, "What caused the fallout that you had with J. D. and Ben Fielder?"

The big man became angry and rapped his knuckles on the table. "Brewster was starting to become ornery. I saw him do some things that just weren't right. J. D. and Ben carried on with some crazy shit that was just downright mean and cruel. What they were up to was just about to drag me down. If they're jumpin' off the rails, I don't want any part of it. I swear to Jesus, I should've boxed their ears."

"So, are you telling me that you've never done any crazy shit that was just downright mean and cruel?" Cheryl leaned back in her chair.

Willy looked down at the dessert plate and stabbed away at the tiramisu with his fork as if he was trying to injure the tasty innocent treat.

Cheryl said, "Willy, are you okay?"

"Pardon me for a moment, Cheryl," Willy said. "I have to use the restroom. I'll be right back."

The restroom was a 'one-holer', which afforded Willy the opportunity to lock the door behind him. He peeled off his clothing and carefully scrutinized the fabric of his blouse to make absolutely certain that the permanent stain of blood on his torso was not leaching through his skin and onto his clothing.

Willy Mammon remembered that he had murdered a prisoner of war in Vietnam. Willy Mammon remembered that he had pulverized the leg of a defenseless man who had been handcuffed to the leg of a table at the police station. Willy Mammon remembered the scriptures as recorded in John 8:7 and he suddenly felt a twinge of hypocrisy and guilt.

When he returned to the table, Cheryl asked, "What's wrong, Willy? You're drenched with sweat!"

"You're correct, Cheryl," Willy said. "I have to make things right with my good buddies."

"You know," Cheryl said, "they have a three-hole pitch-and-putt golf course over at the VA Annex in Bellaire. As you're a service-connected 'Nam vet, you can use those facilities over there any time you want. You should get together with Brewster and Fielder, and the three of you can take out your frustrations on a little white ball."

"Never played golf before," Willy said defensively, "and those other boys would probably just laugh at me."

"Now, I'm already a licensed nurse. You're going to be a doctor someday, are you not?" Cheryl asked. "You better learn how to play golf now because that's what doctors do on Wednesday afternoons. No man of mine is going to be sitting on the sidelines of life just because he's, well—"

"I believe the word that you are looking for is 'black,' is it not?"

—◦◦◦❦◈❦◦◦◦—

At the University of Houston, the Dalton twins had settled into the fall semester of their junior year. Unfortunately, the severe headaches had worsened for D' Shea, and she secretly feared that something was quite wrong. Denial can only last so long before the truth rears its ugly head. Earlier in the summer, the headaches were only intermittent. By the fall of 1980, the headaches were becoming chronic, and the pain was tormenting her around the clock.

On campus, one of D' Shea Dalton's friends suffered an encounter with poison ivy and developed a nasty rash on her arms and legs. The physician at the University Health Center had placed the young woman on a course of the steroid medication known as prednisone in an effort to make the extraordinarily uncomfortable rash recede. After her outbreak of poison ivy had abated, the young coed offered D' Shea the rest of the prescription to see if it might help with her headaches.

D' Shea found a pharmacology book at the library and learned that prednisone was a powerful anti-inflammatory medication, and she thought the steroid could cool off her daily headaches, nausea, and vomiting. D' Shea was pleasantly surprised to find that just one twenty-milligram prednisone tablet was completely successful in controlling her crushing headache symptoms. Unfortunately, the steroid medication was only a finger in the dike. The powerful medication allowed D' Shea to complete the first semester of her junior year without further difficulty. If she could get through the semester, she thought everything else would fall into place. She promised herself that she would eventually make an appointment to see a neurology specialist. All she had to do was to hang tough until the end of December.

Nog was starting to slowly heal up from his leg injury, but he was still in a cast and on crutches. When the Wooly Mammoth had thrown himself across Nog's right leg, both the cartilage and the anterior and posterior cruciate ligaments, which essentially comprised the hinge mechanism of the right knee, were completely sheared away.

To compound his injury, Nog also suffered a fracture of the proximal tibia bone. After his injury, the police simply threw him out of the police station and into the back alleyway with the explicit intent that the car thief would have to fend for himself.

After his injury, Nog was able to hitch a ride to the emergency room. Once there, he told the doctors a fabricated story that he had merely fallen down a flight of stairs. Nog underwent orthopedic repair as a noninsured charity case. The orthopedist who helped in the management of Smeg Nog's care was none other than the hippie, stoner, surfer dude from California named, Dr. Bay.

When the orthopedic doctor in training first met Smeg Nog, the resident physician said, "It's way cool, man. Dig this, gnarly dude. The bone can clone!"

Where had Nog heard that expression before? After his leg was pulverized in the interrogation room, his assailant, the Wooly Mammoth, had made the same unusual proclamation. There was no way that it was simply a coincidence. Nog slowly smiled and nodded when he came to the realization that everything in the universe was connected somehow. Surely, his assailants must have been associated with the Gulf Coast College of Medicine in some capacity. With that realization, seeking revenge against the perpetrator who had permanently crippled him had become a much easier task.

Nog was unable to participate in any "inventory acquisition" for the chop shop, and his partner in crime was under considerable pressure.

"When are you going to get well?" Big asked.

"You ask me the same goddamn question every day, and I always give you the same goddamn answer. I'll get well when I get well."

"Don't get snippy with me, you little maggot!" Big exclaimed. "I'm totin' all the mail here."

"I'll make it up to you as soon as I'm able."

"I never gave you the green light to steal that Caddy on your own accord," Big said.

"Well," Nog explained, "if that Caddy wasn't saddled with crappy brakes, I would've pulled it off."

"Something doesn't make sense to me," Big said. "How did you skate without having *any* formal charges levied against you?"

"Just lucky, I guess."

Big had no idea that the pistol that had been used to execute Uncle John's wife and Feral Cheryl's father during the botched cigar store robbery was now in the hands of the police. If Big Nig had realized the pistol was undergoing ballistic testing, he would have killed Smeg Nog on the spot and fled to Mexico.

Smeg Nog kept his mouth shut and hoped the confiscated weapon would not come back and bite either of them in the butt for the brutal execution-style murders that they had committed twelve years earlier at the cigar shop on South Main.

In October, it became quite obvious to J. D. Brewster that Felix Dunhill had discontinued bathing altogether. On morning rounds, Dung's colleagues would make certain that they were more than an arm's length away from the malodorous student who at that point in time had become a venerable pariah.

Dung was still saddled with the humiliating designation of being a lowly mushroom. No matter how hard he tried, he just couldn't earn the promotion to the rank of scut puppy. Dung was the only team member who was subjected to daily pimp and pone torment. At the two-week mark of the one-month rotation, he repeatedly suffered ignominious defeat and had been thoroughly pimped every time he was intellectually challenged. His overall fund of knowledge was modest at best, and he was not able to win even one round of the competition.

Initially, Dr. Price would openly ridicule Dung with a barrage of obscure clinical questions. At the mid-rotation mark, Dr. Penn and Dr. Marek Cannon smelled blood in the water (as well as Dung's body odor) and seemed to relish in the student's downward spiral.

On one occasion after pitching a shutout, Dr. Penn said, "Felix, your nickname is certainly deserved. I can't believe it, but you're zero for sixteen in the pimp and pone challenge. You're worthless. I guess you're going to be a mushroom for the rest of your miserable life. I don't give a damn if your father is an attending on the rehabilitation unit. If you can't win even one pimp and pone contest, I'm going to make sure you don't get any credit for this rotation. I'm certain that nepotism is the only reason why you got admitted to this medical school in the first place."

"If you go running off to your daddy," Dr. Price said, adding further insult to injury. "Don't even think about asking him for an end-around promotion to scut puppy status, I'll mow you down so fast that you'll end up shitting your brains out all over the floor!"

Well, that was it. Unable to fend off the attacks that were now coming from all sides, Felix Dunhill was irreparably broken. From that point on, Dung never took off his white consultation jacket. In fact, he would even sleep in it. Perhaps, if he never took it off, it would somehow magically make him a better student. Whenever a body fluid or stain appeared on the consultation jacket, Dung circled the stain and wrote down the offending material and the date of the stain as a memento!

Until the twenty-first century, the football helmet was used as a weapon. High school and college athletes who played defense were taught to use the facemask and the crown of the helmet to inflict pain and injury when tackling opponents. This technique would invariably leave gashes and discoloration on the headgear. These marks, stains, and gashes served as venerable badges of courage.

A running back might think twice about trying to block down on a defensive end in a game if his opponent was wearing a helmet covered with gashes and paint chips that marred the stripes and decals that adorned the headgear. It was implicit that an opponent wearing such a marred helmet was one mentally and physically tough hombre.

As it turned out, Felix Dunhill was only trying to create the illusion to his internal medicine team through the imagery of his filthy white consultation jacket that he was a mentally and physically tough medical student—and perhaps a man not to be trifled with. Unfortunately, it was nothing more than a smoke screen that percolated from the perpetually lit cigarettes that dangled from his lips.

At first, Dung's bizarre mannerisms were a big joke to everybody. Sadly, nobody realized that Felix Dunhill had been mortally wounded—and an injured animal is a very dangerous animal indeed.

Antonio Mendez was an undocumented migrant. No, that's not correct. Anybody who's in the United States without proper documentation and has come into this country to specifically perpetrate criminal activity north of the Rio Bravo is an *illegal alien*. There's no need for using euphemistic bullshit liberal verbiage at this juncture. Although he was a member of a violent criminal enterprise known as the *SM-31 Banditos*, Mendez allegedly wanted to apply for work as a gardener in the wealthy and predominantly black community of Riverside Terrace, immediately east of the Texas Medical Center. He told the police when he was arrested that he only wanted to drop off his resume at the stylish four-bedroom home where he was seeking employment. Unfortunately, the homeowners were out of town on vacation, and the house was all locked up as tight as a drum. Well, what was Mendez supposed to do if nobody was at home? There was no sense in ringing the doorbell at 3:16 in the morning.

The only viable option Mendez had was to use a crowbar to pry open a skylight and leave his resume on the dining room table. Yeah, that's the ticket. While he was inside the home, he found that the family had an entire silverware set that had become very tarnished, in addition to many other valuables in the vacant home that appeared to be somewhat dusty. As Mendez was a courteous follow, he gathered up all the expensive items that he could find and then he wrapped them up in a bed sheet. He told the police that he planned to haul away the various luxuries and give them all a proper dusting and thorough polishing before he returned the treasured heirlooms to their rightful owners.

Being a very thoughtful and gracious gentleman, Mendez had left all the lights off to make certain that he didn't awaken or disturb any of the adjacent neighbors while he was quietly applying for a new job in the wee hours of the morning. Wow. What a nice guy. Every woke liberal should have a neighbor like this man. In any event, he had unfortunately fallen down the stairwell in the darkness and severely fractured his ankle. He tried to leave the home through the front door, but the security system was triggered as soon as he tried to limp away with his bundle of valuables.

After he was arrested and charged with burglary, which was probably just a big misunderstanding on the part of the evil law enforcement authorities who were obviously predominantly white and cruelly saddled with overt racist ideations, the alleged criminal was brought to the Gulf Coast University Hospital for an open surgical reduction and internal fixation of his fractured extremity. If convicted of a felony, Mendez would have been deported to Mexico. For that reason, he had received pro bono legal counsel from the overtly racist, anti-American, Mexican supremacy group known as "Hispanics Without Borders." This group had an inflammatory, anti-Anglo motto: *"Para los Mexicanos, todo. Para los Gringos, nada."* Needless to say, if the tables were turned, and this was a white supremacy group, a similar inflammatory, anti-Hispanic motto would likely have caused riots in the streets.

Postoperatively, Mendez developed a blood clot in his lower extremity, and the orthopedic surgeons requested a consultation from the internal medicine physicians to help manage the thrombotic event. Dr. Price assigned Dung Dunhill to the case, although Dunhill couldn't speak Spanish and the patient knew little if any English. After the resident physician started the patient on an intravenous blood thinner known as heparin, Dung went back into the patient's room and tried to conduct an interview without any success.

"Hey, Brewster," Dung said. "I've heard that you speak Spanish."

"No, but I speak Mexican," Brewster replied. "In our society, that's even a better commodity. How may I be of service to you?"

"I've been assigned this joker who suffered a veno-occlusive thromboembolic event after he underwent an ORIF repair of a fractured ankle. I'm trying to get some history from this guy, but I can't make heads or tails of what he's trying to say to me. Frankly, he scares the crap out of me. He has some really nasty tattoos on his face, and I don't know what they mean."

"I'll help you figure out what this guy's all about," Brewster said.

Upon entering the room, Brewster asked Antonio Mendez about his true intentions on why he crossed the border illegally. The student received more than a snoot full of hostile but nonetheless honest answers. After gathering a history of events, Brewster turned to Dunhill to explain what was going on. "This man says that he belongs to a gang that calls themselves 'SM-31'. I, for one, have never heard of these *banditos*," Brewster reported. "Have you?"

"Nope—neither have I!"

"In any event, if we don't treat him with the deferential respect that he believes that he deserves, his associates will come by and pay us a rather unpleasant visit," Brewster explained.

"Is that so?" Dung asked. "What will happen to us?"

"It won't be pretty," Brewster answered. "His friends will hack us up with machetes—but not before they gouge our eyes out with a grapefruit spoon."

"Nice!" Dung said. "I have absolutely no intention of dancing a tango with a bunch of drug dealers. Why was this guy sent here to our facility without a prison guard? This bastard's not even in handcuffs!"

"Beats the shit out of me," Brewster answered. "Out on bail, maybe? He claims that his gang members constitute the first wave of the 'Reconquesta.' Above and beyond basic low-life criminal activity, he states that his gang has come here across the border to repatriate the Southwest part of United States back to Mexico. He says the gringos are pussies and we can't do shit about it."

"Why in hell do we let people like this into our damned country?"

"Well, technically, I don't think this hombre was sent an engraved invitation to cross the Bravo," Brewster answered. "Check this out— this asshole just said we need to learn how to speak Spanish because someday, in the near future, we'll again be under the rule of Mexico. He said that Anglos are an inferior ethnic group, and he refuses to answer any further questions. Good luck, Dung. I think I should leave this room before I try to choke the shit out of this guy."

As Brewster headed toward the door, he turned to Mendez and rudely explained to him in Spanish that if Mexico didn't want to lose a third of its territory to the gringos, then Mexico shouldn't have declared war on the United States back in 1845. In English, Brewster added one final insult. "To the victors goes the spoils. Deal with it, fuck wad! When the criminal justice system is done with your sorry ass, you'll eventually get shipped back to Mexico. *Adios, muchacho*."

Brewster was totally unaware of the effect his hostile reactionary response would have on his emotionally challenged colleague because, at that point, Dung was starting to place much greater faith in the *clinical* justice system than the *criminal* justice system. After Brewster left the room, Dunhill elected to dispense a generous measure of retribution by swapping out the intravenous drip of the anticoagulant called heparin with a simple bag of normal saline. Nobody would ever realize what Dunhill had accomplished as the student removed the adhesive medication identification label from the bag containing heparin and placed it upon the bag that contained only normal saline. The student quickly disposed of the real bag previously medicated with heparin into a trash bin to make certain that his ruse would remain clandestine.

In the morning, Antonio Mendez developed bilateral pulmonary emboli. The criminal visitor to the United States started to suffer from stabbing pleuritic chest pain, and he was also expectorating bloody phlegm.

Felix Dunhill was secretly delighted with his own vicious handiwork. The clots that had showered into the patient's lungs would leave him permanently injured. Mendez was now a pulmonary cripple who would be afflicted with chronic shortness of breath and eventual pulmonary hypertension. Upon the eventual deportation of Antonio Mendez back to Mexico, his residual poor pulmonary reserve ensured that the SM-31 gang member would never again be able to try to illegally sneak back into the United States. Ultimately, the violent gang member would be eventually doomed to suffer a premature death from right-sided congestive heart failure while languishing in a filthy, roach invested Mexican prison. So sad…

Brewster had his own patients to attend to at that time. Mr. Harold McCord was an octogenarian who had a remarkable claim to fame. The frail patient was a former ground crew member of the "Valiant 38" that had flown Spad biplanes for the Lafayette Americaine division of the Escadrille during World War I. When Brewster learned that McCord had personally known James Doolittle, J. D. had made a point to learn everything he could about what Mr. McCord remembered about the "War to End All Wars".

Unfortunately, Father Time was starting to have an adverse effect on Harold's mental faculties, and he was starting to demonstrate a variety of bizarre behaviors. On the day he was admitted to the hospital, Mr. McCord had crawled into the emergency room as if he were a quadruped. He had a large cardboard sign around his neck that said: "Hello, my name is Harold McCord. I have a dangerous cardiac arrhythmia called 'Atrial Fibrillation.' Please help me." Mr. McCord had apparently forgotten to take his digoxin anti-arrhythmia medication for several days, and the consequence of this oversight was the early morning onset of a rapid, irregular heart rate and associated hypotension.

It appeared that Mr. McCord was beachcombing with a metal detector when he found a dead bottlenose dolphin that had washed upon the shore and was in the advanced stages of decomposition. The dead cetacean was being consumed by hungry crabs, seagulls, and large turkey vultures that had swooped down to partake of the feast. Sadly, Mr. McCord had erroneously believed that one of the carrion-consuming buzzards was a large chicken, and he grabbed the bird by its feet and took it home to eat for supper. The doomed buzzard, for its part, could only hiss and flap its wings in protest to a pending untimely demise that would no doubt be a rather undignified terminal event.

When the elderly gentleman presented the bird to his wife to prepare for supper, she said, "This is the ugliest chicken I've ever seen. It don't got no dad-burn hair on top of its hair, but I'll cook it up rare just as you like it."

No form of fowl should ever be consumed raw or rare, especially a buzzard that dines exclusively on carrion. Also, since chickens don't have hair (and neither do buzzards for that matter), it would have been safe to assume that Mrs. McCord, like her husband, was also a taco shy of a combo platter at that point as a consequence to her advanced age. In any event, it was the foulest-tasting fowl that either of them had ever consumed. After dinner, Mr. McCord suddenly developed abdominal cramps in addition to diarrhea, and that's when he decided to turn in early that evening.

The following morning, the multiple episodes of nocturnal diarrhea had left him very lightheaded. He tried to stand, but he felt as if he was about to faint.

"Harold, your atrial fibrillation has flared back up," his wife said. "I'll bet that you've forgotten to take your digoxin medicine again. I want you to put the cardboard sign back around your neck and drive up to the emergency room at the Gulf Coast University Hospital to see if they can fix you up again. Now remember, when you drive the sedan, it will be necessary for you to turn your head and body sideways. You might pass out if you sit up straight in the car."

Harold McCord carefully followed his wife's instructions since she seemed to know best about these delicate matters. When he drove up to the emergency room, he had to lean so far to the right that his level of vision was just above the dashboard. If he had tried to sit straight up in the car seat, he most assuredly would have blacked out! His blood pressure was so low from the cardiac arrhythmia that he would not have been getting enough blood perfused up to his brain if his body was in an upright position. Some urban thugs passed him on the road, and the hoodlums thought he was driving with the "gangster lean." They honked at the old man and gave him an enthusiastic thumbs-up!

Upon Harold's arrival at the emergency room, Dr. Frank Barber was able to put the elderly patient back into a normal cardiac sinus rhythm with a loading dose of digoxin and IV hydration. The patient was subsequently admitted to the internal medicine service under the care of Dr. Cannon's team. It was necessary to have Mr. McCord's residual electrolyte abnormalities, caused by the previous multiple episodes of diarrhea, completely corrected before the patient could be safely discharged back to his domicile.

"Brewster, listen up," Dr. Penn said. "This crazy coot is eight hundred years old. If his ticker goes on the fritz again, it'll be time for this buzzard-eating old buzzard to get transferred to the eternal care unit and have that up-close and personal conversation with Jesus that he so readily deserves. I'm not about to pounce on this old boy's chest. We'll just end up breaking every bone in his thorax. We're not going to hit him with any juice either if he decides to code on us or ultimately degenerates into vent fib. Make him DNR. Do it now."

Brewster had investigated why Mr. McCord was not a candidate to receive medical care through the VA Hospital. As it turned out, Mr. McCord served as an American in the French Air Force and was technically considered to be a foreign legionnaire. Therefore, he was not a candidate to receive benefits from the VA system. Brewster had taken upon himself the task of writing a letter to Mr. McCord's congressman in an effort to voice his complaint about this unjust matter. Sadly, it appeared that Brewster had forgotten a fundamental rule that Dr. Colima had previously and most emphatically once taught him: no good deed goes unpunished.

Mr. McCord failed to get any benefits from the VA system, and Brewster's letter found its way to the IRS. Upon further investigation, the IRS discovered that the elderly couple had not filed income tax returns for the past several years. Now there was going to be hell to pay.

The three great universal lies are as follows: *I love you, The check's in the mail,* and *I'm from the government, and I'm here to help.* As it turns out, there's also a *fourth* great lie concerning any given male individual who may be on the receiving end of an act of fellatio who makes a fallacious promise that he'll attempt to refrain from inducing an acute gag reflex in the person on his or her knees in front of him.

Perhaps, however, that salacious tale of woe should best be reserved for another time and another place...

Ben Fielder had to extricate Dr. Price from a potentially dangerous situation. A member of the outlaw motorcycle club, the Mexican Marauders, was recovering from a myocardial infarction after ingesting a considerable amount of cocaine. This stimulant had become an extremely popular illicit drug back in the 1980s. The gang member was known as "Moritz the Mouse," and his motorcycle club had become intricately linked to the Calle Vampiro drug cartel. Although the motorcycle gang members were given strict instructions not to recreate with any product that was being shipped north across the border, the rule was rarely followed.

When the patient was transferred from the intensive care unit back up to the med-surg floor prior to a planned discharge from the hospital, Dr. Price walked into the patient's room at a most inopportune moment. Moritz the Mouse was being sexually serviced by his "old lady" at the time. "Young lady, you can't be doing this now!" Price warned. "Mr. Moritz has just had a heart attack, and if you get him too agitated, he might extend his infarct!"

The muscular and tattooed "old lady" dismounted her biker boyfriend and charged at Dr. Price. "Listen to me, you fat bastard! I was just about to come like a banshee, and you ruined a very romantic moment. I'm going to cut you and bleed you out right here and right now, and do it real quiet like!"

"Okay," Ben Fielder said as he entered the room just in time to save the day. "Everybody needs to take a chill pill right about now! Dr. Price, I believe it would be the better part of valor if you simply disappear."

"I'll do just that!" Price said.

"Before you leave, there needs to be a quid pro quo mutually beneficial arrangement if I'm indeed going to save your sorry ass from getting stomped by this dude's beefy old lady," Fielder added as he pointed to the couple on the hospital bed.

"Anything," the intern replied. "Name your price."

"I'll cool this dude's tool, but only if you promise to get your boot off the back of my neck," Fielder said. "You need to offer Brewster and Dunhill the same gracious considerations. Go light on us from here on out, damn it! Deal?"

"Deal."

As Fielder strong-armed Dr. Price out of the room, he profusely apologized to Moritz the Mouse and his girlfriend. "Price won't be back. Ever. Now—we good?"

Fortunately, the medical student was able to successfully defuse the rather volatile situation. Blessed be the pacemakers.

After Fielder encouraged the couple to complete their romantic task at hand, the Mouse said, "String Bean, you did me a solid. I owe you big time. If you ever need me and my club to take care of any problems for you in the future, just let me know."

"That's a rather generous offer," Fielder said.

"You're welcome to stay and watch us finish up. My old lady doesn't have any teeth because I busted them all out a while back with a mallet. If you'd like, I'll make her give you a hum job! I'll have her gum on your noodle until your head starts to sweat drops of blood. Nothin' better than gettin' a 'hummer from a gummer'! Know what I mean, String Bean? Whowee!"

"Whowee!" Fielder answered. "Thanks for the offer, man, but I've got more rounds to make. Someday, however, I might take you up on your offer for help if I ever get into some kind of a jam somewhere."

Russian Bear had reluctantly accepted the assignment of following Gerta Braun. She had been hospitalized with an infected diabetic foot ulcer that required antibiotic therapy and surgical debridement. His personal reservations about seeing the patient stemmed from the fact that she was, well—a German. Although the World War II had been over for thirty-five years, there was still a feeling of residual animosity between the Russian and German people. Nonetheless, the Bear was ready to try to break the ice.

"Mrs. Braun, you're now fifty years old," Bear noted. "You must have been only a teenager during the Great Patriotic War. What do you remember about the whole ordeal?"

"I can tell by your accent that you're Russian," Gerta replied. "I'm sorry for what the Fatherland had done to the Motherland, but perhaps you and I should both talk about it."

"Perhaps we should," Bear said. "Were any of your immediate family members involved in the conflict?"

"My father was a sniper with the Fallschirmjager 4 Kompanie that served under Von Paulus at Stalingrad in 1942," Gerta answered. "When Georgy Zhukov annihilated the Sixth Army Group, my father never came home. I don't know what happened to him. The last thing that I know was that he was in a firefight at Orlovka when 4 Kompanie fell. Tell me about your family. I'm certain they must have also fought in the war."

Russian Bear said, "My father survived the war, but his twin brother did not. His name was Yuri. He was killed by sniper fire at Orlovka in 1942 when the Red Army liberated Stalingrad."

"Oh my God!" Gerta exclaimed. "You don't think that it's possible that my father was the sniper who—"

"Well, what does it matter now?" Bear interrupted. "It was war, and the Allies and Germans tried to exterminate each other. What else is there to say?"

"I was fifteen years old and living in Dresden in February 1945," Gerta said. "I was there when the Allies firebombed my beloved city. I remember seeing a tornado of fire that swept through the heart of town."

"That sounds terrifying, quite frankly."

"You have no idea," Gerta said. "The wind was so strong that people were virtually being swept up into the fire vortex. They were being incinerated alive! I remember seeing a man run out of his house. He was on already on fire, and he was carrying his infant daughter on his shoulders."

"Did they escape?"

"Sadly, no," Gerta answered. "He didn't realize the asphalt in the street had become soft and gelatinous like hot lava. He got trapped in the liquefied asphalt and started to cook from the bottom up."

"I recently saw a bumper sticker on a car that said, 'War is not good for children and other living things.'"

"Indeed," Gerta said. "In any event, the war was certainly not good for that man and his baby girl. While he was screaming in agony, he tried the hold his baby above his head to spare her from the inferno, but his efforts were futile."

"You were a personal witness to all of this?"

"With my own two eyes," Gerta said. "As he was rendered into sizzling grease, he finally could no longer hold up his infant any longer—and she slowly slipped into the boiling asphalt. I will never forget her bloodcurdling scream and the odor of her being cooked alive."

"Although the German people were our enemy, I don't think that I'll be able to get that story out of my mind for the rest of my life," Bear said. "I … I'm so sorry."

"Upon the firebombing raid of Dresden, thousands of my fellow civilians ceased to exist in just a momentary blink," Gerta said as tears welled in her eyes. "Well, what does it matter now? It was war, and the Allies and Germans tried to exterminate each other. What else is there to say?"

What else was there to say? Perhaps J. D. Brewster was correct all along in his cynical theological postulate that God had simply backed the wrong primate.

# 9

# THE SPA

When the calendar rolled over to Monday, November 3, 1980, Brewster and his three colleagues went to the VA annex in Bellaire to start their second rotation on their internal medicine clerkship. Brewster felt especially honored to have an opportunity to help provide medical care for the men and women who had dedicated so much to make the United States the most powerful country the world had ever seen.

The only problem was that the VA hospital system was run by the federal government. The government was barely capable of delivering mail, protecting America's borders, or staying the hell out of the lives of the average American citizen, much less providing health care for our country's valiant veteran population. Like anything else that the federal government had ever done, the VA system was fraught with fraud, waste, and ineptitude. That's why the VA Hospital had been given the ignominious nickname of "the Spa."

The term *spa*, in the medical vernacular, does not connote an environment conducive to industrious labor. On the contrary, the word is reflective of atmospheric inertia where administrative sloths shuffle forms and requisitions about with the self-delusion that such mundane activities have any true meaning. Nonetheless, the VA annex in Bellaire was supposedly a powder-puff location to do a powder-puff clerkship, since the facility had a fully equipped gymnasium and a three-hole pitch-and-putt golf course.

Brewster believed, like so many other Americans, that something was fundamentally wrong with the country at that time in history. He loved his country, but he loathed his government. The following day would be Tuesday, November 4, Election Day. It would be the first time Brewster and many of his colleagues would have an opportunity to cast their votes to help determine the direction of the country. Brewster had initiated an informal survey of his classmates, and he could not find anybody who would willingly admit to the heinous intention of voting for that spineless and bitter bumpkin peanut farmer named Jimmy Carter. Brewster's spirits had been levied by the prospects that there were still Americans with functioning brains. Perhaps his fellow Americans had finally come to realize that the country under Carter had become cloaked in a shroud of pessimistic impotence.

Even Russian Bear had detected a positive vibration that the country was on the threshold of a change for the better. The Bear announced that he and Larisa would host an old-fashioned party with beer and hot dogs at their apartment to usher in Ronald Reagan if he indeed became the president-elect. Brewster offered to bring two cases of an American brew to contribute to the celebration.

Brewster thought a party would be a perfect opportunity to get a better handle on the nature of his reserved colleague who was a refugee from the Soviet Union. After all, without the Wooly Mammoth, Brewster felt that he needed another moral barometer to hash over problems with besides the agnostic Ben Fielder.

Compared to its urban counterpart in Houston, the VA annex in Bellaire was a palatial edifice. There was a specific reason for that. At the time, each individual VA hospital received an allocation from the government based upon the average length of patient hospital admission days. The longer a patient stayed in the hospital, the more money the VA facility could expect to receive from Uncle Sam as an operational stipend. Therefore, based on the bizarre rules established by the federal government, the objective was *not* to make a veteran patient well and try to expedite his or her discharge back into the community at large, but to keep the patient in the hospital for as long as possible.

The national average for length of stay in the VA system was a rather paltry twenty-four days, but the VA annex in Bellaire had purposefully blown that national average statistic clear out of the water with a median length of stay of up to thirty-eight days! That astounding statistic was the third best in the country, and that was why the VA annex in Bellaire had prospered at the expense of good patient care and squandered taxpayer dollars. It would be a statistic that would make any American proud, right?

The chief of medical services at the VA annex in Bellaire was Dr. Morris Mackenzie, a retired army major. Called up into the military during the last year of the Korean War, Dr. Mackenzie had served all the way through the Vietnam conflict and was able to take a full retirement with benefits in 1973. Over the past seven years, he worked for the VA system. Starting out in Albuquerque, New Mexico, he was able to jump over to Texas. He ran the program in Bellaire for the past two years. He was an associate professor at the Gulf Coast College of Medicine, but if the truth be told, he had never set foot inside the university campus located at the Texas Medical Center.

Because the Baylor College of Medicine had wrapped up a long-term working relationship with the VA Hospital in Houston, the Gulf Coast had to settle for the junior annex facility in the suburbs of Bellaire. Dr. Mackenzie was essentially the liaison that bridged a relationship with the Gulf Coast College of Medicine training program, which allowed students, interns, and residents a foot in the door at the VA annex. It was a mutually beneficial relationship. The VA Hospital received a workforce of students and physicians in training, and the university received a much-needed affiliate institute where students and young physicians could receive additional medical education beyond the boundaries of the Texas Medical Center.

Spending his entire medical career within the confines of the military and VA system, Dr. Mackenzie was well aware how wasteful and inefficient the federal government had actually become. He accepted the reality of his own peculiar situation and considered himself to be little more than a small cog in a machine that was operated by a tyranny of unknowing and uncaring micro-cephalic bureaucrats. He looked upon his job with the same lack of enthusiasm that many jaded senators inside the Beltway would secretly profess about their own despised constituents. The primary job was to "bring home the bacon." Oink, oink, squeal, squeal, little piglets! Fill up at the pork-belly trough of misallocated tax dollars.

Dr. Mackenzie's premeditated act of being inefficient had resulted in keeping patients in the hospital much longer than was ever actually required. If doing so meant there would be more funds allocated to his beloved VA annex in Bellaire, then so be it. Mission accomplished, and a job well done. Why not game the system? Hell's bells—every scumbag, deep-state player sloshing through the swamp of the ineffectual federal government seemed to be doing the same thing. Nice, eh?

On the first morning of their new rotation, Brewster and his colleagues met Dr. Mackenzie and their new resident, Dr. Lisa Barron, in the medical conference room.

Dr. Mackenzie said, "Look, I'm not going to try to learn anybody's name. I truly don't give a shit about who any of you are as students, much less human beings. I'm going to be on the level with you in that this is a very straightforward rotation to get through. I've *never* failed anybody who's rotated here at the VA annex, but it should be noted that I've *never* awarded anybody with an honors grade either. This is a government-run facility, and we pride ourselves on inefficiency. Don't be in a rush in getting anybody well or getting anybody discharged from this facility in a timely fashion. Those lofty goals may be aspirations at the Gulf Coast, but here at the VA annex, we pride ourselves in mediocrity. If anybody is planning on getting into the Alpha Omega Alpha medical school honor society, it ain't gonna happen here on this rotation." He leaned back in his chair and looked at Russian Bear. "I don't know what your name is, but for this rotation, you'll be known as 'Willy."

Russian Bear said, "No, I'm Ilya, but my friends call me Russian Bear. There's a large black man in my class with the name Willy, so you can't refer to me by that name. That's just not right. It would be most disrespectful to me, and it would be most disrespectful to the person in my class who already has the name, Willy! You may call me Russian Bear if you please."

Dr. Mackenzie said, "No, that doesn't please me one damn bit, dumbass! Your name is Willy, understand? Don't argue with me. I suggest that you get used to it."

With a huge grin, Russian Bear pointed at the attending and said, "захлопни ебальник и иди на хуй! Сейчас въебу тебе в жопу так, что ты поперхнешься моим сапогом, ебаный ублюдок."

"You just said something to me in Russian, didn't you? What in hell did you just say to me? Tell me right now what just belched out of your pie hole—and you better tell it to me in English!"

Russian Bear said, "I believe a rough translation of what I said into the English language is, 'Have a nice day!' if I'm not mistaken."

McKenzie glared at Russian Bear for several moments before he turned his attention to Felix Dunhill. "For the love of Jesus, you smell like an ashtray and look like some inebriated, down-trodden hobo I once saw hanging out in an alley way after being kicked out of the local chapter of the Salvation Army. Your name is 'Poor Boy' for the duration of this rotation."

Felix Dunhill clenched his fists and glared back at the attending physician. Felix accepted the fact that he may have been little more than a pile of dung, but he was no Poor Boy.

Brewster suddenly realized that Dr. Mackenzie was naming his colleagues after the characters from the 1969 song, "Down on the Corner," originally recorded on the Fantasy record label by "Cosmo"

Clifford, Stu Cooke, and the Fogerty brothers. The four members of the rock and roll group were collectively known as Creedence Clearwater Revival.

"So, I would surmise that my colleague, Mr. Fielder, is going to called 'Rooster.' After all, he tends to cackle a bit when he's annoyed," Brewster said. "If that's the case, 'Blinky' will be my moniker, and I accept it proudly."

Dr. Mackenzie leaned forward and stared at J. D. Brewster. "I've been warned about you. You must be J. D. Brewster, I'll venture. Frankly, I really don't want to know your name either, but nonetheless, you must be the former brainiac who's been known to brew up trouble on every rotation he's ever been on. I'll tell you how it's going down," as he pointed at Ben Fielder. "This anorexic, frayed wad of dental floss will be called Blinky."

"Excuse me, sir, but does that name end in the letter 'y' or an 'ie'?" Fielder asked with a smirk.

McKenzie failed to answer Fielder's question and directed his attention back to Brewster. "You'll be known as Rooster," Dr. McKenzie said. "After all, you have the reputation of being a cocky sumbitch, and the name Rooster rhymes with your last name. Don't piss me off. Am I clear? Dr. Barron has a list of the patients she is going to distribute amongst you four individuals. We will meet here for morning report in this room at eight each day. Get to work—and don't bother me. All questions and problems must go through Dr. Barron."

Brewster sighed when he realized he was going to be in another verbally abusive but perhaps relatively mundane clerkship rotation. If the VA system was in search of mediocrity, Brewster was ready and willing to deal it out in spades.

On election night, nearly a dozen medical students and their wives and girlfriends were gathered around the television in Russian Bear's apartment. Every time the political correspondent announced that a state had been won by Ronald Reagan, a cheer erupted. When it was clear that Ronald Reagan was about to become the president-elect in a land slide victory, Russian Bear conducted the gathering of patriots in a heartfelt rendition of "God Bless America."

As Brewster gave Stella Link a celebratory hug, Russian Bear approached with his wife. "Hello. I'm glad you were both able to come to my party. Thanks for bringing the cold beer. I want to introduce you to my lovely wife, Larisa."

Brewster could not help himself and immediately slipped into his usual full-throttle, obnoxious modus operandi. "My, oh my! I must say, Russian Bear, your wife is drop-dead gorgeous. She doesn't look anything like what you had described her to be. You said that she had a unibrow and a receding, simian-like forehead."

Brewster reached out and planted his thumb across Larisa's brow ridge and said, "I don't understand. You have two distinct eyebrows and they're not connected in the middle like Russian Bear had previously described. Oh, wait—that's my mistake. I remember now that Russian Bear was talking about how his new Latvian *girlfriend* from the respiratory therapy department looked like—not the appearance of his *wife*." Brewster laughed and slapped his thigh as if he had just told a funny joke, but oddly, nobody else was laughing. "Wow," Brewster said. "If I could crack myself up like this for hours on end, why on earth would I ever need the company of other human beings?"

Larisa's jaw dropped open, and she turned to Russian Bear and loudly scolded him in Russian.

Russian Bear put up his hands and was prepared to ward off what appeared to be an eminent frontal assault.

Larisa stormed out of the room with the Russian Bear in pursuit, all the while trying to explain the situation.

Stella Link stared at J. D. Brewster with mouth agape. "What the hell is the matter with you? So, you don't need my company, do you?"

"I was just joking."

"You're a pig!" Stella proclaimed. "Why am I even here with you? You disgust me! Go back there right now and apologize to that young woman. Did you think that was funny? She didn't deserve to hear what just spewed out of your filthy mouth. How dare you speak to somebody in such a fashion? Do it now, damn it!"

Brewster refused to budge or even look at Stella at that point.

Russian Bear and Larisa calmly returned to the living room as the party was starting to wind down. Larisa walked up to Brewster and ran her hands over his scalp. She then turned to her husband and nodded with a scowl.

Russian Bear walked behind Brewster, grabbed the back of Brewster's trousers at the belt line, and yanked hard while Larisa looked down the back of Brewster's undershorts. She seemed to be disgusted with what she had witnessed after she carefully scrutinized Brewster's coccygeal region, just north of his ass end. Russian Bear pulled up a chair from the dining room table and requested that Brewster take a seat. Brewster also complied when Russian Bear ordered him to take off his socks and shoes.

Larisa nodded again and turned to her husband. "I'm sorry that I ever doubted you, my darling. You were right. Mr. Brewster is indeed the Devil incarnate. My husband and I will pray for you, J. D. Brewster. I'm certain that we can find a Russian Orthodox priest here in Houston who knows how to perform a ritual exorcism."

When Brewster and Stella Link were leaving the party that night, Russian Bear smiled at Brewster and whispered a dire warning. "I've learned an expression from the time that I moved here to America. They say that 'payback is a bitch'!"

In the near future, Brewster would readily attest that this particular American expression was quite true.

Brewster and his colleagues were about to meet fascinating American heroes they would remember for the rest of their lives. Brewster was assigned to a patient named Buck Rodgers, a Korean War veteran afflicted with stage-4 metastatic prostate cancer that had become resistant to hormonal manipulation. Prostate cancer has the peculiar predilection to predominantly metastasize to the bones, and generally the bones fill up with metastatic disease before the cancer has an opportunity to invade the visceral organs. Once prostate cancer spreads to the bones or other locations, it is not thought to be curable by radical prostatectomy surgical procedures or radiation treatment. Since prostate cancer cell survival is, at least initially, highly dependent upon the presence of the exogenous circulating male hormone called testosterone, physicians have known since the beginning of the twentieth century that performing an orchiectomy (surgical castration) is effective in controlling metastatic prostate cancer for two or maybe three years in patients afflicted with this dreadful disease. Even patients with advanced metastatic prostate cancer can achieve complete remission if surgical or chemical castration is employed to eliminate the circulating male hormones.

Despite aggressive hormonal manipulation, most patients afflicted with metastatic prostate cancer will develop a clone of cancer cells that can grow quite nicely without the presence of any circulating systemic testosterone. This is referred to as "castrate-resistant" prostate cancer. At the end of Brewster's career many years later, any practicing cancer specialist would have an entire armamentarium of drugs to treat hormone-dependent and subsequent castrate-resistant prostate cancer, but that was not the case in 1980.

Buck Rodgers had already failed surgical castration, and the two-year clinical remission he had enjoyed had come to a rather disappointing conclusion. He had developed multiple new bone metastases that were quite painful. As long as there were no visceral metastases, a patient with metastatic prostate cancer can live for quite a long time. Unfortunately, the quality of life in that situation may be rather poor as one might expect.

The free radicals, as the physicians from the radiation oncology service were nicknamed, tried to "spot-weld" the painful metastatic foci with external beam radiation therapy, however this treatment modality was met with only marginal success at best. As soon as the radiation oncology service completed radiation therapy on one site, a new painful metastatic lesion would show up almost immediately at another location. The radiation oncology service now believed it was doing nothing more than chasing its own tail.

The medical oncologist in the VA annex in Bellaire believed that changing the hormonal milieu in some way, shape, or form could extend the survival of Mr. Rodgers a bit longer. With that line of thinking, he was placed on a female hormone called diethylstilbestrol, which was also known as DES. That drug was later found to induce unwanted and potentially lethal thrombo-embolic, veno-occlusive events. Mr. Rodgers had developed gynecomastia as a consequence of the DES treatment. In layman's terms, gynecomastia is the abnormal and oftentimes painful enlargement of a man's breast tissue. Mr. Rodgers was not particularly happy with his clinical course, and he decided to abandon the DES treatment.

When Brewster met Mr. Rodgers, he noted that the patient had a below-the-knee amputation of his right leg. There was no mention in the patient's medical record as to why this distal extremity had disappeared. "I can see that your right leg below the knee has been amputated at the mid-tibial region," Brewster said. "Is this a consequence of your prostate cancer or from some other problem?"

"No," Rodgers replied. "It was actually a gift from the North Koreans."

"Good God in heaven—tell me what happened," Brewster said. "It's a very happy story that will make you grin from ear to ear, but I rarely tell it to anybody," the veteran said with a sardonic smile. "Since you asked, I'll let you know. My F-86 got into a dogfight with a MiG-15, and I lost. I think I must have been up against a Chinese or Russian fighter pilot since they were consistently better fliers than the North Koreans. Anyhow, I bailed from my jet and parachuted down. Landing with a parachute can be tough stuff. It's like jumping from the top of a six-foot ladder onto a hard tarmac. I didn't break anything, but I sprained my ankle. I was immediately captured by the North Koreans, and they realized that I had injured my right foot. All they had to do was leave me alone, and I would have been walking fine in a few days or so. The North Koreans didn't see it that way. They dragged me into a barn and hacked my leg off with a wood ax. After that, they seared the end of my stump with a red-hot branding iron to stop the bleeding."

At the end of his career, Brewster would remember that the ensuing query would be the most idiotic question he had ever asked another living human being. "That sounds terrible," Brewster said. "Did they torture you?"

Mr. Rodgers furrowed his brow and—on one leg—hopped over to where Brewster was sitting. When he got within an inch of Brewster's face, he whispered, "Listen to me very carefully, you dumbass. They cut my fucking leg off with a wood ax and then they seared my bloody stump with a branding iron! Does that sound like a vacation trip to Disneyland to you?"

"I, well, I'm—"

"Ah, forget it," Buck said. "To be honest, that was my very best day as a prisoner of war. It went downhill from that day forward. Although I only had one leg, I had to pick cabbage—and my quota was no different than any other prisoner of war. If I did not produce, I would be severely beaten. Perhaps it would not have been so bad if I'd at least been given crutches, but that was not the case. It's hard to pick vegetables while hopping around on one leg in a muddy, shit-filled cabbage patch."

"How long were you a POW?" Brewster asked.

"One year, four months, sixteen days, and five hours, but who's counting?" Buck Rodgers answered. "I really didn't think I was going to survive. At one time, the North Koreans seemed to have forgotten to pick me up at the end of the day after working in the cabbage patch. I waited for several hours since I thought it was a trap. When it got dark, I thought I would try to escape. For several days, I crawled on my hands and knees back toward the thirty-eighth parallel. I was close enough to hear the voices of U.N. troops, and I thought I was saved. Sadly, nothing could have been further from the truth."

"What happened?"

"I crawled over a rise in the road, and there to meet me was one of the cruelest prison guards I had ever dealt with. He was sitting in a lawn chair with a truncheon, just waiting for me. After he had beaten me, he shoved the baton up my ass—and then he made be crawl all the way back to the prison camp. The guard made it clear to me that if the baton fell out of my ass on the way back to the prison camp, he would run me through with a bayonet. When I made it back to the prison camp after four days of crawling on my hands and knees, he pulled the truncheon out of my backside and beat me with it yet again."

"As hard as all of this is for me to hear, I need to know about these things. I'm an amateur historian," Brewster said. "Perhaps I'm in the wrong line of work and I should be teaching history at a college."

"Perhaps you should," Buck said. "I am afraid that most young people in this country don't know anything at all about the United States of America and what it truly means to be an American. You see, I don't actually know how many North Koreans we had killed in that conflict, but it was not enough if you ask me. General Douglas MacArthur was correct—we should have dropped the bomb on all those nasty bastards and exterminated them as a race. I hope it does not seem to you that I'm a racist or that I still holding a grudge about all of this."

"No, not at all," Brewster said with a shrug. "What else you remember?"

"Oh, it only gets better," Buck answered. "The prison guards would feed us the most vile and rancid gruel that you could ever possibly imagine. I'm sure that they would piss and shit in the food that they served to us. We weren't allowed to make any sound at all while we ate. If we did, we'd get skewered. From time to time, while we were eating dinner, a North Korean guard would come into the hut, hold a gun to the head of one of the prisoners, and pull the trigger. Nine times out of ten, the guard would shoot a blank round just to see if any of the prisoners would make any noise. If any of the prisoners sounded out or screamed in fear, he would end up a dead man."

"Well," Brewster said, "that was nine out of ten times. What happened during the one out of ten times?"

"One out of ten times, they would proceed to blow the brains out of somebody who was sitting at the dining room mat for no apparent reason at all. When that happened, we couldn't do or say anything or make any kind of objectionable sound whatsoever. If the fellow who was sitting beside you was suddenly executed and chunks of his brain, skull, and shit like that ended up falling into your bowl of gruel, you just had to eat it all up as if nothing had ever happened. If you tried to fish out any bits of brain matter or skull out of your food, the slopes would run you through. Nice, eh?"

It had not happened to Brewster in quite some time, but he suddenly lost the vision in his left eye. The more Buck Rodgers expounded on his tale of horror, the more agitated Brewster became. The pervasive shroud of evil and hatred that Brewster had noted while he was doing his clerkship on the burn unit returned with all its fury. Nonetheless, he was compelled to finish his interview. After all, if Brewster considered himself to be a historian, he had to be brave enough to learn everything he possibly could about what Buck Rodgers had experienced. To cap it all off, the medical student was about to be reminded the peculiar lesson than that everything in the universe is somehow connected.

"As you know, my name is Buck Rodgers. That name is actually on my birth certificate. There was a fellow in the prison camp who was a friend of mine from Wink, Texas. His name was Flavius Gordon. His nickname, as you would probably guess, was 'Flash Gordon.' I suspect we became friends because of our peculiar names. Neither one of us had ever considered ourselves to be space cadet heroes, however. One day, several dog-eating, slope-headed gooks came into the hut, and a Red Chinese army captain was with them."

"What did that bastard want?"

"Beats me why they picked on Flash that day, but they wanted to put him through another round of interrogation. That was the last I ever saw Flash Gordon. Before he disappeared, he told me that he had a fiancé in Houston, and he made me promise that I would look her up after the war and deliver to her a dozen yellow roses if he was not lucky enough to make it home. Her first name was Irene, and her last name sounded Italian. God forgive me, but I didn't remember what her last name was when the war ended. After all, it wasn't like I had a pencil and paper and could jot down any notes. I was never able to keep my promise. To this day, I feel guilty about that."

When Brewster's vision returned to his left eye, he stood and excitedly said, "Her last name was Segulla! She was a nurse who used to work at the Gulf Coast University Hospital, and she told me she was engaged to a man named Flavius Gordon at the onset of the Korean War. She died a few months ago after she was assaulted in the parking lot at the university hospital complex."

"I remember reading about that story!" Buck said. "It was all in the newspapers. So, that woman was Gordon's fiancée? Damnation! What a horrible thing. I still think about my old friend. I still don't know if it was the filthy Communist Chinese or godless North Korean animals who may have had their way with him, but he never came home. God forgive me, but I pray that he died quickly. I know exactly what happened to our American servicemen who were interrogated by the enemy during the war. After all, I went through it too. You know, a lot of those prisoners of war of never came home. You don't think any of our boys are still being held by those Communists after all these years, do you? For what purpose could our boys still be held as captives? Well, what else can I say?"

For Brewster, it was just another inexplicable soul-shaking occurrence of déjà vu. What possible message was the universe attempting to convey to him? Brewster was continuously being pummeled over the head with recurrent phrases and recurrent circumstances, and it was clearly not a coincidence. Brewster thought that God was trying to get his attention, but to what end? *Perhaps I'm supposed to be an avenger*, he thought.

Buck Rodgers held fast to his conviction in the end that that he had made the right decision when decided to abandon a course of aggressive cancer management. The patient entered a brand-new program at the VA annex that was called "hospice". He was certainly amenable to signing a DNR code status. "Brewster, let me tell you something. Despite all that happened to me during the war, I've done my best to be a righteous man. I've fought the good fight, I've finished the race, and I've kept the faith…"

Russian Bear had been called down to the Life Support Unit, which was basically a glorified urgent care setting at the VA annex. An elderly World War I vet, Helmut Gross, had showed up with a raging urinary tract infection. As the patient was running a fever of 103.5 F and was developing hypotension with bilateral flank pain, it appeared that the patient had a much more serious acute condition than just a simple bladder infection. Clinically, it would appear that he had pyelonephritis, an infection in the kidneys. Once admitted, the resident physician, Dr. Lisa Barron, started intravenous antibiotic therapy.

Men have external plumbing and are generally not supposed to get urinary tract infections. For Helmut to have developed urosepsis, there must have been something wrong with his "radiator." The term "radiator" was used by the medical students as a nonspecific description of the genitourinary system. The urology resident, I. P. Stream, was called in to assess the patient and he found that Helmut possessed an enormous prostate with associated lower urinary tract obstructive symptoms. Once the patient eventually recovered from his kidney infections, a transurethral resection of the enlarged prostate would be the next order of business.

Elderly patients with urinary tract infections often present with acute delirium, which was clearly the case with Mr. Gross. After the night shift nurse completed her rounds, the patient slipped down the stairwell and escaped onto Rice Avenue.

A Code Silver was broadcast over the loudspeakers and the Bellaire Police Department was notified. Fortunately, a prowl car spotted the deranged ancient man as he ambled into a busy intersection while pushing a front-wheeled aluminum walker. The police gently placed the frail and confused gentleman in the back of the squad car and brought him directly back to the VA annex. Upon readmission, soft restraints were utilized to keep the patient from wandering away again.

The following morning, the VA administration went into a histrionic war dance about the status of Helmut Gross. For certain, Mr. Gross was a World War I veteran, but it was discovered that he had actually fought for the Kaiser! The administration demanded that Dr. McKenzie's team discharge the patient immediately. There was no way Dr. Mackenzie was going to allow a clerical error to have an adverse outcome on the all-important patient length of stay data.

If Helmut Gross was forced to be discharged or transferred to some other facility after just one day in the VA system, it would throw a wrench into the precious census statistics. Dr. McKenzie needed to manipulate the situation, but he realized that he would only inflame the circumstances if he approached administration on his own accord.

The answer to the dilemma was a simple act of forgery. Russian Bear created a false service record report that indicated that Helmut Gross was a double agent during the war.

When the falsified document was presented to administration, Dr. Lisa Barron explained to the bean counters that the patient's military service record had, up until that very moment, been classified information—and only an act of Congress released the patient's service record to the VA system!

The VA administration said they would have to look into the matter, but because of lassitude and the snail-like pace of completing any meaningful work on behalf of the federal government, Mr. Gross was long out of the hospital before any irregularities had been noted. Dr. McKenzie's precious statistics had not been adversely affected, which was obviously much more important than simply doing the right thing for an elderly and delirious man, irrespective of which side he fought on during World War I.

After his most recent stint as a wily rascal who committed an overt act of forgery to specifically create a fictional military record out of a bolt of whole cloth, Russian Bear was now finally corrupted. Sadly, he was now starting to seamlessly fit right in with his new American colleagues.

# 10

## I TOOK CARE OF THEM

"Thanks for this invite in tackling a round of par three, Willy," Brewster said. "Frankly, I didn't think I'd ever hear from you again."

"Don't try to overplay your hand with me, Brew," the big man warned. "If you think for one minute that you and Fielder somehow weaseled a fancy way to get off of my shit list, then you boys got another thing comin'. Why don't you just look at it as a round of golf—nothing more and nothing less?"

"Swell," Brewster said. "Apparently you now hold me in the same high regard as one would have for say, I don't know–maybe a dead 'possum."

"Well," Willy laughed, "you're in the ballpark."

Rip Ford pulled a golf ball out of his bag and said, "Are you worth a tinker's damn at this game, Brewster?"

"Only if I play by my own rules." Brewster replied.

"Well, would you care to elaborate?" Ben Fielder asked as he slipped a white leather golf glove upon his left hand.

"Well, it is quite simple. Anything on the green is a 'gimme', I generally tee up in the rough, and a loss of ball is penalty enough.

On a three-hole par three like this, I should be able to break a hundred easily."

"So, in other words, not only do you suck at this, but you also cheat?" Fielder concluded.

"Twenty-four seven—and 365," Brewster answered. "You should know me by now."

As Willy Mammon teed up his ball on the first hole, he said, "It looks like the 'token black man' gets to take the first swing. After all, I'm the one who invited you jokers to tag along. Should I consider this an honor—or are you pasty boys just attempting to assuage your own guilt. After all, the blue-eyed, white-devil slave master has kept the black man down for so long, has he not?"

Ben Fielder put up his hands together to form the letter T. "Time-out. Tell me more about this 'token black man' scenario of which you've just now spoken. Is this some kind of an acute clinical calamity—or would you consider it more of a chronic condition? In fact, does your own father even know that you happen to self-iden-tify as a *black* man?"

Ford looked over to Brewster for clarity. "Brew, tell me what you think."

Brewster lit up a Churchill and said, "Nobody ever told me that the big colored man was indeed a black man. Damnation! I just did *not* see that coming. I'm sorry, but that's all news to me. I simply thought that he was just some poor big bastard afflicted with an excessive production of melanin in his skin. Hell's bells— if I thought for one minute that the guy was black, I sure as shit wouldn't be hanging around with him. So, Ford, why on earth would we want this guy to tee up first? After all, he's allegedly a *black* man."

"He's never hit a damned golf ball before," Rip answered. "I just want to laugh my ass off when he takes his first swing."

Willy Mammon reared back with a nine iron and slapped the ball. It must have been blind luck or hidden talent because the ball landed within eight feet of the pin. He dropped the club, raised his arms, and crowed with pride. "Take that, bitches!" He danced around the tee box while the other men looked on in stunned silence.

"All right, it's my turn," Fielder said. "I'm going to drop my ball inside the mark where Willy's ball landed. Watch and learn, ladies." Ben took a swat, but he didn't hit the ball with a clean strike.

When he toed the target on the tee, the golf ball zoomed off into the parking lot, only to shatter the windshield of Brewster's Mustang.

Rip Ford and Willy Mammon howled with delight as they interlocked their arms and circled around J. D. Brewster in an Irish jig.

Brewster looked over to Ben Fielder and scowled. "You did that on purpose. What in hell is the matter with you?"

"No … I swear to God … it was an accident," Ben said. "I couldn't do that again in a million years—even if my life be depended on it!"

"Well, you can't prove it to me. I have a portrait of Abraham Lincoln in my wallet that says that you did that on purpose!"

"I'm taking a mulligan." Ben teed up for a second attempt and hit another ball from the tee box, but the dimpled white sphere yet again sliced right into the windshield of Brewster's prized Mustang, which was quietly minding its own business on the adjacent parking lot.

J. D. looked up to the heavens and realized God was having a good laugh at his expense. By that time, his three golf buddies were rolling on the ground and laughing hysterically.

Brewster took a five-dollar bill out of his wallet, threw it on the ground, and walked off without saying another word. One by one, the golf clubs in his bag fell out of his bag, leaving a trail to his car like the crumbs left behind by Hansel and Gretel in the forest.

Helen Beachwood was a long-retired army nurse who was consigned to the Pacific Theater of Operations in World War II. In the ETO, nurses might have been found only a few miles from the front lines of combat, but that was certainly not the case in the Pacific. There was a great fear that the Japanese adversaries would brutalize any nurses who may have been captured in combat. For that reason, the closest that any army nurses had gotten to actual combat was in the Philippines after that island chain had been recaptured by General Douglas McArthur.

Helen was battling metastatic colon cancer that had spread to her liver. By 1980, the drug 5-fluorouracil had already been around for two decades, but it was still the only marginally effective palliative chemotherapeutic agent that was available to be utilized against this particular malignancy during that era. Helen had been admitted to the hospital after her last round of cancer treatment because of diarrhea that resulted in dehydration and electrolyte problems. She also developed terrible ulcerations involving the mucous membranes inside her mouth. This was a curious complication, since she had received several doses of this specific chemotherapy in the past without any previously recognizable serious adverse reactions.

Ben Fielder was assisting with her management when he received a call that the patient wanted to speak with him.

"Will you be truthful with me?" Helen Beachwood asked. "I've pressed Dr. McKenzie and the resident, Dr. Barron as to what's really going on inside me. I feel like I'm just a number and not a human being anymore. Nobody will give me a simple explanation about my clinical situation, and I keep getting the brush-off. Am I ... am I going to die from this?"

Fielder took Mrs. Beachwood by the hand and looked at her, directly in the eyes. "Yes, Mrs. Beachwood, this is unfortunately a terminal illness. Most patients with metastatic colorectal cancer that has spread to the liver or the lungs are dead within six months of diagnosis if they elect not to take any palliative treatment or if the treatment they are receiving is ineffective. From what I know, the chemotherapy you are on is being used as only a single agent in a palliative setting. At best, it's only marginally effective. It might buy you a little bit of time, but I can't really say how much time that you'll have left on this planet. That's between you and God."

"Mr. Fielder," Helen said, "I thought you told me the other day that you didn't even know if God actually exists."

"Frankly, I don't," Fielder said, "but nonetheless, I've told you the truth about your medical condition as best I understand it."

"I thought as much." She sighed. "I understand that you're an amateur historian and know a lot about World War II."

"No," Fielder replied, "you must be confusing me with my colleague, J. D. Brewster. Would you like me to call him in to see you? After all, he's right down the hall."

"Yes, please do," Helen answered. "I have some things I want to get off of my chest. I want you both to hear what I have to say."

Fielder found Brewster and brought him into Helen's room. "Hello, Mrs. Beachwood. My name is Brewster. I've not met you before, but I assure you that it's my honor to do so. My mother was also an army nurse, but she served stateside during the war. She was actually charged with taking care of German prisoners of war, and she was stationed right here in Texas. What would you like to chat about?"

"As you probably know, brutal things were done to the American marines who were captured by the Japanese at the Battle of Iwo Jima and Okinawa. These poor boys were not necessarily killed outright. Sometimes, the Japanese would make examples of them to try to scare off and demoralize the other American servicemen. The marines who were captured would be blinded, skinned alive, disemboweled, or have their arms, legs, and genitalia hacked off with samurai swords—and worse. The Japanese would make certain that these men would survive long enough to be found by their comrades. When they were found alive, they were flown out to the Philippines after being stabilized on one of the offshore hospital-support ships. Do you know what I did when these darling boys were brought to me? Well, let me tell you what I did. I, well—I took care of them."

"I'm sure that you were an excellent nurse and that you took care of them as best you could," Fielder said.

"You don't understand what I am saying!" Helen screamed. "Listen to me, goddamn it! Pay attention to what you're about to hear! I didn't say that I took care of them. I said that '*I TOOK CARE OF THEM!*' She buried her face in her hands and wept passionately.

Ben Fielder bit down on his knuckles, and Brewster opened his eyes as wide as he could and waved his hand in front of his face. Yet again, he had temporarily lost the vision in his left eye.

Helen asked a question, and it was not rhetorical. She truly needed an answer, but spiritual ministry was outside the wheelhouse of the two young medical students. "My time is coming soon," Helen said. "How do you think God in heaven will judge me for taking care of my boys? I need to know. I've asked for his forgiveness, but I haven't heard any replies. Why won't he answer me? I hope he won't judge me too harshly. What do you think will happen to me when I die? Will I be punished? I'm afraid. I'm so very afraid."

Helen, desperately searching for redemption and salvation, had just made a confession in the dark.

Brewster and Fielder sat in stunned silence. Tears began to stream down Brewster's face, but he couldn't let Fielder see that he was beginning to weep. It would have been a sign of weakness. The Gulf Coast College of Medicine didn't tolerate any signs of weakness. It probably would have been relatively safe for J. D. to have let down his guard just a bit at that time because— unbeknownst to Brewster— Fielder was also crying.

Unfortunately, each witnessed act of brutality and unembellished recollection of horror pushed Brewster and his colleagues further down a dim and thorny path where the demons of humanity's lesser nature had dwelled.

As the Greatest Generation passed into the annals of history, it's now well recognized that a basic and fundamental keystone of World War II was racism. The Nazis were delusional in their adherence to concepts of Aryan superiority. Here is the score in the European Theater of Operations: millions upon millions of dead Jews, Russians, Gypsies, Slavs, Serbs, and Romani. This does not even count the other people the Nazis considered to be undesirables, including Freemasons, Communists, homosexuals, and the mentally and physically challenged. It's been estimated that between five thousand and twenty-five thousand black people were living in Europe at the onset of World War II. What happened to them? At the end of the conflict, the remnants of this modest human population of African origin could no longer be found. Sadly, this is history that's understood all too well.

How does this compare to what happened in the Eastern Hemisphere? The Pacific Theater of Operations, above and beyond a war of imperialism, was essentially a war of ethnic and racial discord.

The Japanese also considered themselves a superior race, and they did their best to match their Nazi counterparts in their own extermination programs in the Pacific Rim. Here is the score in the Pacific Theater of Operations: millions upon millions of dead Chinese, Koreans, Filipinos, Malaysians, Indonesians, Burmese, Indians, and Indo-Chinese.

These appalling figures do not even count the other people the Japanese considered undesirable: Muslims, English, Dutch, Americans, Australians, New Zealanders, Sikhs, Russians, and even a handful of unfortunate Jews who were trying to flee extermination in Europe and only ended up making the mistake of finding themselves in the Far East. Wow! Talk about jumping out of the piss pot and straight into the fire…

The atrocities the Japanese committed during World War II were as ghoulish as they were widespread. At least 5,725 Japanese were indicted for war crimes. Of those convicted, most went to prison. However, some of the crimes that were committed were so ghastly that at least 920 of these villains received justice at the end of a rope.

People of all stripes are tribal by nature and inherently fearful and prejudicial against other racial and ethnic groups. As that's a shameful but indisputable character flaw deeply woven within the fabric of the human condition, none of these above-noted horrific statistics should sadly come as a surprise to anyone.

Woodrow Bright, a former member of the Pacific War Crime Tribunal's legal team, was a retired army attorney. Although he only served on the tribunal from the end of 1945 until 1948, that three-year period had changed his life forever, and it was a change that was decidedly not for the better. Woodrow had learned of information concerning war crimes that was so shocking and disturbing that much of the prosecutorial evidence concerning these acts of human brutality have never been—and will likely never be—released for general public consumption.

Like a motion picture reel on a continuous loop, he could never escape what he saw or learned. He resorted to the consumption of one bottle of vodka per week for thirty-two years in an effort to overcome his chronic insomnia and depression. Needless to say, his alcohol consumption was not particularly efficacious in the management of his post-traumatic psychological afflictions.

After developing cirrhotic liver disease, Woodrow Bright had become a "frequent flier" at the VA annex. He suffered from periodic complications of chronic alcoholism manifested by upper gastrointestinal bleeding from esophageal varices and ascites that periodically required management by the paracentesis procedure.

Dung Dunhill was assigned to help in the management of Mr. Bright, but since he was still stuck with the designated rank of a mushroom, he was not authorized to participate in procedures. An administrative error, however, allowed Dunhill to be subjected to further emotional trauma.

The patient had a markedly distended abdomen from the fluid that had accumulated and basilar rales were noted in the left lower lung field. Dung correctly assessed that the patient may have been developing a complication of pneumonia superimposed upon the patient's underlying liver failure and ascites.

He called Dr. Barron for instructions, but she was not available that afternoon. As the resident was getting a painful cavity filled at the dentist's office, Dunhill was forced to call Dr. Mackenzie for guidance. "Dr. Mackenzie, I know you don't like to be bothered, but this is the student you know as Poor Boy. Dr. Barron's not here today, and I'm not certain what I should do about a patient."

After explaining to the attending physician about Mr. Bright's clinical condition, Dr. Mackenzie answered, "I want you to call in that dumbass, Rooster. He knows how to tap bellies. Afterward, have the patient's nurse call me, and I'll authorize a chest x-ray to see what's going on with his lungs. It's getting late. You better call me when you know what the chest x-ray looks like. Am I clear?"

After hanging up the phone, Dung called J. D. Brewster.

Brewster came in and said, "I shouldn't be doing this because you're just a mushroom, but I guess rules were made to be broken.

I'm going to teach you how to tap somebody's belly, so next time the opportunity arises, you'll be able to handle it if it is okay with your intern or resident physician."

Once the transparent yellowish fluid was starting to drain out of Mr. Woodrow Bright's abdomen, Brewster gave Dung additional instructions. "When you're done—and this patient goes down to get his chest x-ray—call me. We'll need to look at the film together. We need to make sure we let Dr. Mackenzie know what's going on before the end of the day—or he'll chew on our ass during tomorrow's morning report."

Upon Brewster's departure, Dung was obligated to find out what happened during the war crime trials that had taken place after World War II. After all, a thorough patient history was mandatory during every admission. Since Dung was already on the threshold of a major meltdown, however, he perhaps should have let sleeping dogs lie. What Woodrow Bright was about to tell him, in the words of the 1960s rock and roll star, Janice Joplin, would just "tear another piece" of Dunhill's heart.

"We rounded up some very bad hombres after the war," Woodrow Bright explained. "I remember seeing photographs that had been secretly taken by a Christian missionary at Nanking when the Japanese invaded. I can't make this shit up. I saw pictures of Japanese soldiers using Chinese infants for bayonet practice. The babies would be thrown into air and then impaled upon the end of the soldiers' bayonets. The picture showed the soldiers laughing and smiling while they were doing it. I swear I'll never get those pictures out of my mind no matter how long I live. Did you know that the divine emperor, Hirohito, authorized all of that?"

"Was that the worst of it?"

"You tell me," Woodrow said. "The Sikhs from India had fought for the British, and we found a mass grave where hundreds of them were stacked up like cordwood. The Japanese had actually taken a hammer and roofing nails and tacked their turbans down to their skulls before they buried those poor bastards! The Sikhs still had their turbans hammered into their brains when their corpses were exhumed. Nice. How could somebody do that to a fellow human being?"

"I wish I could attribute something like that to the moral ambiguity of warfare," Dung said, "but I believe some things happen as a consequence of the evil that already dwells deep within the collective heart of what we call mankind."

"We arrested several Japanese soldiers who were overtly involved with cannibalism," Woodrow said. "I shit you not! It would generally take about three days for the Japanese to eat a human being, and the victim was kept alive throughout the process. At first, the subject would have his arms and legs hacked off with a samurai sword. Then they would burn the ends of the stumps to keep the victim from bleeding to death. The extremities were consumed first, and then the torso of the victim would be put in an open pit—so he could not try to roll away and escape."

"Are those the kinds of cases you prosecuted?"

"That, and much more," Woodrow said. "You haven't heard half of it when it comes to human cannibalism. On the second day of the grisly human feast, the Japanese would generally eat the victim's face, including the eyes, ears, nose, and tongue. On the third day, the officers would consume the prisoner's internal organs, including the liver and heart, and these items were eaten raw like sushi. Sadly, the internal organs would be harvested while the victim was still very much alive. Fortunately, only a few captured American servicemen were cannibalized. It would seem that the Japs preferred 'brown meat' since most of the victims were Asians. Probably the greatest satisfaction I ever had on the tribunal was when we prosecuted members of the 731 Unit."

"Never heard of it."

"The 731 Unit was the Japanese biological warfare agency," the patient explained. "Countless victims were exposed to infectious diseases and poisonous substances in an attempt to develop weapons of mass destruction. The Japanese military doctors were actually involved with this heinous activity long before the Nazis started doing the same type of research. Unfortunately, victims were also subjected to live vivisections without anesthesia. The Japs and the

Huns must have been cut from the same cloth, eh? Can you guess who authorized the creation of the 731 Unit?"

"Hirohito?"

"Bingo!" Woodward exclaimed. "Although future historians might actually debate this matter, it was Emperor Hirohito who ordered the creation of the 731 Unit. That's an indisputable fact as far as I'm concerned. You know, to this day, I'm not sure why the Japanese named their biological warfare agency the 731 Unit. Perhaps it has the same significance to the Japanese as, oh, I don't know, what John 3:16 means to us. Scratch that. Don't pay attention to my righteous rant. I suppose that I'm just being a racist right about now."

"Nah," Dung said. "Not as far as I can tell!"

"Speculate one way or the other as far as I'm concerned," Woodrow said, "but I certainly am *not* about to apologize for how I feel. I can't get over it. I don't want to get over it."

"Maybe there are some things that a human being is just not supposed to 'get over' as you say," Dung added.

"My only regret about World War II is that we only used two atomic bombs. We should have dropped a third one on Tokyo and vaporized Emperor Hirohito. Was it a sin to incinerate innocent women and children with Fat Man and Little Boy?"

"The morality, or lack thereof, concerning the use of atomic weapons should only be judged within the context of the times in which they were deployed," Dunhill opined. "I've heard my colleague Brewster argue that without a time-specific historical lens, any other conclusion would likely result in a bastardization of human history."

"Frankly, I don't give a shit anymore. As you may or may not know, Tokyo was the third original planned nuclear target that had been drawn up by the 509th Atomic Bomb group. If the Japanese had not capitulated after Nagasaki, Emperor Hirohito's compound was in the queue to get nuked next. It would have been done as soon as another plutonium bomb had rolled off the assembly line at Los Alamos. To this very day, I still feel hatred toward Emperor Hirohito. Right or wrong, I blame him for everything. I'm ashamed that we didn't have the balls to indict that lemon-skinned little coward as a war criminal at the end of the conflict."

"Well, don't be bashful," Felix said as he completed the paracentesis procedure and pulled the catheter line out of Mr. Bright's abdomen. "Why don't you tell me how you really feel about the whole matter?"

"How much were you able to drain out of my belly this time?"

"About two liters. I hope you're feeling better. Do you have anything else to add before we send you down for your chest x-ray and see what is going on in your left lung?"

"When the Japanese withdrew from Manila," Woodrow Bright explained, "they butchered a hundred thousand people. It was clear that the Japanese looked upon the Filipinos as belonging to an inferior race. The Japanese official who oversaw the war crimes was a low-life, dickwad named General Tomoyuki Yamashita. He and his associate chief of staff, Akiro Muto, were both convicted and sentenced to death. I was furious with my colleague, Colonel Harry E. Clark, because he was assigned to be the defense attorney for General Yamashita at the trial."

"Why was that an issue?"

"He could have turned down the job, but for some reason, Harry Clark accepted the task at hand. In retrospect, I'm quite surprised that he actually tried to do a good job as the defense attorney for these bastards. In any event, justice was served in the end as Yamashita and his ilk eventually got the noose. I was not the chief prosecutor for that particular trial, as I was consigned the collateral case against the Japanese marine captain who authorized the notorious Raping of Ermita."

"What was that about?" Dunhill asked.

"Four hundred young girls, some no older than twelve, were rounded up from the Ermita district of Manila and summarily gang-raped by the Japanese. Many of the young girls were then subsequently butchered. Nice, eh?" Woodrow explained. "The Japanese officer responsible for that particular atrocity was convicted and sentenced to death by hanging in February 1946. I made the one big sin during my brief career on the war crimes tribunal and still have misgivings about it."

"What might this 'big sin' have been?" Dunhill pressed for clarity.

"My big sin was that I allowed the Filipinos to carry out the execution without supervision. The surviving citizens of Manila built a hundred-foot scaffold with a ninety-foot rope. By the time they completed the edifice, it was too late to change anything. The project had taken on a life of its own. The condemned man's final words were, 'Why are you doing this to me? They were only Filipinos!' To the very end, the man apparently had no remorse for the barbarity that he allowed his troops to commit."

"I'm surprised that this Japanese officer was unrepentant until the very end."

"Why would he bother to seek redemption or perhaps even salvation?" Woodrow asked. "In his mind, the Filipinos were an inferior, subhuman race! When the lever on the gallows was pulled, the platform fell from underneath the officer's feet. The captain fell at an acceleration rate of thirty-two feet per second per second. I'm certain you're able to guess what happened next. Once his body hit the end of the rope, he was decapitated. It was the most extraordinary thing I had ever seen. His headless body bounced upon the ground, and then it came back upright on its two feet! The headless corpse proceeded to run around clockwise in a semicircle for a few moments before it fell on its right side, but the legs continued to twitch! I can't make this shit up."

"That doesn't seem plausible!"

"You weren't there. Gospel truth, I tell you," Woodrow professed. "The roar from the crowd was unbelievable. It sounded as if I was in the bleachers of a college football game and the home team had just scored the winning touchdown. The Filipinos ran out, grabbed the headless corpse, and carried it out into the forest. The dead man was swept away as if he were merely a tray of beverages hoisted on high by waitresses in a busy pub. God knows what they ultimately did to that nasty bastard's body. What does that tell you?"

Felix Dunhill began to laugh hysterically. "What it tells me is that justice was served!"

"What I said was not supposed to be funny!" Woodrow Bright said. "Nevertheless, don't get me wrong. I've always loved the Filipino people. They were always good to me, and I've never forgiven the Japanese for the sins and crimes that they committed during the war."

"How could you forgive them?" Dung asked indignantly. "After all, forgiveness wasn't your assigned responsibility. As best I can tell, your job was to ensure the dispensation of *justice*— not the dispensation of *mercy.* There's no shame in what you did. You should have taken great pride when that war criminal finally took a big swan dive from that execution scaffold!"

"Damnation, son! You sound like a Texan who's all hat and no cattle," Woodrow said. "So in the end, do you think that you could have done better at a job like mine?"

"Hands down," Dung chuckled, "and I would have enjoyed doing it!"

After Mr. Bright was sent down for his chest x-ray, Brewster and Felix Dunhill went down to the radiology department to look at the film. It was already 3:16 PM, and the radiology department was going to close up as tight as a drum at 4:00 PM sharp. The VA annex was run like a post office. Nothing of substance could ever actually get accomplished after four in the afternoon, but the students had plenty of time to complete their task.

The head radiology library clerk was a peculiar little histrionic malingerer who was known as Slow Joe. Sadly, Joe exemplified precisely what was wrong with the entire VA system. Joe worked behind the counter at the film library reception area, and no house staff members, much less students, were ever allowed to look for any x-ray films on their own accord. Only a designated x-ray clerk was allowed to retrieve any films or dictated reports that needed to be reviewed. When it was in the middle of a working day, that policy was just fine and dandy. However, all the x-ray clerks would go home at four o'clock at the end of their afternoon shift. If you needed to find an x-ray report or film after that time when the radiology suite had already shut down, you were stone-cold shit out of luck. This policy was detrimental to patient care, but whoever said the VA system had anything to do with patient care?

Slow Joe didn't like to be spoken to, and he had a big poster in the reception area: "Do Not Talk to the Clerk. Silence Must Be Maintained at All Times!"

The only way to convey a petition for Slow Joe to find an x-ray report or film was to physically write down the request on an index card and then hand it to him without making any eye contact.

Slow Joe would then go into an amazing and annoying ritualistic dance. He would study the card for a long time by holding it up close to his face and then at arm's length. He would repeat these gyrations after removing his reading glasses. He would periodically sneer at the written request and then slam it down on the counter in front of him. Finally, after five or six minutes of studying the writing on the card as if he were an Oxford linguistic scholar trying to translate the Hindu Bhagavad-Gita from its original Sanskrit into modern English, he would slowly shuffle off to the library area.

Oddly, Slow Joe would never take the index card with him. He would invariably leave it on the counter, but he never remembered what had been written on the note in the first place. After disappearing for another five or ten minutes, he would shuffle back to the counter, pick up the index card, and study it yet again. This whole dreadful process would be repeated over and over. It would often take Slow Joe an hour or more to find an x-ray report or film, and that extraordinary amount of time required to execute such a mundane task would be no different for Brewster and Felix Dunhill when they came down to the radiology department to find the chest x-ray results on Mr. Woodrow Bright. Slow Joe could never be reprimanded for his sloth-like work habits because he was unionized.

On Slow's third trip to the counter, it was already 4:53 PM.

Felix Dunhill said, "Listen to me, you useless old sod! Why don't you take the goddamn index card with you when you wander off into the back library area? If you did that, you wouldn't forget what the fuck you were trying to accomplish in the first place. For Pete's sake, pull your head out of your ass!"

Oops! That was not a particularly good move on Dung's part. Slow Joe cupped his hands over his ears as if he was in brain-splitting agony. After he had composed himself, he came around to the other side of the counter and slammed his hand against the poster.

Maybe Slow Joe was a functional mute who had been afflicted with hyperacusis syndrome. Just as likely, Slow Joe was a functional mute who had been afflicted with a high titer of bullshit, and he was just trying to game the system. As a symbolic gesture to show the hostile student who was really in charge, he purposefully left the card on the counter yet again when he disappeared into the netherworld where the x-ray films were stored and cataloged.

Brewster and Dunhill looked at each other in astonishment when, at 4:00 PM sharp, all the lights in the film library were suddenly turned off. The door that led to the film storage area was then immediately closed and locked from the other side.

Without a word, Dunhill turned his back to the clerk's desk and propped his butt upon the counter. He swung his legs over to the other side and jumped down into the reception area.

Brewster handed Dunhill a fire extinguisher that he had appropriated from the hallway wall.

Dunhill grabbed the fire extinguisher and used it as a sledgehammer. He repeatedly slammed the fire extinguisher against the doorknob in an attempt to break into the film library area. On the third blow, the door gently swung open. Dung took one step into the back region and immediately found the x-ray that they had been looking for.

The diagnostic imaging study was right on top of a pile of other film jackets in a bin that had been cryptically labeled "TO BE". Perhaps "TO BE" was simply an in-house designation to the radiology staff that the batch of film jackets in that particular labeled bin still needed "to be" read. Perhaps, "TO BE" was simply an in-house designation to Slow Joe that the batch of film jackets in that particular labeled bin needed "to be" ignored.

Upon review of the x-ray, an alveolar infiltrate was noted in the patient's left lower lung field, which seemed to be consistent with an early pneumonia. These findings were conveyed to the attending, Dr. Mackenzie, who promptly called in a telephone order to the medical floor to instruct the nurse to place the patient on antibiotic therapy.

The following morning, Dr. Mackenzie wanted to know if Poor Boy and Rooster knew anything about the mayhem that occurred in the film library during the preceding evening. Brewster and Dunhill simply looked at each other and shrugged.

Later that morning, Brewster and Dunhill made a follow-up visit to the radiology film room library and discovered that the carnage that they had left in their angry wake had already been cleaned up and immediately repaired by the Spa's maintenance crew. Compelled to return to the scene of the crime, it was an absolutely amazing thing to behold that the door lock appeared to be as good as new. It was certainly frustrating that the rest of the VA system, allegedly responsible for actual patient care, didn't work with such efficiency. Dumbfounded, Brewster and Dunhill stared into the radiology reception area as if they were gazing upon an intersession of Divine intervention.

They sat in silence for several minutes and pondered the mysteries of the universe in addition to the inexplicable operational priorities of the Veteran's Administration health care-delivery system.

Finally, Brewster asked, "What in hell happened over yonder?"

"Nothing. I assure you—not a damned thing happened in there today."

PUS
BLOOD
URINE
SEMEN

# 11

## MELTDOWN

Thanksgiving fell on November 27 in 1980, and the students who were working on their clerkship rotations were looking forward to a four-day break. Their next rotations were scheduled to begin on the first Monday in December. Since J. D. Brewster was a direct descendent of William Brewster who had come over with the Pilgrims on the *Mayflower*, Thanksgiving had always been important to him. His mother, Helliarma, was going to host Thanksgiving dinner that year.

There were going to be no less than eight guests, including Brewster and Stella, Bill and his wife, Cathy, Uncle John, Feral Cheryl, the Wooly Mammoth, and Rudolph Valentino Mammon. Helliarma was quite nervous about inviting "colored people" into her home, so she planned on making a point of keeping an eye on everybody so that none of the silverware would end up missing.

Uncertain if her non-white guests were familiar with the proper use of indoor plumbing, Helliarma had lined the guest bathroom floor around the toilet with several heavy-duty, jumbo trash bags. She secured the plastic bags to the floor with duct tape as a preemptive strike against any anticipated untidy happenstance. After all, if the target ring was erroneously missed by any visitors whom she perceived to be culturally primitive individuals, cleanup would have been a relatively easy task without the need to employ a full-blown haz-mat emergency detail that would have required the evacuation of the entire neighborhood.

Mother Brewster would cook a turkey, but everybody else would have to bring a side dish for the feast. The one traditional staple J. D. Brewster was quite skillful at conjuring was praline-style candied yams. He made certain to prepare a large enough serving to accommodate all the guests. Rudolph Valentino Mammon had planned on bringing a pumpkin pie, but he decided on bringing a homemade sweet potato pie. That was a good deal for all the guests since a delicious sweet potato pie could beat the pants off of a Yankee pumpkin pie any day of the week and twice on Sunday!

It was time for Brewster to try to make sure that the axe had been deeply buried with the Wooly Mammoth. "Say, Willy, I hear that you have just wrapped up a pediatric rotation and your mandatory family practice gig. Cheryl tells me that you're finally going to begin your three-month internal medicine rotation at the VA annex in Bellaire. I'm sure you'll do well and will be ready to get a promotion to stud status sooner than later. I hope you and I are able to do a clerkship again together someday."

"Thanks," the big man succinctly replied.

"Are things now cool between us?" Brewster asked. "I know some of the crazy stuff Fielder and I did may have seemed a bit juvenile, and I do apologize for that. Maybe you and I can go back out to the VA annex sometime and take on that three-hole pitch and putt again. As I painfully recall, I never had a chance to even take a swing at the ball."

"Stop right there!" Willy said. "Time to be serious. I know it's in your nature to go around and brew up trouble, but you need to act like a full-grown man from now on and keep your weird shit on a short leash."

"Okay, Willy. You can count on me," Brewster replied as he crossed his fingers behind his back.

The holiday was the first opportunity for Bill to meet Stella Link, but Brother Bill did not find favor in his younger brother's new consort. When the very first inconspicuous opportunity availed itself, Bill took J. D. for an attempted intervention. "Look, I know that you have never had a real girlfriend before, but do you know what you're doing? I see now that you have been dating a fat, old, hippie, dinosaur loser chick who must be at least ten years older than you are. She even wears plastic flowers in her hair. How lame is that? Oh my God. Are you kidding me?"

J. D. started to sing a refrain from a rock and roll song originally recorded by Eric Burdon and the Animals from about fifteen years earlier: "It's my life—and I'll do what I want!"

November was an important month. Stella Link had just turned thirty-three, and it was the twentieth anniversary of Mother Brewster's widowhood. If Charles Dickens had penned his master-piece, *Great Expectations*, in the later part of the twentieth century, Helliarma Brewster would have certainly been the perfect inspiration for his tragic character, Miss Havisham. Helliarma was trapped in a strange time warp, and nothing had changed in her house since her husband had passed away years before.

As a case in point, a square pane of glass had been knocked out of the front living room window when a late summer storm uprooted a dying sycamore back in 1960. A strong wind had driven a thick, broken limb from that tree directly unto the front of the home. Woody Brewster was busy preparing for his run for a seat on the Houston City Council, and the broken glass was never replaced. Instead, the broken pane had been temporarily patched with a small piece of plywood that had been caulked into the frame. That tempo-rary patchwork was now twenty years old.

Bill brought a new pane of glass and window caulk to make the overdue repair. "Mom, I have a big surprise for you. I'm going to finally repair the broken window that's in the living room!"

To everybody's dismay, Helliarma replied, "No, you'll do no such thing! Don't touch anything in my house. Do you understand?"

"What are you talking about?" Bill asked.

"This is the exact condition the house has been in since your father passed away. This is exactly how I want it."

"It is a damned house," J. D. said, "not a shrine!"

"Once I'm dead and gone, you and your brother can fight over what little I own, but for now, everything must remain the same.

Am I clear?" She turned to address Cathy and Stella. "My husband, Woody, died twenty years ago this month—on Sunday, November 13, 1960. Did you know my husband was a personal acquaintance of the Houston Oiler quarterback, George Blanda?"

"So I've heard," Stella said as she wiped beads of perspiration from her brow. "Please excuse me momentarily, everybody. I have to use the restroom once again."

"You're like a leaky faucet, Stella," Brewster joked. "Maybe I need to call in a plumber."

Stella glared at her boyfriend as she left the table.

"That's a fact," Mamma Brewster continued. "Woody and Rudy would meet Blanda from time to time over at a club not far from Hobby Airport … the Blue Tone. In the 1960s, there were stories in the newspaper that Blanda may have been involved with gambling while he was still with the Houston Oilers, but those were just unsubstantiated rumors." She looked directly at Rudy Mammon and asked, "Those were just rumors, weren't they, Rudy?"

Rudolph Valentino Mammon failed to answer the question.

J. D. said, "Look, Mom, this is ancient history."

"Not to me," Helliarma said. "This all happened as if it was just yesterday. After Sunday brunch, I went to take a nap while Woody and the boys watched a football game on television. I remember that the Houston Oilers were playing the Los Angeles Chargers that Sunday. The Oilers happened to lose that contest, but it was a very close score in the end as I recall."

"Why do you torture yourself like this?" Cathy asked.

"Maybe my husband made a wager on the outcome of that game, but I don't know for sure," Mother Brewster said. "Anyhow, while I was taking my nap, he died from an apparent heart attack. It was the fault of William and J. D. that my husband died that day, and it is their fault now that I'm a widow now."

"Stop!" Bill said. "Enough already."

"If they had only awakened me from my nap, I would have been able to resuscitate him. I was a nurse, you know."

J. D. and Bill had heard this hyperbolic maternal harping all their lives. Bill finally said, "As you should recall, Mother, you gave us strict instructions that you did *not* want to be awakened under any circumstances. We were just following your orders. That's all on your head if you plan on playing the blame game today."

"Are you serious, Mrs. Brewster?" Stella added upon her return from the restroom. "What you're saying makes no sense at all. How could you possibly blame your children for Wood's death twenty years after the event?"

"Well, it was their fault, I tell you! I knew how to deal with medical emergencies. When I found Woody on the floor, the boys were sitting beside him. They were both crying—like they knew that they had done something wrong."

"Okay," J. D. said. "Let's just air it all out right now. Why don't you just tell the entire neighborhood that my brother and I purposefully murdered our own father? Happy freaking Thanksgiving, everybody!"

"It's plain to see," Helliarma continued. "You boys knew that your father had just keeled over dead. You kids should've awakened me! He must have been dead for at least an hour by the time I awakened from my nap."

J. D. rolled his eyes and shook his head. "I'm sick and tired of hearing this story. Thanks, Mom. I really appreciate these unfounded accusations that you've levied against William and me. Nice. For goodness sake, listen to what in hell you're saying!"

"When I found your father dead on the floor," Mother Brewster said, "I picked up my Jack LaLanne jump rope, and I wanted to beat you boys with it, but that pesky neighbor, Sister Buena, somehow appeared and stopped me from doing it. She was the one who actually called the ambulance, but I guess it didn't matter by then. It was already too late. Woody was gone. Nothing else in life has mattered to me ever since."

The guests stared at Helliarma in stunned silence.

"The following Thanksgiving—a year after Woody passed away—I tried to murder my sons," Mother Brewster added in a nonchalant manner. "William was six years old, and J. D. was around four by then."

"I missed that," Rudy said. "My hearing must be goin' bad."

"No," Helliarma said. "Y'all heard me correctly. Do you boys remember when I asked you to play hide-and-seek with me on that Thanksgiving Day? I told you kids to get into the oven, but you ignored my order. You boys *always* disobeyed me. If you had only done what I simply asked, I would have flipped the lever and then I would have gassed you rascals, but no! You both got scared and hid behind the living room curtain. Does that ring a bell?"

J. D. and Bill simply stared at each other in shame.

"When I pulled you boys out from behind the curtain, I had just managed to wrestle you both back into the oven and turn on the gas when Sister Buena again appeared from out of nowhere. She said, 'Helliarma, it smells like you have a gas leak!' She shut off the gas lever behind the stove and pulled you boys out from the oven. She hauled you boys out into the yard to get some fresh air. As I recall, I may have tried to kill you kids two or three other times after that occasion, but I was obviously never successful."

"Well, if at first you don't succeed, try and try again!" Uncle John said.

J. D. Brewster went acutely blind again in his left eye, and it lasted for more than five minutes, which was the longest he had ever experienced the loss of visual acuity. Fortunately, the symptoms were again transient. After several anxiety-filled minutes, he slowly recovered his eyesight, but he had not previously known that his mother had indeed contemplated murdering her very own offspring on more than one occasion. It was shocking to him that she had spoken about the macabre matter with such candor.

Sister Buena had saved Brewster from being physically abused at the day care center. Not only that, but she somehow always magically reappeared whenever Brewster's life—or his brother's life—was in peril. None of it made any sense. His mother referred to Sister Buena as a neighbor, but that couldn't be the case. After all, J.D. lived in that house until the time that he had moved away to college. J. D. knew everybody who lived on the street, and he didn't recall any neighbor named Sister Buena. He would make a point to talk to Bill about this peculiar matter. In any event, the very few family ties that he had left in what was turning out for him to be a very bizarre life had continued to erode.

After a prolonged period of silence, the wooly one said, "Boy, J. D., your candied yams sure are special." The other guests quietly nodded in approval.

J. D. Brewster, Bill, and their two companions excused themselves and quietly, but quickly, walked toward the front door. Before Bill departed, he purposefully dropped the replacement pane of glass that he had thoughtfully brought on top of the dining room table. All of the other visitors pretended not to notice that anything was awry when the windowpane shattered and shards of glass were showered upon the roasted turkey, which at that point had not even been carved and served up to any of the guests.

Mother Brewster was in her eighties by the year 2000 when the Houston Museum of Modern Art made it a point to borrow all her living room furniture for a special public event. Her belongings were put on display to exemplify a middle-class, mid-twentieth-century domicile in an exhibit that was called "Life in Texas in the Twentieth Century."

Your Witness News had even done a happy human-interest story about how Helliarma had made a living museum out of her home with all her furnishings that dated back to the mid-1950s. Sadly, nothing could have been further from the truth; paying tribute to the mid-twentieth century was a concept that had never entered Mother Brewster's mind.

Upon the death of her husband, Helliarma Brewster's life also succinctly ended on the early afternoon of November 13, 1960. Sadly, her home had become little more than the deep hidden passageways of the pyramids where dead pharaohs could be surrounded by the furnishings and accouterments that they had accumulated during their brief life spans as Egyptian rulers. Perhaps such material trappings could offer some kind of comfort if one anticipated that in the afterlife, a soul would only be relegated to a lonely eternity entombed in utter silence and darkness.

Helliarma Brewster had developed homicidal ideations after she became a widow. From a psychiatric standpoint, she suffered from chronic situational depression with superimposed psychopathy from which she would never recover. Be that as it may, a fundamental question remains: Can homicidal ideations be an inheritable trait?

Years later, J. D. Brewster would wonder if his own maladjusted behavior, evil actions, and poor life decisions were a matter of nature, nurture, or a combination thereof. In any event, that would be the last time J. D. would ever pay his aging mother a visit at his old childhood homestead. As it would turn out, it would also be the very last Thanksgiving celebration that Brewster would ever share with any of his few friends or remaining family members…

"Hello, Dr. Beathard," Brewster said as he sheepishly entered the office of the research scientist. "I've not seen you since Dr. Holcombe went away on sick leave. I thought I'd come by and find out if there's any way I can resurrect my participation in the dual training program. I still hope to get my PhD by the spring of '83."

"I can't see how that's going to happen, Brewster," Beathard explained. "The soonest you'll be able to ramp up on a new research project will be July of next year. You'll have to at least complete this current year of clinical clerkship training as things now stand. Besides, you don't currently have a viable research project to jump back into. Sadly, you squandered an entire year, and you'll have to start over from scratch."

"Well, I'm formulating some new ideas," Brewster said. "I just need to make a pitch to Dr. Sassman about it."

"Fair enough, but realistically you won't be ready to break out of here until '84 at the earliest—unless you can find a new project that you can ramp up in a year or less. Can you live with that?"

"We'll see."

"By the way, a couple of Iranian fellows came by administration and were looking for you. Know anything about it?"

"No," Brewster said as he tried to hide his alarm. "It must be a mistake. I don't know any Iranians except for my friend, Mehdi, who works in food services."

"Well," Beathard said, "they *insisted* that they knew who you were—and they made it clear to me that they very much wanted to give you something."

On Monday, December 1, Fielder and Russian Bear were watching TV while waiting in the vinyl lounge for Felix Dunhill and Brewster to arrive in order to start their third and final month on the mandatory internal medicine rotation.

Upon Brewster's arrival, Fielder asked, "How are you, Brew? Did you enjoy Thanksgiving break?

"If I was doing any better, they'd bronze me, put me over in Hermann Park, and then let pigeons shit all over me. That's how well I'm doing. By the way, what in hell are you watching, Russian Bear? Are those people on the screen a bunch of snake worshipers?"

The television show featured a white-haired televangelist with an enormous double jelly-rolled pompadour who was flinging around venomous serpents held high above his head.

"No, no, you have to watch this with us," Fielder said. "This is the 'Rectal Roberts Ministry Hour,' and this dude's about to perform an exorcism on one of his parishioners."

"Hold on there, pencil dick," Brewster said. "Regarding spiritual matters, I thought you were a bona fide agnostic."

"Past tense," Fielder replied. "I've had a new spiritual awakening! You should be happy for me."

"Be that as it may," Brewster said, "who's this Rectal Roberts character? If I had to venture a guess, he looks like a Southern Baptist preacher all jacked up on amphetamines and anabolic steroids."

"Evidentially, he must be a bit like Oral Roberts," Fielder replied. "However, from what little I know, I'd have to surmise that Rectal is not quite as an accomplished faith healer as old Oral. The members of Rectal's television-based congregation have given their minister a reverential nickname."

"Pray tell."

"They call him the Righteous Rectal Vault!"

"Is that so?" Brewster asked.

"After all," Fielder explained, "it would seem to me that this Rectal preacher must start at the bottom and then slowly work his way up—if you catch my meaning. Other than that, all I know about this minister is that he's originally from some crappy, shithole place, filled with incestuous and ignorant peons. He broadcasts his show out of his hometown of Hope, Arkansas."

The three students watched with utter amazement as the television preacher slipped on a pair of brass knuckles and steeled his resolve to spiritually clean the clock of a little old paraplegic lady. The misfortunate parishioner had struggled with a pair of withered and useless lower extremities as a consequence to some type of catastrophic chronic neurological condition. Whatever the noxious malady was that had chronically afflicted the pilgrim with lower leg weakness, it was a disease process that had sadly rendered the ancient woman crippled, and with at best, very limited mobility. Now strictly confined to one of the Salvation Army's bargain-bin refurbished wheelchairs (itself crippled with a warped left wheel) the pious parishioner came to Rectal Roberts in search of redemption and perhaps even salvation.

"In the name of Jah-heeez-us-uh-huh," the televangelist proclaimed, "I cast you out, you evil agent of Satan!" After receiving a mighty blow from the brass knuckles, the little old lady flew out of her wheelchair and bounced unconsciously across the floor of the church sanctuary. The congregation went wild with a pious and repetitive chorus of "Hallelujah!" as they fervently rammed their right fists repeatedly into the air toward the spiritual Pied Piper known affectionately as The Righteous Rectal Vault. The image would be clearly reminiscent of a by-gone era to any fledgling historian who had even the vaguest familiarity with the Nuremburg rallies of the 1930s.

Fielder and the Russian Bear started to shout with enthusiasm and gave each other high fives.

"You boys need to turn this crap off right now!" Brewster exclaimed. "First off, the name 'Jesus' is *not* pronounced with five syllables. Second, I think this is going to give Christianity a bad name if somebody else walks into the Vinyl Lounge right about now."

"Oh, you are so wrong, grasshopper!" Fielder laughed. "This is some good, old-timey Gospel, I tell you."

"The more I think about this, Brew," Russian Bear said, "the more I'm certain that you'd likely benefit from a prayer session with this Rectal Roberts individual. He's asking the television audience to send in money to an off-shore P.O. Box located in the Caribbean islands. He says that he needs our money right this very minute! I'm thinking that Fielder and I should ship off a few dollars today to this very important spiritual ministry. Although he prefers cash, he also apparently accepts Master Card and Visa."

"Yes indeed," Fielder added, "but not American Express for some unclear reason. If we slip this guy a couple of Jackson notes, maybe, just maybe, he could perform a low-budget exorcism on your sorry ass. Hallelujah! Praise the Lord and pass the ammunition."

"So, it's come down to this, has it?" Brewster asked. "Apparently you boys believe I'm in dire need of some kind of hocus-pocus, evangelistic exorcism! I'll have you know that I'm *already* a man who tries to walk the straight—"

"Yeah, yeah, yeah," Bear interrupted. "We've heard it all before."

"I've got it all figured out," Fielder said. "You'll just have to drop your trousers and plant your penis upon the TV screen—and then you'll be healed! Before you do it, however, I would recommend using a clean piece of cloth to wipe the lint off the screen."

"The purpose being?" Brewster asked as he folded his arms.

"Otherwise, you might experience static electricity that might give you a rude shock on the end of your pecker. I'd bet that would make you cry like a little schoolgirl! Come to think of it, that might be good for you, no?"

Brewster shook his head in disgust and said, "A pox on all of you! I swear that you're a band of sacrilegious heathens!" If the truth be told, Brewster was painfully aware that he and his colleagues were already spiritually lost.

Upon the arrival of Dung Felix, the four students headed up to see the infamous Dr. Harrison Reed. It had been months since Brewster had encountered Dr. Reed, the head of the MD/PhD dual-training program, and Brewster was somewhat concerned that the hostility they had for each other would somehow be rekindled.

When they entered the conference room to meet the attending and his new resident and intern, Dr. Reed acted as if he had never even met J. D. Brewster before. Apparently, Brewster ceased to exist the moment he was no longer actively engaged in any type of research project.

Dr. Reed said, "Gentlemen, my name's Dr. Harrison Reed. I'll be your attending for your last mandatory rotation on the internal medicine service. I hope you'll find this experience both intellectually and physically challenging. Unlike your other rotations where you've been on call every third or fourth night, I'm going to have you on call every other night. As there are four of you, this should not be much of a hardship. Your resident this month is in her third year of postgraduate training, and her name is Dr. Hillman. Your intern on our team is Dr. Clarke. I've been informed that one of my students this month, Mr. Felix Dunhill, has never passed a pimp and pone challenge."

"Well," Dunhill said, "it's not been for the lack of trying."

"Batter up!" Dr. Reed said. "Here's the first pitch. What is the malignant cell—and what is the immunoglobulin subtype—that's associated with Waldenström's Disease?"

Felix Dunhill replied. "The malignant cell is considered to be a plasmacytoid lymphocyte, and the monoclonal immunoglobulin is subtype M, I do believe."

"I do believe you're correct!" Reed replied with a smile. "He got a base hit, everybody. Here's the second pitch. Name at least three etiologies associated with cancer of the pancreas."

Dunhill answered, "Chronic alcohol abuse, diabetes mellitus, and chronic recurrent episodic pancreatitis are known to be some of the etiologies for cancer of the pancreas."

Realizing that victory was at hand, Dung's three colleagues clapped their hands and cheered him on.

"You can do this, Dung," Brewster said. "If you need help on the third question, don't be afraid to ask somebody from the bleachers to pinch-hit for you if it's necessary."

"You're doing quite well right now, young man," Dr. Reed stated. "Let's see if you can hit a grand slam on the third question. What intracellular eukaryotic parasite was responsible for the majority of malaria cases during the Korean War?"

"I'll bet this is a trick question," Felix said. "I know that the most common cause of malaria among American serviceman during the Vietnam War was caused by *Plasmodium falciparum*, but Vietnam is in the tropics, and that war was fought on or about the seventeenth parallel. The border between North and South Korea on the more temperate peninsula is about 1,500 miles to the north of Nam, at about the thirty-eighth parallel, although frankly the border between North and South Korea runs at a bit more of a diagonal course, and it's not exactly horizontal to the equator per se. Be that as it may, I've based my calculations on the fact that one degree of latitude is approximately sixty-nine miles and that there's a twenty-one-degree difference in latitude between the Korean peninsula and Vietnam. Therefore, I'm guessing that the *Plasmodium* species most responsible for most of the cases of malaria among American serviceman during the Korean War was most assuredly a different organism than *falciparum*. If that's the case, I have three other blood-borne eukaryotic intracellular parasites to choose from. I've got my fingers crossed, and I'm going to make a blind-ass guess that it was likely *Plasmodium vivax*."

"Well, my young ward, you've just hit a grand slam—and I just got poned!" Dr. Reed said. "I believe congratulations are in order to you. Through a rather brilliant deduction, you finally won a pimp and pone challenge, and you've just hit a grand slam to boot. Not only that, you did it against the titular head of the MD/PhD dual training program. As everyone will attest, I'm the smartest attending at the Gulf Coast College of Medicine, so I must say that you did quite well indeed."

Felix Dunhill started to cry while his colleagues were patting him on the back and congratulating him. Felix finally said, "Does this mean I've finally graduated from being a mushroom to being a scut puppy?"

Dr. Reed said, "Oh, heavens no. Normally, I'd issue a field commission of scut puppy to a student at this time right on the spot, but because you're a slob and currently wearing a filthy consultation jacket, you'll be stuck as a mushroom for the duration of this rotation as far as I'm concerned. There's nothing you can possibly do to change your miserable lot in life. I hope you enjoy your time on this clerkship."

"Wait!" Felix said, "That's not fair."

Dr. Reed pointed at Dung Felix and started to laugh. "I know your father is an attending on the rehab unit. Do you think he's proud of you right about now? To the contrary, I suspect he's truly ashamed to have you as a son."

Dunhill made a fist and was about to pound Dr. Reed's face into a bloody pulp, but he suddenly felt a stabbing pain radiating through his right trapezius muscle group. He turned sharply and saw that Russian Bear was firmly pinching the posterior aspect of the base of Dung's neck in an attempt to defuse the situation.

"Let go, Bear!" Dung demanded.

Bear wouldn't relent, and he continued to apply painful pressure against his colleague's trigger point until Dung raised his hands in submission.

Dr. Reed gave an order to the resident, Dr. Hillman, to divide up the patients on the service among the four students, and it was time for them to get to work. Felix Dunhill was instructed to assist the intern, Dr. Clarke, on a very difficult case of postpartum eclampsia involving a critically ill young woman in the ICU who was only twenty-seven years old.

Eclampsia is a serious and potentially life-threatening disorder manifested by hypertension, proteinuria, cerebral edema, seizure activity, renal insufficiency, and possibly cerebral hemorrhagic events. It's a rare complication seen in pregnancy, and it can occur in the immediate postpartum state. The disorder is thought to be a consequence of placental insufficiency, and the disorder seems to be immunologically mediated. The coagulation cascade can be activated, and there are reductions of normal vasodilators in circulation. When this occurs, pathological vasoconstriction and maternal end-organ damage may be the ultimate result.

The woman was transferred from the obstetrics service to the internal medicine service to help manage the renal failure, pulmonary insufficiency, blood-clotting abnormalities, and hypertension that was seriously out of control. The intern, Dr. Clarke, brought in the nephrology service to begin emergency dialysis.

The pulmonary service was needed to massage the ventilator settings, and the neurology service was also needed to assist with uncontrollable epileptic conniptions that were not responding to conventional anti-seizure medications.

The cardiology team assumed management of the patient's severe hypertension, and the obstetricians were needed to assist with postpartum vaginal bleeding.

When an apparent micro-angiopathic hemolysis was noted and the patient was found to be destroying her own platelets and red cells, the hematology/oncology service was also employed to initiate plasmapheresis in conjunction with plasma exchange, which had to be carefully juggled between the dialysis procedures.

Dr. Clarke and Dunhill actually performed a masterful job of orchestrating the input from no less than six subspecialty services. Finally, the patient's severe hypertension was brought under control with powerful intravenous blood pressure-blocking agents in conjunction with fluid removal that occurred during the dialysis procedures. Unfortunately, the patient nonetheless experienced a catastrophic intracranial bleed and suffered a cruel and horrific demise. The intern and student, Felix Dunhill, had valiantly worked nonstop for thirty-two hours to try to sustain the young woman's life. When the patient finally expired, Dunhill and Clarke collapsed with utter exhaustion.

Sadly, a mole inside the hospital released information to Antonia Alabaster and the Your Witness News team that the very first case of

death ever recorded at the Gulf Coast University Hospital as a consequence of complications of postpartum eclampsia had occurred, and
the story was covered by both the newspaper and television media.

A physician in the small community of Lake Jackson, Texas,
heard the report about the young patient's untimely death, and he
became livid because he was the doctor who had referred the patient
to the Gulf Coast for tertiary medical care to begin with. He believed
that he should have at least been given the courtesy of a telephone
call about the patient's death and not learned about the details of her
demise from the newspaper or the television.

"Reed? What in the blue blazes is going on up there at that
goddamned medical school of yours? I just got clobbered by that
patient's family members after they found out that the young woman
died. The surviving family members learned about it while they were
watching the evening news. Do you hear me? The media reported
that she kicked the bucket before your staff even had the decency to
give me a call. What's the matter with you people? I was the referring
physician, for Pete's sake! You people at the Gulf Coast are as useless
as a teat on a boar hog!"

"Wait," Reed said. "Didn't you get a telephone call from the
house staff when she died?"

"Hell no! Listen carefully to me, Reed: I'm *never* going to refer
another patient to your hospital ever again! I've known you from
our days together at the UTMB, but in the future, I'd sooner piss
down the hole that you just crawled out from before I'd send another
patient back over to your facility to receive tertiary care! Oh, by the
way–have a nice day."

The following morning, any normal, decent, and compassionate attending would have offered kudos to Felix Dunhill and Dr.
Clarke for their heroic efforts in trying to keep the woman alive.
Their superhuman efforts with mind-numbing sleep and food deprivation should have been given praise and accolades from the administration. However, the Gulf Coast College of Medicine was not a
normal medical school—and Dr. Harrison Reed was not a normal
attending physician.

Dr. Reed generally spoke in a low tone with a raspy voice, but he nonetheless was able to berate his internal medicine team mercilessly. "I want to know something. Who was the dumbass who forgot to call the referring physician when the patient finally expired? Clearly, one of you lazy bag of bones thought it was more important to try to catch a nap when the patient died instead of giving the referring physician the courtesy of a telephone call. The blame falls squarely on your shoulders, Mr. Felix 'Dung' Dunhill."

"What?" Felix protested. "I do every damned thing that I'm told to do. If somebody had mentioned that task to me, I would've been happy to have taken on that specific assignment. I was totally unaware that such a responsibility would've fallen upon the shoulders of a lowly, subhuman, scumbag mushroom such as me. If I had only known that it was my responsibility to call the referring physician, I assure you that it would've been handled differently."

Dunhill stood motionless at the edge of the conference table and waited to be crushed by another verbal barrage.

"Excuses are like assholes," Dr. Reed said. "Every loser like you has one, but nobody else wants to see it."

Felix Dunhill soon initiated an in-house referral program known as the "Black Thumb Consult Service." Essentially, if one of his colleagues encountered a cantankerous or troublesome patient, Dunhill would encourage his fellow students to kindly submit a Black Thumb Consult request. Once Dunhill received such a requisition, he would pay a visit to the troublesome patient to make a formal recommendation as to the most expeditious way to terminate the patient's life. His fellow student colleagues thought it was all in good fun, but Dunhill was serious about the task at hand.

Ben Fielder assisted Dr. Hillman with the management of a very unusual case of metastatic breast cancer. For years, the middle-aged patient in question had noted a large mass in the upper outer quadrant of her left breast that had expanded in size and became quite painful over time. The patient was reluctant to see a physician because she thought that the mass was, well-cancer! As it turned out, her intuitive diagnostic skills were rather commendable. Eventually the carcinoma eroded through the skin and became a malodorous, fungating ulcer. As her left axillary lymph nodes became contaminated with metastatic breast cancer cells, she developed horrific edema involving her left upper extremity.

The swelling was so severe that it got to the point where she couldn't even move her left arm, and the now-useless appendage became affixed to her rib cage. The tumor actually created a stalactite-like land bridge and invaded the medial aspect of her upper left arm by direct extension! None of the crab-pickers on the oncology/hematology service had ever seen a breast tumor extend to the ventral aspect of an upper arm by direct invasion before. It was akin to something from a monster movie.

The patient was afraid that her husband would eventually discover the ulcerating mass, but she had to keep her malady a secret. She pretended she no longer loved her spouse, and she moved into the guest bedroom so he would not discover that her left breast was literally rotting away. One day, the husband become suspicious and caught his wife taking a shower. When he saw that his beloved partner was being eaten alive by an angry crab beast that was emanating from the upper/outer quadrant of her left breast, he forcibly brought her to the Gulf Coast University Hospital for admission and management thereof.

Biopsies confirmed that the tumor was a classic infiltrating ductal, high-grade adenocarcinoma. Back in 1980, looking for hormone receptors on breast cancer specimens was a brand-new laboratory parameter at the Gulf Coast. It was soon confirmed that the tumor was positive for estrogen and progesterone receptors, which meant that it could readily be theoretically managed by relatively nontoxic antihormone treatment in the form of a new drug called tamoxifen that had been on the market for two years. Oddly enough, the patient had ordered Ben Fielder not to say the word "cancer" in her presence. He was only allowed to use the word "tumor." If he ever said the word "cancer" when he was making rounds with the internal medicine team, she believed it would jinx her with, well—cancer!

The crab-pickers from the hematology/oncology service had come down to talk to her about palliative radiation treatment and tamoxifen, but she wouldn't agree to any of it. She said she only wanted "natural" treatment.

"I know that there's a universal cure for cancer," she said.

"That's the craziest thing I've ever heard," Ben Fielder replied.

"It's true. You damned doctors are keeping it a secret because of the vast medical/pharmacological/industrial complex."

"I'm sorry, madam, but doctors and their family members also contract cancer and die from it—just like everybody else."

"Lies! You want to promote illness and disease instead of health and wellness!"

"You win, lady," Fielder said. "After all, it's your funeral."

Ben Fielder voiced his considerable frustration over this bizarre case with Felix Dunhill. Fielder had jokingly requested that Dunhill do a formal "Black Thumb Consult" on this angry individual.

"Anybody who's too stupid or too fearful to actually hear the word *cancer* deserves our contempt," Dunhill said. "Anybody who is too stupid or too fearful to actually accept a relatively benign and nontoxic cancer treatment in the form of an oral antihormone pill definitely deserves a formal evaluation from the Black Thumb Consult Service! I'll have extensive formal recommendations on how to expeditiously snuff this psychotic bitch placed upon her chart by the early morning."

Fielder had no idea that Dunhill would actually write up a rec-ommendation on how to terminate the patient's life. Dunhill placed the written consultation in the permanent medical records and left it on the chart for all the other clinicians involved with her case to read: "A 100 mL injection of air into the patient's venous system should result in an acute, lethal air embolism. The Black Thumb Consult Service would like to thank you at this time for allowing me to assist you with the management of this difficult case. Please let me know if I may be of service to you in the future or, if you so desire, that

I should personally proceed with initiating my formal therapeutic recommendation at this particular time to promptly terminate this individual's life."

At the end of the first week in December, the resident physician, Dr. Hillman, was notified that an evil prison inmate, E. Rockholder, was being admitted from the outpatient GI service for the evaluation of a mass that had developed in the right lobe of his liver. He also had an elevated tumor marker found in the blood. The alpha feto-protein tumor marker is frequently associated with primary cancers involving the liver, and patients with cirrhotic liver disease are at risk of eventually developing this type of malignancy.

It was explained to the resident physician, Dr. Hillman, that Brewster had previous unpleasant encounters with this specific patient. As J. D. was not particularly comfortable with providing further medical care for this hostile and evil individual, Dr. Hillman had to acquiesce to the student's request for an exemption.

Hillman informed Felix Dunhill that he would be assigned the case once the patient reached the med-surg floor. The plan was to make sure that the ascites was sufficiently drained out of his abdominal cavity to allow a CT-guided biopsy of the liver mass to be safely performed. Since Brewster was a stud and Dunhill was a lowly mushroom, Dr. Hillman would rely upon Brewster to assist Dung with the paracentesis procedure, especially since Brewster had extensive experience in tapping ascites out of abdominal cavities.

"I heard that E. Rockholder has been convicted of murder and is an extraordinarily nasty and vile human," Felix Dunhill said.

"You're wrong about that," Brewster said. "How so?"

"He's not human," Brewster replied.

"Perhaps he might benefit from a Black Thumb Consult if that's the case," Felix suggested.

"If anybody deserves a Black Thumb Consult, this is indeed the creature."

"What can you tell me about this guy?"

"Listen to me," Brewster said. "This monster, this … this *ghoul*, is pure, unadulterated evil. I actually don't think he falls within the spectrum of where one might find other *Homo sapiens*. I've come to the conclusion that he must truly be demonic! He committed multiple cases of vehicular homicide. He was involved in a rear-end collision that ended up incinerating a pair of three-year-old twins and their mother. The woman's husband, who witnessed the whole ordeal, was driven to commit suicide."

"Wow!" Felix said. "I can't wait to meet this guy."

"E. Rockholder also ran over a person who was changing a flat tire on the 610 Loop. This Rockholder guy is a DiSPOSe, and he has non-A, non-B hepatitis with end-stage cirrhotic liver disease," Brewster explained. "A needle stick from Rockholder ended up infecting a young nurse who worked at this hospital, and she eventually died from the infection. What's really sick and twisted about this beast is that he truly enjoyed watching all these people suffer and die. He'll tell you that himself—and in no uncertain terms."

"It sounds like that it will be a challenge to do a history and physical on this scumbag."

"No!" Brewster said. "Pay attention to me. Do *not* talk to him. He'll get inside your head. When he does, he'll permanently fuck up your immortal soul in a major league way. I'm serious. Dead serious. I took care of him about five months ago when I was doing clinical research, and he almost drove me to homicide. There's a corrections officer named Arby Fuller, and we actually planned on murdering this nasty Rockholder son of a bitch when he was in the hospital this past June. I taught you how to tap a belly on the last rotation, so you know what to do. If you think you might need some help tonight, let me know. Once you get started, I'll pop my head in to see how you're doing. Whatever you do, be careful. *Do not talk to this man!* Am I clear?"

"Crystal," Dung Felix replied.

The correction officer, Arby Fuller Jr. had been assigned to bring Mr. E. Rockholder back to the Gulf Coast University Hospital. Fuller pushed Rockholder onto elevator at the same time Stella Link was riding up to her office in the Psychiatry Department.

Although she was a complete stranger, the serial killer began to berate Stella without mercy.

Arby Fuller took out his nightstick and waved it in front of E. Rockholder's face without saying a word. Then, and only then, the felon briefly shut his mouth.

The elevator doors opened on the next floor, and J. D. Brewster entered the lift with a box of jelly doughnuts under his arm. "Oh my God!" Brewster exclaimed. "You are two of my most favorite people in the whole world. Arby, I haven't seen you in a long time. We need to catch up with each other."

"I'm well, Brew, but I wish I could say the same for my dad."

"What gives?"

"He has acute CHF. He's in the VA annex in Bellaire. Believe it or not, the Wooly Mammoth has been assigned to his case. Everything in the universe appears to be connected somehow."

"So it would seem."

"Don't be a turd, Brewster," Arby said. "You haven't even formally said hello to your girlfriend yet. If you don't do it soon, she'll end up being *my* girlfriend next!"

After they shook hands, Brewster turned to Stella and said, "Hello, girlfriend. You're looking good today! Would you like a jelly doughnut?"

"I'll pass," Stella said with a frown. "Whenever I eat sweet things lately, I just don't feel good."

"Suit yourself, doll face," J. D. said. Up until that moment, he had tried his best to ignore his old nemesis who was wearing an orange prison jumpsuit and was handcuffed to the arm of the wheelchair he was sitting in.

The prisoner finally spoke. "Hello, Brewster. Did you miss me?"

"Hello, asshole," Brewster said. "Frankly, I'm sad to see that you're still alive."

"Are you coming up to my room to give me a blow job?" Rockholder asked hopefully.

"As long as you keep your mouth shut," Brewster said, "your admission to the hospital on this occasion should go rather smoothly."

"I see now that you have been dating a fat, old, hippie, dinosaur loser chick who must be ten years older than you are. She even wears plastic flowers in her hair. How lame is that? Oh my God. Are you kidding me?"

"Shut up, Rockholder!" Brewster exclaimed as he suddenly experienced another soul-shaking déjà vu event. After all, his brother, Bill, made the exact same word-for-word editorial comment about Stella over the Thanksgiving Day holiday.

Rockholder looked over at Stella and said, "Come over here and lick the sweat off my gonads, you nasty, syphilitic whore. Your boyfriend likes to suck on my ball sack, and I'll bet you will too. Stella, you fat pig, I need a smoke!"

"Shut up, Rockholder! I am not going to tell you again," Brewster said.

"Stella, you fat pig, sit on my face!"

While nobody else was looking, Stella took a ballpoint pen out of her purse and attempted to stab the felon in his left eye. Rockholder dodged the assault and blew Stella a kiss in return.

"Arby, I'm truly delighted to see that Mr. E. Rockholder is getting readmitted to the hospital today!" Brewster sarcastically exclaimed.

"Sorry to do this to you, Brew. I thought somebody from gen pop would have given the old boy a shiv once word got out—by accident, no doubt—that Rockholder had killed two children. The prisoners in gen pop don't readily cotton up to baby killers," Fuller said with a sly nod. "Unfortunately, our chicken-shit warden put him in isolation, allegedly for his own protection."

Brewster laughed. "I wonder how Rockholder's little secret got out into the general prison population?"

"Beats me," Arby answered with a grin. "So sad though, don't you think?"

"Don't worry about it, Arby. I'll make sure Rockholder gets the treatment he deserves." Brewster bent over and softly whispered something into the vile murderer's ear.

"Prisoner abuse! Prisoner abuse!" Rockholder protested. "I've just been threatened!"

Arby Fuller took out his nightstick and struck it against the prisoner's knee, which caused him to bellow out in pain. Fuller said, "There are three other people on this elevator besides your sorry ass, and nobody witnessed any prisoner abuse."

Stella Link smiled at Brewster when she got off on her floor and said, "J. D., I trust that you'll personally take care of this man." She winked at him as the elevator doors closed behind her.

Brewster was somewhat surprised at what Stella Link said, and even the encephalopathic serial killer clearly understood that he stepped over the line. However, it would not stop the prisoner from verbally tormenting his caretakers.

When the elevator doors opened on the med-surg unit, Arby Fuller pushed the patient to the registration desk to get him squared away into his hospital room.

That night, at five-minute intervals, E. Rockholder would shout, "Stella, I need a smoke! Stella, sit on my face!"

Brewster had given Felix Dunhill very sage advice about restricting conversations with E. Rockholder. Unfortunately, Dunhill failed to take these strong recommendations under advisement.

Rockholder had a specific request for Dunhill. "Before you suck the fluid out of my belly, would you do me a favor?"

"Okay," Dunhill answered. "What kind of favor?"

"Well, I've been in solitary confinement for quite some time. I never have anybody to talk to anymore, and I get lonely. I'd like for you to sit for a spell so I can just visit with you for a little while. I like you, Dunhill. I feel like we're long-lost friends! I'd really like to tell you my life's story first. After that, I'll let you drain my belly."

"Hang on there, Dung," Arby Fuller interjected as he pulled out his nightstick and tapped it upon the end of Rockholder's hospital bed. "This isn't my first rodeo. I heard Brewster give you explicit instructions not to talk to this guy. Trust me, amigo. You should heed that warning."

"It'll be okay, Mr. Fuller," Dunhill replied. "I might as well listen to what Rockholder has to say to me before I get this scheduled paracentesis procedure started."

"Your funeral, pal," Arby said.

"You and Brewster are acting like a couple of old maids," Dung said. "I might as well hear what this turd has to say to me. It should be interesting. After all, I've got all damned night to be here, and that'll leave me with a lot of time to kill."

"Yeah," Arby said. "That's *exactly* what I'm afraid of."

At the VA annex in Bellaire, the Wooly Mammoth was about to learn that everything in the universe was connected somehow. According to the peculiar and nihilistic theological convictions of J. D. Brewster, God had long ago abandoned human beings as they were no longer worthy of his attention. If that was the case, somebody was going to have to explain to Willy why God had bothered to overtly make an open indictment against the big man for the mortal sin of viciously murdering a prisoner of war during the Vietnam conflict.

When Arby Fuller Sr. was admitted to the annex for congestive heart failure, a dose of diuretics was administered.

"Sir, I see by your service record that you received a Bronze Star for valor while fighting in World War II," Willy stated. "It's indeed an honor to meet you. Would you be willing to share with me what happened?"

"I'm going to tell you something that I am not very proud of," Mr. Fuller replied. "I didn't deserve a Bronze Star. Perhaps I should send the damned thing back. On December 17, 1944, during the Battle of the Bulge, something ghastly occurred. Members of Kampfgruppe Pieper, which was part of the First SS Panzer Division, had massacred no less than eighty-four American prisoners of war at Malmedy. Most of the victims were shot in the back of the head, but some of our boys had been beaten to death. Others had been stabbed with bayonets. I'm ashamed to tell that we were no longer going to take any SS members as prisoners of war. Any of them we captured after the Malmedy Massacre—and straight through until the end of the war—were butchered like hogs."

"Were you personally involved with any of that?"

"I most certainly was," he said. "We dragged one SS member out into the forest and actually crucified the Nazi bastard before we lit him up with a torch. We had become Caligula! We got away with that crime, and nobody ever found out what we had done. We also retaliated against several German prisoners of war at Chenogne on January 1, 1945. I am ashamed to say that I received the Bronze Star for my participation in that unholy event. We had captured a young member of the regular Wehrmacht, but he was not a member of the SS. It didn't matter—we wanted blood."

"What happened?" Willy asked

"When the soldier came out of the woods, it appeared that he only wanted to give up. Before we grabbed him and tied his hands behind his back, he waved a white piece of cloth and shouted, 'Surrender! Surrender!' He said this over and over again in perfect English. We charged forward to secure the scene. He was a young man of slight build who looked to be about my age when I went off to the war. The prisoner smiled and bobbed his head up and down while repeating the word *surrender*. Perhaps that was the only English word he knew. He had no idea what was going to happen next. I pressed against his torso, which was intended to instruct him to lay back. He did this without hesitation. I saw a small silver crucifix around his neck. He was a Christian. Well, I… *I took care of him*. Do you know what I mean?"

"*Of course I know what that means!*" Willy thought. "*History repeated itself for me in Vietnam!*"

"We were told that the enemy were all a bunch of Godless atheists and that it would be proper for us to kill as many as we possibly could. I took a towel from around the back of my neck and put it under his head. He smiled and bobbed his head slightly. He thought it was an act of kindness."

"Stop, Mr. Fuller," Willy said. "I know what happens next."

"How could you?" Mr. Fuller asked. "I've never met you before, and I've never told you this story prior to now."

"You don't understand!" Willy exclaimed. "I lived this entire exact event in Vietnam! It would seem to me that this same damned sin continues to be repeated over and over again!"

"Well, then, you'll understand. I got down on my knees beside his head and lunged across his face to muffle his screams. My buddy took his bayonet and slowly, but thoroughly, thrust the knife in an upward direction right below the prisoner's breastplate. There was no coming back from what we had done."

"I'm sorry, Mr. Fuller. I don't feel well right now. I'm going to find the men's room, but I promise that I'll try to be back in just a few."

Willy went straight to the restroom to put some cold water on his face. He pulled off his shirt to take a look at his torso. The red stain on his chest and abdominal wall seemed to have grown bigger. In reality, he was the only one who could see the bloody curse. An old folk tune called "Where Have All the Flowers Gone?" by the Kingston Trio was playing softly over the speakers in the men's room.

Willy Mammon suddenly felt as if he was under direct scrutiny from the Creator, and he began to weep. He painfully realized that he was a naked and vulnerable soul on the threshold of being perpetually cursed for what he had done amongst the vines and the ferns of a remote, dark, and steamy tropical jungle in another time and another place.

If the same crimes are perpetrated by sinners again and again, then maybe Willy was already cast into hell! Inexplicably, the big man was terrified that his life was entrapped on a repeating loop of celluloid. Perhaps he was sadly doomed to revisit the same act of evil that he had committed in Vietnam over and over for an eternity, amidst the realm of the eternally damned…

The corrections officer watched with bemused interest as Felix Dunhill was emotionally overwhelmed by the horror that E. Rockholder had committed against other human beings. Dunhill had already been primed to commit acts of violence as a consequence of the abuse from attending physicians, residents, and interns over the past several months. By the time Dunhill was ready to perform the paracentesis procedure on E. Rockholder, the student was an unbridled force of fury.

"Didn't Brewster and I give you fair warning?" Arby asked. "Didn't we tell you not to talk to him? Well, we did indeed as I recall. Welcome to the club of perpetual nightmares, Dunhill. After you insisted on having a pleasant little chat with this convicted killer, Rockholder is now living rent free inside your brain. You've been corrupted just like the rest of us, buddy boy! It serves you right, you stubborn asshole!

"Shut up, Arby!" The medical student demanded. "I'm in no mood for any of your goody-two-shoes, sanctimonious bullshit right about now."

Dunhill looked over his shoulder and noticed that Nurse Missy Brownwood was standing at the threshold with folded arms and an exasperated look of utter disgust upon her face as she glared at the prisoner with toxic contempt.

"Missy, can you stay out of this room tonight?" Dunhill asked. "I'll need to be alone with this dirt bag for about an hour or so."

"If you are going to do exactly what everybody thinks that you boys should have done a long time ago," Missy replied, "then I'll keep the coast clear for you. I've been assigned to be Rockholder's nurse tonight, so I'll make certain that this goes off without a hitch. Are you sure you can handle this job, Junior?"

"He's going to handle this job whether he likes it or not," Arby interrupted. "He has no choice in this matter. This is all on his head. He's already crossed the threshold into darkness, and there's no going back now from what needs to be done."

"I'm sorry that I ever learned about the people he killed in the past," Dunhill lamented. I'll never be able to get that out of my mind. What he told me will haunt me for the rest of my life. That's something I'll just have to live with."

"That's where you're wrong, Felix," Missy softly whispered as she reached out to touch Dunhill's arm. "You see, Rockholder told me that very same story on his last admission. Frankly, I can't even live with myself now as it is!"

"Bless you, Missy," Dunhill replied with compassion. "You're a good person."

"Well, I won't be after tonight," Missy opined. "Sadly, I'll be going straight to hell someday, just like everybody else in this room. Before I leave, do you need anything else to get the task at hand successfully accomplished?"

Dunhill sadly shakes his head, and then he discharges the nurse with a slight wag of his left index finger before pointing toward the door without saying another word to her. Missy Brownwood nods and quietly departs the room, closing the door behind her.

Felix didn't bother to prep the abdomen of E. Rockholder with Betadine swabs or use any lidocaine anesthetic before he began the paracentesis procedure. "This is going to hurt! Don't move." He took a scalpel and stabbed Rockholder in his abdominal cavity directly below the umbilicus, gouging out a huge hole that was the diameter of a quarter.

Rockholder screamed in pain.

"I'm going to suck you dry now. I've got this medical equipment all set-up and jury-rigged like a wet-sump Shop-Vac!" He took the tonsillar suction device that was used to clear secretions out of the back of the patient's throat and jammed it directly into the abdominal cavity of the prisoner as far as it would go. Once done, he hooked up the device to high-vacuum wall suction and told the nurses to stay out of the patient's room that night.

When Brewster finally looked in on Dunhill's progress later that evening, all of Rockholder's abdominal ascites fluid been sucked out of his abdomen—and also half of the felon's entire intravascular volume!

"I can't find a pulse!" Brewster said as he examined the lifeless patient.

"I wouldn't expect so," Dunhill replied cheerfully. "He's not breathing either!" Brewster exclaimed.

"Well, my intention was to perform a power-assisted paracentesis procedure on E. Rockholder until his respirations completely ceased. To be truthful, by your just-rendered objective observations, no doubt fortified by your very own rather renowned astute clinical acumen, I think my desired therapeutic end point has already been successfully achieved, do you not?"

The corrections officer, Arby Fuller, looked on with a gleaming smile as if he had just eaten a whole pecan pie in one sitting. "For shit's sake, Brew! I figured even a lame-ass medical student such as you should be able to readily recognize a dead body when you see one!" Arby exclaimed. "Frankly, I'm surprised you haven't started mouth-to-mouth resuscitation on this nasty bastard as of yet. Go ahead—knock yourself out. Don't let me stop you from contracting some lethal, untreatable, and as of yet unidentified hepatitis virus from this filthy dirtbag."

"Good God, what have you done, Felix?" Brewster asked.

"Well, I sucked him dry," Dunhill replied. "In fact, I mummi-fied the son of a bitch! You were right. He was an evil beast. If you ask me, I just did the world a big favor. You can thank me later, Brew."

Brewster turned to the corrections officer and said, "Holy shit, Arby! What do you have to say for yourself? You were in here— and you let all of this happen?"

"I have no idea what you're talking about," Fuller said as he cast his eyes toward the ceiling and unsuccessfully attempted to stifle a smirk. "I'm just a humble, God-fearing corrections officer, and I know little if anything about the practice of medicine. If you ask me, everything went 'according to Hoyle' except for the fact that the patient had not signed onto a DNR code status designation before Mr. Dunhill magically turned Mr. E. Rockfucker from a swollen, orange pumpkin into a shriveled, orange raisin. Hell's bells, Brew. Be it far from me to interfere with any technically complex and intellec-tually challenging medical procedure!"

Brewster's eyes became as big as dinner plates. "Do you mean to tell me that this guy is still supposed to be a full-court press? Shit, oh dear! We have to mop up this mess and then sanitize this crime scene —pronto!" He put on a pair of gloves and helped Dunhill flush several gallons of body fluid down the toilet. He pulled the tonsillar suction trocar out of the dead man's abdominal cavity and hid the evidence in a red biohazard bag.

After the patient's dead body had been tidied up a bit, Felix Dunhill asked, "Should we now call a code blue now?"

"No, not yet," Brewster responded. "We're going to orchestrate a Mr. Pibb code for this joker. Arby, you need to hold down the fort. I'll bring you back a cold soda. In the meantime, Mr. Dunhill and I are going down to the basement to dispose of any incriminating evidence. If any of the nurses try to enter, just tell them to stay the hell out because we're doing a procedure. Tell them that the patient is in the can and he's shitting his brains out. Tell them that the patient hates nurses and wants to rape them and murder their children. Tell them the room is contaminated with a highly contagious and aerosolized form of the non-A, non-B hepatitis virus. Tell them that the patient's busy flogging the dolphin. Hell, Arby, tell them anything! Just keep them out of this room for a while!"

Brewster and Dunhill disposed of the tonsillar suction trocar and vacuum line in the incinerator room, and then they grabbed a couple of cans of Mr. Pibb from the refrigerator in the Vinyl Lounge. They casually walked across the street to Hermann Park, consumed the refreshing beverages, and then they each puffed on one of Brewster's Churchill cigars. When they were finished, they returned to the scene of the crime with an extra can of soda for Arby Fuller.

"*Now* it's time to call for a code blue!" Brewster said.

Dunhill went out to the nurse's station to inform the front desk that Rockholder had suffered a sudden cardiopulmonary arrest. As soon as the code blue alert was announced, Dr. Hillman and the night shift resuscitation team rushed to Rockholder's room with the crash cart.

"I have to step back from this case," the code team leader from the emergency room said as soon as he recognized the identity of the dead man. "Look—I know this filthy son of a bitch. He's threatened me with physical violence in the past, and there's clearly been a breach in the doctor-patient relationship. You'll need to run this code on your own, Dr. Hillman. Knock yourselves out, boys and girls. I'm gone! Give me a call once he's officially pronounced dead, dead, and then dead some more! I'll be down in the ER."

"Will you hump back up here and do the death summary paper-work if Rockholder doesn't pull through this code?" Dr. Hillman hopefully asked.

"Oh, *hell* no," the code team captain responded. "I just want to come back up here and piss on his corpse once he's been declared. I was friends with the late nurse, Kelli Krause, who died because of this filthy pig a while back. Kelli once told me she was lonely and she asked me out on a date just before she passed away. I turned her down. All I had to do was to pull the trigger and say yes, but I rejected her offer for some reason or another. Why did I do that? All I had to do was to–"

The code team leader quickly turned away before he finished his personal, painful and soulful confession and went back down to the emergency room to attend to other business at hand.

"If I have to take over as code team leader, so be it," Dr. Hillman said. "I'll have y'all know right now that this guy's a dirtbag. He has terminal end-stage liver disease and he might actually have liver cancer as a consequence to his infection with chronic non-A, non-B hepatitis. He has multiple convictions for vehicular homicide, and he's a baby killer. He's facing life in prison without any chance for parole. I can tell you right now that I'm not inclined to run a full-court press."

Dr. Hillman looked at Brewster and Dunhill and said, "Do you boys know what a Mr. Pibb Code is?"

"I don't think we know what that particular expression means," Brewster lied.

"Well, this is what we're going to do," Dr. Hillman said. "We're all going down to the cafeteria to drink a cold soda before we come back up here and run a sham code on this guy. I want to make completely sure that he's as dead has a dodo bird before we actually run the code. If any of you boys or if any members of the code team would like to go outside and smoke a cigarette before we come back up here and run the resuscitation drill, this is the time to do it. Take a long break and enjoy yourselves. Catch a cat-nap for all that I care."

"Gee, I don't exactly know about all of this," Dunhill replied while feigning moral outrage. "It sounds a bit unethical for us to do something like that."

Arby Fuller began to laugh so hard that tears were streaming from his eyes.

"No, it's not ethical," Dr. Hillman said. "Get over it, pigpen."

Brewster said, "Well, Dr. Hillman, I guess it would be okay if Dunhill and I grabbed a cold Mr. Pibb and went over to smoke a cigar at Hermann Park. Would it be okay with you, Felix?"

"I suppose so," Dung answered. "I just want to make sure that nobody thinks that I somehow provided substandard medical care on the dearly departed."

"You're exonerated," Hillman replied with a sigh.

"In fact," Brewster said, "it would also appear that Mr. Fuller's job as a corrections officer is finished here for the evening. Perhaps he would like to join us. He must be deeply saddened over the passing of not only such a model prisoner, but also such an exemplary human being whom he's intimately known for such a long time."

Arby bit his lower lip. "As you can tell, I am pretty upset that Rockholder has passed away. Sadly, for the past several months, he was held in solitary confinement because the other prisoners found out he was a baby killer. That was supposed to have been kept a secret, and I have no idea who could have released that kind of information to the general prison population."

"So, Rockholder actually turned out to be a credit to the white race," Dr. Hillman said with a malicious sneer. "Is that what you're trying to say?"

"I know that Big Tom, Nick the Shiv, and Joey the Bull at the Sharpstown Correction Facility were looking forward to having Rockholder released back into the general population," Arby said. "Like me, they must have thought that he was a truly fine fellow. I really think I need to go across the street to Hermann Park and have an ice-cold beverage and a nice big cigar to assuage my grief about the whole matter. Rockholder will be dearly missed!"

"Fair thee well upon thy arduous journey into the good night, my sweet prince!" Brewster said as he harshly rubbed his knuckles across the dead man's sternum.

At Hermann Park, Arby Fuller removed his nylon windbreaker and stuffed it under his shirt to make it appear as if he were pregnant or otherwise had been afflicted with a severe case of ascites as a consequence of end-stage liver disease. He managed to pull off a perfect vocal impersonation of the late E. Rockholder's raspy voice when he proclaimed, "Come over here, you filthy bastards. Suck my balls!"

Brewster started to howl with laughter.

Dung picked up a stick from the ground and stabbed at Arby's distended abdomen. "No! I'm not going to suck your balls, but I'll nevertheless suck you dry, raisin boy!"

Although it was a dark and twisted macabre celebration, the impromptu party over the inadvertent death of the evil E. Rockholder was the most fun that the three men had experienced in quite some time.

Brewster embraced the fact that he was now already in advanced stages of spiritual decomposition. He was becoming as dark and twisted as the depraved celebratory event that he orchestrated at Hermann Park that evening. In the recent past, Brewster had rightfully criticized E. Rockholder for his participation in the death of many other people. How could Brewster now look at himself in a mirror and actually think that he was somehow any different?

On the following morning, Felix Dunhill's Black Thumb consultation note that had been placed upon the chart of the obstinate woman with metastatic breast cancer finally came to the light of day when Dr. Harrison Reed was reviewing medical records. When Dunhill was called up to the attending's office, Dr. Reed had already realized that Felix Dunhill must have experienced a complete psychological meltdown.

"Mr. Dunhill," Dr. Reed began, "I've called you to my office to let you know that your student position at the Gulf Coast College of Medicine has been terminated, effective immediately. This decision is irrevocable and final."

"You think it's funny, don't you?"

"Actually, I do indeed. These two men who are here from the university's security service will escort you off the premises."

Dunhill flew across the desk, threw the professor out of his chair, and then pressed his thumbs into Dr. Reed's eye sockets in an attempt to murder the attending physician. "I don't see you laughing now, you weasel-fucking son of a bitch!"

The security detail's choke hold saved Dr. Harrison Reed from certain death. The bodyguards physically hauled the hapless and perpetually disheveled student from the campus without any further histrionic outbursts.

Dung simply disappeared. Nobody would ever see him or hear from him ever again. His name was never even spoken of following his fateful dismissal from the medical school. In the end, it was as if the spiritually broken student named Felix Dunhill had never even existed.

# 12

# GRAY MATTER

rewster," Medhi asked, "are you taking extra precautions to look out for your own safety?"

"What in the devil are you talking about?"

"You need to start paying attention to what's going on in the world," Mehdi said. "You can't go through life this disconnected from everything that's swirling around you."

"I'm not in the mood for a game of twenty questions right now," Brewster replied.

"A day or two before Thanksgiving, three of the Iranian terrorists tried to escape from jail. One was immediately recaptured, but the other two got away. Federal marshals are combing Houston for the two fugitives as we speak. Believe it or not, these two jokers were recently seen lurking about the Texas Medical Center just a few weeks ago."

"Damnation!" Brewster replied. "At the beginning of my last rotation, Dr. Beathard told me that two Iranian fellows were looking for me. I didn't think much of it at the time. What in hell would they want with me?"

"I don't know for sure," Medhi said, "but if I were you, I'd grow a pair of eyes on the back of my head."

"I'll take that under advisement," Brewster replied, "but I should at least be safe within the confines of this medical complex.

After all, there's extensive security here at the Gulf Coast, and I really don't think I'll have anything to worry about."

"Famous last words…"

The internal medicine rotation under the tutelage of Dr. Reed wrapped up on Christmas Eve, and the students were about to get more than ten full days of vacation. The next clerkship was not scheduled to begin until Monday, January 5, 1981.

Brewster, Fielder, and the Russian Bear decided to stay together as a team for at least the next two mandatory rotations during January and February. They planned to rotate through the neurology and the neurosurgery service together during that time. The Gulf Coast College of Medicine had always structured the mandatory neurology and neurosurgery services in a back-to-back fashion in an attempt to integrate the experience of both the medical and surgical management of diseases that involved the nervous system.

After the disturbing Thanksgiving dinner at his mother's house, Brewster had endured about as much family interactions as he could possibly tolerate for quite some time. Stella Link had invited Brewster up to her family's farm near Waco, but Brewster convinced her to stay in Houston and have a quiet celebration without any family drama or family trauma.

Since Thanksgiving, Stella had informed her boyfriend on more than one occasion that she had not been feeling well. She was starting to develop symptoms of progressive carbohydrate intolerance with associated fatigue in addition to polyuria and polydipsia. Excessive sugar intake was causing increased urinary frequency and increased fluid intake. Stella's persistent thirst just could not be quenched. Sadly, Stella's blood sugar was starting to spiral out of control.

In addition, she was starting to experience the troublesome symptoms of numbness and tingling involving her feet and occasional stabbing sensations on the plantar aspects of her toes. If Brewster had been paying closer attention, he would have realized that Stella was developing peripheral diabetic neuropathy. Her elevated blood sugar was starting to damage her body. Stella tried to convey her concerns about these problems to her boyfriend, but Brewster was rarely able to see the big picture.

"Sweetie, sometimes I have the sensation that ants are biting the bottom of my feet, and I have to get up to urinate two or three times every night," Stella said. "This has been going on now for the last few months, and I'm afraid something's wrong. What do you think is going on?"

"Oh, it's probably nothing," Brewster replied. "I want you to hurry up and open the Christmas present I gave you! I can't wait because I know it'll make you happy."

Stella tore into the wrapped Christmas present, which turned out to be a two-pound box of chocolates. It was the worst possible gift that Brewster could have given her. Stella lied when she said that she was delighted. "You're such a dear to me!"

Brewster secretly hoped he could push Stella's weight up to a stout 240 pounds, which he thought would be ideal for her. He was totally oblivious to the fact that he was contributing to the premature demise of a friendly, cheerful, and morally righteous woman whom he had truly cared for. Stella was actually Brewster's better half, as she was everything that he wasn't. Sadly, Brewster possessed a perverted and selfish concept of baroque, Rubenesque beauty. His insistence that Stella should pack on even more weight would eventually turn Stella's small arteries into lead pipes that were clogged up with fatty, greasy plaques. Stella Link's vascular system was rapidly becoming physiologically much older than the thirty-three years that she had lived upon this planet, and it was just a matter of time before the organs that were downstream to those clogged arteries would be in serious trouble…

On January 5, 1981, Ben Fielder showed up at the Vinyl Lounge to discover that Russian Bear and Brewster were enjoying a box of jelly doughnuts.

The anesthesiologist, Dr. Ron Chelsea, was front and center in the lounge, serenading an imaginary audience with his signature song, "Who Shot That Hole in My Sombrero?"

"To what do we owe this on honor?" Fielder asked. "It must be a special day if we're getting a visit from Ron Chelsea and a box of jelly doughnuts to boot!"

"It's a special day indeed!" Chelsea replied. "In fact, I'm going to bring a box of doughnuts to every ward and every floor to celebrate my divorce. I just got a call from my attorney that it'll be finalized by the end of the day. How good is that?"

"It seems strange to me that you'd want to celebrate such a somber event with jelly doughnuts," Russian Bear noted. "Perhaps, in your case, I should say *sombrero* event!"

"Listen boys, jelly doughnuts are near and dear to my heart," Dr. Chelsey said. "I just don't give them out in some willy-nilly fashion. Did I tell you about the time I was surrounded by a band of wild, bloodthirsty Injuns?"

"Well, this should be a good one," J. D. said with a laugh. "Please, Ron, tell us all about it."

"I was leading a wagon train into the Trans-Pecos wilderness when we were suddenly set upon by the mountain warriors of the Lack-a-nookie tribe. It should be noted that up until just recently, this tribe had never successfully been pacified. I was just about to get scalped when I broke out a baker's dozen box of jelly doughnuts and a thermos of Kona coffee. I'm certain that you boys know that Kona coffee is the best in the world."

"Smooth?" Fielder asked.

"Velvet!" Chelsea said. "The leader of the tribe, Chief Beaucoup Pecker, broke out a peace pipe and loaded up a bowl of 'Purple Monkey Shit' for us to puff on. After we had polished off that box of doughnuts, we all took a nap! After we crashed, Chief Beaucoup Pecker changed his mind about me and was about to give me a very close shave with a tomahawk! Fortunately, his daughter, Stinky Beaver, petitioned her father to spare my miserable life."

"What in the world could a Stinky Beaver find of value in a redneck like you?" Brewster asked.

"I am a man of undeniable charm!" Ron boasted. "At the time, I was saddled with a damned time-share condominium over on Shit Creek. As luck would have it, I was able to successfully pawn off that useless vacation property to Chief Beaucoup Pecker, and when we shook hands, I went on my merry way. I still get a Christmas card from his lovely daughter every now and then, and I also make a point of buying 'Purple Monkey Shit' brownies from the tribe whenever they have a fund-raising event."

"I'm certain that we'll never find this story in the annals of American history, but I must say that I enjoyed your tale nonetheless," Brewster said. "However, I suspect that Native Americans might issue a rather strong rebuttal in the editorial section of the *Houston Post* if they ever hear about *any* of this story."

"No doubt about that!" Ron said.

"Russian Bear is correct in his humble observation that a divorce is not necessarily something to celebrate, right?" Fielder asked.

"After I had that gold-digger, soon-to-be ex-wife sign a nuptial financial agreement, I ended up spending my entire marriage on the living room sofa! I swear if I ever get lonely in the future, I'll never get married again, no question about that. I'll simply rent somebody for a short-term, meaningless relationship. I wouldn't even want to know her last name. Her first name would have to be something like 'Bubbles,' or 'Sunshine,' or some shit like that. In any event, the only affection I received during that entire fiasco of a marriage was from my 'Blow-Up Betty Blow Job' love doll. She was manufactured in Thailand. Betty was dangerous though."

"Battery or electric?" Bear asked.

"Funny you should ask," Chelsea replied. "She operated on a 120-volt motor with a 50-amp fuse that plugged into a wall socket. Sadly, Betty was factory-equipped with only a 2-pronged electrical plug, lacking a good ground-default connection. One day, Betty developed an electrical short. Once the synthetic silicone little man in the canoe got a bit damp from a vigorous and intimate romantic interlude, Blow-Up Betty ended up turning my pecker into a deep-fried and unidentified appendage! There was only one way to tell that the nubbin in my boxer shorts was indeed the incinerated remains of my own putrefied pecker."

"How's that?" Brewster asked.

"It was because there was a residual small tuft of singed curlicues at the stem. Whowee!"

The students laughed and replied in unison, "Whowee!"

Ron was a renowned, beloved, bawdy, and self-deprecating humorist. It was quite clear to all who had known him that the mold was definitely broken when the one and only edition of Dr. Chelsea had originally rolled off the celestial assembly line long ago.

The neurology rotation was slated to begin at ten o'clock at the outpatient neurology clinic, and the students were assigned to work with Dr. Sergio Balbona.

While waiting for their new attending to arrive, Russian Bear mentioned that he was a fan of the NBA. Although the Houston Rockets would end up having a mediocre season, they would eventually make it into the playoffs before falling in the championship series to the Boston Celtics that year.

"I enjoy the spectacle of American basketball," Russian Bear said. "I would very much enjoy seeing a professional basketball game someday."

"Well, I'm glad you're becoming Westernized!" Fielder proclaimed.

Brewster took Fielder aside to plan an impractical joke on their naïve Slavic colleague. "Bear's a good guy, but in my humble opinion, he's taking life far too seriously. He's acting as if our very existence on this planet actually means something."

"Dude never smiles," Fielder observed.

"If he did, his face would probably crack and fall right off from his skull and end up getting glued to the sticky yellow mouse-trap paper strip on the floor near the microwave oven," Brewster opined.

"Maybe it's time for us to further his corruption and truly make him as cynical and jaded as we are," Fielder said.

"Look Ben, we might be going straight to hell over what I'm about to suggest," Brewster said, "but I have an idea."

A plot was hatched to prank the Russian, and there was very little time to spare.

When the new attending arrived, Dr. Balbona said, "Half of our work will be inpatient in the hospital setting but half of our work will be here in the outpatient clinic where we're starting today. My neurology resident, Dr. Payne, will assign the patients that you're scheduled to see here in the clinic today. After you take a history and perform a thorough neurological examination on these patients, you will present the cases to Dr. Payne and he'll subsequently relay the information to me. I know that this medical school has reputation for being a hard and cold place, but it's my intention to make this rotation enjoyable for you. If you have any questions, please do not hesitate to talk to me at any time. I have an 'open-door' policy. Mr. Brewster, I do believe I owe you a cigar and a Cuba libre!"

Wow, that was a refreshing policy to hear, especially after what the students had previously experienced over the last several months.

Russian Bear was assigned to see a patient who had been worked into the schedule without an appointment. The patient had been sent up from the emergency room, and the neurology service had been asked to see this patient on an emergency basis. The patient worked for the natural gas company, checking meter readings for monthly residential utility billing.

A mishap had warranted an emergency visit. It's a sad fact that just about every single invertebrate critter that crawls on the ground in Texas is potentially dangerous. This is especially true for the dreaded pus-moth caterpillar, which is considered one of the most toxic insects in North America. An innocuous-appearing fuzzy bug, a pus-moth caterpillar will nonetheless cause excruciating pain if it crawls upon the flesh of an unwitting human being.

People who have been stung by this nasty varmint will attest that the pain is at a level of eleven on a scale of one to ten! Its neurotoxic sting may cause temporary paralysis in the limb of an individual who is stung. Headaches, nausea, vomiting, respiratory distress, and symptoms that may be indistinguishable from an acute myocardial infarction have also been reported in patients who have tangled with this fiendish, furry, creepy-crawler. As misfortune would have it, one of these potentially dangerous caterpillars was crawling up into a tree to envelop itself into a cocoon to metamorphose into a moth by springtime. Upon stumbling on a branch, the creature had fallen directly upon the right wrist of the unfortunate meter reader.

When the patient's right arm caught on fire, he looked down to see that he was being stung by an evil, fuzzy assailant that he immediately recognized. He made the mistake of grabbing the creature with his left hand and casting it onto the ground before squashing it like, well—like a bug. This action, however, resulted in the meter reader getting stung on his left hand, also.

When Russian Bear walked into the room, the patient was in agony. The victim said it felt as if the skin was being stripped off of his right arm and from the palm of his left hand. He had developed a palpable erythematous eruption on his skin where the insect had stung him, and he was starting to experience abdominal cramps with nausea. When vital signs were obtained, it was found that the patient was hypotensive and had tachycardia.

"I understand you may have been attacked by some kind of poisonous creature," Russian Bear said. "I'm from Russia, and I'm not very familiar with the dangerous types of animals that live in this strange place called Texas. What exactly happened to you?"

Russian Bear was not aware that the pus-moth caterpillar was a scourge in the Southeast and was known by a variety of different names including the "flannel moth caterpillar," the "wooly slug," and the "possum bug". In Texas, it was often referred to as an "asp". In light of the toxic symptoms a sting from this highly venomous insect may perpetrate, *asp* is probably the most accurate description of this larval form of an insect that is scientifically and taxonomically cate-gorized as the *Megalopyge opercularis.*

When the patient reported that he had been stung by an asp and that his distal upper extremities had become acutely paralyzed, Russian Bear misinterpreted what the man was saying. The Russian Bear thought the man had been bitten by a venomous snake and he immediately got the resident and attending physician involved in the patient's care while he made an emergency call to the Texas Poison Control Center.

When it had been clarified that the patient had been stung by an "asp caterpillar" and not an "asp viper," it was nonetheless still considered to be an emergency since the patient had developed bilat-eral upper arm paralysis with hypotension, and he was in excruciat-ing pain.

Dr. Balbona was furious at the ineptitude exemplified in the emergency room in regard to the medical management—or lack thereof—that the patient had received upon his arrival to the Gulf Coast University Hospital. "Gather around, children. It's time all of you learn an important concept that falls under the realm of profes-sional courtesy. Listen, Bear; when this patient was sent over to us from the emergency room, you should have rejected the case from the very start."

"I believe this is an appropriate case for us to take care of down here in the outpatient neurology suite," Bear said, "is it not?"

"You're wrong!" Dr. Balbona said. "This emergency room refer-ral was nothing more than a dump."

"What do you mean?" Brewster asked.

"A dump is when a patient is inappropriately shipped over to somebody else's turf when the referring team is otherwise perfectly capable of handling the medical matter to begin with. A medical professional with a conscience should never dump on a colleague. By the same token, you boys need to man up and make sure that nobody ever takes advantage of your good nature. If a colleague ever tries to dump on you, it's your responsibility to push back hard."

"That seems rude to me!" Bear said.

"Does it now? For all intents and purposes, a dump is the most supreme act of rude behavior within the confines of our profession. A doctor insults another caretaker when a dump occurs, and it's generally the consequence of ineptitude, laziness, or some combination thereof. Don't ever turf a dump, boys! By the same token, don't ever accept a dump. Am I clear?"

After thoroughly washing down the patient's extremities with rubbing alcohol and applying ice packs, the patient was administered a dose of intravenous morphine, Benadryl, and a dose of the universal anti-inflammatory panacea of catabolic steroids. The patient was subsequently admitted to the neurology ward for further observation and management. Fortunately, the patient's paralysis subsided over the next forty-eight hours.

Anybody who was involved with the patient's care at that time learned three valuable lessons: never turf a dump, never accept a dump, and a pus-moth caterpillar should always be killed on sight, no questions asked!

When J. D. Brewster went into the next patient's room, he was stunned to see that it was none other than Tiny Tucker, the director of automotive engineering at Dick Dowling University.

"Tell me, Mr. Brewster," Professor Tucker asked, "do you still own that hot rod Mustang my automotive class assembled on your behalf a few years ago? If you do, be honest with me. Did you ever really put your foot into it?"

"Tiny, I'm very happy to see you—but not necessarily under these circumstances. Yes, I still own the Mustang, but I've only wrapped it up to about 140 miles per hour. I was just past the Stuckey's rest stop on Interstate 10 between Houston and San Antonio. It had a lot more under the hood, but I lost my nerve and didn't take it any faster than that. What on earth brings you to the neurology clinic at the Gulf Coast College of Medicine?"

"I have Lou Gehrig's disease," replied the old automotive wizard, "and I'm afraid I'm going to die from it—likely much sooner than later. I'm in for a follow-up visit today. I've actually battled this disease now for quite some time, but I kept my illness a secret while I was at Dick Dowling University. Sadly, I was forced to retire early. Over the past year, I've needed a wheelchair because I've lost power in my legs. I'm also troubled by painful involuntary muscle spasms. Dr. Payne wrote a prescription for Valium to help control the symptoms. It appears to be working only modestly, but I need a refill nonetheless. What do you know about this disease?"

"Quite a bit, actually," Brewster replied. "Lou Gehrig's disease, also known as amyotrophic lateral sclerosis, is a horrible neurological degenerative disorder where the motor neurons that control muscular function die off over time."

"As in my case," Tiny confirmed.

"Most of the patients who acquire this disease from hell will eventually succumb from suffocation when the diaphragm, which controls the movement of air into and out of the lungs, finally becomes paralyzed as an end-stage event."

"You win a Cuban cigar, Brewster!" Tucker beamed. "It's quite frightening to realize I'll eventually die while gasping for my last breath of air."

"Lou Gehrig's disease is a rare disorder that only afflicts two out of every hundred thousand people. There's a rare familial form of this peculiar illness, but the etiology is idiopathic in 95 percent of the cases."

"I need to tell you something strange, Brewster," Tiny Tucker said. "When I was first diagnosed with this disease, I went to see a neurology specialist at the Scott and White Clinic."

"Great place," Brewster said, "and even a better reputation."

"This doctor I saw was considered the expert for Lou Gehrig's disease in the southern part of United States. He was a big wheel, and the only patients he saw at his clinic toward the end of his career were patients who had contracted this thing you medical professionals call amyotrophic lateral sclerosis."

"He must have been a big wheel indeed," Brewster said.

"Guess what happened to this doctor." Tucker asked.

"Don't tell me—"

"You guessed it!" Tucker exclaimed. "He died this past summer from amyotrophic lateral sclerosis! I shit you not. What are the odds of that? That's the reason I'm here for additional treatment, although I still have a profound amount of faith in the folks at Scott and White. Do you think Lou Gehrig's disease is caused by an infectious agent or is otherwise transmissible from one person to another?"

The odds must have been astronomical; it would be an extraordinary coincidence that a neurological specialist taking care of patients with Lou Gehrig's disease would one day contract Lou Gehrig's disease and then actually die from that very specific, rare illness. The likelihood of that anecdote being merely a clinical coincidence was probably numerically far greater than the odds of the spontaneous appearance of intelligent life upon the face of the planet Earth. Although this degenerative neurological disorder has never been proven to be a horizontally transmissible disease process, Brewster would always remember Tiny Tucker's cautionary story.

"I want to be the master of my own fate," Professor Tucker said. "I'm afraid of the thought of dying by suffocation when my diaphragm fails. I'm absolutely terrified of that happening to me. What should I do?"

Brewster made certain that the door to the exam room was completely closed when he said, "I'm glad to hear that the Valium is helping you with the muscle spasms. I'll ask Dr. Payne to give you a refill, and I'll make sure he gives you enough pills to last the entire month. Tiny, you have to promise me that you'll be very careful with this medication. A whole month's supply of Valium could be dangerous. If you *accidentally* take a whole bottle of these pills at one time, and then you *accidentally* chase it down with a fifth of hard liquor of your choice, you'll go to sleep and you'll never wake up. Do you understand what I'm trying to tell you?"

Professor Tucker smiled. "So, let me get this straight. If I *accidentally* swallow a whole bottle of Valium at one time, and then I *accidentally* chase it down with a bottle of select premium and expensive, Highland, single-malt, twelve-year-old Scotch poured into an engraved whisky glass and then consumed on the rocks with a lemon rind twist in one sitting, I'll go to sleep and then I'll never wake up?"

"That's correct," Brewster answered. "Are you absolutely certain that you fully understand the important information that I just conveyed to you?'

"You're crystal clear, Brewster," Tucker said. "You may rest assured that I'll be *very* careful with Dr. Payne's prescription, and I won't screw this up."

"Good luck, Professor," Brewster said. "It was truly an honor to have made your acquaintance so many years ago."

"God bless you, my son," Tucker said. "You were always a fine lad. It's really not a coincidence that I ran into you today. Everything in the universe seems to be connected somehow. Goodbye, Brewster. I hope you'll live a good life and that you'll always be a good man. Promise me that you'll always drive above the limit if and when you have the opportunity to do so!"

Brewster reluctantly allowed Tiny Tucker to give him a hug, but the student was painfully aware that he would never see his old professor again.

Brewster excused himself to the men's room where he washed himself down with germicidal soap. He lathered up his entire body to be on the safe side. There was no sense in taking any chances after coming into physical contact with somebody afflicted with amyotrophic lateral sclerosis—even if there was only a one in a trillion chance that it was a transmissible disease.

Professor Tucker's obituary was published in the *Golden Triangle Tribune* that very weekend. It appeared that the popular former director of automotive engineering at Dick Dowling University had died in his sleep from complications of Lou Gehrig's disease.

Brewster wept when he learned of Tiny Tucker's demise. He shed tears of sadness for the passing of the affable automotive wizard who had engineered the transformation of Brewster's old Mustang into a rocket ship. He shed tears of joy that Tiny Tucker made it to the finish line in life as a man who was able to die on his own terms…

The following day, Stella Link visited the neurology clinic to see Ben Fielder. She had specifically made an appointment to be evaluated for the numbness and tingling sensation in her feet, which was becoming quite a problem. It felt like the soles of her feet and her toes were being bitten by angry fire ants. She told Fielder about her chronic thirst and frequent urination, but she made him promise not to tell Brewster about her appointment at the outpatient neurology facility.

"I know the Gulf Coast College of Medicine doesn't tolerate any signs of weakness," Stella said. "I need to make sure J. D. doesn't find out that I have a weakness."

"I believe that you've likely developed adult-onset diabetes mellitus," Fielder explained. "For cryin' out loud, it's an *illness*, Stella, not a *weakness*."

"Can't prove it by me," Stella answered. "If J. D. thinks I'm damaged goods, he might leave me!"

"Aren't you underestimating your boyfriend just a bit?"

"No," Stella said as she sadly shook her head. "No, I'm not."

"I'm sorry you feel that way, but I assure you that Brewster will never know you were here in the clinic to see me today."

"For now," Stella said, "I have to pretend that everything is just fine. I must be strong. I have no other option." The culture at the Gulf Coast College of Medicine had become so perversely militaristic that Stella Link was compelled to feel that way.

Fielder brought in the intern, Dr. Payne, and it was quickly confirmed that Stella was suffering from diabetes mellitus as a consequence of her chronic morbid obesity. A referral was made to the outpatient internal medicine clinic to have her disease properly managed.

Stella had developed what was known at the time as "Syndrome X." In modern times, it's referred to simply as the metabolic syndrome, and it's manifested by obesity, hypertension, hypercholesterolemia, and type 2 diabetes mellitus. Unfortunately, with the expanding waistline of many Americans, this syndrome is now the most common endocrinological disorder in the United States.

"I tell you what," Ben said, "I'll keep this a secret between you and me, but you must help Brewster and me play a joke on Russian Bear. Up in your office, do you have one of those computer gizmo devices where a person can type up statements and documents and then edit it right on the monitor screen?"

"Why, yes," Stella replied. "It's a new computer system called a *word processor*, and I'm still learning how to use it. You're wrong though if you think I'm going to help you boys play a joke on Russian Bear. I told Brewster it is time for him to grow up and act like a man. I know you're still dating Missy Brownwood, and she'd be most upset if she knew you were still doing childish things like playing practical jokes on people."

"I assure you that what Brewster and I are planning on doing to Russian Bear is not going to be a *practical* joke," Ben said. "It's going to be a most *impractical* joke—and you owe me big-time right about now!"

"I guess if I'm buying your silence," Stella said, "I at least owe you something."

"Quid pro quo, madam!" Fielder said.

Stella reluctantly agreed, and she and Fielder went to her desk in the Psychiatry Department.

At the end of the day, Ben Fielder called Brewster and invited him to come to the Psychiatry Department to initiate the prank. When Brewster arrived, he instructed Stella to type up a letter of invitation to Russian Bear on Stella's new word processor.

The sham letter would be addressed from the Russian-American Friendship Society, and it instructed Russian Bear to present the letter to the will call window for the Houston Rockets versus Portland Trail Blazers game on January 10. The letter stated that Bear would be given two complimentary tickets to attend the game—and he would even have a chance to meet several of the players on the court after the game.

After Stella begrudgingly completed the letter, Brewster and Fielder gave each other a high five. They put the letter in Russian Bear's mail slot and waited for the fireworks to begin.

On Friday morning, Russian Bear was dancing around the Vinyl Lounge as if he were on a cloud.

"What's up with you, Russian Bear?" Brewster asked. "You're flopping around like a Slavic lunatic."

Russian Bear waved the letter in front of Brewster's face. "I have some really good news, and you're not going to spoil it today—no matter what you say. I received a letter from the Russian-American Friendship Society, and I've been awarded two free tickets to the Rockets game tonight! Before the neurology clinic starts this morning, I'm going up to the med-surg floor to tell my wife. This is beautiful. I'm going to take Larisa on a date to see a professional basketball game! Is America a great country or what?"

Ben Fielder said, "Oh, yes, this is a great country, indeed. I hope you and your wife have fun at the Summit basketball game."

That night, Russian Bear and Larisa presented the letter to the clerk at the will call window at the basketball arena.

The clerk seemed to be a bit confused, but she took the letter to her manager.

"Well, the letter looks legitimate," the manager said, "but I don't see that anybody left tickets for these two people. I don't want to cause some type of international scene, especially now that the Soviet Union and United States are butting heads against each other over which country can leave the biggest turd in the cat box."

"How do you want me to play this?" the clerk asked. "Since we're not even close to a sellout tonight, scrape up a pair of tickets in the cheapo seats and get them the hell out of here. Make sure you give them a postgame courtside pass and set up a two-minute photo-op with Rudy T. I'm sure he won't mind."

In the Vinyl Lounge on the following morning, Russian Bear showed his colleagues the Polaroid shot that he and Larisa had taken with a Rockets player. "It was a wonderful thing to watch," Bear said. "The Rockets won the game by just one point, and it was all very exciting. We met Rudy Tomjanovich. He told us he was of Croatian descent, but that's almost as good as being a Russian!"

Fielder asked what had happened at the game.

"Larisa and I just followed the instructions on the letter," Bear explained. "We took the letter to the designated window at the arena, and they gave us two tickets and a postgame, courtside pass. It was the most fun we've had in quite some time."

On their way to the outpatient neurology clinic, Fielder and Brewster were baffled. The two students could only look at each other with bewilderment and a shrug of frustration.

The Dalton twins had only one more week of vacation before the start of the spring semester.

D' Shea cupped her hand over the side of her face and said, "Oh my God. It feels like my eyeball is about to pop out of my head!"

She fell to the ground and had a grand mal seizure.

D' Nae called for an ambulance, and D' Shea was hauled off to the emergency room at the Gulf Coast University Hospital for evaluation.

D' Nae went into full-on, self-recrimination mode for not forcing her sister to see a neurologist sooner.

The emergency CT scan revealed a large tumor in the right frontal and occipital lobe of D' Shea's brain. The tumor mass looked like a giant grass burr with surrounding edema, and it was most likely an aggressive malignant process.

For the past few months, D' Shea had been taking the prednisone from her friend, and it had temporarily reduced the peri-tumoral edema. The frequent, severe headaches and left arm weakness had magically subsided as a result of her daily dose of the steroid medication.

Unfortunately, D' Shea would learn that the beneficial effects that a patient may receive from taking catabolic steroids for a malignant brain tumor are, at best, only temporary. After receiving a loading dose of Dilantin to try to prevent future seizure activity and a large dose of additional steroids in the form of intravenous dexamethasone, D' Shea was admitted to the neurology floor.

J. D. Brewster was about to get another lesson that would remind him that everything in the universe was connected somehow. Upon entering D' Shea's room, Brewster could not help but recognize the distinct familiar facial features he shared with the twins.

D' Shea said. "So, you've come to meet me and help find out what is going on inside my aching noodle? If baby girl and I have never met you before, why do you look so dad-gum familiar?"

All three people in the room had bright green eyes, broad foreheads, and a distinct left temporal nevus.

"Well, well, well, what do we have here?" D' Nae said. "I tell you what, baby girl, we have us a white boy in this room who must be our doppelganger. He's cute as a bug!"

D' Shea jumped out of her hospital bed and wheeled over her IV pole to take a better look at Brewster. Without a word, she pulled him over to the bathroom mirror. The sisters aligned themselves on either side of Brewster's face for a side-by-side-by-side comparison. The three individuals opened their mouths and stuck out their tongues. They examined each other's teeth and eyes carefully, and they inspected the familial mole that each had on their left temple region.

While Brewster and the two sisters were visually inspecting each other, the mother of the twins arrived with a bouquet of flowers.

When Lilly saw J. D. Brewster, she said, "Oh my God. Are … are you a ghost?" She reached out to touch Brewster's face and began to weep. "Well, you seem to be a living human being. I need to know something. Are you the son of the Woody Brewster?"

"I am indeed," Brewster replied.

"My twin sister, Iris, and I were, well—*friends* with your father back in the day," Lilly said. "We would often run into him at the Blue Tone. Iris died from a brain tumor many years ago, and now I'm told that my baby girl has the same thing. If you're on this team to help take care of my daughter, promise me you'll do a good job. After meeting you today, I just can't stay."

"Madam, are you not feeling well?" Brewster asked.

"I have to go home and sort things out," Mrs. Dalton said. "I'm sorry for that. What's going on here must be happening for a reason.

Okay, girls, if your father comes up here in a little while for visit, don't let him know that there's a young white man named Brewster who'll be looking in on the case. Just do that for me— and don't ever ask me any questions about all of this."

After giving J. D. Brewster a big hug and a soft kiss on his cheek, Lilly Dalton continued to cry and hastily retreated from the room.

D' Shea turned to Brewster and asked, "What in hell was that about? It sounds like Momma and Aunt Iris may have been cavorting about with Frosty the Snowman before she met Daddy. Oh my God! Do you think that they were doing a tag-team match with some wild white boy?"

"That would appear to be the case," D' Nae said. "That's disgusting! If that's the truth of the matter, it doesn't mean one damned thing. Our daddy is our daddy—even if we turned out to be a cup of coffee with cream. I can't speak on behalf of baby girl over there, but I'll have you know that I'm still a cup of coffee—no matter what. Dig that?"

Brewster thought, *The facts are inescapable and undeniable. The twins must be my half-sisters!* He believed that the better part of valor was to play dumb. "I really don't know what that was all about. I suspect that your mother is confusing me and my late father for somebody else."

"Yes, you're probably right," D' Nae said. "I'm certain that our mother is confusing you and your late father with somebody else. That's my story, and I'm sticking to it. No offense, Mr. Brewster, but a person like you would certainly be hard to explain to a large family gathering on Thanksgiving Day. I know for a fact that some of my kin are rather doubtful that you uncouth and uncivilized white folks are even familiar with the proper use of indoor plumbing! Five will get you ten that if you ever came over to our house for a visit and you had to up and relieve yourself, Daddy Dalton would make you go outside and pee on the oleander bush in the backyard. Gospel truth, I tell you."

"No doubt," Brewster said.

D' Shea said, "I can assure you, kind sir, that you would not be exactly welcomed with open arms, if you understand my meaning.

So, if an old hound dog is asleep on the porch, don't go poking a stick at it. Nonetheless, for what it's worth, baby girl and I both think you're cute as a bug!"

The times being what they were, perhaps denial was the best way to negotiate through the awkward obstacle course that the three individuals had found themselves in.

On Monday, D' Shea would have her case presented before the experts to try to determine the best course of action for managing her perilous clinical state.

Mr. Pablo See was a wealthy hotel owner who had married a peculiar woman whom J. D. Brewster would come to believe was the most idiotic human being he had ever met in his entire life. In her earlier years, the woman was known by her maiden name: Banana Pillow. Above and beyond her stupidity, the woman's only other claim to fame was that she was named the "Miss Hot-Fire Spark Plug" calendar girl in 1955. When she married Pablo, she decided to take on a hyphenated last name, and from that time on she would be forever known as Nana Pillow-See. Her premature, heavy leonine facial creases from chronic marijuana abuse forced her to get multiple face-lifts, and her permanent smile was as taut as a trampoline. Sadly, the multiple plastic surgery procedures also rendered a perpetual look of surprise, or perhaps terror, upon her synthetic face.

Mr. Pablo See suffered a catastrophic embolic cerebral vascular accident while he was in the bathroom at his home. He collapsed in the shower stall, and as Nana Pillow-See had neither the intellect nor the insight to call 911, she simply left him in the bathroom for several days. When he voided or moved his bowels, she would simply turn on the shower head and hose him down.

As she was vaguely concerned about his nutritional status, she would pry open his mandible up to three times a day and attempt to jam a can of peaches or mixed fruit cocktail into his mouth. She would then try to force the food down into his gullet with the end of a wooden mixing spoon.

Unfortunately, the brain-stem stroke that her husband had experienced had left him essentially paralyzed with what is medically referred to as the *locked-in syndrome.* Every attempt at feeding him resulted in the material entering his right main-stem bronchus. The food eventually filled the right middle lobe of his lung.

The tasty and refreshing admixture of fruit, which had been canned in heavy-fructose corn syrup and fortified with 100 percent of the daily recommended allotment of vitamin C (amongst other essential nutrients), had unwittingly been forced into the doomed man's pulmonary tree.

In an effort to round out his meager diet, Nana Pillow-See would occasionally throw in a carton of blueberry yogurt or eight ounces of spicy salsa *fresca caliente* and *ceviche del mar.* After all, her husband loved oysters and scallops that had been marinated in lime juice with *chile tepin.*

The toxic capsaicin levels in the tiny *chile tepin* may exceed a hundred thousand Scoville units. If so, the vicious little pepper might be hot enough to denature pulmonary alveoli and other vital internal organelles!

Antler Weezle and his pathetic, homely, and nearly anorectic wife, Puma Imakween lived next door to Nana Pillow-See, and they came by for a visit because Weezle had just been released from prison after being convicted of exposing his reproductive member to a young teenage boy.

Puma was a former power-hungry congressional staffer. For years, rumors circulated throughout the Beltway that she had no fewer than three family members who had belonged to the Islamo-fascist terrorist organization known as the Islamic Fatherhood.

This treacherous organization had been established in Cairo in the early 1920s. The Islamic Fatherhood had vowed that it would not rest until the flag of the Crescent Moon was flying high over the White House.

Antler and Puma were hosting a block party that was funded by lobbyists for the nefarious pedophilic political action organization known as the Texas Man-Child Association for Love (TEMCAL). Pablo and Nana Pillow-See happened to be on the invitation list.

Weezle, whose nickname in prison was *"Carlos Peligro,"* had asked Mrs. Pillow-See where her husband had been since nobody in the neighborhood had seen him for quite a while.

Nana told him that her husband had collapsed in the bathroom and that he had been there for several days!

"This sounds terrible," Puma said. "We better go in there to find out what is going on."

"Well," Mrs. Pillow-See replied, "you'll have to open *up* the shower to see what is *in* the shower!"

Nana rode to the emergency room in the ambulance with Pedro. She wore a tight, leopard-skin miniskirt and slip-on pumps that were adorned with clusters of tiny fuzzy dice. Her horn-rimmed glasses were encrusted with sparkly sequins, and the only part of her body that was more vacuous than her silicone-impregnated breasts was the galactic space between her ears.

The CT scan of the patient's brain confirmed that the doomed hotel magnate had a catastrophic brainstem stroke. The subsequent chest x-ray revealed a secondary lethal complication: a complete whiteout of his right lung. The pulmonologist used a bronchoscope to evacuate enough fruit cocktail from the patient's lung to feed a family of six.

Since the ICU and the med-surg unit were full, the patient had to be admitted to the neurology service after the patient's first course of broad-spectrum antibiotics. Patients cruelly afflicted with the locked-in syndrome from a brain stem stroke are only able to blink and move their eyes up and down to communicate.

The attending physician, Dr. Balbona, held the opinion that Mr. See had suffered a lethal event, especially in light of the aspiration pneumonia caused by the inhalation of peaches, pears, grapes, and maraschino cherries.

The neurology chief asked Dr. Payne and Brewster to have a frank conversation with the patient about considering a DNR code status, and they reluctantly complied with this request. The patient's wife was in the room when Dr. Payne and the student tried to explain that the patient's recovery was not expected.

Pedro conveyed to Brewster and Dr. Payne by a series of blinks that he was prepared to accept a DNR code status, and this order was subsequently initiated at the nurse's station.

Before leaving her husband's room to get a pedicure in North University Place, Nana Pillow-See asked, "Do you boys think my husband will be well by Friday?"

"No!" Dr. Balbona harshly declared.

"I hope that's not the case," Pillow-See said. "We've been invited to a block party by a Houston socialite, Antler Weezle, and his wife. They're having a wiener roast in their backyard. Can you imagine? Say—I'll bet you can't guess what Antler's secret nickname is. Since he's such a puny specimen of a man, his moniker is, 'Ant-Kneed.' Isn't that a stitch?"

"Frankly," Brewster replied, "I couldn't care less."

"The party is going to be called the Ant-kneed Wiener Roast."

"What?!" Brewster asked. "Oh, for shit sake, lady, just never mind."

J. D. Brewster and Dr. Payne looked at each other in stunned silence. There was no sense in trying to explain anything to a person who had the intellectual capacity of a gnat. Despite that fact, Nana Pillow-See was still at least smart enough to one day consider a run for the United States Congress as a Democrat, but of course, that's really not saying very much.

On the day Ronald Reagan was sworn in as the fortieth president of the United States, the Iranians released the American hostages in Tehran. Just like that, the whole ordeal was over.

It was a fascinating and tasty slice of history, and many Americans wondered exactly what Reagan would have done on his first day in office if the Iranians had been stupid enough to continue to hold American citizens in captivity.

Although nobody living today could ever be sure of what Reagan would have done, many speculate that he would have pulled a sixteen-pound sledge out of the tool shed and pounded the fucking Iranians into hammered shit.

Brewster wondered if the two Iranian terrorists who had escaped from jail—and who were still at large in the greater Houston area—would simply give up and go home. That was his fervent hope. After all, they couldn't possibly still hold a grudge just because Brewster was directly responsible for their apprehension to begin with, now could they?

The secretary for the Russian Consulate in Houston was having trouble with heavy snoring and intermittent late-night episodes of respiratory cessations. She was admitted to the neurology service at the University for an overnight EEG and sleep study to make certain that she was not having episodes of a medical disorder known as nocturnal sleep apnea.

In modern times, an evaluation for sleep apnea generally takes place in a specialized sleep laboratory, and the procedures are usually managed by a pulmonologist and not by a neurologist as was the case during the 1980s.

Russian Bear was able to readily communicate with the middle-aged patient who was erroneously thought to have a very limited command of English. Unbeknownst to the members of the medical staff, this Russian woman's ability to speak the English language was actually quite good. Once the electrodes were pasted upon the patient's scalp for the EEG sleep study, the Russian Bear brought in J.D. Brewster to meet the patient for an initial introduction.

Brewster wanted to be gracious, and he asked his Russian colleague to teach him a rudimentary pleasantry in order to at least be able to tell the patient to "have a nice day" before she was scheduled to depart from the hospital the following morning.

After the two medical students had left the patient's room, Russian Bear tried in vain to teach Brewster to say something in

Russian, but Brewster's ability to pronounce Russian words was apparently quite poor. Finally, Bear gave up and said, "Brewster, you're a dumbass. You're clearly not smart enough to be a Russian. I'm going to have to spell this out for you." He used the Cyrillic alphabet to write out a phrase on an index card: "иди на хуй!" He gave the index card to Brewster and said, "In the morning, before this patient gets discharged from the hospital, I want you to be here in the room with me. I'll make sure that my wife, Larisa, is here too. I want you to smile and hand the patient this card. I'm certain that the patient will be absolutely stunned when she reads this note!"

"Well, what does this mean in the English language?" J. D. asked. "It is a very common greeting that Russians say to each other," Bear replied, "and frankly, we enjoy saying this happy and polite expression, not only to other Russians, but to every other person in the world, regardless of their race, religion, or country of origin. On a personal note, I really enjoy saying this expression directly into someone's face if they're from Germany. After all, the Russians are *very* friendly people."

"What?!" Brewster asked, "Not so much if you ask me."

"It's typical for you Americans to always underestimate Russia," Bear said. "After all, you've only done it for the last thirty-five years. Hell, Brewster, you people don't even give us Russians the credit we deserve for devising the scientific periodic table of elements, or for even putting the first man on the moon!"

"What?!"

"Well, I'm certainly not making any claims that the cosmonauts ever returned to Earth or actually even *survived* the landing on the moon when they finally got there for that matter, but that's neither here nor there," Bear said. "The point is, the Russians got their first!"

"What?!"

"In any event, to answer your question, let me explain it to you as best as I can. I believe in the English language, the written phrase means, 'It was a pleasure to have made your acquaintance!' Just hand her the card and wait for the surprised look on her face."

"That's really quite generous of you, Ilya!" Brewster said. "You Russians really are something else."

"You have no idea!" Russian Bear laughed. "Just give this note to the patient, and it'll put a smile on my face … uh, forgive my poor choice of words in your native tongue. I meant to say that it would put a smile on *her* face."

Brewster was a notorious prankster, but this time, it was his turn to get pranked. He failed to realize that he had just been sandbagged!

On the following morning, Brewster, Ilya, and Larisa went to say goodbye to the patient before she was discharged from the hospital and returned to work at the Russian consulate.

Brewster smiled and handed the woman the index card with the mysterious Cyrillic greeting.

Without a word, the patient got out of bed and started looking about the room for something that could possibly be used as a lethal weapon. She found her metallic bedpan and smacked Brewster upside the head!

"I want you to know that my country has a very large arsenal of atomic weapons and a ballistic missile-delivery system that's fully capable of eradicating all life as we know it from the entire face of the planet Earth," she said in perfect English. "I assure you that we're not afraid of using these weapons if we have to, young man!"

Brewster suddenly realized that he was on the ass-end of an impractical joke when Ilya and his wife pointed at him and started to laugh.

"I've learned an expression from the time when I first moved here to America," Russian Bear whispered. "They say that payback's a bitch!"

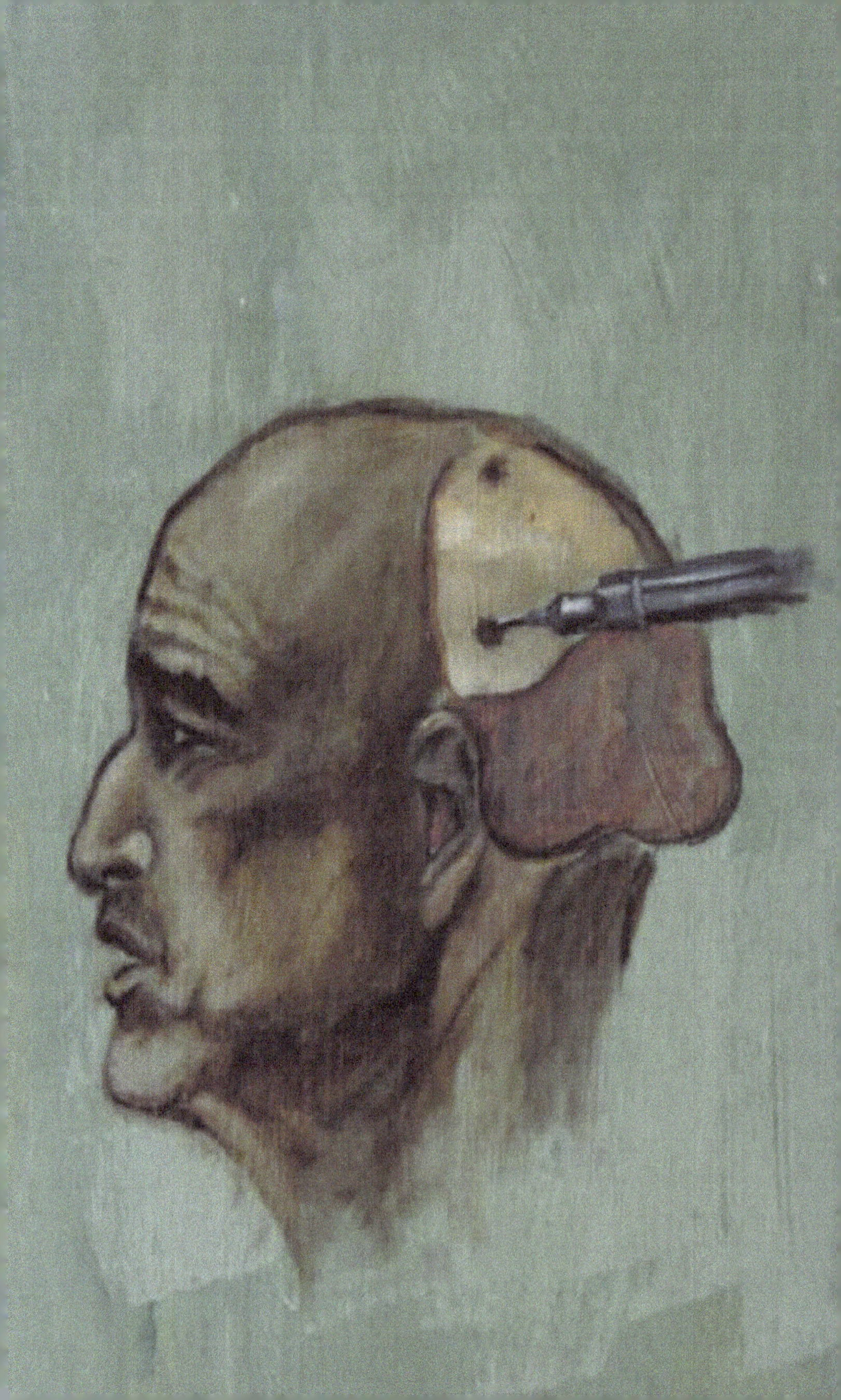

# 13

# BURR HOLE

On February 2, the three students switched over to their bookend rotation for one month of indentured servitude in neurosurgery under the tutelage of Dr. Horacio Hurt and his second-year fellow, Dr. April May. As was customary, Dr. Hurt baptized the students with a pimp and pone session.

Hurt looked at Russian Bear and said, "Batter up, young man! Here's the first pitch. There are at least five recognized hereditary neurocutaneous syndromes that may be associated with neurofibromas and cerebral cortical lesions. You're at the plate. See if you can name at least three of the five syndromes."

Russian Bear had been given a heads-up from a student who had previously rotated through the neurosurgery service that Dr. Hurt would likely ask about the hereditary neurocutaneous syndromes. Therefore, Russian Bear already knew the answer. He replied, "Neurofibromatosis type 1, Neurofibromatosis type 2, and Bourneville's disease are three examples of neurocutaneous syndromes that may be associated with tumors involving the peripheral and central nervous system."

Dr. Hurt said, "You, sir, are bona fide genius! Here is the second pitch. Tell me which of the following environmental factors have been definitely linked as a recognized etiology that may be contributing factors of primary brain tumors: tobacco consumption, alcohol, and/ or electromagnetic radiation."

Bear was also ready for the second question. "None of the environmental exposure factors you've mentioned have ever been confirmed to clearly be associated with primary tumors of the central nervous system at this time."

"I can tell you right now, boys, if your Rooskie friend here answers the next question correctly, he's going to get a field commission promotion to the rank of stud right here on the spot! Look, Bear, you might be a godless commie, but you're one smart man!"

"Here is the third pitch. For patients afflicted with aggressive primary brain tumors such as glioblastoma multiforme, what is the median survival post-resection and external beam radiation treatment?"

"It's a most dismal disease process, and the prognosis is terrible," Russian Bear answered. "The median survival is only on the order of twelve to eighteen months."

Years later, Brewster would look back and remember the details of this particular pimp and pone session when he was coming to the end of his less-than-illustrious medical career. Sadly, he would realize that the median survival rate for that particular primary brain cancer had not gotten much better.

Dr. Hurt thrust both of his arms in the air and said, "I just got poned! Russian Bear, you are now officially a designated stud. Congratulations!"

Brewster and Fielder grabbed Russian Bear under each arm, hoisted him several inches off the ground, and gave arousing cheer. A celebration was in order. Brewster and Fielder promised to take Russian Bear and Larisa out to dinner to celebrate Valentine's Day.

Dr. Hurt explained that the patients who received care on his neurosurgery service were an admixture of individuals who had experienced brain injuries from both open and closed insults to the skull and also unfortunate souls afflicted with primary or metastatic brain tumors that required neurosurgical debulking.

Because of early rheumatoid arthritis changes involving his hands, Dr. Hurt was steering his practice away from spinal surgery at that point in his medical career. The only other neurosurgeon on staff at the Gulf Coast who had the procedural skills to perform spinal surgery was a man named Dr. Jack DeRippa, but he was on sabbatical at the time. Nonetheless, Dr. Hurt promised to allow the three medical students to have an opportunity to participate in the management of a patient undergoing a spinal procedure if an appropriate case availed itself. Through prior arrangements made with the University of Texas Medical School at Houston, which had a superlative neurology and neurosurgery service, Dr. Hurt made certain that no neurosurgical patient would "fall through the cracks."

After a thorough scrutiny of the medical care delivery system model previously established by Kaiser Permanente on the West Coast, the Gulf Coast College of Medicine created its very own nascent HMO program. The only draw-back to the HMO delivery system was that enrolled patients had to receive *all* their medical care through the Gulf Coast institute. By and large, the program worked quite well except for the rare occasions when patients needed to receive medical care outside of the staff physicians who worked at the Gulf Coast College of Medicine. Joe Diddly was such a patient who was about to encounter a world of trouble when he needed emergency surgery that could not be performed at the Gulf Coast University Hospital in a timely fashion.

Mr. Diddly had a herniated lumbar disc with associated symptoms of lower extremity paresis. As this was considered to be a neurosurgical emergency, the patient was transferred from the Gulf Coast to Hermann Hospital, which was the primary medical care facility associated with the University of Texas Medical School.

"Listen up, boys," Dr. Hurt explained to his three medical students. "Mr. Diddly is going to get a decompression laminectomy at Hermann Hospital this afternoon, and I've been given the administrative clearance that'll allow y'all to scrub in on the procedure."

"Who will we be working with over there?" Fielder asked. "The neurosurgeon's name is Dr. Wolfgang von Scheiß Kopf,"

Dr. Hurt replied. "Now look, Russian Bear, there are some things that you need to know about this guy before you simply tip-toe over to Hermann Hospital."

"Well, is this guy a Nazi, or what?"

"Not exactly," Hurt answered, "but his father was an SS physician who was a liaison officer with the Nazi Party and the Leben Kur, AG, pharmaceutical firm during the war."

"You expect me to work under this shit head?" Bear asked. "After all, I've been told that an apple doesn't fall from a tree. Is that not correct, Brew?"

"Personally, I wouldn't know anything about that," J. D. answered rather defensively.

"Just be polite, stay out of the way, and don't fuck up anything while you're over there," Dr. Hurt instructed. "After all, you boys should look at this adventure as a field-trip."

While at Hermann Hospital, Fielder, Brewster, and Russian Bear watched the surgical laminectomy procedure with great interest when the telephone in the operating suite suddenly began to ring. The telephone was answered by an assistant scrub who broke away from the procedure. "I've got some jack-ass insurance rep on the line from the Gulf Coast HMO. She doesn't speak English very well, but from what I can discern, she wants to talk to the individual from the Gulf Coast who's allegedly in charge of this operation."

Obviously annoyed, Dr. Scheiß Kopf looked up at the three students and said," I don't have time for this crap. One of you boys needs to field this call and sort out what in hell the problem is. Draw straws if you have to."

When Brewster drew the metaphorical short straw, he flipped the phone into speaker mode in order for everybody in surgical suite to hear what was going on. "Hello, madam. My name is Brewster. How may I help you?"

"My name is Hunanundan Kualalampoon. I'm an insurance rep for the Gulf Coast HMO. What are you doing to Mr. Diddly?"

"I'm not doing anything to him *per se*," Brewster answered. "He's getting an emergency decompression laminectomy courtesy of the neurosurgery service here at Hermann Hospital."

"Why is he not to getting his surgery performed at the Gulf Coast University Hospital?"

"Dr. DeRippa from our facility is on sabbatical. From what I understand, he's the only neurosurgeon at the Gulf Coast who's able to do this kind of work. He's not available now."

"Why didn't you wait to do the operation until Dr. DeRippa was back from his vacation?"

"Look, lady," Brewster explained. "The patient in question has a nasty herniated disc and he started to experience paralysis of his lower extremities. Now I'm just a dumb-shit medical student, but I was informed that this type of neurological complication from a herniated disc is a bona fide neurosurgical emergency. If this poor bastard doesn't get fixed right away, then Joe Diddly could find himself in the deep end of the diddly-squat. He might be left with a permanent paralysis!"

"If that's indeed the case," the HMO rep asked, "why wasn't he referred to another medical facility that could do this kind of procedure on an emergency basis?"

"He *was* referred to another facility," Brewster tried to explain in vain. "Just this very day, he was sent emergently from the Gulf over here to Hermann Hospital. As we speak, the patient is in the prone position and the back-crackers are performing a laminectomy procedure on him right now!"

"Well, if Jack DeRippa is not available to do the laminectomy, then I insist that the patient get transferred from the Gulf Coast to another competent facility to have the surgical procedure done properly! I'm giving you explicit instructions that you must transfer the patient over to Baylor. The operation should be done at that university, and not at the Gulf Coast."

"Baylor?! What in hell are you talking about?" Brewster asked. "The patient is not *at* the Gulf Coast. He's already been transferred to the U.T. I was informed by Dr. Hurt that there was a preauthorization approval for the surgery to be done here at the University of Texas, not at Baylor. Listen to me very carefully. I want you to break out your English-Sanskrit dictionary and try to comprehend what I'm trying to explain to you. He's at U.T. already, and he's in the middle of getting an operation done this very moment! Would you like to speak to the neurosurgeon doing the procedure? I'll ask him to give you a shout on the speaker phone if that would help matters any."

"Just a moment," the rep said. "I have to talk to my supervisor."

"Take your time," Brewster replied. "Go have a pow-wow with Gunga Din if you must. I've got all damned day. Just be sure to pull your head out of your ass somewhere along the way and brush up on your limited comprehension of the spoken form of English. I don't know where in hell you're calling from, but surely you must have been colonized by the Brits at one time or another awhile back. After all, those slimy limeys planted the Union Jack in just about every damned corner of the third world, as far as I can tell. To be frank, what amazes me right about now, is that the Brits didn't leave you with a better command of the King's tongue while they were busy raping your countryside and plundering all your natural resources back in the 19th century. I'm actually quite surprised that England even left you jack assess with a pot to piss in."

After seventeen minutes of silence, the rep finally returned to the telephone. "These are my final instructions to you. You must discharge the patient from the Gulf Coast University Hospital and transfer the patient over to the Baylor Medical Center immediately. I've already taken the liberty to arrange the transfer. An ambulance will be over directly to pick up the patient from the Gulf Coast facility. You can thank me later. Don't argue with me about this matter anymore! I'll have you know that you're a rude young man, and I'll report your insubordinate behavior to the medical school. I'll make sure that you'll have a permanent black mark on your record if it's the last thing I'll ever do!"

At that point, the neurosurgeon went ballistic. Dr. Scheiß Kopf broke away from the procedure and stormed over to the wall mounted telephone and screamed into speaker. "Listen to me, you brainless polliwog! Hang up the goddamned phone right now, Mrs. Harpoon, or whatever the fuck your name is! If you call back before I'm finished with this surgical procedure, I'm going to hunt you down and back-hand you with vicious pimp slaps until you slip into an irreversible coma and you end up on a ventilator! Am I coming in loud and clear?" Russian Bear was right–the apple didn't fall far from the tree.

After the telephone call was over, it was time for Dr. Scheiß Kopf to give J. D. Brewster some advice. "You need to learn to be more polite the next time you speak directly to an insurance representative."

"Is that so?"

"In fact, you should pick up a few Russian phrases along the way," Scheiß Kopf suggested. "After all, your colleague, Russian Bear, just taught me a thing or two while you were on the phone. I've been practicing to say, 'иди на хуй!' Russian Bear said it directly to my face. From what I've been told, it's a polite expression that the Russians especially like to say to people of Germanic origin."

"What?!"

The decompression laminectomy turned out to be a success and Mr. Diddly was eventually discharged from the hospital without further complications. Sadly, the patient eventually got a huge medical bill from the Gulf Coast HMO because he received out-of-service medical care from an alleged unauthorized facility. It would take years of litigious combat until the matter was finally settled equitably in the patient's favor.

Brewster would often wonder throughout the rest of his dismal career if a national single-payer health care system that was funded and subsequently implemented by the federal government could have possibly performed any worse as an insurance arbiter than what he had witnessed from the Gulf Coast HMO regarding their abysmal management of the patient known as Joe Diddly.

The good Sam Aria was accustomed to helping anybody in need. In the past year, as a recent example, he brought Dora Garza to the hospital when he found her aimlessly wandering about in his neighborhood. At the time, he knew it was the right thing to do. Unfortunately, Sam had not met Dr. Blomeo Colima, who had completed his fellowship training the prior year. Dr. Colima would have surely admonished Sam for engaging in such foolish behavior. After all, no good deed goes unpunished. If Sam had continued to try to live his life by adhering to silly, archaic, Judeo-Christian principles of spreading exemplary platonic love, charity, and kindness to his fellow human beings, he would certainly deserve to be severely brutalized for such reprehensible and nefarious activities. After all, organizations such as the radical Society for the Freedom from Religion openly detest such overt practical applications of theistic spirituality! It was just a matter of time before Sam would be violently reprimanded for such inappropriate benevolent behavior. That time occurred on the first Friday in February as Sam was leaving the parking lot at the El Parador Supermarket.

Smeg Nog still had a limp and wore a knee brace, but he was back in action with his partner. The two career criminals had devised a new scam to acquire additional automotive inventory for their chop shop. Smeg Nog was lying on the ground in front of the strip mall, and Big Nig was leaning over him, appearing as if he was attending to a man who had fallen ill in the parking lot. Their signature assault weapon, a three-quarter-inch threaded lead pipe was securely hidden in Smeg Nog's sleeve.

Sam Aria jumped out of his car, ran up to the two men, and said, "Is your friend ill? I'm here to help if I can."

"Skew me, my man, do you know where da white wimmins at?" Big Nig replied.

Sam Aria replied, "I'm sorry, but I don't under—"

Before he could complete his response, the lead pipe slammed into the side of his head. As he fell to his knees, Sam cried out, "Why are you doing this to me?"

The second blast created an open head wound and drove Sam straight into the pavement.

Big Nig pried the car keys from the fingers of the dying man and said, "Why? I'll tell you why. 'Cause you ain't like me, taco bender! Can you dig that?"

———◦◦◦◦►◉◄◦◦◦———

The neurosurgery team had already been alerted that an emergency case was arriving by ambulance. The good Sam Aria was immediately hauled away to the operating suite, and Dr. Hurt, Dr. May, and his students attempted to extract the broken skull fragments that had compressed the patient's brain and caused massive intra-parenchymal bleeding.

Upon stabilization, Ben Fielder was assigned to help follow the case. In the intensive care unit, steroids and a nondigestible sugar called mannitol were utilized to reduce the elevated intracerebral pressure. Sam required ventilator support to keep his lungs aerated since he was unable to breathe on his own accord.

After several days without improvement, the neurology service under Dr. Payne rendered a consult. The EEG confirmed that the patient was brain-dead. The patient's wife had kept a vigil at her husband's bedside for the entire time he had been hospitalized.

Dr. May and Mr. Fielder spoke to the patient's wife about the prospects of discontinuing aggressive management and having the patient declared a DNR code status. To the dismay of the neurosurgery service, the patient's wife refused and demanded that everything be done to keep her husband alive.

Dr. May took Ben Fielder aside. "When the brain fails, the heart will soon follow. If Señor Aria's spouse is insisting on a full-court press, we'll pull the trigger when the time comes. What difference will make? If she's insistent on staying here the entire time, we won't be able to run a slow code or suck down a can of Mr. Pibb before we call the code blue. When we eventually run the code, it will have to be by the book. I want you to gently talk to her again about an organ harvest when the time comes. It will take some diplomacy on your part, but I'm sure you can get it done."

At that point, Señora Aria was at least amenable to the idea of her husband being an organ donor. After all, he was the most generous human being that she had ever known, and she was certain it was something he would have wanted to do. Within four days, the good Sam Aria went into cardiac asystole. A codeblue was called, and when the resuscitative efforts were unsuccessful as expected, Dr. Gray's organ-harvest team was waiting on the sidelines.

"Brewster, you need to come with me," Dr. Gray said. "I need an extra set of hands on the harvest team—and you know the ropes."

"Wait!" Brewster said. "I need to get this cleared by Dr. Hurt first."

"No time for that," Dr. Gray said. "I'll have you back in the saddle with the skull crackers before Dr. Hurt can even ask, 'How do you shit?' Fair enough? Let's go."

Ben Fielder was feeling quite despondent and wanted to visit his girlfriend to decompress. Missy and Ben planned to meet across the street at Hermann Park for an impromptu picnic lunch.

On her way down the stairwell, Missy ran into Dr. Harrison Reed. Dr. Reed considered himself to be a "switch hitter," and he had no intention of going through life with one hand tied behind his back. There was a persistent rumor that Harrison Reed molested a motorcycle gang member named Moritz the Mouse at the Astrodome a while back, and the professor of medicine got a well-deserved thrashing for his impulsive sexual indiscretions. One would think that a person should learn from his or her mistakes, however that apparently was not the case for Dr. Reed who was completely unaware that he was about to step into the spinning blade of a buzz saw.

"Well, hello there, little schoolgirl! I've had my eye on you for quite some time. In case you weren't aware of this fact, I happen to be the director of the MD/PhD training program here at the Gulf Coast College of Medicine. I suspect I'm the smartest person that you've ever met. I can tell right now that you're ready to throw yourself at me, and your desire to have sex with me in this stairwell is quite understandable." He grabbed Missy, pinned her against the wall, and started to fondle her violently.

Missy slapped Dr. Reed across the face.

Harrison Reed retaliated by punching Missy in the mouth. Before leaving the stairwell, he said, "You better put some ice on that."

When Missy met Ben Fielder at Hermann Park, she had a fat lower lip. When she told Ben what had happened, he suggested that she go through the proper legal channels to file a complaint with the medical school and the hospital administration, although he was furious beyond measure.

Missy thoughtfully and accurately filed the complaint the following day, but she had no idea that the tables would be turned against her. She was about to learn a painful lesson: the loftier the position in the hierarchy of life that a misogynistic sexual deviant is able to carve out for himself, the greater likelihood the predator will be able to skate away from any societal repercussions.

Missy was taken into a conference room and accused of making sexual advances against Dr. Reed! She was told in no uncertain terms that she would be terminated on the spot if there were any further romantic advances made toward the physician.

If going through the proper channels had failed so miserably, it was a foregone conclusion that Missy Brownwood and Ben Fielder were going to have to seek retribution against Dr. Reed through the occult underground clinical justice system…

"Brewster, where in hell have you been?" Dr. Hurt asked upon Brewster's return from the organ harvest. "Have you been jerking off in a broom closet again?"

"I'd never do that, Dr. Hurt," Brewster said.

"Never?"

"Well, rarely would be a more accurate response, I suppose," Brewster answered. "I got called away by Dr. Gray to lend a hand with his organ-harvest team when Sam Aria died."

"I didn't give you permission to abandon ship like that! Pull another stunt like that, and I'll pull your stud rank."

"I thought it would be a good deed to help out where I was needed," Brewster said.

"No good deed …"

"Yes, Dr. Hurt," Brewster said. "Sadly, I know the rest."

"Get the Dalton girl transferred over to the neurosurgery service," Hurt ordered. "It's time we crack open her noodle and scrape that nasty crab out of her skull."

Axel Kurtz treated himself to surfing lessons in Corpus Christi, Texas, on his twenty-fifth birthday in August 1978. Unbeknownst to most folks who've never tried surfing, the sport can be quite dangerous. Although serious injuries are not all that common, there are neurosurgeons who've worked their entire careers on the Hawaiian Island chain while attending to individuals who've sustained serious head, neck, and spinal fractures while participating in the sport. Surfing is harder than it looks, and it requires a considerable amount of athletic skill and balance. Unfortunately, Axel Kurtz was endowed with none of those prerequisite physical attributes.

After multiple tries, Axel finally caught a wave, and he was quite proud of his accomplishment when he was able to stand upright upon the big board. His surfing coach had instructed Axel to simply fall off the board when the wave began to peter out. Axel was feeling brave and tried to turn his board back into the wave to extend his ride. That turned out to be a big mistake since Axel didn't see the adjacent young man on the personal watercraft crashing over the swell.

The closed head injury Axel sustained left him in a vegetative state for the better part of two and a half years. By the winter of 1981, his fiancée had left him. Sadly, even his family members rarely came by to see him at the nursing home where he was receiving long-term custodial management.

The neurosurgeons kept an eye on Axel since he would periodically run into problems with post-traumatic hydrocephalus. Although a ventricular-peritoneal shunt was surgically placed years before, the decompression tube device occasionally malfunctioned or clogged up with mucoid or cellular debris. Other times, the shunt would need to be revised because it failed to operate properly for some obscure reason or another. His admission to the hospital in February 1981 was one of those unfortunate occasions.

Russian Bear had been assigned to look in on Axel and found it sad that the patient had no friends or family members visiting him. The patient was in a vegetative state and was not verbally communicative. Axel's eyes were open, and he would spontaneously blink, but the only sound he made was a repetitive clicking of his tongue.

Despite the patient's neurological limitations, Russian Bear was nonetheless compelled to speak to the unfortunate individual. "I suspect that you've never heard the song, 'Midnight in Moscow', sung in the original Russian language. I would like to sing that for you now since I suspect you might be feeling a bit lonely inside this empty hospital room." Bear had a beautiful baritone voice and sang a wonderful rendition of the classic Slavic tune.

After completing the song, Bear noticed that somebody named Gideon had visited the patient and left a Bible on the nightstand. When he picked up the Bible and departed from the patient's room, his intent was to take the book directly down to the hospital's lost and found department. After all, Bear held in his hands what he thought was a rare and valuable treatise that was no doubt a most important item to the individual who had mistakenly left the book behind.

Sister Buena intercepted him in the hallway and said, "Where are you going with that Bible, young man? It's perfectly okay to leave it in the patient's room—or you could keep it for yourself if you'd like."

Although the Gulf Coast College of Medicine Hospital was a private secular institution, it was hospital policy to make sure that there was a Bible in every patient's room.

"I'm a floating nurse from the temp pool, and my boss sent me here to pray over Axel and bestow a blessing upon him," she said. "Why don't you join me?"

Other than his unfortunate isolated television viewing of the pseudo-Christian, fraudulent and greedy, charlatan "holy-roller evangelist" from Hope, Arkansas named Rectal Roberts, Russian Bear had only vague concepts of Christianity since organized religion had been actively suppressed by the Soviet Union for the past sixty-three years. After all, religion was nothing more than an opiate for the masses. Nonetheless, Bear thought that Sister Buena's suggestion was indeed a capital idea.

After plowing through a rotation in pediatrics and a less-than-fulfilling stint on a family practice rotation, Willy Mammon decided to do an elective on the ear, nose, and throat service. Although the rotation on the burn unit was a physically and spiritually draining experience, the big man felt drawn to surgery for some reason, and perhaps a surgical subspecialty would be a potential field of endeavor for him to pursue after his graduation from medical school.

Curl Floyd was a middle-aged gentleman who had chewed tobacco since Little League. He preferred a slab of brick tobacco to the sweetened leaf chew that came in aluminum pouches. A real Texan will either bite right through the plastic wrapping to take a plug of brick tobacco or use a blade to cut out a chunk to munch on. Curl invariably used his trusty, rusty pocketknife to cut out a plug of tobacco, leaving no doubt to any observer that Curl Floyd was a vine-swinging, testosterone-laden, macho hombre.

Unfortunately, his chronic tobacco habit resulted in the development of a squamous cell carcinoma on the floor of his mouth two years earlier. At the time of his original diagnosis, back in '79, he was found to be already doomed by an unresectable, stage IV-b disease process with pulmonary metastases that was deemed incurable and refractory to oncological intervention. His aggressive cancer appeared to be totally unresponsive to a variety of different types of multi-modality treatments.

After Curl experienced cancer progression following radiation treatment for palliative intent, the crab-pickers signed the patient onto an experimental in-house clinical trial, GCH-HNSCC 80-01. This protocol utilized the conventional drug, 5-fluorouracil, which had been commercially available for twenty years, and an experimental drug called, methyl-GAG, which was added to the protocol. What an absolutely beautiful name for an experimental chemotherapeutic agent! The patient appeared to have experienced disease stabilization for the better part of half a year, but he sadly suffered from a rapid expansion of his tumor over the two months prior to his presentation to the ear, nose, and throat service for what should have been a routine follow-up outpatient visit.

When the Wooly Mammoth examined the gaping hole that had appeared in the right anterolateral aspect of the patient's neck, which was caused by the tumor, he saw the most horrific cancer he had ever seen during his limited clinical experience. Sadly, the malignancy exceeded anything that had been described in any textbook that he had ever read.

The patient had a large open wound on the right side of the neck that extended through the floor of the mouth. The foul, putrescene gas that emanated from the wound could actually be seen briefly as a faint yellow haze when the gauze dressing was unpacked from the hole in the patient's neck. Floyd's tongue, floor of the mouth, and right side of his mandible had completely disintegrated. The hole extended directly into the trachea, and the patient's sternocleidomastoid muscle was completely gone. It was a shock to see that the patient's carotid artery and jugular vein were completely exposed, and the vascular structures were pulsating in the open hole on the side of the patient's neck! The jugular vein and carotid artery were enveloped by a thin rim of tumor, much like sausage casing.

Since the patient was on a registered experimental protocol, it was the duty of the crazy crab-pickers consigned to the Department of Experimental Chemotherapeutics to try to squeeze out as much life as they possibly could from the dying man. They actually asked the ear, nose, and throat service to ligate the carotid artery and jugular vein to prevent a blowout! Doing so would result in a catastrophic cerebrovascular accident that would have caused left hemiparesis, but the patient would have likely lived for another week or so. Quality of life be damned. Statistically, something like only a modest one or two-week improvement in overall survival might have been a make-or-break situation as to whether an experimental agent would see the light of day—at least from the standpoint of the Food and Drug Administration.

By the time that the attending physician, Dr. Seth Stringer, had heard the wooly one explain the bizarre request that the crab pickers had petitioned, a trickle of blood was already oozing from the hole in the patient's neck. The idea of actually ligating a patient's jugular vein and carotid artery was so outrageous that the diddly-squat slammed directly into the spinning blades of the proverbial fan.

"Willy, tell those crab-pickers that I'm going to stick my foot so far up their collective asses that they'll be able to taste the leather on my shoe! As his carotid/jugular complex is already starting to break down, I anticipate that Mr. Floyd is going to be transferred to the eternal care unit tonight. I want you to stay in there with him until it happens. We don't have a resident or intern on my service this month, so if anything gets out of control—or if the patient becomes uncomfortable—you must call me immediately."

Willy called down to the laundry service to find out if there was a maroon bath towel anywhere in the hospital. All three maroon towels were reserved for Dr. Harrison Reed's private washroom. If that was indeed the case, there was only one person Wooly Mammoth could trust in the acquisition of said items, and that person was none other than J. D. Brewster.

"Yes, I know where the washroom allocated to that son of a bitch is located," Brewster said. "It's adjacent to the conference room. In addition, I know for a fact that there's no lock on the door to his private little spa."

"How do you know that?" Willy asked.

"I make a point of pissing in his sink whenever the opportunity arises," Brewster explained. "I can get those special towels for you in a jiffy, big boy."

Within ten minutes, Brewster appeared with the three maroon bath towels.

"Brew, I need you to dampen all the towels in the sink with very warm water and then set them at the ready on the Mayo table," Willy instructed.

"What the heck are you doing?" Brewster asked.

"Patience, my pasty friend."

When the cancer had finally finished chewing a gaping hole through the right carotid/jugular complex of Curl Floyd, a bright-red blowout that would have made the Hawaiian Kilauea Volcano envious, had suddenly exploded. An admixture of arterial and venous blood suddenly blasted across the floor of the hospital room.

The patient panicked when he began to exsanguinate, as he realized that his time on earth was drawing to a rather rapid and genuinely unpleasant conclusion.

Willy calmly packed a damp warm towel across the patient's neck, and when it became saturated with blood, he applied the second towel. The patient calmed down when he could no longer see his own blood spilling upon the hospital bed, floor, and walls. Willy didn't need the third towel because by then, the angels came down from heaven and took Curl Floyd back home.

Dr. Seth Stringer was so impressed with Wooly Mammoth's compassionate intervention that he gave him a field commission to the rank of stud before the night was over.

For some reason, Willy Mammon was not particularly proud of how he had earned his newfound status. He placed the bloody towels in a red biohazard bag and asked Brewster to deliver the bag back down to the laundry room. "These towels need to be thoroughly washed and dried before Dr. Harrison Reed becomes any the wiser about this situation," Willy instructed.

Brewster cheerfully complied, but he took the biohazard bag containing the maroon towels straight down to the laboratory incinerator to be destroyed. While out and about on this devious mission, Brewster gleefully sang the song made famous by Walt Disney's Seven Dwarves: "Whistle While You Work."

Brewster scrubbed in on the craniotomy and resection of the large malignant tumor invading D' Shea's brain. During the surgical procedure, Dr. Hurt and his fellow in training, Dr. April May, communicated to each other with a volley of blue expletives.

It was Brewster's job to stand to the side, hold a suction device, and occasionally remove blood and debris from the surgical wound without actually touching the brain. Neither Dr. Hurt nor Dr. May had informed Brewster at any time during the operation how things were actually going, but J. D. intuitively knew by the cursing that ensued from the attending and the fellow that the cancer could not be completely excised.

Toward the end of the operation, Dr. Hurt said, "Well, goddamn it, is that the best we can do?"

Dr. May said, "I think I can burn out a little bit more at the deeper aspect, so I want to try to go just a little bit longer."

"You're more than welcome to go down swinging," the attending said, "but we're never going to achieve clean margins."

After a few moments, Dr. May threw down the electro-cautery Bovie tool in disgust. "I guess that's the best we can do! Maybe we should just cut out her entire brain and replace it with a fucking lap sponge in light of all the good that we've done for her today."

"April, sometimes our best is not much better than shit on a shingle," Dr. Hurt said. "You have to be able to accept that. I never told you when you signed on as a neurosurgical fellow that this was a particularly happy line of work. Deal with it." He looked directly at Brewster and said, "Help April close up. She'll tell you what to do. I'm going to suck my balls up around my throat and be a man. I'm going out into the waiting room to tell the family that, despite our best efforts, we had to leave behind a considerable amount of residual cancer."

"This is bad," Brewster said, "isn't it?"

"There's just no way that any more of the tumor could be surgically removed without putting the young woman's life in jeopardy. I can't tell you what a cheerful conversation that this is going to turn out to be."

The final pathology report indicated that the patient had a very high-grade primary brain tumor, and it was a glioblastoma multiforme. This nasty animal was considered to be the most aggressive primary tumor that could develop within the confines of the central nervous system.

Dr. Hurt instructed Dr. May to order a follow-up, post-craniotomy CT scan that would be the baseline imaging study to be utilized as the new postoperative point of reference. The attending also had a new set of questions for the medical student. "Brewster, step up here, front and center."

"Sir?"

"Are there currently any effective chemotherapy protocols available that might be beneficial for a patient who's status post a craniotomy and partial surgical debulking procedure to manage a GBM tumor?"

"I don't know."

"Brewster, what is the time interval needed for postoperative recovery from a craniotomy before the crab zappers would be comfortable with the employment of adjuvant external beam radiation treatment?"

"I don't know."

"Did the crab zappers ever get their hands on that new LINAC gun that they've been waiting for—or are they still dicking around with that old, inferior cobalt machine from the dark ages?"

"I don't know," Brewster answered. "Congratulations, Dr. Hurt. You just pitched a shutout!"

"What?!" Hurt asked. "This isn't a game of pimp and pone, you dumbass! I don't know the answers to these questions either. Go talk to the crazy crab-pickers in the Department of Experimental Chemotherapeutics and find out if there are any systemic protocols that are available through the TROG or FROG study groups. When you're done with those guys, talk to the crab zappers. We're definitely going to need some answers from the free radicals about postoperative XRT. Get to it, son."

Upon recovery from her craniotomy, D' Shea Dalton had a ton of questions. "Brewster, do you think I can stay alive long enough to earn my undergraduate degree? I finish up at the University of Houston in the spring of 1982, which is only about sixteen months from now. I understand the median projected survival for somebody with this type of brain cancer is only about a year or a year and a half at best. Do you know what's sad?"

"I can think of a thousand—"

"Right on!" D' Shea said. "As for me, I've never even had a boyfriend. I'd ask you out on a date, but since you may turn out to have some kind of kinship with me and baby girl, that would just end up being some kind of weird, hillbilly, cracker, inbred, white-trash bullshit, would it not? Sorry, I meant no offense."

"None taken. However the likelihood of—"

"Damn straight, skippy!" D' Shea said. "It's strange that I never really knew any white people before, but you seem okay to me—as best as I can tell. I certainly have no realm of experience about what other white people are like, but you're, well, like a regular human being from what little I know about you. I guess I didn't know what to expect about white people before I met you, as I made a point to avoid your kind as long I could in my life. Listen to me just go on and on. As you can probably figure out, baby girl and I can never shut up. One of the nurses, Missy Brownwood, says that you're a man who likes to hear the sound of your own voice. She said that you're the kind of person who will take the time to speak ten words in any given situation when a simple yes or no would readily suffice. I guess baby girl and I are the same in that regard. If you're also like that, it wouldn't surprise me in the least!"

Brewster said, "Missy Brownwood talks—"

"I need you to sit down and story-talk with me, J. D. It would sure be nice if you'd open up a bit. You seem awfully quiet right now. Here I am, all by my lonesome, and I'm pouring out my heart and soul to you. While I don't expect you to be a Chatty Cathy, it would nevertheless be nice if you said something once in a while."

"I'd be happy to try to squeeze in a—"

"Anyhow, even if you and I were not any kind of kin to each other, it might not be too realistic to think that you and I could ever go out on a date. Do you know what I mean?"

"If you would just let me—"

"That is exactly what I am talking about! Maybe it's none of my business, but do you think you could ever go out on a date with a black girl?"

"Well—"

"I knew it! Please tell me—are white girls different than me?"

"Why would you think—"

"That's spot on and so righteous, brother! How are they different?"

"From a scientific standpoint, the chromosomal arrangements of *Homo sapiens* across different ethnic and racial groups are all the same as best I know," Brewster replied. "As I'm a white man from the South, that's actually hard for me to admit, but it nonetheless appears to be the truth. I've heard some geneticists argue that, unlike sexual gender, race is a *social* construct and not *biological* reality. If that's indeed the case, I would like to think that someday I'd be brave enough, despite the pressures of our current peculiar social circumstances, to accept the fact that you and your sister are likely—"

"Thank you! There it is, pardon the pun, in black and white and zebra stripes for the whole world to see!" D' Shea said. "I'm happy to hear that. I had no idea that *any* white people felt that way. As you've noticed, I have green eyes that are the same color as yours. I had really nice, tight, springy hair before my surgery. It was so soft. It felt really nice. I've been told that I'll stay permanently bald once I get the radiation treatment and that my hair will likely never grow back."

"Wait! Your hair could possibly—"

"Don't tell me about the bad news. I already know about it," D' Shea said. "It will only make me sad. I've wondered what it would be like to have straight hair like some white girls have, but I was happy with the hair that I had. I need to tell you a secret— baby girl likes you a lot. Would you go on a date with her instead of me just because I could end up completely bald?"

"Why would you think that a *real* man would—"

"Would that matter to you? I mean, do you think I'd look okay if I had to go through life wearing a wig or a bandana on top of my head?"

"How could—"

"Of course! That is exactly what I am talking about! If I had ever gone out on a date with a white boy, Daddy would go purple monkey shit on me. Maybe, though, he'd feel different about it if he knew I only had a year or so left to live. After all, what difference could it possibly make to white people, black people, the universe, or even God? Why aren't you saying anything? You're making me do all the talking."

Brewster picked up a roll of surgical tape, tore off a strip, and plastered it across her lips. "I'd go out on a date with you—white or black, nappy or bald, skinny or fat! Well, to be honest, I prefer fat girls. Nonetheless, if you packed on a few pounds, I'd do it just as long as you didn't make me listen to any of that disco crap that you and your sister used to listen to on the radio! Deal?"

D' Shae peeled the tape off her lips and laughed out loud. "I don't know about this premonition I've had for a while, but for some reason, I think I am getting closer to the finish line of my life. If that's so, my only regret is that I missed a chance to be loved. If it had happened, even for a fleeting moment, I think I would truly feel that my life was complete. I guess it just wasn't meant to happen for me."

"Stop right there," Brewster said. "You're just starting this journey."

"No, J.D., I see it differently. I'm lonely, and I hope that doesn't happen to you too. It's the awareness of our own mortality that gives our very lives any meaning at all. What do any of us have? If a person is lucky, maybe he or she will have about a number of four score or so spins around the sun. That's it. That's all we get."

"Now, eighty years of life may be too many for some people but not enough for others," Brewster said.

"True, but I can't help but be philosophical about all of this. No matter how much time any of us are allotted, I believe we're all called to find some tangible mission that's righteous and good."

"Have you found yours?"

"I most certainly have," D' Shea answered. "Once any of us recognize that this Divine calling may be our destiny, it's our duty to try to accomplish this calling to the best of our God-given abilities. Have you found yours?"

"The longer I look, the more elusive it's become."

"That just means you haven't been looking hard enough," D' Shea replied. "This commission to such a purpose gives our lives a deeper meaning. This is my conviction. Should we not also strive to pursue love and happiness along the way of this mystical journey, no matter how fleeting? I suggest you consider the same."

Brewster couldn't afford to let D' Shea see the tears that were streaming down his face as a consequence of another soul-shaking déjà vu event. To do so would be a sign of weakness. After all, the Gulf Coast College of Medicine didn't tolerate any signs of weakness.

Brewster hugged D' Shea as he pulled her close, and gently rubbed his chin back and forth over the top of the bald spot on her scalp, which had been shaved for the surgical craniotomy. After all, Brewster's beard was also comprised of really nice, tight, and springy hair…

On Valentine's Day, reservations for a party of eight were made at the Seven Samurai in North University Place. The Wooly Mammoth and Russian Bear were being honored by Ben Fielder, J. D. Brewster, and their dates for the important promotion to the full rank of stud. Of the eight people in attendance, the Wooly Mammoth, Feral Cheryl, Russian Bear, and Larisa had never eaten at a sushi bar before.

Cheryl expressed concern about the prospects of consuming uncooked seafood. "Explain something to me. Is there not some risk about getting parasites like worms, liver flukes, and evil shit like that from eating raw fish?"

"Why, absolutely!" Ben Fielder exclaimed. "Before I started eating sushi, I weighed in at about 425 pounds. In fact, I was at one time a professional sumo wrestler and had an excellent career. Geisha girls were really hot for me. I was the stunt double in the Japanese monster movie *Dr. Smeg Versus the Atomic Cockroach*. After I picked up a few intestinal tapeworms from eating raw fish, I dropped down to this svelte and debonair 163 pounds that now constitutes my current fighting weight."

"You're such a dork!" Missy said.

"Honest!" Fielder said. "I'm six feet three inches tall, and I must admit that I look pretty dashing right about now—if I do say so myself. If you pick up a few tapeworms along the way, it's a bonus as far as I am concerned!"

Missy Brownwood buried the heel of her shoe into the top of her boyfriend's foot.

Ben Fielder was not only full of industrial-strength BS, but it was also clear that he was hanging around J. D. Brewster far too much. Apparently, being inflicted with hyperbolic BS was a transmissible disease process-much like tapeworms!

Stella Link was having her diabetes and hypertension managed at the outpatient internal medicine clinic, but Brewster had no idea about any of it. Stella kept her medical problems—and management thereof—a secret from her boyfriend, but Stella was now starting to lose weight. She was down to 192 pounds.

"You look fantastic, Stella!" Missy said. "You're really trimming up."

"What're you saying?" Brewster asked. "I just thought Stella was buying bigger sizes in the anticipation of packing on a few more beautiful pounds."

"You're an idiot," Feral Cheryl said.

"Stella, are you trying to drop a few pounds here and there without telling me?"

When Stella looked away, Brewster realized something was out of sorts. He was not about to tolerate his girlfriend losing any weight. In fact, he had openly expressed his desire to see her up to about 240 pounds. Brewster was determined to get to the bottom of what was going on.

Willy Mammon turned to Brewster and said, "I don't know anything about this sushi stuff. I'm not all high-toned and sophisticated like you are, J. D. Tell me, what's good to eat at this place?"

"Everything tastes good," Brewster answered, "however I would definitely avoid trying to eat the sea cucumber. If you don't know what a sea cucumber is, it's an invertebrate echinoderm that looks like a giant turd that rolls around blithely on the ocean floor. I tried it once, and I immediately puked. It happened to taste like shit with the subtle tones of vintage twat rot."

"For once in your life," Stella pleaded, "don't be a pig."

"When I put the squishy sea creature in my mouth, it felt like I was trying to choke down a thick slab of cold snot!" Brewster elaborated. "I never actually swallowed the damn thing. I basically just gargled with it for a moment before I blew beets all over the sushi boat. I had chunks of squid shooting out of my nose!"

Stella Link buried the heel of her shoe into the top of her boyfriend's foot as Missy Brownwood furrowed her brow at Brewster. "Come to think of it, the Wooly Mammoth just professed that you were all high-toned and sophisticated. Well, you can't prove that laudatory acclamation to me."

Stella whispered a specific secret request to the waitress.

When the head chef presented an enormous sea cucumber on a turkey platter, Brewster opened his wallet and threw all of his cash on the table. He fled the restaurant alone, trying to suppress the waves of nausea and bitter water brash that was now burning the back of his throat while the other guests at the table howled with laughter.

While Willy Mammon paid a visit to the ATM across Fannin Street, Big Nig and Smeg Nog were actively casing the Texas Medical Center for additional automotive inventory for their chop shop.

Smeg Nog turned to his accomplice and said, "Well, well, well, as I live and breathe, there's the big black bastard who crushed my leg eight months ago. I do believe it's payback time!"

Big Nig said, "If that's the guy, we better hurry up and get across the street. Put your mask on."

The masks that the two thugs wore as disguises appeared to have been appropriated from *The Lone Ranger*.

Big Nig crept up behind the Mammoth and said, "Skew me, my man. Do you know where da white wimmins is at?"

Willy turned around and saw two men with black masks that covered their faces. "I'm sorry, gentlemen, but Halloween was four months ago."

Smeg Nog took the lead pipe from his associate and smashed Wooly Mammoth's skull. As Willy fell to his knees, Smeg Nog peeled back the mask and sneered, "It's way cool, man. Dig this, gnarly dude. The bone can clone!"

Willy's field of vision began to tunnel, but he could nonetheless feel the hot, gritty sidewalk against his face. Before he lost consciousness, he heard his two assailants arguing with each other.

"Why did you take your mask off, you dumb shit?" Big Nig asked, as the two assailants fled the scene. "They have a video camera at that ATM, and your picture might have been taken! You're getting careless, my man."

"Why you always ridin' me?"

"Because you're going to get pinched someday, and I'm going to laugh my ass off when it happens."

Big Nig would not be laughing if the careless behavior of his partner in crime would end up bringing in the authorities just a little bit closer for an eventual unpleasant visitation followed by a life-long incarceration, or worse!

The emergency room had to order a second CT scan on the brain of Wooly Mammoth since the big man suffered a grand mal seizure in the giant imaging doughnut machine. The tonic/clonic seizure distorted the quality of the picture from the first computerized axial tomography study. The quality of the second imaging study was much better and clearly showed a massive subdural hematoma and a left-sided depressed skull fracture. The bleeding was occurring between the inner table of the skull in the outer layer of the brain, and it was compressing Willy's gray matter. The wooly one soon slipped into a life-threatening coma.

Ben Fielder and Russian Bear assisted Dr. Hurt and April May in performing the surgical burr hole into Willy's skull to facilitate the evacuation of the intracranial bleed. J. D. Brewster held Feral Cheryl's hand tightly in the waiting room while Willy was undergoing the emergency surgery.

Dr. Hurt went out to the waiting room and said. "It's too soon to tell, people. If he does pull out of this, he'll have long and rocky road ahead."

Willy would be out of commission for several weeks, but at that time, nobody knew if he would be left with any permanent, debilitating neurological sequelae.

Several days after his surgical craniotomy, two detectives from the Houston Police Department paid Willy a visit, but the big man was obviously reluctant to tell them about anything that had occurred. After all, how could Willy possibly tell the two police officers the details concerning the fracture he previously inflicted upon Smeg Nog's leg during the prior summer?

"Okay, Willy," Detective Watt asked. "Did you recognize either of the men who assaulted you?"

"Nope."

"That's it?" Culp asked. "Is that all you want to say?"

"Nothing else to say," Willy replied.

"A little canary told us that you were acquainted with a man named Darryl Hewritt last year after his attempt to steal your father's Caddy went sideways. We find it odd that no criminal charges were ever filed against this fellow. The precinct at the North University Place happens to be like the Wild West," Watt said. "My partner and I have heard about the crazy shit that goes on over there."

"Don't know anything about it."

"Is that so?" Culp asked. "Maybe just a little bit of police squad justice happens over there from time to time. What do you think? After all, some shady things also happen at the Gulf Coast College of Medicine from what we've heard. Ever since this place opened in '71, rumors have been floating around about a clandestine clinical justice system. Any comments?"

"Don't know anything about it."

"Tell me," Watt asked. "When was the last time you saw Darryl Hewritt?"

"Don't know the man."

"Is that so?" Culp asked. "After all, the security cameras at the ATM machine captured a few grainy pictures of somebody who looked an awful lot like the man who tried to steal your father's Cadillac last year. We know that because the North University Place shipped a World War II Walther P-38 to our office for a ballistic assay, and that gun was previously in the possession of the man named Hewritt. So, be honest with us. You must at least know one of the men who assaulted you."

"Asked and answered."

Willy's father was present during the interrogation and pressured his son for not only clarity but also for complete disclosure. "Willy, you have to come clean about all of this. Tell these men what you know. You have to be straight up with them— no matter the consequences."

"You got it all wrong, Pops," Willy said. "I don't know shit about shit."

"Tell me something, Willy," Detective Culp said. "You're not going to do something stupid like trying to hunt down these bastards and dispense your own personal brand of vengeance, are you?"

"Now why would I do that?" Willy asked. "After all, I'm a man who has the utmost faith in our own clinical justice—uh, oops!—I meant to say, our own *criminal* justice system…"

By the time Willy Mammon returned to his clinical clerkship rotations, his dream of a career as a surgeon was forever dashed. The subdural hematoma had left him with a seizure disorder that would be poorly controlled for the rest of his life. It would remain a problem for Willy despite a variety of anti-seizure medication regimens. Sadly, a future seizure event would eventually end his life when he was driving his daughter to college in San Antonio years later.

After he was assaulted in February 1981, it would be many years before Willy would be granted a driver's license again. Without being able to drive and being physically at risk for recurrent seizure activity, Willy would never be considered a good candidate for a surgical residency program. That was a very hard pill for Wooly Mammoth to swallow, and he became deeply embittered about his unfortunate circumstances.

On the last day of the neurosurgery rotation in February, Antonia Alabaster and the Your Witness News team arrived to the neurosurgical unit to conduct an interview with Mr. Axel Kurtz. The patient had just awakened an hour earlier after being trapped in a deep coma for more than two and a half years!

Mr. Kurtz seemed to be completely awake and alert, and he appeared to have no residual neurological deficits after being in a vegetative state for such a long period of time. That was quite remarkable since the surfing accident he was involved with had resulted in a 50 percent loss of the bilateral frontal lobes of his brain.

During the interview, Mr. Kurtz wanted to specifically thank the medical student who had sung to him in Russian. He recalled the song with great clarity, and it inspired him to awaken from his coma. He said he needed to meet the man who sang to him!

When Russian Bear saw the television report in the Vinyl Lounge, he was totally unaware at the time that Mr. Axel Kurtz had awakened from his vegetative state earlier that very morning. Bear had scrubbed in that day to observe two neurosurgical procedures. By the time lunch rolled around, he didn't have the opportunity to make any patient rounds on the neurosurgical floor.

"Did you see that, Brewster?" Bear asked. "Oh my God. I think I saw miracle! This is the same patient I was assigned to look after earlier this month. This guy's been in a coma for more than two years! Tell me you saw that! Let's go upstairs so I can see him again right now. I have to talk to this guy and confirm what happened to him with my very own two eyes."

"Calm down, Bear."

"You can't just blow this off, Brew," Bear said. "It would be sacrilegious to do so! Come upstairs with me right now. Let's see this guy together."

Brewster shook his head as he plopped down on the sofa with a hot burrito that he had just removed from the microwave. "If there's such a thing as a miraculous awakening, it's likely a consequence of the patient having his ventricular-peritoneal shunt revised by Dr. Hurt—nothing more and nothing less."

"Once again," Bear said, "you're missing the big picture."

"Miracles do happen, but you never know who's been chosen to be the witness. I guess I just wasn't supposed to see this one."

# 14

## MARDI GRAS

J. D. Brewster's clerkship tract was two months ahead of schedule since he had received elective credits for his infectious disease and gastroenterology rotations during his ill-fated year of research. The electives had been surreptitiously scored while he was working in futility in the MD/PhD dual-training program.

He had to take four more mandatory clinical rotations— psychiatry, family practice, obstetrics/gynecology, and pediatrics—to complete this phase of his medical training. Unfortunately, the current schedule would only permit him to complete a family practice and psychiatry rotation by the end of June. The pediatric and obstetrics/gynecology rotation would have to be jammed into the second and final round of his clinical training program. For most medical students, the second year of clinical experience was totally comprised of elective rotations. As Brewster had time to spare, he decided to take a month off from the clerkship rotations and see what kind of trouble he could stir up down in the research laboratory.

As it turned out, several of his classmates had planned a road trip to Mardi Gras that month, and there was no way in hell that he would miss out on that party. Even though he had completed his undergraduate work in the Golden Triangle of East Texas, he had never even paid a visit to the Crescent City, much less to Mardi Gras.

Brewster's first stop would be to see his cherished mentor, Yeshua Rabbi. "Hello, Professor Rabbi. I wanted to come by and find out what kind of progress you've been making on your new research project. I've not really had an opportunity to talk to you since the university pulled the plug on our hepatitis vaccine study."

"Well, if it is not J. D. Brewster! Please come in, my young ward, and have a seat. I would like you to visit with me for a moment." Dr. Rabbi looked up from his desk. "I've been apprised of more than a few unsettling stories about you, Mr. Brewster. For the love of God, tell me that the rumors aren't true!"

With the index and middle finger of his right hand crossed behind his back, Brewster replied, "Why, Dr. Rabbi, I have no idea how those nasty rumors have circulated throughout the Gulf Coast College of Medicine. I'm just trying to keep my head down and my nose firmly planted upon the grindstone to get through life as best I can—just like everybody else. So, tell me, how are things with your shingles vaccine study?"

"This particular virus seems to be an easier entity to work with compared to the hepatitis B virus and infinitely easier to work with than the still-unidentified non-A, non-B hepatitis virus. I'm subjecting the virus to a variety of chemical baths at this time to see what it will take to denature it before we subject any animal models to direct inoculation procedures. This particular study is facing financial constraints. If I don't come up with some concrete data by the end of the year, they may pull the plug on the project. I have a backup plan, however. If the rug gets yanked out from under me yet again, I want to investigate the possibility of creating a better rabies vaccine."

"How do you plan on doing that?" Brewster asked.

"I'll be using the skunk as a viral host. I think it would be much easier to work with than bats. If so, this might be right in your wheelhouse. Please make a point of paying a visit to Rip Ford. He's working with Bookman on the GRID syndrome project. From now on, please stay in touch, my son."

"I will this time."

"Just between you and me, the head of the Department of Psychiatry strikes me as being a most peculiar fellow. Well, your girlfriend is his secretary. Has Stella Link ever told you anything about Corka Sorass?"

"Oh, as a matter of fact, she has," Brewster answered. "A few weeks ago, she informed me that Dr. Sorass had two sisters who didn't survive the war. Byda, Beeda and their parents were hiding behind a false wall in a garage when they were discovered by the Gestapo. I don't have to tell you what happened next."

The Rabbi turned pale, closed his eyes, and rolled his face up toward the ceiling. When he finally opened his eyes, he said "Excuse me, J. D., but I must cut our visit short. I suddenly have a *very* important phone call to make. You must go down the hallway and visit Rip Ford now. Thank you for the information that you've given me. I can't tell you just how crucial this matter may turn out to be."

Brewster was curious about the Rabbi's alarming behavior, and the student elected to quietly stand out in the hall beside his former mentor's doorway to listen in on the "important phone call." Professor Rabbi asked for long distance information and requested to be connected to the Simon Wiesenthal Center in Los Angeles.

"I know your organization has only been operational for the past three years," the professor spoke into the telephone, "but it's very important that I talk to somebody in the War Crimes Division—immediately!"

When Brewster heard somebody walking down the hallway, he quickly turned away to pay a visit to his old research associate, Rip Ford. From what had just occurred, Brewster suddenly suspected that Corka Sorass may have been somehow involved in some rather nefarious activities years ago. It would certainly warrant a bit of snooping on Brewster's part to find out exactly what was going on.

When Brewster had arrived at Rip Ford's workstation, Rip was wearing a gray motorcycle cap that was likely stolen from Marlon Brando when he starred in the 1953 classic *The Wild One*. Brewster said, "All you need now is a 1950 Triumph motorcycle, and you'll be ready to join the Mexican Marauder motorcycle club!"

Ford looked up from his workstation and said, "Hello, dumbass! I was wondering how long it would take for you to come back down to the bowels of the research center. Did you miss me?"

"Ford, I've missed you like a thrombosed external anal hemorrhoid spritzed with *salsa fresca*! Fill me in on how things are going with Dr. Bookman's Gay-Related Immunodeficiency Disorder research program. What's it like working with Parker Coxswain?"

"He's a bona fide genius."

"So I've heard, but I know for a fact that the guy is a major league goofball."

"Parker's bat-shit crazy, but at least he seems to be not half as nuts as you were, Brew. I'd swear that you'd not believe the weird shit that's going on around here right now. Good God in heaven, it's so odd that I am certain you'd feel right at home if you came back and worked in the laboratory and resurrected your PhD training program."

"What gives?"

"Bookman received a monetary grant from the group known as Gays Without Borders. This organization wants us to prove that the GRID syndrome is an infectious disease, and that it's *not* necessarily an illness that is restricted to the gay community," Rip explained.

"Why would they care one way or another?"

"This organization believes that there's a stigma associated with homosexual activity. At least it's frowned upon by the majority of Americans who are living a straight lifestyle," Rip added. "This stigma would be amplified if the GRID syndrome is going to turn out to be a disease process that only afflicts homosexuals."

"What are you supposed to do about the data?" Brewster asked. "Make up shit along the way?"

"No, but Gays Without Borders believes it's imperative for us to prove that straight people are also at risk of acquiring the GRID syndrome," Rip Ford explained. "I can tell you right now that this sounds more like a political agenda than a medical or scientific inquiry."

"Why should you care?" Brewster shrugged. "Does it present any particular ethical challenges?"

"Unfortunately, if we go down this path of research, I'm going to encounter the same problem we faced last summer when Hank Holcombe tried to shoehorn us into doing inoculation experiments on the big primates. Incidentally, we still have the big boys incarcerated in the lockdown kennel, and I get to visit them from time to time."

"I trust that are simian friends are well."

"Check this out," Rip added. "I'm not necessarily saying that Bookman is going to create a conflict of interest, but he's also working on getting a federal grant to try to prove that the GRID syndrome is *not* an *infectious disease* at all, but perhaps it's a *lifestyle disease*! I shit you not. Uncle Sam has inquired if we can figure out a way to actually prove that the GRID syndrome is spread from person to person by the simple act of getting a rigid, one-eyed trouser snake rammed up a happy, horny ass-end."

"A *lifestyle* issue?" Brewster asked. "You can't be serious!"

"I can tell you right now that this sounds more like another political agenda witch hunt and not a medical or scientific inquiry. I don't know how he's going to pull this off, but Bookman and Parker are planning on playing both ends against the middle since Gulf Coast intends to accept funding from both extremes of the political spectrum. I just hope I don't get my left testicle caught in a vise over all of this."

"Since I'm missing my left testicle already, I don't really have a point of reference, per se. However, if you are making money for the medical school, I don't think anybody will be casting stones at either of you for any alleged conflict of interest. Data is data. Let the cards fall where they may."

"What makes you think it's so easy?" Rip asked.

"A professor of atmospheric sciences at Dick Dowling University was given a grant by the Green People organization," Brewster said. "He was asked to prove that the temperatures were falling on the planet because of man-made global cooling. These fruitcakes believed the next ice age will arrive in about two decades, around the year 2000. The professor took the research grant that was offered, but the Green People were furious when he published an independent report that refuted the hypothesis that the activity of mankind was responsible for temperature changes on our planet. Do you see?"

"Yeah," Ford said. "It's just like I thought. I can see my left testicle getting caught in a vise over this."

"Maybe not," Brewster said. "There are political agendas, and there are scientific agendas. These differing objectives often fail to intersect on any recognizable plane of existence. Speaking of still being in existence, what can you tell me about Hank Holcombe? Have you heard anything about how his cancer treatment is going?"

Rip Ford looked down to the floor and said, "In December, Uncle Hank underwent high-dose chemotherapy and had an autologous bone marrow transplant. Hank has no living relatives, so he had to be his own donor. In my humble opinion, an autologous transplant is like getting an oil change on your car but not putting on a new oil filter."

"How so?"

"It just didn't make sense how they managed his case," Rip said. "Unfortunately, the transplant was done when Hank still had active and measurable disease. The bone marrow transplant was not performed as a *consolidative* procedure while he was in remission. It was attempted as a *curative* procedure. Sadly, it doesn't work that way. The problem was that Uncle Hank had never gone into remission to begin with!"

"Never?"

"Can you believe that shit? No chemotherapeutic protocol has been particularly effective, and his lymphoma has apparently been giving the crab-pickers the middle finger the entire time! Anyhow, I've been informed that the transplant procedure, as expected, has already failed—and his disease has come back with a vengeance. He declared himself to have a DNR code status recently, so no heroics will be done when his time comes. The only intervention he'll receive now is additional XRT to try to keep a lid on his dreadful pruritis."

"I can't believe I am hearing this," Brewster said.

"The last time I paid him a visit in his home, he had already clawed off several layers of his own skin," Rip said. "You need to make a promise to me right here and right now—if I ever contract any weird shit like the nasty crab that's eating Uncle Hank alive, you'll take me out, throw me in a dumpster, put a cardboard box over my head, and administer a lethal dose of elemental lead right into my cerebral cortex with a high-velocity lead-injection devise, preferably one that has a nine-millimeter bore or larger."

"Look, Ford; I love you like a brother," Brewster said. "In fact, I'd be willing to do you a big favor and just shoot you right now! Consider it a prophylactic, preemptive strike. That's fraternal love right there, buddy boy. You just say the word, and it'll be a done deal. I promise you'll never see it coming."

"Wow!" Ford laughed. "With friends like you, who needs enemas? I know you're trying to get through life without actually living, but you need to man up and pay Uncle Hank a visit with me."

"Will do."

"Don't just patronize me—and don't just pay me lip service either," Ford said. "We have to pay Uncle Hank a visit before he kicks the bucket. Do you understand?"

Nobody who had met Uncle John would have ever guessed that the man, at one time, had true musical talent. For most of his life, Uncle John appeared to be sullen and slow. Periodically, he would have manic episodes where he would stay awake, composing music for weeks at a time. After Erna and Rex were murdered in his cigar shop, John showed no further interest in life except for the obligation he felt to try to raise Rex's daughter, Cheryl, as best he could.

Before the war, John attended Carnegie Tech on a full-ride musical scholarship. John was proficient in piano, violin, and the French horn, and he was also a marginally gifted composer in the genre of marching music and eighteenth-century Italian and Western European classical symphonic orchestration.

In 1940, John could not have picked a worse time to accept an exchange student position offered through the Conservatorio di Musica Classica di Napoli. Of course, the United States did not enter World War II until December 7, 1941, but Europe was embroiled in the conflict much earlier. In the spring of 1941, John decided to have a picnic on a hillside that overlooked the militarized refueling station in Naples for Karl Dönitz and his Kriegsmarine Unterseeboot wolves which had been preying upon Allied merchant and military vessels in the Mediterranean Sea.

John was composing music at the time, and he was totally oblivious to the submarine base. The Gestapo however, did not see it that way, and Uncle John was thrown into one of Mussolini's political dungeons for half a year without a trial. In October, the State Department was able to negotiate John's release and orchestrate his repatriation back to the United States.

If the State Department had not been successful at that point, John likely would have likely died in prison during the European hostilities since Germany declared war on the United States in December of 1941 after the Japanese attack upon Pearl Harbor. Upon his return, it was discovered that John had acquired tuberculosis while languishing in a dank dungeon. Because of his illness, John was never able to complete his formal musical training, and complications from tuberculosis kept him out of World War II. John was treated at a tuberculosis sanitarium in Arizona at a time when the only known treatment was surgical deflation of the lung to try to starve oxygen away from the aerophillic mycobacterium organism that was the etiology of the scourge.

John finally recovered long after the war had ended, and hard work and exercise finally brought him back to his fighting weight and pre-tuberculosis physical condition. John tried his hand at jazz music, and he even briefly tried to collaborate with the vibraphone maestro, Lionel Hampton, in the early 1950s, but Hampton felt that John's style of composition was rigid and too heavily influenced by classical structure.

As John's application of entrenched musical composition theory was not suited for the free-flowing jazz movement, he went on to compose the fight song for Dick Dowling University. After failing in a last-ditch attempt at becoming proficient in the West Coast, cool-jazz sound as exemplified by the Dave Brubeck Quartet, John finally abandoned his musical career and worked as a postman for several years before acquiring the ill-fated cigar shop in Houston.

Did bona fide miracles occur in ancient times? According to biblical tradition, that would appear to be the case. Hanukkah is celebrated by those who pay homage to ancient Hebraic traditions. According to deuterocanonical and other historical references, Judaism was outlawed by the conquering ruler, Antiochus IV, in 167 BC. The Holy Temple in Jerusalem was defiled by polytheism when a statue of Zeus was erected and swine were sacrificed at the site.

After a successful revolt in 165 BC cast out the Hellenistic oppressors, the temple had to be ritually cleansed and rededicated. The high priests issued a decree that part of the cleansing ritual would require burning oil for eight days and eight nights, although only one day of oil was available for the consecration.

A miracle occurred when the one allotted day of oil burned for the entire eight days and eight nights. To this very day, the nine-candle menorah is as much a symbol of Judaism as the Star of David. For all intents and purposes, Hanukkah is a celebration of an intercession of Divine providence that had occurred two millennia ago.

Do miracles occur in modern times? People who do not believe in miracles never met Uncle John's 1966, two-door, light blue, three-on-the-tree Dodge Dart that was powered by a rather anemic 225 CID slant-six engine.

In all the years that Uncle John owned the car, he never checked the battery, put air in the tires, changed the oil, flushed the radiator, replaced the factory-installed ignition points, spark plugs, or condenser under the distributor cap, replaced the plug wires, flushed the differential, checked the brakes, or performed any other sort of routine maintenance that most automobiles required. In fact, Uncle

John's crappy Dodge Dart had not been washed or vacuumed in fourteen years.

The tread on the tires had worn out to the point that John was actually driving about on the tires' bias-ply fabric backbone. John didn't pay insurance for the car, update its license plate, or get the annual safety checks required by the Texas Department of Public Safety. Talk about miracles!

The Dodge Division of the Chrysler Motor Company may have produced some really decent automobiles at one time or another, but one might venture that there's absolutely nothing that has ever rolled off the assembly line that could ever hold a menorah to Uncle John's Dodge Dart.

Uncle John's car had probably exceeded its projected life expectancy by, oh, fourteen years or so if one considered the maintenance and upkeep the vehicle *never* received. The only accessories that Uncle John added to his miraculous vehicle were the steer horns that he affixed to the front grill and a twelve-gauge shotgun he kept in the trunk. After all, Uncle John never knew when it would be necessary to break out the old scatter-gun and blast some dipshit blue-belly carpetbagger into smithereens.

Every March, the Greek Orthodox Church would host its spring fund-raising bazaar. John went every year because he enjoyed getting absolutely plastered on the bitter Greek wine that was served. If anything good can ever be said about Greek wine, it's that it has some long-legged, oily gams when you roll it about in a four-ounce, wax-papered Dixie cup.

John parked his car and was walking toward the festival when a man pulled up and said, "Hey, Doc, I'm new around here, and I am trying to find the Greek festival. Could you give me directions? It looks like you might be going in the same direction!"

Uncle John said, "I can tell that you're not from around here. In fact, you sound like Bugs Bunny! Are you from New York?"

"Wow! I didn't realize my accent was that thick, but you're correct. I'm indeed from New York.'

"What in hell are you doing here?" John asked.

"My business has just transferred me down here to Texas."

"Well, do you like it here?"

"I can't tell you how happy I am to be right here in the Lone Star State."

"Gee," John said. "That's too bad."

Uncle John walked to the back of the Dart, opened the trunk, pulled out his shotgun, and said, "I'll show you how to get to the Greek festival. Eat a load of this buckshot, you Yankee varmint son of a bitch!"

As the shotgun began to blast away, the interloper sped off as fast as possible. Fortunately, as John was apparently a lousy shot, none of the blasts from the 12-gauge hit its mark. John calmly reloaded his weapon, put the shotgun back into the trunk, and then he ambled off to the festival as if nothing had happened…

Emboldened by the fact that there were no apparent consequences to the sexual assault that Dr. Harrison Reed had attempted to perpetrate upon Missy Brownwood, the director of the MD/PhD dual-training program was determined to have his way with the young woman once and for all. After all, nobody could refuse somebody who was as smart as Dr. Reed had professed himself to be.

Dr. Reed had drawn an elaborate caricature of himself dressed up like Fred Flintstone, riding upon a triceratops dinosaur and brandishing a club. The object of the caveman's attention was an image of a very naked and very voluptuous Missy Brownwood running through a primordial forest, trying to escape the sexual predator in hot pursuit.

From an artistic standpoint, the cartoon was actually quite excellent. From an ethical standpoint, the cartoon was actually quite repulsive. If Harrison Reed was trying to woo Missy Brownwood, it had quite the opposite effect when Reed taped the cartoon upon the refrigerator door in the nurse's break room.

Missy pulled the offensive cartoon off the refrigerator door and briskly marched off to administration to complain that Dr. Harrison Reed was engaged in more overt sexual harassment, and this time, she had the evidence. She demanded that the unwanted advances cease immediately.

Once again, the administrators told Missy that she was blowing things out of proportion and that she should have a sense of humor about the whole matter. After all, Harrison Reed was an up-and-coming power broker and fund-raiser in the Democratic Party.

What was Missy to do if she was being sexually harassed by somebody who held a lofty position at the hospital and medical school, and curried a great deal of influence with a political party that valued partisan ideology over what was right and what was wrong?

One evening, Missy was walking out to her car in the employee parking lot when Harrison Reed pounced upon her. He dragged her to his metallic blue BMW 3.0 CS and pushed her inside. Missy was terrified, but when Dr. Reed tried to rape her, the professor remained completely flaccid. In retrospect, he turned out to be no Bill Clinton! Reed was simply unable to have his way with Missy as he had planned.

Missy quickly lost all her fear of Dr. Reed as soon as she realized that he was little more than an impotent, raspy-voiced, and squinty-eyed old bastard with an atrophied and nonfunctional reproductive member. "Is that the best that you can do, you dirty old sod?" Missy laughed. "You disgust me. Just wait until I tell all the nurses up on the med-surg unit that you tried to rape me with a flaccid pecker that was so small and flimsy that you probably had to borrow it from an achondroplastic gnat!" Missy began to sequentially gangster slap Harrison Reed in the face, submitting alternating sequential blows with her open palm and then the back of her hand. She cackled malevolently each time she administered a sharp blow to the face of the sexual deviant. "Let me know when you have had enough, you pig!"

Harrison Reed was incapable of fending off the defensive blows that Missy Brownwood had heroically levied upon his face because he was too busy slinging his puny pecker from side to side in a futile attempt to stimulate an erection. Finally, he had the wherewithal to grab Missy's hand, and he bit it hard enough to break the skin. He pushed her out of the car and sped away with his favorite boxer shorts, replete with a colorful print of multi-flavored Gummy Bears, hanging down around his ankles!

Missy went back inside the hospital to find Ben Fielder, and they went to the North University Place Police Station to file an assault complaint against Harrison Reed. When she showed the officers the bite mark on the dorsum of her right hand, it was finally enough evidence for an arrest warrant to be issued.

When he was brought down to the police station for booking, Dr. Reed glibly uttered a watertight alibi. His secretary would attest that her boss had stayed in his office all night long completing paperwork when the alleged assault had occurred. When Dr. Reed's secretary said that she would testify to this statement in a court of law, the district attorney decided not to proceed with the indictment—and the criminal charges were quickly dropped.

Missy Brownwood developed a serious cellulitis infection on the dorsum of her hand that warranted a brief admission to the hospital for intravenous antibiotic therapy. After all, human bite injuries can be very serious, and an infection from the usually benign saprophytic mouth-dwelling microbes can easily damage the extensor tendons that run through the top of the hand. Then again, who could ever really be sure of the type of toxic microbes that might have taken up residence within the foul confines of the oral cavity of the sexual deviant named, Harry Reed?

As Missy feared retribution from Dr. Reed, she elected to be admitted at the adjacent Hermann Hospital at the Texas Medical Center instead of the Gulf Coast University Hospital where she was employed. She received appropriate treatment, and fortunately she quickly recovered from the infection.

Ben Fielder confided with his girlfriend that something drastic had to be done because Dr. Reed would likely hound her until she was fired or forced to resign. Perhaps it was now time for Ben to call in a marker from a rather vicious and violent individual and his fellow motorcycle gang members who had specifically promised the medical student in the recent past that he was owed a great personal favor…

The anesthesiologist, Ron Chelsea, "passed gas" during a routine oral surgery procedure for the ENT service. After the custodial crew cleaned up the surgical suite, Ron went back into the operating room to recover his stethoscope, which he had inadvertently left behind. In the empty OR room, Dr. Chelsea saw that the tank of nitrous oxide, also known as laughing gas, had not yet been locked back up in the extruded steel cage where all the volatile gas cylinders were stored at the end of the day. Ron thought, *"What the hell? I should really know what my patients experience when they inhale laughing gas. I'll try just one little snort. After all, what harm could it do?"*

The following morning, Ron Chelsea's lifeless body was found on the floor of the operating room. He had collapsed beside an empty canister of nitrous oxide anesthetic gas. The news of his death spread through the hospital like wildfire. More than two dozen students gathered in the Vinyl Lounge to commemorate his passing. A spontaneous rendition of "Who Shot That Hole in My Sombrero?" was sung by all. Some medical students were thoughtful enough to bring Bandito pizzas from Taco Hell and several boxes of jelly doughnuts.

More than a hundred people showed up for Ron's funeral, but his ex-wife made no effort to attend. Ron's only living relative was his single mother who had never married. She asked Brewster if he would be so kind as to give her a ride home after the funeral service ended.

After the minister read the twenty-third psalm, the congregation departed. Ron's mother, J. D. Brewster, and two of his student colleagues lingered at the gravesite to pay their final respects.

Unfortunately, Willy Mammon was still recovering from his craniotomy, and he was not feeling well enough to attend the graveside memorial ceremony.

Russian Bear looked down at the casket, which had already been lowered into the ground, and said, "Dr. Chelsea, you were a strange and funny man. You made me laugh even though, most of the time, I had no idea what you were talking about. I'll surely miss you."

Ron's mother sat down on the edge of the grave and dangled her feet into the rectangular hole. She pulled a flask out of her purse and started to guzzle it. "You know, I never really liked Ron—and I never wanted him as a son."

"What are you saying?" Brewster asked.

"When I thought I was barren," the drunken woman slurred, "I believed that I was finally free to have a good time with anyone I wanted, but then—pow! I got pregnant with him just like that. I never knew who his father was, and it could have been anybody with the way that I was going at it, all hot and heavy at the time. I swear, junior, I'd jump in the sack with every throbbing pecker that I could wrap my loins around!"

As she set her near-empty liquor flask upon on the ground, Ben Fielder said, "That's one of the most disturbing things that I've ever heard a parent say about their own child. You disgust me! You didn't deserve to have a son as good as Ron."

"You didn't know him like I did," she replied. "He was always telling ridiculous stories just to make people laugh. He was a silly and useless little man."

"No, you don't understand," Russian Bear said. "The ability to make somebody else laugh is a gift. If you don't know that, then I feel sorry for you."

"Buzz off, dipshit," she said. "I don't need some Euro-trash foreigner like you giving me a sermon. Somebody better take me home. I need one of you big boys to lay the timber to me tonight. If one or more of you jerk-weeds are up for the job, have at it. As best I know, my twat is as clean as a whistle. After all, I don't have any open sores in the camel toe and I haven't noticed any itchy chiggers or shit like that fixin' to set up camp in my short hairs."

Brewster and his colleagues looked at each other in stunned silence. J. D. took his left foot and pushed Ron's mother down into the hole.

When she landed upon top of the casket lid, she cried out, "Somebody better get me the hell out of here! I didn't want to be this close to Ron when he was alive—much less now that he's actually dead. Get me out of here, damn you!"

Ben Fielder kicked the flask down to her. "Wrap your lips around the opening on that damned thing. Maybe if you suck real hard, which I know that you're fully capable of doing, you may be able to nurse out another drop or two of the liquid sustenance that your body so desperately craves."

She writhed about like a box turtle that had been flipped over on its back while she reached out in futility to find her precious liquor flask among the confines of the open grave.

As the three men departed the cemetery, Brewster was obliged to pay is own personal homage to the twenty-third psalm. "Yeah, though I walk through the valley of the shadow of death, I shall fear no evil. After all, if you manage to piss me off from here on out, I'll just have to stomp your sorry ass into the dirt."

The inspired author of Proverbs 16:17 who wrote that "idle hands are the devil's workshop" may have had J. D. Brewster in mind. The morally challenged and rebellious medical student was a troublemaker, and he likely always would be, as it's impossible for a tiger to change its stripes. Brewster had absolutely no intention of spending the month of March, 1981, engaged in any meaningful or constructive endeavor whatsoever.

As personal freedoms erode over time, it's sadly conceivable that the Constitution of United States could be cast aside in a dark, dystopian future. If this unspeakable tragedy would ever happen, our country would likely be ruled by a malevolent or demented dictator.

In such a nightmare scenario, troublemakers like J. D. Brewster with idle hands would be rounded up and simply worked to death at gunpoint. After all, a police state could *never* allow somebody like Brewster to have any time off. The threat to the social order would just be too great to allow a mischievous hooligan like Brewster to have any free time when reactionary and revolutionary schemes might be hatched to overthrow the state in a violent manner.

Therefore, it was clearly a foolish idea for the militaristic Gulf Coast College of Medicine to allow Brewster to have the whole month of March off for a vacation because it afforded the socially maladapted medical student an opportunity to settle a long-festering score with the sadistic head of the burn service. Finally, Brewster had enough free time to achieve this lofty goal.

An announcement in the *Houston Post*'s public transaction section declared that Dr. Blaze Street had planned to turn his eighty-acre family ranch near Palestine, Texas, into a private deer-hunting game preserve. The newspaper had given the exact legal description of the property in question and had even listed the plat map's numerical legal heading. Brewster hatched a malicious scheme, but he realized that he was going to be facing a difficult task. Nonetheless, it was too important a prank to let anybody else in on the elaborate plan or on its intricate execution.

The first thing Brewster had to do was to go on a field trip to visually inspect the parcel in question. When he arrived in Palestine, he found that Dr. Street's property had an abandoned oil well that had been capped off decades ago. The spoil area around the wellhead must have occupied at least fifty thousand square feet. It was time to confer with Brother Bill about the rules and regulations regarding environmental contamination from an oil field accident.

Brewster took several photographs of the site before he returned to Houston. When he got back to his apartment, he called his brother at the Tenneco Oil and Gas Company to see if a few questions could be succinctly answered.

"If a large oil spill or oil field accident occurs that may result in a potential danger to the environment, would such an event fall under the jurisdiction of the Environmental Protection Agency?" J.D. asked.

"The federal government would only get involved if an oil spill places a federally controlled area of land or waterway at risk," Bill explained. "Otherwise, an oil spill would be addressed by the Texas Railroad Commission. An oil field accident is only considered problematic if the spill is greater than five barrels of oil."

"How much crude does that work out to be?"

"About 250 gallons," Bill answered.

"How much oil in an accidental spill would be enough to create a permanent spoil area that's much bigger than an acre?"

"A whole acre or more?" Bill asked. "You're now talking a shitload—"

"If a catastrophic accident occurs, would it be the landowner or the entity who owns the mineral rights that would have liability and end up paying the piper?"

"The entity who would be responsible for cleaning up an oil field spill would be the well operator—not the landowner or mineral rights owner," Bill said. "Once an operator has received a certified letter from the Texas Railroad Commission that an environmental infraction has occurred, the offending party must take action within two weeks or less. If no cleanup efforts are initiated within that two-week period, the guilty party would face fines of up to ten thousand dollars per day until the remedial work to clean up the spill has been completed."

"Wow!" J. D. said. "That's terrifying."

"What are you up to?' Bill asked. "Please don't tell me that you're neck deep into one of your bullshit pranks. If you are, I don't want any part of it."

J. D. put his hand behind his back and crossed his index and middle fingers. "Now, look here. I have turned over a new leaf, and I'm walking the straight and narrow. Do me a favor. I found a piece of property that I would like you to look into. It has a very large spoil area that must be on at least an acre, and that just doesn't seem right to me. I've seen other spoil areas in east Texas, and they seem to be considerably smaller."

"What's so important about all of this?" Bill asked.

"I think something bad happened at this particular well site. The ground is completely barren of vegetation. It's just nasty out there, and it stinks to high heaven with the odor of petroleum fuel. I'd venture that if somebody threw a lit match on the ground out there, the place would go up like napalm. The site has an old wellhead that looks like it was shut down years ago. The cap's quite rusty, in fact. I'm going to give you the plat map number of the parcel, and I would like you to tell me when the well was operational, who owned the mineral rights, who was the licensed operator, and what year the well was shut down."

"You'll owe me big-time," Bill said. "Anything else?"

"I also need you to tell me if there was any record of a large oil spill or blowout that occurred on the site that was legitimately reported to the Texas Railroad Commission."

J. D. had the information he requested by the end of the week, and it was quite interesting. The well had been capped off and abandoned in 1967, but there were *no* legitimate reports or any information about a catastrophic major oil spill or blowout accidents in the past. Certainly no violations had been previously submitted to the Texas Railroad Commission that would have accounted for a spoil zone of over an acre in size prior to the time that the wellhead had ended its production run. In light of the incriminating photographs, it meant only one thing: the oil well operator committed a major crime by not reporting the accident to the Texas Railroad Commission years ago!

The land and mineral rights were owned by the Blaze Street Family Limited Partnership, and Dr. Blaze Street, Jr. was the director of this still legal and active entity. The on-site operator for the entire time that the wellhead was operational was surprisingly still in existence. The name of the company was the "Chestnut Mare Oil Production Company."

According to the secretary of state, which was the legal body that had overseen corporate and business entities, this company was never incorporated. The sole owner of the business was Mr. Blaze Street, Sr., who was still alive in his seventh decade of life. Without the protection of a corporate umbrella, any liabilities incurred by the oil production company would be essentially passed on directly to the Street family!

It was turning out to be a beautiful situation—as far as J. D. Brewster was concerned. Is there such a thing as Karma? If not, Dr. Blaze Street was about to get bit in the ass by something that looked an awful lot like it. In fact, a large and untidy dyspeptic possum was about to shit all over Dr. Blaze Street's personal retirement nest egg.

Stella Link had taught Brewster how to use a word processor. All he would need was an example of the official letterhead from the Spankham, Tilley, and Hertz law firm. Brewster wrote a sham letter to the law firm asking for information about which defense attorney in their group had legal expertise in defending a potential client who had been accused of smuggling automatic weapons, drugs, and underage prepubescent prostitutes across the border with Mexico.

J.D. promptly received a less than polite rejection letter from the law firm, informing him that this particular group of upscale attorneys would *never* consider handling a reprobate the likes of Brewster. This was all fine and dandy; the only thing Brewster needed was a copy of the firm's letterhead—and now he had one.

The next item on the agenda was to craft the prank letter to Dr. Street. Brewster had cut off the top of the letterhead and photocopied it onto a blank sheet of paper. He then crafted a sham letter that appeared to have been sent from Spankham and his associates.

The prank letter stated that the law firm was representing a group of concerned citizens in the Palestine area who had strong concerns that the eighty-acre sheep ranch owned by the Street Family Limited Partnership was heavily contaminated by a previously unreported major oil field accident. The group had ostensibly hired the attorneys to draft a formal complaint with the Texas Railroad Commission about the matter. Copies of the photographs of the spoil zone were included with the prank letter to add gravitas.

When Dr. Street received the prank letter via registered mail, he drove directly downtown to the law office of his own attorney to find out what this matter was all about. Dr. Street's legal counsel could not get any confirmation that Spankham or his associates were openly working on such a matter.

Dr. Blaze Street then drove straight to Spankham, Tilley, and Hertz. He barged into the office of Mr. Tilley, dragged the attorney across his desk, and threw him upon the ground. He took the fake letter and stuffed it into the mouth of the senior partner. Dr. Street returned to the Texas Medical Center before the police arrived at the scene of the assault. Mr. Tilley was startled but uninjured. He pulled the letter out of his mouth and quickly realized that his firm had nothing to do with the document, or about Dr. Street's ire, for that matter.

When the police arrived at the Texas Medical Center, Dr. Street was immediately apprehended. "You're under arrest and charged with assault and battery," the officer said as he placed Dr. Street in handcuffs.

Tilley's law firm was determined to make Dr. Street's life completely miserable. Mr. Hertz was a social acquaintance of Martin Zinfandel, the titular head of Your Witness News consumer protection team.

"Martin? This is Javier Hertz. Long time no see. I was wondering if the investigational journalists on your team would be interested in looking into a major oil spill that occurred up in Palestine but was never reported to the Texas Railroad Commission. It seems that the culprit involved is a professor at the Gulf Coast College of Medicine at the TMC. Juicy, huh?"

"Thanks for the tip, Javier," Zinfandel said. "My team is already on it!"

Zinfandel's crew of reporters confirmed that a major oil spill previously occurred on Dr. Street's sheep ranch. Since the catastrophic accident had placed the environment in considerable jeopardy and the event had never been reported to the Texas Railroad Commission, there was now going to be hell to pay! Dr. Blaze Street was suddenly about to get a "Spankham, Tilley, Hertz".

More than thirty students and their spouses or significant others made the chartered bus ride to New Orleans for Mardi Gras. Willy

Mammon was still out of commission, but Brewster, Stella, Fielder, Missy Brownwood, and the Bear and his wife had all made the trip. Everybody who had gone on the Mardi Gras trip put ten dollars in a cookie jar on the bus, and it was going to be given away to the individual who was able to collect the most beads at the festival. It's a long-standing tradition for the citizens of the Crescent City and the visitors who come for Mardi Gras to exchange plastic beads, throw beads, hoard beads, wear beads, buy beads, and sell beads throughout the extravaganza.

During a parade, thousands of beads were being thrown out into the crowd, and the medical students were aggressively pushing and shoving other people out of the way to get a crack at winning the six-hundred-dollar jackpot. Many of the beads landed in the branches of the trees that had lined the boulevard, and a medical student named Bobby Dalles unwisely climbed into the trees to pull down the beads trapped amongst the higher branches. Unfortunately, one of the members of the New Orleans Police Department was not particularly amused by what Bobby was doing. The officer grabbed him by his right ankle, pulled him out of the tree, threw handcuffs on him, and hauled him off to the hoosegow. Bobby was charged with public intoxication and disorderly conduct, and the jackpot had to be used to spring his bail.

Later that evening, several students inadvertently ended up in a strip joint that featured hermaphrodites. After one particularly titillating exhibition, a dancer approached Russian Bear and Larisa and invited them both to shove a dollar bill up his/her ass.

Larisa was a bit stunned to witness a human being who had the nicest and best-proportioned pair of breasts that she had ever seen and also the nicest and best-proportioned penis that she had ever seen. "I must ask you— from a biological standpoint of sexual gender, do you consider yourself to be a man or woman?"

"Honey, tonight I'll be whatever you want me to be!"

The dancer turned to Russian Bear, expecting monetary compensation for the rendered performance, but the Bear said, "Before I came on this trip, I took my soiled clothing down to the laundromat. I was watching my shirts tumble about in the dryer, and I became so mesmerized that I just kept putting in one quarter after another. The clothing kept going around and around and around until I ran out of money."

The dancer bent over, gave Russian Bear a big kiss, and handed him a dollar bill. "Honey, tonight you need this more than I do."

Stella Link acquired the most beads by the time the celebration had drawn to a conclusion. Although there was no longer any prize money left over to award her for this magnanimous triumph, she felt as if the victory was one of the greatest accomplishments of her entire life.

Before it was time to return to Houston, the group decided to have brunch at a famous restaurant in the French Quarter. Parker Coxswain had a full beard in Houston, but by the time the students showed up at Brennan's Restaurant, Parker had completely shaved the left side of his face. He had also picked up a chef's hat somewhere along the way, and he was wearing it proudly. He was perhaps the only student other than J. D. Brewster who was always on the prank prowl.

During brunch, Coxswain saw a young couple sitting at a nearby table. The gentleman appeared to be inebriated as he ambulated toward the restroom with a most irregular gait.

Parker moved over to the young woman who was alone at the table. "Madam, I hope you're enjoying my restaurant." He sat down directly across from her and completely devoured the food that had been brought for her gentleman guest while he was using the toilet.

With a fake French accent, Parker said, "You are so beautiful!" He began to kiss her hand as if he was the reincarnation of Pepé Le Pew, putting the moves on the feline object of his wanton and hormonally driven copulatory desires.

Parker found a pygmy palm tree fern in the corner of the restaurant. Although it must have weighed more than fifty pounds, he picked up the plant and brought it to the woman's table. "You're so beautiful that I want to give you this palm tree. Please take it home as a gift from me, the head chef at Brennan's, to you, the most beautiful woman I have ever seen!" He returned to his rightful seat with the other medical students before the woman's date returned from the bathroom.

When the inebriated man stumbled back to his table, he quickly realized that his platter of food was empty. He must have assumed that he had eaten the meal himself because he pulled out his wallet, threw several large bills on the table, and then picked up the giant potted plant. He stumbled away with the plant and his girlfriend in tow.

Oddly enough, neither the waiter nor the maître d' tried to stop the couple from absconding with the palm tree and marble vase. Who in the world knows how the witless couple managed to lug the giant potted plant around the French Quarter, much less what they ended up doing with the damned thing? After brunch, the students and their guests clamored back on the bus and sang raunchy rugby renditions, bawdy ballads, and lewd limericks all the way home.

Brewster put his arm around Stella and held her close for the three-hundred-mile trip back to the Bayou City.

"A peso for your thoughts?" Stella asked.

"I'm just not accustomed to feeling this content," Brewster answered. "I hope this feeling lasts a lifetime."

"Enjoy it while you can, lover boy," Stella said. "If there's one thing I've learned from you is that life is a series of hurdles that one must jump over in sequence to eventually get to the finish line of life. However, one never really knows if the challenge that's destined to trip you up happens to be the very next hurdle that's just a little further down the track..."

# 15



## YOU TAX DOLLARS HARD AT WORK

The Calle Vampiro cartel had a very good business relationship with the Mexican Marauder motorcycle club. Once a "coyote" had made a successful merchandise run across the border, he would get compensated by 5 percent of the value of the load, and the club would get another 5 percent as a bonus. Unlike the relationship that other cartel organizations may have had with their own henchmen, if one of the Marauders was ever arrested while conducting business for the benefit of the cartel, the organization would provide a legal defense counselor if the nefarious activity led to an indictment and criminal charges.

As long as the motorcycle gang member kept his mouth shut about the cartel, everything went smoothly. If a shipment was ever lost by police interdiction or if inventory was ever confiscated by border authorities, the cartel would consider such an unfortunate event as part of the cost of doing business. The cartel would generally not retaliate against the motorcycle club member who had been hired to transport the aforementioned illicit recreational substances across the border if the transporter had ever been arrested and incarcerated. This policy also applied to the motorcycle gang member's friends and family under these circumstances.

This benevolent business model, however, had its limitations. If a Mexican Marauder was ever caught with his hand in the proverbial cookie jar, there would be hell to pay—and the club could do nothing to prevent a violent retaliation. In fact, if a gang member was ever caught stealing from the cartel, the guilty party would not be allowed to even physically defend himself at the time of his execution. Moritz the Mouse had a brother named Ernesto who had brought a shipment across the border at Brownsville, Texas. Unfortunately, his load was light by five kilograms, which was enough for Ernesto to face the "Vampiro penalty."

Sadly, the Vampiros eventually found the Mouse's brother. "You know the rules, Ernesto. It's time for you to join us at the hacienda."

Although terrified, it was imperative for Ernesto to maintain a machismo image of strength and resolve. Ernesto said, "I'll come along with you peacefully. You don't have to truss me up like a pig. Why don't you just let me ride in the car? After all, I'm still a man."

"Sorry, but we're not going to allow you to do that. You know the rules, Ernesto."

After he was bound and gagged, the cartel took him back across the border into Mexico. The Marauders, Moritz the Mouse, and Ernesto knew exactly the retribution that would follow, and there was nothing anybody could do to stop the grisly events that were about to unfold.

Ernesto was taken to a large hacienda in Nuevo Laredo and enjoyed an elegant and excellent last meal while surrounded by the Vampiros. Ernesto could not help but notice a peculiar electrically powered surgical instrument on a buffet behind the dining room table. It happened to be an oscillating cranial saw. Although Ernesto had never seen such a device, he was able to readily discern that it would soon be employed to facilitate his pending disassembly.

Adjacent to the peculiar surgical instrument was a razor-sharp knife that had been crafted from obsidian. Believed to have been forged from the flowing hot magma deep within the bowels of the earth by the mythical volcanic demigod, Vulcan, the ancient weapon was the most prized possession of the superstitious collective of the Calle Vampiro cartel.

When dinner was over, Ernesto faced his pending termination with bravery and dignity.

When a Vampiro asked, "*¿Es usted listo, señor*," Ernesto nodded his head in affirmation.

One of the Vampiros behind Ernesto pushed his head forward to examine the posterior aspect of his neck. "Okay, what I would like you to do now is remove your clothes and to lie face down on the table in front of me. Will you promise me that you will stay as still as you possibly can throughout this process?"

Like a lamb being led to the slaughter, Ernesto said, "I will do everything that you ask me to do." He disrobed and assumed a prone position on the table.

Ernesto remained completely still when a Vampiro turned on the electric oscillating cranial saw and plunged the gyrating blade into his spine between the C7 and T1 vertebral body, which had instantly rendered acute quadriplegia. Once done, the Vampiro rolled Ernesto onto his back to allow him to face the ceiling. He was fully conscious and able to speak, but breathing was a moderately taxing experience. "Well, I guess all in all, that did not hurt too badly. It's interesting that I can still move my fingers a little bit! You will be happy to know, however, that I am not particularly uncomfortable at this time."

Although paralyzed, Ernesto was still able to feel sharp pain when one of the Vampiros began to slice away at the anterior aspect of his neck with the obsidian knife. Before Ernesto finally died, he felt a deep, terminal vibratory sensation when the Vampiro turned on the oscillating blade of the cranial saw yet again to finish the task at hand.

Ernesto was completely decapitated when the Vampiro hacked the rest of the way through the condemned man's spinal column. In the end, Ernesto's cervical vertebrae had been violated by a direct transection through the anterior portion of the bony column. All the while, Ernesto was unable to fend off the barbaric assault. Even if he had not been paralyzed at the onset in his own brutal decapitation, fighting back would have only resulted in his pending demise being prolonged into a much more agonizing ordeal—if that were indeed possible.

Although Ernesto was a moderately large man with a body weight of approximately two hundred pounds, it only took a few moments for his beating heart to pump out five quarts of bright red blood onto the dining room table. It was time for dessert. The members of the Calle Vampiro Cartel tore off bits of *pan dulce* from a soft, caramelized loaf that had just been taken out of the oven. The warm bread had a generous topping of sugar and cinnamon. The cartel members dipped the sweet bread into the sanguineous pool on the dining room table before devouring the blood-soaked morsels with great relish.

After dessert, the headless body of Ernesto was dragged out into the street and tied to the bumper of a pickup. The victim was subsequently dragged around on the streets of Nuevo Laredo until the skin had been stripped from the corpse.

Afterward, the dead man's torso was impaled upon a fence post where it had remained until it completely disintegrated through scavenger consumption, predation, and microbial decomposition. Was this all merely a ghoulish, symbolic act of terrorism? Perhaps there was a much deeper meaning to the formal name that the self-ordained Vampiros had bestowed upon their personal ghastly enterprise.

Moritz the Mouse vowed to one day avenge the death of his brother at the hands of the bloodthirsty cartel. Until that future opportunity would avail itself, Moritz had been sadly stripped of any residual emotions. The missing essential component of human compassion rendered Moritz the Mouse the ability to become the perfect enforcer who protected the turf of the Marauders on the east side of Houston from any interlopers who might have become interested in the potentially lucrative local narcotic industry.

There were strict criteria for becoming a Mexican Marauder, which included Latino heritage, ownership of a hog, and a propensity to commit acts of brutality to protect the interests of the club at large. Moritz the Mouse fulfilled each and every criterion with a rather unparalleled curriculum vitae of violence.

Long Unit was a member of a competing outlaw motorcycle club. There were strict criteria for becoming a Prince of Darkness member, which included black heritage, ownership of a hog, and a propensity to commit acts of violence to protect the interests of the club at large. Long Unit fulfilled each and every criterion with his own rather unparalleled résumé of retribution. He knew that the drug market on the east side of Houston was controlled by the Mexican Marauders, but he was big, bad, and black—and he was not about to let a bunch of greasy beaners tell him where he could or could not move a piece of ass or a piece of action. Sadly for Long Unit, Moritz the Mouse would definitely have a contrary point of view regarding that specific, ill-advised personal conviction.

The Mouse had solidified his violent reputation soon after he became a member of the Mexican Marauders. On the sad occasion when he discovered that his old lady was snacking on a gringo, the Mouse took a wooden mallet and bashed her teeth in. Although it turned out to be an extremely effective deterrent to any further acts of sexual infidelity, it left his woman with sharp, jagged, and irregularly broken teeth. After that, getting a hum job seemed to be a much less enjoyable endeavor for Moritz the Mouse.

This untenable situation had been rectified once the Mouse took a pair of pliers and violently extracted the bits of shrapnel that were still embedded in the unfortunate woman's gum line. Moritz found the experience of extracting teeth a thoroughly enjoyable activity, and he would employ oral surgery as a viable means to deter any infringement upon the territory that had been previously staked out by the Mexican Marauders.

Moritz had two bikers under his command, El Jefe and his brother, Tuco. The other members of the motorcycle club referred to the trio as the "Three Mouseketeers."

Through an intermediary, Moritz the Mouse had ostensibly offered to parlay a mutually beneficial turf war truce with Long Unit, and the peace summit would be held at a public forum at the Charlie Chopper biker bar on Telephone Road.

Moritz sent a written invitation to Long Unit: "It is time to stop this skirmish before things get out of control. Come meet me at Charlie Chopper. I know this will be a good time."

As it turned out, Long Unit got dry-gulched on his way to the parlay out on Telephone Road, and he never even took a step inside the bar. A van driven by Moritz the Mouse clipped the rear end of Unit's hog, which caused Unit to lay down his bike and tumble upon the pavement. The Three Mouseketeers poured out of the van and pounced on Long Unit before he had even realized he had been ambushed.

Zip-ties secured Unit's hands behind his back, and he was tossed into the cargo bay of the van. Drivers who passed by the scene averted their eyes to avoid becoming embroiled in an obvious outlaw motorcycle gang turf battle.

Once neutralized, Long Unit was driven to a nondescript warehouse. A dental chair was isolated in the middle of a brightly lit room. Beside the chair, a stainless-steel table held a variety of tools and instruments that any plumber, handyman, or grand inquisitor would have been proud to have owned, including a chisel, a power drill, a hammer, and a huge pair of channel-lock pliers.

The Mouse pointed to the chair and instructed El Jefe and Tuco to firmly secure the "dental patient" before the horrific extractions were to commence.

Unit said, "I thought the letter said I was going to have a good time."

The Mouse replied, "No, you're quite mistaken. The invitation was implicit that *I* was going to have a good time—not you!

Is there any explanation for the horrific abuse Long Unit was subjected to? It's expected that the perpetrators and the victims of criminal activity might have the same ethnic or racial persuasion. After all, violent crime is often an intramural contact sport. However, human beings are tribal by nature. Trans-ethnic and trans-racial crime can be particularly vicious, and this is true, irrespective of whether it's white on black, white on brown, black on white, black on brown, brown on white, or brown on black. Well, if the city of Houston had a respectable Asian, Native American, or even a Micronesian population in 1981, it's highly probable that they too would have been thrown into this hostile mix of tribal warfare. After all, maybe God just backed the wrong primate.

J. D. Brewster brought a bathroom scale to Stella's apartment to try to sort out what was going on with her dramatic weight loss and change in physical appearance.

He threw the scale on the floor in front of Stella and said, "Something's going on with you, and I need to find out right now what this is all about. You're starting to get skinny on me. Get on the scale so I can see what's happening to your weight."

Stella had feared that this day would be coming. She knew her boyfriend would not be happy with the situation. Stella understood that Brewster was attracted to "chunky monkeys" and that there was a chance she would be jeopardizing her relationship with him by attending to her own health needs. She had been diligently losing weight and was down to a relatively svelte 180 pounds. Her blood pressure and blood sugar were now under better control, and she had not felt this healthy in quite some time.

"I already have a bathroom scale, lover boy," Stella said. "How dare you come in here and try to order me around like this?"

"I'm not giving an order," Brewster said. "I just want to weigh something."

"I have an idea," Stella said. "We should weigh your brain and find out how small it really is."

"Stella, I'm not here to fight with you."

"Can't prove it by me," Stella said. "Why don't you take that scale and shove it up your own ass. Your tiny brain is probably already lodged up in there somewhere near your transverse colon!"

Stella Link should have been treated with utmost respect at that point, as the large woman was no doubt completely capable of beating the shit out of J. D. Brewster with her bare hands—and in a dark alley if necessary.

Although usually deferential to Stella, Brewster said, "I'm not fooling around with you, Stella. It's time to get on the scale right now!"

Stella reluctantly climbed on the bathroom scale to reveal that she had lost forty-four pounds in four months.

Brewster was oblivious to the fact that she had previously acquired the dangerous metabolic syndrome. Stella Link was afflicted with hypertension, morbid obesity, hypercholesterolemia, and adult-onset type 2 diabetes mellitus. All these maladies were serious medical problems that threatened to dramatically shorten her life expectancy, but now her physical condition had definitely improved with her extensive and successful weight loss program. Although Stella had kept these medical problems a secret from Brewster, he should have readily recognized the illnesses that had befallen the woman he allegedly cared for.

Brewster sneered at her and said, "When a man gets into a relationship, he hopes his girlfriend will never change. When a woman gets into a relationship, she hopes for the exact opposite outcome."

Despondent over what she felt was rejection, Stella abandoned her new dietary regimen and quit taking her medications to manage her diabetes, hypertension, and high cholesterol. The throttle to the locomotive was again open wide, and it was only a matter of time before the train derailed into a fiery crash.

Lawdy Garth Penn left the Texas Medical Center campus for a one-month rotation at the Spa. Unfortunately, a bizarre event in April 1981 would mark her career with an embarrassing blemish that would be permanently recorded on her formal resident performance evaluation.

Prior to the advent of the cellular telephone era, electronic pagers were routinely utilized to convey information to members of the hospital house staff. An electronic pager from the early 1980s was about the size of a pack of cigarettes and had a spring-loaded clasp that affixed the beeper to the front pocket of the white consultation jacket invariably worn by a member of the house staff.

On one occasion, Dr. Penn utilized a toilet in the women's room at the Spa. Post-micturition, Lawdy Penn stood and hit the lever of the power-assisted flush mechanism to conclude her business at hand. Confirming that God has a peculiar sense of humor, Dr. Penn's electronic pager fell into the toilet bowl just as the 384 milliliters of urine that had been forcefully expelled from her bladder were being swept away into the sewer system of the city of Bellaire.

Thoroughly embarrassed, Dr. Penn reported the mishap to the house-staff administration office where she was immediately placed on administrative leave without pay. After all, an electronic pager simply cannot disappear in the swirling waters of a flushed toilet. This matter would have to be thoroughly investigated by the VA system of administrative bean counters.

The event was eventually reported to Washington, and Congress submitted a formal requisition to the General Accounting Office to scientifically evaluate the situation. It needed to be ascertained as to whether or not such an accident could actually occur to a government-owned electronic pager. After all, the government had paid more than seventy-nine dollars for the electronic communication device.

Two hydrological engineers from the Houston petrochemical firm, Squat and Poot, were commissioned by the federal government to evaluate the likelihood that an electronic beeper could be flushed down an industrial toilet without jamming up the plumbing.

The two engineers tackled the challenging project with the same zeal they had shown when they worked on the plumbing that had provided the cooling for the nuclear reactor on a United States Navy attack submarine. At great expense, a completely transparent, glass, commercial-style, power-flush toilet was commissioned to be constructed by the Toidy Bowl Sanitary Lavatory Consortium along with completely transparent matching sanitary drainage pipes to affix to the experimental crapper.

The enthusiastic hydrological engineers showed up at the VA annex in Bellaire to conduct their experiment. Of course, such a scientific endeavor would have to be performed specifically at that particular facility to match the coefficient of drag, the specific gravity of the target molecular oxygen/di-hydroxide flush load, the suspended particulate composition of the water provided by the local municipality, the atmospheric conditions, the local-regional gravitational forces, and whatever other mumbo-jumbo, bullshit variables that may have influenced the peculiar happenstance that had allegedly occurred on that fateful day when Dr. Penn had inadvertently flushed away her beeper.

A hundred-square-foot steel rebar and concrete platform was constructed three feet above the ground and rigidly affixed to an engineered steel beam and pillar support mechanism that included a novel, heavy-spring, anti-seismic stabilization plate.

The last expensive item mentioned was included to make sure that there were no micro-tremors, much less any high Richter scale earthquake events that could have had an untoward effect on the outcome of this incredibly meaningful experiment on which the fate of the free world had clearly rested. This anti-seismic, spring-loaded stabilization plate was incorporated into the design of the experiment despite the fact that the United States Geological Society had estimated that the likelihood of an earthquake with a magnitude of 6.0 or higher ever hitting Houston was only on the order of about 0.17 percent!

The transparent toilet was then mounted to this stabilized platform, which had been previously covered with the same linoleum type of tile that covered the floor in the bathroom where the catastrophic accident had occurred. When everything was prepared, it was time for the engineers to "let 'er rip!"

The engineers from Squat and Poot performed the experiment of flushing identical beepers to the one that had been lost by Dr. Penn no less than ten times down the transparent toilet and sewage line. On four occasions, the electronic pager was swept away into the makeshift sewer pipe, but on six occasions the beeper simply swirled around the pot before it settled at the bottom of the toilet by the time the tank refilled. As there was only a 40 percent chance of probability that any given electronic pager could actually be flushed down a toilet as a random event, the administration had calculated that there was a 60 percent chance of probability that Dr. Penn had illegally absconded with the beeper for her own personal use. She was forced to pay seventy-nine dollars to the federal government for losing her beeper, which certainly must have been a great relief to the American citizens since the federal government had spent at least $69,666.69 to confirm that there was only a 40 percent chance of probability that Dr. Penn had accidentally lost her electronic pager down the toilet.

The expenditure did not include the cost of the ten beepers the engineers had ended up throwing into the transparent toilet for this extremely important scientific endeavor. Fortunately for the two hydrological engineers from the well-respected Squat and Poot petrochemical firm, the ten beepers that had been employed in the experimental study had been given a predesignated DNR code status. Therefore, at the conclusion of this well-crafted experiment that had a direct bearing on the national security of our great nation, there would be no elaborate efforts undertaken to resuscitate the electronic devices once they had been extracted from the bowels of the seethrough waterworks that had been crafted at great expense by the Toidy Bowl Sanitary Lavatory Consortium. Whew, that was certainly a relief! Your tax dollars hard at work.

Brewster got locked out of participating in either a pediatric or gynecology rotation, which were essentially mandatory to complete as part of his core clerkship experience. Instead, he had to take an elective. There was an opening on the nephrology service with Dr. Regina Clemmons, and Brewster jumped on board along with a third-year medical student, Victoria Campos.

The kidney is an extraordinary organ that is only about the size of a balled-up human fist, and its multiple responsibilities include maintaining the balance of fluid in the body and the excretion of nitrogenous waste invariably generated as a consequence of aerobically catabolized proteins as an energy source within intracellular mitochondria via the Krebs cycle. The kidney also has a third important job as the acting biological rheostat that directs hematopoietic production of red blood cells in the bone marrow by the micro-hormone, erythropoietin.

When the kidney fails and is no longer able to uphold its biological obligations to the organism, it takes a man-made dialysis machine that is the size of a rather large V-8 engine to do only a half-ass job of what a natural kidney can do when it is operating at a peak level of performance.

Brewster and Campos were intellectually challenged by the complex job a nephrologist must undertake to manage patients who require a dependent relationship with a hemodialysis machine to stay alive. Generally, a patient on hemodialysis is a prisoner of the machine. Dialysis is generally administered three times a week to cleanse a patient's blood of nitrogenous waste, and it takes half a day to accomplish each session!

Members of the Mexican Marauder outlaw motorcycle gang would tout the oft-heard expression "Live to ride—ride to live." Well, more than one patient with end-stage renal disease would tout the oft-heard expression, "Live to be dialyzed, be dialyzed to live." If the truth be told, being shackled to a hemodialysis machine was a form of existence and not actually a form of living.

After only two weeks into the nephrology rotation, it became quite apparent to Brewster why many of the patients who are saddled with a life of dialysis maintenance eventually get to the point where they refuse further care and willingly allow themselves to die because of kidney failure. He fully believed that any patients who were brave enough to make that decision remained the masters of their own fate and captains of their own souls.

In 1981, it was unknown that GRID was caused by an RNA retrovirus. Originally thought to be an illness that was strictly isolated to the gay community and transmitted only by homosexual activity, it was finally realized by July 1982 that the disease was also starting to appear among heterosexuals. It was also eventually discovered that it was an infectious disease that was transmissible by other means beyond the realm of sexual activity.

The name of the illness was changed from GRID to AIDS in the summer of 1982 when it was confirmed that blood products and needle sticks could also transmit the potentially deadly virus. The HIV virus does its damage by infecting specific cells of the human immune system, especially the CD4+ T cells. Brain tissue, macrophages, and dendritic cells can also be attacked by this nasty RNA virus.

Once a victim's CD4+ T cells are nearly eradicated by the virus, the body's immunity to other infectious agents is sadly compromised. Patients become susceptible to a host of other pathogens. Unfortunately, patients who have been infected with this RNA retrovirus are also at an increased lifetime risk of contracting cancers, including lymphoma and Kaposi's sarcoma. In modern times, AIDS is fairly well controlled with new antiretroviral medications, and the associated Kaposi's sarcoma is now rarely seen as a complication from this still dreadful illness. In 1981, this same infectious disease, then known as GRID, was invariably lethal with no known effective treatment.

In the early 1980s, it was suspected—but not confirmed at that time—that certain human malignancies might be caused by horizontally transmissible infectious agents. At the end of Brewster's career, multiple pathogens had been recognized to be the direct etiology of several human cancers. The *Helicobacter pylori* organisms had been proven to be the causative agent for some cases of gastric adenocarcinoma and an atypical malignancy known as MALT Gastric lymphoma.

Other examples are subsets of the human papilloma virus that have been associated with cervical cancer, squamous cell head and neck tumors. The human papilloma virus is a sexually transmitted agent. Kaposi's sarcoma, which presents as thick violaceous plaques on the skin, was a disease associated with the GRID/AIDS outbreak in the early 1980s. Of interest, this is also a cancer that has been proven to be caused by an infectious agent, specifically the herpes virus #8.

Kona Flood was only twenty-three years old in the winter of 1981 when he started to suspect that GRID, much like infectious hepatitis, could be spread by sharing needles. He knew of at least two of his contemporaries who were heterosexuals and had nonetheless contracted the disease. The only thing his friends who were infected with this peculiar illness had in common was that they had shared needles while giving each other tattoos. To make certain he would not become a victim of GRID, Kona Flood decided to completely abandon needles when administering tattoos to his friends. He decided to use guitar strings instead. Kona was sadly a product of a mostly inferior public American educational system. He didn't make the connection that it was not the type of instrument that was utilized to create a tattoo (be it a needle or a guitar string, for that matter) but the fact that blood cells and serum could be inoculated by the tattoo process itself, irrespective of what utensil or implement was employed.

By April 1981, Kona Flood had developed large purple lesions on his face and chest. He had foolishly acquired Kaposi's sarcoma and GRID through his unusual practice of using guitar strings to give his friends and himself garage parlor-quality tattoos. Ironically, Kona was a spiritual man, and the disease he acquired was transmitted to him when his friends applied a tattoo of a large crucifix on his back utilizing guitar strings that had been dipped into a bottle of India ink. In retrospect, it made complete sense that he would get infected with this lethal disease while getting a tattoo for such a profoundly pious purpose. After all, no good deed goes unpunished.

When he realized that he was infected with GRID, Kona Flood decided to punch his own ticket by chugging a gallon of antifreeze. Antifreeze, which is comprised of ethylene glycol, is a particularly toxic substance to human subjects. Ethylene glycol, although deadly, is a surprisingly sweet-tasting, syrupy substance. Thousands of cases of poisonings with antifreeze occur every year. Shortly after drinking the antifreeze, Kona felt as if he had become inebriated. The symptoms were akin to consuming a six-pack of cold beer on a hot summer day, but the sensations were soon associated with abdominal cramps and vomiting. Within twenty-four hours of consuming the antifreeze, Kona Flood developed tachycardia, lightheadedness, hyperventilation, and muscle spasms. When the symptoms occurred, he went to bed and thought that he was actively dying. He had even written a suicide note before he had drifted off to sleep.

Within thirty-six hours, Kona was found by his friends, and he was dumped off at the emergency room at the Gulf Coast University Hospital with the sadly ubiquitous "positive taillight sign". Upon his arrival, Kona was already in acute renal failure. As a byproduct of ethylene glycol metabolism, calcium oxalate crystals precipitate in the kidneys, which severely disrupt normal renal function. There have been patients who've survived poisoning with antifreeze via dialysis support until there is eventual long-term recovery of kidney function. However, Kona Flood was facing a lethal illness in the form of GRID, and he refused dialysis. In doing so, he also signed a DNR code status designation.

J. D. Brewster's respect for life and for *Homo sapiens* in general was clearly on the wane, and he was rather ambivalent about the young man's situation. After all, if the patient was ready and willing to abandon aggressive management to specifically and willfully take the mysterious journey into the long night, it was certainly not Brewster's place to stop him from doing so.

As a medical student, Victoria Campos was not yet jaded or otherwise corrupted. She petitioned Dr. Clemmons to intercede and see if there was some legal way to force the young man to receive potentially life-sustaining dialysis treatment—even if it was against his own will. After all, the patient was only twenty-three years old, and he was likely suffering from acute situational depression after learning that he had acquired the disease known as GRID. It was highly likely that his depression could be affecting his judgment in making decisions about his own health care matters.

A libertarian by nature, Dr. Clemmons said, "This is a free country, and as a doctor and as a black woman, it's my opinion that this patient who's making this decision has done so while utilizing his own free will. I suggest that you accept these circumstances. Personally, I reject your argument that his decision is unsound. Facing a similar situation, I suspect that both you and Mr. Brewster might very well consider a similar course of action. If there are patients who are going to die from a disease process, it's their sacred right to make decisions about their own pending demise—no matter what that illness may be. Get over it."

"I warned you that it would shake out this way after he refused to talk to the psychiatry service," Brewster said to Victoria.

"What in hell happened to you, Brewster?" Victoria asked. "There was a time in the not-too-distant past when I thought you were a good human being. As for now, you're doing a fabulous job in building a brick wall around yourself."

"What happened?" Brewster asked. "I figured out how the world really works. I suggest you do the same."

Mr. Flood had agreed to stay in the hospital and have his terminal event happen at the Gulf Coast University Hospital. J. D. Brewster and Victoria Campos were about to learn what it was like to witness a patient's death from end-stage, untreated renal disease.

Upon Dr. Clemmons's departure from the ward, Victoria turned to Brewster and said, "This is pure bullshit. I know Mr. Flood has GRID, but it's my opinion that we may be able to identify what this illness is within the next few years. If so, we might be able to devise an effective treatment or vaccine for this immunological illness. I don't understand why everybody, especially you, lost all hope. After all, Kona Flood is the same age as you!"

"It's not your call, Señorita," Brewster replied.

"Why are you here?" Victoria asked.

"On this rotation?" Brewster probed. "Unfortunately, I'm jammed out of doing my mandatory pediatric and OB/GYN clerkships until after July."

"No, that's not what I asked," Victoria said. "Specifically, why are *you* here?"

"Is this an existential question as to why any of us are here, now that God has likely come to the sad and irrefutable conclusion that He's backed the wrong primate for far too long? If so, then that's indeed a profound celestial mystery."

"You're not a very nice person anymore," Victoria said. "I can tell that you truly despise your fellow human beings. I'm still doing my level best to try to like you. You may still have some redeemable features, but I swear to Jesus, they're certainly getting harder to find."

"Is that the general consensus with my fellow colleagues?"

"I don't know if you give a tinker's damn, but few people, if any, can even stand the sight of you anymore. You're abrasive *all* the time. It's as if you're pissed off at the whole world."

"And you're not?"

It took eight days for Kona Flood to die from renal failure. His creatinine, which was a measurement of the nitrogenous waste in the patient's bloodstream, had risen at an average rate of one point per day. By the time his creatinine had reached a level of 9 mg/dL, malodorous urea was starting to seep out of his pores, and he emanated the stench of a dirty box of cat litter.

The normal creatinine range is 0.4-1.1 mg/dL, depending on the reference laboratory's established parameters. If a patient's creatinine reaches 10 mg/dL, it's generally not considered to be compatible with human life. By the time Kona Flood slipped into a coma, he had developed a crusty precipitation on his skin. This "uremic frost" was his body's last-ditch effort to excrete the nitrogenous waste that could no longer be cleared out by his irreparably damaged kidneys.

Upon Kona Flood's passing, Victoria Campos said, "Well, at least this patient didn't suffer at the time that he finally died."

When Brewster heard this passing observation from his colleague, he had a brief philosophical epiphany. "The root of the word *patient* happens to be the word *passion*," Brewster professed.

"I was actually not aware of that," Victoria replied.

"From its Greek origins, *passion* is derived from the verb *to suffer*. Ergo, to be a *patient* is to *suffer* by the very definition of the word."

"Then should we just accept the fact that suffering will always be a part of the human condition?" Victoria asked.

"Sadly, so it would seem."

Victoria pondered a question that had been bothering her ever since Kona Flood had been admitted to the nephrology unit. "I've never seen a patient with this GRID syndrome before, but I was told that this is a disease that's isolated to the homosexual community. I took a sexual history from this patient when he was first admitted to the hospital, and he was not gay. In fact, as best I could tell, this man was *asexual*."

"Where are you going with this?" Brewster asked with a squint.

"The only risk factor for transmissible diseases that I can ascertain was that he and his friends had given each other tattoos. They had previously shared needles and skinny guitar wires to administer their crude, cutaneous artwork upon each other. To me, it would seem that this is a disease that can be transmitted much like hepatitis B or the non-A, non-B hepatitis, whatever in hell that mysterious disease might turn out to be someday. Brewster, were you aware of that?"

Brewster's eyes grew as big as coffee saucers as he jumped out of his chair and grabbed Victoria by her shoulders. Almost as if he was assaulting her with a head butt, Brewster kissed her hard on the cheek and said, "You're a freaking genius!"

Victoria smiled and wiped her cheek in astonishment while Brewster scurried off to the laboratory to find Rip Ford and Parker Coxswain while they were toiling away on Dr. Bookman's GRID study.

An agent from the Federal Bureau of Investigation showed up at the Psychiatry Department to ask Stella Link about her boss. Stella was repeatedly asked if the department head was from Poland, and each time, she replied—to the best of her knowledge—that Corka Sorass was Hungarian. She did report to the gumshoe however, that the psychiatrist claimed to have had two sisters—Byda and Beeda Sorass—who were tragically lost during the war.

Stella stated that she had been told by her boss that Corka's two sisters and his parents were captured by the Gestapo and likely died in a concentration camp. The federal agent seemed pensive with Stella's answer, but he nonetheless smiled and nodded. He shook Stella's hand when he left, but he asked if she would keep their meeting confidential. Stella agreed, but she thought it was odd that the FBI was investigating her boss. She wanted to discuss it with her boyfriend, but at that juncture, they were still not on speaking terms.

Wooly Mammoth finally returned to the clerkship rotations in April, 1981, after he recovered from his craniotomy. The big man was well into his mandatory gynecology rotation when he performed a supervised pelvic examination in the outpatient obstetrics/gynecology clinic on an elderly lady who was having problems with postmenopausal vaginal bleeding. While performing a bimanual examination on the patient, the wooly one noted a markedly enlarged and lumpy uterus that appeared to be consistent with either a benign fibroid or perhaps locally advanced endometrial cancer.

As Willy turned toward the supervising resident to explain the noted abnormal findings, he entered the tonic phase of a grand mal seizure. He lost consciousness, fell to the floor, contracted his extremities toward his core, and exerted a brief but audible moan. The tonic phase only lasted for a few moments before the seizure event entered the clonic phase. Willy's muscles began to rapidly contract and relax as he convulsed. As his eyes rolled back and his jaw clenched, he bit his lower lip hard enough to draw blood. The big man began to foam at the mouth before he entered the postictal phase, manifested by muscular relaxation and a subsequent sonorous and repetitive gasp to inhale air.

The emergency room found that the blood level of the anti-seizure drug called Dilantin that Willy was taking was indeed at a therapeutic range. This indicated that the Dilantin medication he was taking was no longer completely effective in preventing seizure activity. It would be the task of the neurology service to find new and different drugs to try to keep the seizures under control.

Unfortunately, throughout the remainder of Willy's life, the troublesome seizures would continue to haunt him. After experiencing uncontrolled seizure activity, Willy knew that his dream of being accepted into *any* residency training program after he graduated from medical school was in peril. The only thing left to do was to even the score. He just needed an opportunity to render clinical justice upon Darryl Hewritt and his accomplice— that is, if they could ever be found. Pure hatred now boiled in his psyche. From that point on, every time he had recovered from an acute seizure event, Willy would be seen by his colleagues hanging around the exit stairwell that led into the north employee parking lot.

"Willy, why do I always see you snooping about the back stairwell exit at lunchtime?" Ben Fielder asked.

"From this portal window, I can almost see the entire parking lot. Someday, those two bad boys are going to make a mistake and show back up here on this campus once again."

"Oh, yeah?" Ben asked. "What are you going to do if and when they reappear?"

"What do you think?" Willy asked. "I should've killed Darryl Hewritt a year ago. I won't make the same mistake twice.

Missy Brownwood and Feral Cheryl had been invited down to the security office to witness a humorous loop of tape regarding an event that had been captured on the hospital's closed-circuit security television system. The tape showed Dr. Harrison Reed walking along the hallway of the med-surg unit when he suddenly fell on his face for no apparent reason. He looked like an alpine ski jumper who got too far out in front of his skis, flying with his arms out to his side and his legs poised at shoulder's width. Dr. Reed made no effort to protect himself from the fall, and it appeared that he had simply dropped to the floor like a sheet of plywood that had previously been balanced on edge.

The security guard dialed the tape back and forth over and over to show the event as if Dr. Reed was a spring-loaded jack-in-the-box falling to the floor and then bouncing right back up to an upright position.

"Are you telling me that this is the old bastard who tried to rape you?" Cheryl asked. "Missy, white people are just way too civilized as far as I'm concerned. If that man had tried to do that to me, his body would be rendered into unrecognizable, amorphous, bloody snot. Do you feel me, sister?"

Later that day, Missy Brownwood encountered her tormentor.

"Look, Missy, you and I got off to a bad start. I want to let you know that I find you incredibly attractive and want to get to know you better. Please give me a second chance."

Missy and Ben Fielder had been expecting this type of rapprochement from Dr. Reed. She handed him a prewritten note: "It is time to stop this skirmish before things get out of control. Come meet me at Charlie Chopper. I know this will be a good time."

When Brewster reached the animal lab, he was totally bewildered to see the experimental study that Rip Ford and Parker Coxswain had initiated. Both men wore black leather motorcycle chaps, and World War I-style helmets that Kaiser Wilhelm would have been proud to have owned. If this was not bizarre enough, both helmets were festooned with four-inch pickelhaube spikes!

While Rip Ford popped open ampules of amyl nitrate under the nostrils of the white male lab rats that had been secured in a row on a two-by-six plank of pine, Parker Coxswain proceeded to traumatize the lower gastrointestinal tract of the rats with a standard sheet metal screw until bright red blood poured forth from the rectal vaults of the misfortunate creatures.

Once the vision had returned to J. D. Brewster's left eye, he said, "What in hell are you freaks doing? For the love of Jesus, have you psychopaths joined the Nazi Party since I was here last?"

"Don't pay attention to him, Parker," Ford replied. "Brewster wouldn't know a legitimate scientific experiment if it jumped up and latched onto the end of his shriveled unit like a dog-pecker gnat."

"So, let me get this straight," Brewster said. "You guys are getting little boy-rat laboratory animals stoned on amyl nitrate poppers and then you're fucking them in the ass-end with a sheet metal screw? How can any of this be considered a legitimate scientific experiment?!"

"I'll tell you how." Parker Coxswain furrowed his brow and glared at Brewster. "We just received a $150,000 grant from the federal government to prove that GRID is a *lifestyle* disease that occurs when them there 'homo-satchels' take it up the ass while hitting amyl nitrate poppers—that's how! Now, if you can excuse us, we have serious work to do here."

"This is all bullshit—and you know it!" Brewster said. "I just came down here to tell you that I helped take care of a patient who died from renal failure after he drank a gallon of antifreeze. He was afflicted with GRID, and it appears that the poor dumb bastard contracted the disease in a nonsexual manner. He shared needles and guitar wires with others while he was engaged in tattoos and ritualistic religious scarifications with his friends. Do you understand what I am saying?"

"Go away!" Parker demanded.

"I've come down here to help," Brewster pleaded. "I know it's the right thing for me to do."

"I thought you would've learned by now that no good deed goes unpunished!" Ford exclaimed. "It's time for you to leave, *amigo*."

"It appears that GRID is an infectious illness that can be transmitted much like hepatitis B or perhaps like non-A, non-B hepatitis," Brewster explained. "Listen to me, you idiots! This illness is not a *lifestyle* issue. It happens to be an *infectious* disease issue!"

Parker and Ford had a federal grant, and they were not about to let the truth get in the way of the money that had been bestowed upon them by Uncle Sam. When Parker and Ford turned their backs to Brewster, they jammed their index fingers into their auditory canals and loudly sang, "La, la, la, la, la!"

Are there divinely inspired creations? One might argue that the ceiling of the Sistine Chapel, which was painted by Michelangelo between 1508 and 1512, was divinely inspired since it's considered one of the greatest artistic endeavors in human history. One might argue that "The Messiah," which was composed by George Frederik Handel over a three-week period between August 22 and September 14, 1741, was divinely inspired. After all, it's considered one of the greatest musical endeavors in human history.

One might argue that the Constitution of the United States of America, which was ratified by the founding fathers on June 21, 1788, was divinely inspired. After all, it's considered to be one of the greatest political documents in human history.

Just because a creation at the hand of man may indeed be divinely inspired, it does *not* mean that the creation in question is perfect. The Constitution of the United States was soon followed by the Bill of Rights. Multiple amendments to the Constitution were also needed to overcome previously neglected but nonetheless critical issues that would have a bearing on American citizens. After all, it took the Thirteenth Amendment to the Constitution to rectify the unpleasant truths that had been attributed to involuntary servitude imposed upon residents of African ethnic origins.

There are obvious flaws that exist in the document to this very day. If the Founding Fathers had any idea how members of Congress would pervert their elected posts and anoint themselves members of a North American version of the House of Lords, then term limits would have been incorporated into the original Constitution. If the truth be told, there should be term limits on congressional members and for all the embedded bureaucrats who sadly comprise the deep state within the federal government. Would a swamp by any other name smell as foul?

If the Founding Fathers had any idea how members of Congress would squander taxpayer dollars, the line-item executive branch veto would have been incorporated into the original Constitution. Alas, stupidity and pork barrel payback has become business as usual when it comes to the federal budget. How else could one possibly explain what J. D. Brewster was about to discover?

Furious to learn of the ridiculous federally funded experimental study that Bookman's team was conducting on lab rats, Brewster made his way to Dr. Harrison Reed's office. Brewster was determined to snoop through the file cabinets in an effort to find out what other idiotic programs that the federal government had been funding at the Gulf Coast College of Medicine.

Brewster soon learned that one of the brainiacs had received a large federal grant to determine if laboratory rats could somehow distinguish between spoken words of Spanish from the Italian language. Certainly, the fate of the world's rodent population rested solely on the outcome of such crucial experimental projects.

He also discovered that the Department of Defense had given a huge grant to the university to determine the clinical outcome of dozens of domesticated cats that were shot in the head with a hot smoking round from an AK-47 assault rifle. Brewster was shocked to see the results of that ridiculous study: *all* the feline experimental subjects that had been shot in the head had mysteriously died. There were no survivors. Not one. My, oh my, what a surprise that turned out to be. Nobody could have possibly predicted that unfortunate outcome!

Another federally funded study determined whether nicotine could be recovered from the toenail clippings of individuals who had smoked more than one pack of cigarettes per day. Apparently, the purpose of this study was to see if there was any method to scientifically monitor patients who had allegedly given up the habit of smoking cigarettes. It seemed that the Federal Government believed that it was otherwise impossible to detect if somebody was smoking cigarettes by just taking a random sniff test of somebody's foul, tobacco impregnated breath.

The FDA sponsored another study to determine if the consumption of diet soda had any ill effects on erectile function. Brewster laughed out loud when he realized there might have been an entirely different meaning to the expression of running a "Mr. Pibb" code. If the federal government proved that diet soda could induce erectile dysfunction, the disorder would eventually be recognized by the mainstream medical community as a legitimate medical malady. Brewster would need to make certain that he was *never* going to be the medical student who had to administer mouth-to-appendage resuscitation on any patient who had been acutely afflicted with a flaccid reproductive member because of the consumption of diet soda. There was not enough mouthwash on the planet that was going to make that happen. No, sir!

Brewster also found out that the federal government had issued a hundred-thousand-dollar grant to the Gulf Coast College of Medicine to determine if black males were endowed with larger reproductive plumbing than their Caucasian counterparts. Now, that was a study that somebody could really sink their teeth into. Unfortunately, it was an ongoing prospective evaluation with no published data available for public consumption. Your tax dollars hard at work.

After learning about the aforementioned pointless experimental studies, many of which would eventually render the participant brainiacs with future, highly-coveted PhD degrees, Brewster became even more cynical about his life, his education, his future, his career, and even his citizenship in the United States of America. *"Perhaps one day,"* Brewster thought, *"Texas would be able to successfully secede from the rest of the country and reestablish itself as an independent, sovereign nation."*

After being captured by the Three Mouseketeers, Harrison Reed was blindfolded and dragged into an unmarked white van. El Jefe and

Tuco were eager to learn much more about dental surgery. If their ambitious educational goals could be achieved and ultimately documented with bona fide certificates of achievement signed by Moritz the Mouse, perhaps it would afford El Jefe and Tuco an opportunity to move up in the ranks of the motorcycle club.

When the door to the warehouse opened, the professor's blindfold was removed, but the zip-ties that secured his hands behind his back remained securely in place. Harrison Reed immediately recognized Moritz the Mouse as the man whom he had sexually molested at the urinal in the men's room at the Astrodome the previous summer.

A dental chair was isolated in the middle of a brightly lit room. A stainless-steel table held a variety of tools and instruments that any plumber, handyman, or grand inquisitor would have been proud to have owned, including a chisel, a power drill, a hammer, and a huge pair of channel-lock pliers.

The Mouse pointed to the chair and instructed El Jefe and Tuco to firmly secure the "dental patient" for the dental extractions. The victim quickly realized that he was about to have a very bad day.

"I thought the letter said I was going to have a good time," Dr. Reed said.

"No, you are quite mistaken," Moritz replied. "The invitation was implicit that *I* was going to have a good time—not you!"

Disgusted with the discovery of the overt corruption that was squandering incalculable resources, Brewster went to the washroom to freshen up before he returned to the outpatient nephrology clinic to get back to work. Unfortunately, Brewster was totally unaware that he was being followed by two angry Iranians with a specific violent agenda: revenge.

Mehdi had previously warned Brewster that he needed to be vigilant. Although the men comprising the Iranian terrorist cell had been previously arrested, two of the extremists had recently escaped from jail and were roaming about in the greater Houston metropolitan area. Although a wide drag net had been cast out by the FBI and local authorities to apprehend these individuals, the two terrorists were nonetheless hell bent to hunt down the unwitting medical student and exact their pound of flesh. After all, Brewster had been directly responsible for their original apprehension by the police which ultimately thwarted their dastardly plan to rain down havoc and destruction upon the Houston Ship Channel by blowing up the on-site petroleum storage facilities.

Mehdi previously offered a specific recommendation that Brewster needed to grow a pair of eyes on the back of his head. Unfortunately, this sage advice had merely fallen upon deaf ears. In the end, because Mehdi's wise council was roundly ignored, Brewster was about to suffer the consequences…

TO BE CONTINUED …

# GLOSSARY OF TERMS

(MEDICAL OR OTHERWISE) DNR VOLUMES 1 AND 2

**aerobic organism:** An organism that cannot live or grow in the absence of air.

**aerophilic organism:** An aerobic organism that thrives best in an environment with a high oxygen concentration.

**alpha-fetoprotein:** A serum tumor marker often elevated in some types of testicular cancer and also primary hepatocellular carcinoma.

**alveoli:** The small air sacks in the deep recesses of the lungs where gas exchange occurs.

**Ambu bag:** A compressible hand-operated air-pump device about the size of a football. It is often utilized to temporarily ventilate a patient who has suffered from a cardiopulmonary arrest.

**anaerobic organism:** An organism that is able to live or grow in the absence of air.

**anterolateral thorax:** From an anatomical standpoint, this is the front and side of a person's chest wall.

**antigen:** A foreign material that may be able to insight an immuno-logical response.

**atheromatous plaque:** A fatty deposit within the interior lining of a vessel that can cause vascular narrowing.

**benign prostatic hypertrophy:** A noncancerous enlargement of the male prostate gland.

**big dirt nap:** Dead and buried.

**bilateral mastectomy:** Surgical removal of both breasts.

**bilirubin:** Waste material found in bile. It is formed from the biological breakdown of hemoglobin.

**biopsy:** The surgical sampling of tissue for diagnostic purposes.

**bougie:** A flexible, cylindrical medical instrument utilized to widen an abnormal stricture.

**Bovie:** An electrically powered surgical instrument that can be utilized intraoperatively for both dissection and hemostasis.

**bowel perforation:** A puncture in the bowel wall. If it occurs, it is a medical emergency.

**brady down:** A slang term that means the slowing of a patient's heart rate.

**BRAF:** An oncogene that, when mutated, may drive cancer cells' initiation and proliferation.

**braniac:** A derisive term used to characterize a medical student enrolled in an MD and PhD dual-training program.

**BRCA1:** An inheritable oncogene that may predispose a patient to acquire breast cancer.

**BRCA2:** Another recognized inheritable oncogene that may predispose a patient to acquire breast cancer.

**bronchus:** A major airway pipe that divides off of the trachea to ventilate either lung.

**cannabinoids:** A class of chemical compounds generally found in marijuana that are able to interact with the CBD1 and CBD2 receptors of the human body and perhaps modulate pain perception, appetite, and a sense of well-being.

**cardiopulmonary arrest:** The cessation of a patient's heartbeat and respiration.

**CD4+ T cell subset:** Components of the immune system, these are also known as the T helper cells. The normal count of these cells is in the range of 500 to 1,200 cells per cubic millimeter of blood. An infection with the AIDS virus will result in a diminution of these important cells over time, resulting in a seriously immunocompromised condition.

**cerebral edema:** An abnormal swelling in the brain, which may be a consequence of cancer, stroke, or injury.

**cerebral hemorrhagic event:** A stroke caused by bleeding in the brain.

**chloroma:** A solid or semisolid tumor mass caused by the infiltration of acute leukemia cells into adjacent tissues.

**CHOP:** A four-drug combination used in the treatment of lymphoma cancer.

**choriocarcinoma:** A subtype of cancer that may involve the testes.

**cirrhosis:** A disease of the liver characterized by scarring and fibrosis as a consequence of chronic inflammation caused by a variety of diseases, including viral infections and alcohol abuse.

**clonic phase:** The rapid alternation of muscular flexion and contraction that may occur during a major motor seizure event.

**code blue:** This is an announced hospital emergency requesting a full-court press to try to resuscitate a patient who has suffered a cardiopulmonary arrest.

**code gray:** This is an announced hospital emergency requesting security intervention to assist an individual who is being physically assaulted.

**code silver:** An unauthorized patient elopement event.

**communist:** A disciple of an economic system wherein the collective welfare supersedes individual merit. Although it is an immoral wealth-redistribution ploy that has failed every single time it has ever been tried anywhere in the world, it is still the cornerstone of flawed liberal and progressive ideology.

**Cowden's syndrome:** An autosomal-dominant inherited disorder characterized by an increased risk of certain forms of **cancer**.

**creatinine:** A component of nitrogenous waste. Levels of this material found in the blood reflect kidney function.

**CXR:** An abbreviation for "chest x-ray."

**decerebrate:** An abnormal body posture characterized by extension of the extremities that occurs after serious head injury.

**dermatode:** A derisive slang word used to describe a dermatologist.

**dermatome:** As it pertains to the field of dermatology and plastic surgery, an electric-powered surgical device that is able to shave off a thin, rectangular section of skin to be utilized during a skin-grafting procedure.

**dendritic cell:** A component of the immune system that presents processed antigens to T-cell lymphocytes in an effort to ramp up an immunological response to a biological entity that may be a hazard to the host organism.

**DiSPOSe:** A derisive patient designation that stands for a "drug-seeking piece of shit."

**DNR:** Do not resuscitate. This is a designated declaration indicating that a patient declines to receive any heroic revitalization attempts in the event of a pending cardiopulmonary arrest.

**doink:** The act of engaging in a casual sexual encounter. Sadly, as readily confirmed through my own personal experience, the frequency of getting doinked appears to be inversely proportional not only to a man's chronological and physiological age but also to a man's fasting glucose, cholesterol, and serum hemoglobin A1-C levels. Please note that there is an intellectually inferior term utilized in certain parts of the country that are still afflicted with such extensive problems as hookworm and inbreeding (including Eau Claire, Wisconsin, as one recognized specific location). The phonetically similar word *boink* has been erroneously uttered aloud from time to time. I can sadly confirm that this particular archaic malapropism has been mistakenly utilized by the unwashed and the unenlightened even within the context of our current modern era of running water and flush toilets.

**ECOG:** Eastern Cooperative Oncology Group.

**ECOG performance status:** A standardized measurement of a patient's symptoms and ability to participate in life activities. An

ECOG 4 indicates that a patient is bedridden and no longer capable of independent living.

**EDTA:** An abbreviation for ethylenediaminetetraacetic acid, generally referring to a specialized blood-collecting tube.

**embolism:** A vascular obstruction caused by a clot that has migrated downstream via blood flow from its site of origin.

**endometrium:** The inner layer of the female uterus.

**endorphins:** Naturally occurring, self-generated analgesics.

**epinephrine:** Adrenaline. The primary acute stress hormone released during fight-or-flight situations. It is produced in the adrenal glands.

**epispadia:** Also known as the pee-in-your-own-face syndrome. This is a disorder wherein urinary flow exits from the dorsal (topside) aspect of the penis as opposed to the normal urethral exit at the tip of the corona.

**erythematous:** An overt red discoloration.

**erythropoietin:** A sialic acid protein produced in the kidney that regulates red cell production in the bone marrow.

**eschar:** A thick, fibrous scab that forms over the site of a severe cutaneous burn injury.

**excoriation:** A linear cutaneous scratch mark. **estrogen:** The primary biological female hormone. **eternal care unit:** Heaven.

**eukaryotic organism:** A more advanced cellular structure that has a defined nucleus.

**frequent flier:** A derisive term used to describe a patient who makes frequent and oftentimes inappropriate visits to a hospital's emergency room.

**gamete:** Either a male (sperm) or female (ovum) haploid cellular entity that is able to engage in conjugation with an opposite sex gamete to form a zygote in the act of biological reproduction.

**gastrotomy:** A surgical opening into the stomach, generally done for the purpose of exploration.

**Genesis 6:5–6 (King James Version):** "And God saw that the wickedness of man was great in the earth, and that every imagination of the thoughts of his heart was only evil continually. The Lord regretted that he had made human beings on the earth, and his heart was deeply troubled." Cross reference to *Dr. Blow's Honeybun Diet* 3:16 : "It looks like God backed the wrong primate."

**geographic rash:** A generally large, flat cutaneous lesion that is much bigger than a macular eruption.

**glioblastoma multiforme:** An evil and generally lethal primary brain cancer.

**gradeaux:** A nasty, slimy, malodorous sludge that is a wetter version of grunge.

**GRID:** Gay-related immunodeficiency syndrome. In the early 1980s, this was the name of the disease now known as AIDS.

**grunge:** A drier version of gradeaux.

**gynecomastia:** An abnormal enlargement of male breast tissue. Gynecomastia is not an uncommon problem among men being treated with antihormone therapy for metastatic prostate cancer.

**gyri:** Convolutional contours of the brain.

**halitosis:** Butt breath. It is bad breath that is even worse than the ass end of a dead hippopotamus.

**hematoma:** An extravascular bleed into tissues or organs. In layman's terms, a hematoma is a "bad-ass" bruise.

**hematocrit:** A measurement of the percentage of whole blood that is comprised of red cells.

**hemoglobin:** The oxygen-carrying respiratory protein found in red cells.

**hepatitis B:** A subset of an inflammatory infection of the liver caused by a specific DNA-type virus.

**hepatocytes:** Parenchymal cells of the liver.

**hepatology:** The discipline that involves the study of the liver.

**hepatorenal syndrome:** A potentially life-threatening illness that results in the degradation of both the liver and the kidneys.

**HER2/neu oncogene:** An oncogene responsible for a tyrosine-protein kinase component of an epidermal growth factor receptor. Amplification of this oncogene may result in the development and progression of an aggressive form of breast cancer.

**HIPAA:** The 1996 Health Care Insurance Portability and Accountability Act. Sadly, it was a HIPAA regulation that prevented John Q. Public from ever learning what type of multiple sexually transmitted diseases which previously infected the serial sexual abuser known as William Jefferson Clinton. Although inquiring minds want to know, it is only a matter of speculation as to what caused his male plumbing to rot off at the curly cues.

**homo-satchel:** The Trans-Pecos dialect's pronunciation of the word *homosexual.*

**hydrocephalus:** An abnormal condition of the brain wherein an excessive amount of cerebral spinal fluid accumulates within the ventricles. This abnormality may or may not cause an increase in intracranial pressure.

**hyperacusis syndrome:** An abnormal condition manifested by excessive sensitivity to noise.

**hypercholesterolemia:** Elevated cholesterol level.

**hyperpigmented lesion:** A skin abnormality manifested by enhanced coloration compared to the normal surrounding tissue.

**hypocapnia:** A low systemic carbon dioxide level, which may result in an alkalotic condition manifested by an elevated pH.

**hypopigmented lesion:** A skin abnormality manifested by diminished coloration compared to the normal surrounding tissue.

**hypospadia:** Also known as the pee-on-your-shoe syndrome. This is a disorder wherein urinary flow exits from the ventral (back-side) aspect of the penis as opposed to the normal urethral exit at the tip of the corona.

**hypotensive state:** Low blood pressure.

**hysterectomy:** Surgical removal of the female plumbing.

**idiot:** A "woke" moron. See *liberal.*

**immunological seroconversion:** A clinical situation that is tantamount to the recognition of an antigen by the immune system, with the possible conveyance of immunity.

**inflammatory breast cancer:** An aggressive form of breast cancer that presents with inflamed and erythematous skin overlying the malignant breast.

**integument:** Skin.

**John 8:7 (King James Version):** "He that is without sin among you, let him cast the first stone."

**John 19:34 (King James Version):** "One of the soldiers with a spear pierced His side, and forthwith came there out blood and water."

**Kaposi sarcoma:** A cutaneous malignancy that generally appears as a violaceous plaque associated with AIDS. This is a cancer caused by herpes virus 8.

**keloid:** A firm, nodular, hyperplastic scar.

**liberal:** A lower life-form that appears to believe in the misguided concept of wealth redistribution and identity politics which only sees the color of person's skin and not the content of their character. The end result is that a person defined as a liberal has a compulsion to give away free stuff to other people, as long as the commodities being dispensed among others were previously owned by conservative individuals and, specifically, not previously owned by liberals. See *idiot*. See also *Communist* and *prokaryotic microbe*. If any readers think otherwise, I would kindly like to refer them to the glossary of Russian terms at the end of this section.

**Luke 10:30–32 (King James Version):** "A certain man went down from Jerusalem to Jericho, and fell among thieves, which stripped him of his raiment, and wounded him, and departed, leaving him half dead. And by chance there came down a certain priest that way: and when he saw him, he passed by on the other side. And likewise a Levite, when he was at the place, came and looked on him, and passed by on the other side."

**lymphadenopathy:** Pathologic lymph nodes affected by some type of disease process, including cancer and infections.

**lymphoma:** A cancer involving the lymphatic component of the immune system.

**lyophilization:** Cryodesiccation. A preservation technique utilizing freeze-drying methodology.

**macrophages:** The garbage-disposal cells of the reticuloendothelial system. Macrophages are large extravascular cells derived out of monocytes that purposefully leave the circulatory system and enter into tissue spaces. The job of the macrophage is to eat bacteria, foreign material, and cellular debris. The monocytes and macrophages are good guys to have around.

**macular eruption:** An abnormally pigmented, flat cutaneous eruption.

**MAI:** *Mycobacterium avium intracellulare* bacterium.

**Mallory-Weiss tear:** A pathological rent that may occur at the gastroesophageal junction as a result of violent episodes of vomiting.

**Matthew 5:29 (King James Version):** "And if thy right eye offends thee, pluck it out and cast it from thee."

**MEK:** Mitogen-activated protein kinase. MEK1 and MEK2 are extracellular signal pathways that may often drive cancer initiation and proliferation if enzymatic dysregulation occurs.

**melanin:** Pigmented indole polymers that provide coloration to the integument and hair.

**melanocytes:** The pigment-producing cells found in the integument.

**mesenteric lymph nodes:** Lymph nodes found within the intra-abdominal area.

**metastases:** The appearance of cancer that has spread far from its primary site of origin to other body areas via the lymphatic system or blood vessels.

**mets:** An abbreviation for foci of metastatic cancer.

**microangiopathic hemolysis:** A small-vessel disease process manifested by protean features that may include the abnormal rupture of red cells, fever, a low platelet count as a consequence of blood-product consumption, and maybe even kidney and brain damage.

**microcephalic:** The pathological affliction of having a tiny brain. See *liberal.*

**monoclonal immunoglobulin:** An abnormal concentration of a repetitively produced immunoprotein that may be a harbinger for a variety of different diseases, including Waldenström's disease, multiple myeloma cancer, and lymphomas.

**mushroom:** A lower-life-form fungal reference utilized as a derisive nickname to describe an inexperienced medical student.

**mycobacteria:** A Gram-positive, aerobic, acid-fast bacteria. Tuberculosis and MAI are two examples of infectious diseases caused by microorganisms designated as mycobacteria.

**myeloblast:** The bone-marrow-residing parent or precursor of white cells consigned to myelogenous lineage. An overabundance of abnormal myeloblasts is the classic hallmark feature of acute myelogenous leukemia.

**NCCN:** National Comprehensive Cancer Network.

**necrotic:** An adjective that describes biological material as dead and in state of active decay.

**nephrotoxic:** A substance that is potentially dangerous to the kidneys.

**neurocutaneous syndrome:** A constellation of neoplasms that involve both the nervous system and the skin.

**neurofibroma:** A tumor involving the peripheral nervous system as a consequence of the disorderly, abnormal proliferation of Schwann cells. The Schwann cells provide the insulator matrix of the nerve sheath.

**nephrotoxic:** A substance potentially injurious to the liver.

**nevus:** An often pigmented cutaneous lesion that is an aggregation of melanocytes. Atypical nevi are often precursors to melanoma cancer.

**non-A, non-B hepatitis:** An infectious entity that is now recognized as hepatitis C.

**norepinephrine:** A secondary acute stress hormone.

**omentum:** A rubbery, membranous tissue found in the abdomen that acts as a shock absorber for the internal organs.

**oncogene:** A gene that, when often mutated or amplified, has the potential for cancer initiation and proliferation.

**orchidopexy:** The surgical fixation of a mal-positioned testicle to its proper location and orientation within the scrotum.

**orchiectomy:** Surgical removal of the testicles.

**osteomyelitis:** A bone infection.

**pallor:** A pale discoloration of the skin.

**papular eruption:** An outbreak of cutaneous lesions that are well defined, solid nodules but are considerably smaller than a dermatological plaque.

**paracentesis:** The removal of an abnormal accumulation of fluid within the abdomen.

**paraplegic:** Paralysis of the lower extremities.

**parasite:** A life-form that can only survive by drawing its nutritional support from another living entity. See *liberal.*

**parenchyma:** The cellular matrix of a specific gland or organ.

***peligro*:** Spanish word for *danger.*

**petechiae:** Punctate red hemorrhagic spots that may appear on the skin, conjunctiva, and mucous membranes.

**plaque:** In regard to a dermatological condition, a relatively large, abnormal, raised, and palpable cutaneous lesion.

**plasmacytoid lymphocyte:** A relatively mature and differentiated B-cell white blood cell subtype that is a precursor to the plasma cell. The cancer cells associated with Waldenström's disease are an abnormal clonal aggregation of plasmacytoid lymphocytes.

**port-a-cath:** A central venous access device that is surgically placed in the body to facilitate the administration of intravenous medications, including chemotherapy for the treatment of cancer.

**postictal phase:** A somnolent state that may occur after a major motor seizure event.

**proctoscope:** A longer version of the anoscope.

**progesterone:** The secondary biological female hormone.

**prokaryotic microbe:** A primitive form of bacteria that lacks a defined nucleus.

**proprioreception:** Spatial orientation.

**proptotic:** Bug-eyed. As an example, go to Google, and look up a picture of the late English comedian Marty Feldman.

**prostatectomy:** The surgical removal of the male prostate gland. **proteinuria:** The abnormal presence of protein in the urine. **pruritus:** An itchy sensation.

**psychogenic blindness:** A stress-induced, psychiatric dissociative disorder manifested by self-limited unilateral or bilateral loss of visual acuity.

**PTEN gene:** An oncogene that drives the production of dephosphorylate proteins. Mutation and amplification of this gene can cause human cancers.

**pyelonephritis:** A kidney infection.

**radical nephrectomy:** The surgical removal of a kidney, often done for cancer treatment.

**rales:** An abnormal auscultatory finding in the lung that has the sound of a sharp crackle. This is often a consequence of either congestion of the alveoli or fibrotic scarring involving the lungs.

**respiratory alkalosis:** An elevation of systemic pH as a consequence of tachypnea and hypocapnia.

**rubor:** The presence of a red discoloration of the skin.

**scut puppy:** A midlevel medical school rank. A student with this designation has at least a modest amount of clinical skills and intellectual prowess.

**seborrheic keratosis:** Scaly, superficial cutaneous lesions that appear as a consequence of dermal senescence.

**seminoma:** A subtype of cancer that may involve the testes.

**sepsis:** The presence of toxic, pathogenic microbial organisms within the bloodstream.

**serosanguinous:** A bodily fluid that is an admixture of blood and watery serum. See reference noted at John 19:34.

**solar keratosis:** A scaly precancerous skin lesion.

**spot weld:** A colloquial expression for radiation treatment.

**stud:** The highest rank a medical student can achieve prior to graduating. The word *stud* in and of itself is a neutral word and has no gender or sexual orientation, insinuation, or connotation of any sort. If any readers think otherwise, I would kindly like to refer them to the glossary of Russian terms at the end of this section.

**sulci:** The normal grooves and fissures found on the surface of the brain.

**tachycardia:** Rapid heart rate.

**tachypnea:** Rapid breathing.

**testosterone:** The primary biological male hormone.

**thromboembolic cerebral vascular accident:** A stroke caused by a clot occurring in the blood supply to the brain.

**thromboembolic veno-occlusive event:** A blood clot occurring in the venous system.

**tonic phase:** A state of continuous muscle contraction that may occur during a major motor seizure event.

**transient ischemic attack:** A completely reversible ministroke event.

**Trendelenburg position:** A supine body position in which the pelvis is at a higher elevation than the head, usually achieved with a forty-five-degree decline of the head and thorax. This position is often utilized to increase blood flow to the brain during an episode of symptomatic hypotension.

**trichobezoar:** A hair ball.

**triple-negative breast cancer:** An aggressive and poor-prognosis form of breast cancer. The cancer cells in this particular subset of breast cancer lack estrogen receptors and progesterone receptors, and there is no amplification of the HER2/neu oncogene.

**TURP:** Transurethral resection of the prostate. This urosurgical procedure is undertaken to manage benign prostatic hypertrophy. A slang term for a TURP procedure is *Roto-Rooter job*.

**urosepsis:** A septic event originating in the urinary tract.

**vasoconstriction:** A reduction in the caliber of a blood vessel.

**ventriculoperitoneal shunt:** A long, surgically placed internal drain that is able to diverge an abnormal accumulation of fluid in the brain into the free space of the abdomen. It's a recognized treatment utilized by neurosurgeons in an attempt to manage hydrocephalus.

**vesicular eruption:** A cutaneous eruption manifested by an outbreak of fluid-filled, blister-like lesions.

**VIP:** A crude slang acronym for "ventilated, intubated patient."

**vitreous intraocular material:** The gelatinous material found in the posterior chamber of an eyeball.

**vivisection:** The dissection of biological entities, including human beings (as was brutally performed upon prisoners of war by the evil doctors who collaborated with the World War II biological warfare Japanese Army 731 Unit), done while the unanesthetized experimental subjects were still alive and in agony. Nice. Perhaps this is another example indicating that God may have backed the wrong primate.

**XRT:** X-ray therapy or an all-inclusive term for some type of radiation therapy.

**yolk sack (tumor):** A subtype of cancer that may involve the testes.

**Z-track:** The introduction into a body cavity of a needle that purposefully follows an irregular path to prevent a postprocedural fluid leak.

**zygomatic arch:** Part of the skull that protects the eyeball.

# GLOSSARY OF RUSSIAN TERMS

захлопни ебальник и иди на хуй! Сейчас въебу тебе в жопу так, что ты поперхнешься моим сапогом, ебаный ублюдок: There are two possible translations for this Russian expression:

1) Shut up, and go fuck yourself! I'm going to stick my foot so far up your ass that you will be able to taste the leather from my shoe, you nasty bastard.
2) Have a nice day!

иди на хуй!: There are two possible translations for this Russian expression:

1) Fuck off!
2) It was a pleasure to have made your acquaintance!

# ABOUT THE AUTHOR

A native of Houston, Donald W. Hill, MD, FACP, graduated from Trinity University in San Antonio, Texas, in 1978. After completing his medical school training at the University of Texas Medical School at Houston in 1982, Dr. Hill completed his postgraduate training in internal medicine, hematology, and oncology at the University of New Mexico in Albuquerque in 1987. At the time he composed this novel, Dr. Hill had completed thirty years of medical practice that included working in multispecialty clinics, solo practice, and everything in between, including academia and clinical research. A fellow of the American College of Physicians, Dr. Hill is a published scholar, but this is his first attempt at a work of fiction. Although approaching the end of his medical career, Dr. Hill was still in practice in Hawaii when he crafted this novel. A self-described angry man safely nestled behind a superficial, amiable facade of banality, Dr. Hill felt compelled to write this novel in an attempt to make peace with God, the universe, and the practice of medicine. Only time will tell whether these lofty objectives have been achieved.

# WHAT OTHERS ARE SAYING

Sadly, I was the historical eyewitness to much of what was written. Frankly, I was uncertain if I ever wanted to take another unpleasant trip down memory lane. After all, some things, like the dead, should remain forever buried. However, with the interjection of dark humor, I found myself laughing and crying at the same time.

—S. Carol Maple, LPN, Casa Grande, Arizona

A darker twenty-first-century version of *The House of God* on steroids. It will be a big fix to any junkie addicted to the genre of medical drama.

—Kelli Terrell, Tucson, Arizona

Thoroughly disturbing, thoroughly captivating, and, in the end, thoroughly satisfying. If Fyodor Dostoyevsky had penned *Crime and Punishment* in the twenty-first century, it would be this novel.

—Vicky Atkinson, RN, Kona, Hawaii

A fascinating glimpse into the dark underbelly of the medical profession. A must for anyone looking for intrigue, mystery, and a compelling read. It would appear that the more unsavory elements of our society should have much more to worry about from the underground clinical justice system than from our own official criminal justice system.

—J. C. Sullivan, Tucson, Arizona

Kudos, Dr. Hill. A complex modern masterpiece that probes not only the roots of good and evil in the heart and soul of human beings but also humankind's perpetual quest for spiritual redemption and, ultimately, perhaps even salvation.

—C. Darter, Tucson, Arizona

Be prepared for a trip into a dark realm where the demons of humankind's lesser nature may dwell.

—Wynn Madden, Tucson, Arizona

Dr. Hill accurately captures the dehumanization of students during the medical education process during the last half of the twentieth century. The American public should hope its next generation of physicians will arrive with less pathology.

—James F. Gardner, MD, San Antonio, Texas

In the introduction, the author suggests that if any readers become disturbed by the time they have digested this novel, a hot shower and bright sunshine may prove to be an effective antidote. If that were only true.

—Judy Kahler, RN, Kona, Hawaii

*DNR* is brilliantly disturbing—a throat-grabbing retribution ride with witty, hard-hitting social commentary. Realistic fiction cleverly elevated by a healthy dose of sarcasm!

—Big Tom Cavaretta, Phoenix, Arizona

# ABOUT THE SERIES

The DNR Trilogy is a dark yet compelling set of novels that are rife with moral ambiguity where dispirited medical personnel conspire to brutally murder a vicious hospitalized killer. *No Good Deed* is the second novel in this trilogy.